James Stewart

Recollections of the Early Settlement of Carroll County

Anatiposi

James Stewart

Recollections of the Early Settlement of Carroll County

Reprint of the original, first published in 1872.

1st Edition 2023 | ISBN: 978-3-38213-355-9

Anatiposi Verlag is an imprint of Outlook Verlagsgesellschaft mbH.

Verlag (Publisher): Outlook Verlag GmbH, Zeilweg 44, 60439 Frankfurt, Deutschland
Vertretungsberechtigt (Authorized to represent): E. Roepke, Zeilweg 44, 60439 Frankfurt, Deutschland
Druck (Print): Books on Demand GmbH, In de Tarpen 42, 22848 Norderstedt, Deutschland

RECOLLECTIONS

OF THE

EARLY SETTLEMENT

OF

CARROLL COUNTY,

INDIANA.

BY

DR. JAMES HERVEY STEWART,

County Clerk for Twenty-five Consecutive Years.

"Should auld acquaintance be forgot,
And never brought to mind."—*Burns*

CINCINNATI:
PRINTED BY HITCHCOCK AND WALDEN,
FOR THE AUTHOR.
1872.

Dedication.

To all of the

OLD SETTLERS,

WHO HAVE

DEVELOPED THE MATERIAL AND GENERAL INTERESTS

OF

CARROLL COUNTY, INDIANA,

This Work

IS MOST AFFECTIONATELY DEDICATED

BY

James Hervey Stewart.

PREFACE.

WHEN the author wrote and published the first call, requesting the early settlers of Carroll County to assemble in 1855, he little dreamed that a book would grow out of the meetings of the early pioneers.

The author having been appointed secretary of the society organized at the first meeting, he took down in writing the substance of the remarks made by the members at the annual gatherings, and thus a mass of facts, connected with the early settlement of the county, accumulated in his hands. The items of information acquired in this way, in the opinion of the members of the society, were too valuable to be lost, and the idea then suggested itself, that the only way for their preservation was to have them printed in a book. As very many of the persons who took part in the early meetings of the society are now dead, the history each one gave of the incidents connected with his settlement in the county could not now be obtained from any source.

The biographical sketches, it seems to the author, can not fail to be interesting. These statements were taken from the lips of the several persons as given to the writer, and, of course, are authentic.

It was thought that the publication of the list of the soldiers, who served in the wars of 1846 and 1861, would add interest to the book, and the author has been at great pains to make the list as accurate as possible.

As this work has been prepared in moments snatched from his official duties as clerk of the court, and from his professional duties since the expiration of his term of office, he is aware of its many imperfections.

The most of the manuscript has been written for some time, and remained untouched until now. In fact it might have lain much longer had not my brother-in-law, the Rev. John O. Foster, of the Rock-river Conference, Illinois (author of "The Life and Labors of Mrs. Maggie Newton Van Cott," the lady evangelist), kindly offered to take the work and superintend its publication.

JAMES H. STEWART.

INTRODUCTION.

A SHORT time since, DR. JAMES H. STEWART placed in our hands a manuscript, the principal part of which was prepared before the late war.

On looking it over, there was unmistakable evidence of its great local value for Carroll County, Indiana.

The scenes herein described are of sufficient interest to attract the lover of romance, while the few remaining "old settlers" will be glad to see their names permanently recorded, and a brief sketch of their early struggles.

And to the kindred of those who have gone before, this book will speak, with a silent yet potent speech, of those who opened the lines of travel, and with heroic efforts changed a wilderness into a city, and beautified all the land.

The farmer, the mechanic, the physician, the attorney, and the clergy, all have a record here, that will be of great value in years to come.

It was not necessary to bring all of the lines of events down to the present date; but, "having established the corners and corrected back," the rest of the work may be done in subsequent years.

It is very fitting to close the volume with the soldier's muster-roll. Of many we say:

> Their deeds are passed; their work is done,
> Their marching and their might;
> The step they took while here below,
> Is changed from left to *right*.
> But hark! we can not call for those
> Whose crimson tide is shed;
> Their lights went out at tattoo's beat,
> To glow again with wonted heat,
> At the reveille of the dead.

In the two wars named, Carroll County bore no mean part. Would that at the county-seat there was a monument in proportion to the high honor the soldiers deserve! But their names must not perish from our pages, nor from our memories.

Dr. Stewart has done his work well. He declined to furnish the reviser a sketch of his life, though often requested; yet the correct steel portrait, and the memory of his efforts for nearly two generations, as he has helped to develop Carroll County, must suffice.

The genial face of Abner Robinson will please familiar friends, and the well-cut picture of the court-house can not fail to satisfy. With assurance that the book will be a valuable souvenir, we close with a few thoughts of

FORTY YEARS AGO.

TUNE—"*Auld Lang Syne.*"

> "In what a wondrous age we live,
> Not many seem to know;
> But few the mighty change perceive,
> Since *forty years ago.*

Our fathers never had a dream,
  When things moved on so slow,
Of what the boys would do by steam,
  Not *forty years ago.*"

Our *warmuses* and *roundabouts*
  Gave plenty room to grow,
And boys were strong and rugged then,
  Full *forty years ago.*
The "youngsters" dressed in *homespun* clothes,
  And made but little show;
And "*linsey woolsey*" dressed the girls,
  Some *forty years ago.*

Those girls could spin and knit and weave,
  And have as good a beau
As any lady's heart could wish,
  Since *forty years ago.*
And grandpa's heart was always green,
  Although his locks were snow;
And grandma knit and darned the socks,
  Some *forty years ago.*

But time has *deadened* many a tree,
  And "*logged up*" many a row,
Since we began to clear the land,
  Some *forty years ago.*
And when the "*covered wagons*" come,
  And we are called to go,
We'll settle in a *better land*
  Than *forty years ago.*

JOHN O. FOSTER.

May, 1872.

RECOLLECTIONS

OF THE

Early Settlement of Carroll County,

INDIANA.

CHAPTER I.

ON the 21st day of December, 1824, Government land was purchased in the office at Crawfordsville, which afterward formed the boundaries of Carroll County, Indiana. The following persons made the first purchases between December 21st and 27th, 1824: David Mount, Daniel Baum, Samuel Williamson, James Thornton, John Beard, Henry Robinson, Jesse Clark, and Hugh Manary.

Henry Robinson and his son, Abner Robinson, were the first settlers. A narrative of the emigration of these families from their former home near Dayton, Ohio, can not fail to be interesting. The following account of the journey and incidents connected with the first settlement, is taken from a paper read by Abner Robinson to the "old settlers'" meeting, on the 9th day of June, 1855.

On the 12th day of October, 1824, Henry, Hezekiah, and Abner Robinson, with their families, accompanied by Joseph Clymer and his son, and a Mr. James French, started for the Wabash Valley. On passing through Richmond and Centerville, they were annoyed by the croaking predictions of "ill luck" uttered on all sides. "You will never get through," says one. "You will die if you go to the Wabash; every one that goes there dies in less than a year," joined another. "You will never get along with that wagon, 'Old Sampson;'" referring to a wagon for hauling saw-logs, used for a great many years after the settlement by the family in this county.

From Centerville the route lay through Jacksonborough, two or three miles north of Newcastle; thence to Makepeace, or "Old Bucktown," on White River; thence down the south side of the river, through Andersontown, to Strawtown. From Strawtown to Thornton was a dense wilderness, and for three or four days the party suffered greatly for want of water. After crossing White River, the party had much trouble in finding their cattle; nor did they recover all of them for several days, they having evidently been driven off by some marauders.

On the fourteenth day after commencing their journey, they were much rejoiced at again seeing corn-fields and log-cabins; this was in the vicinity of where Lafayette was afterward located. The inhabitants were greatly pleased at the arrival of "new-comers." At this place Hezekiah Robinson left the party, and purchased a residence near Crawfordsville, Indiana.

Such members of the families of Henry and Abner Robinson as were not otherwise employed, had five or six weeks in which to look for land. There was much difficulty in "looking for land" in what now constitutes Carroll County, for they had no other directions than to follow the *Indian trail*, which in many places would not admit of two horses abreast. All provision, camp equipage, etc., had either to be carried on the back or on horses from the settlement before mentioned, about twenty-five miles from the point were Delphi now stands.

In accordance with the advertisement (at the land sale), the *lowest* number of section, township, and range was first offered. The first land sold was E. ½, S. E. ¼, Sec. 20, T. 25, R. 2 W., and was purchased by Henry Robinson, on the 21st day of December. Most of the "squatters" purchased their land with little or no advance on Government price.

The Quakers near Richmond had made up their minds to make a settlement on this part of the Wabash. They made a mistake in the order in which the land was to be sold, which accident prevented Carroll from being a Quaker County.

The Robinsons, having secured the land for their future home, proceeded to cut a wagon-road and build a cabin. For this end, on Tuesday, the 28th day of December, 1824, Henry Robinson and his two sons, Abner and Coleman, assisted by a Mr. Starks and son, cut out a road, taking their ox-team along. On the first day, after a hard day's work, they crossed Wild-cat Creek, and encamped in the evening on the bluff. Not knowing the situation of the country, they did not obtain a very good crossing. On the 29th, the party left Wildcat, and commenced cutting their way through a dense forest, without pilot or guide, avoiding the creeks running toward the river on the left, and the swamps on the right. During this day Benj. D. Angell (father of Dr. Angell, of Pittsburg,) overtook the Robinsons, and remained with them two or three days; encamped on the evening of the 29th, about one mile beyond Sugar Creek. Thursday, the 30th, they proceeded with the same caution as on the day before, and were overtaken by a Mr. John I. Davidson (for many years afterward a leading citizen of Tippecanoe County), and encamped that night on "Walker's Branch," or "Bridge Creek." They passed a cheerful night in company with the new friends. Friday, the 31st, they started early, and had considerable difficulty in crossing an almost impassable swamp that ran parallel with Deer Creek, three-fourths of a mile south of Delphi. Arrived about the middle of the day at their proposed new home (the farm now owned by General R. H. Milroy), the first thing was to find a section line, to ascertain if they were right, and fix the encampment; then, having cut a few bushes, concluded the day, the month, and the year.

Saturday, January 1, 1825, found the party in a wilderness, without a house, in an inclement season of the year, the nearest neighbors twenty-five miles away, and provisions growing scarce. It was no time to be idle. The persons who had overtaken them on the road had all gone on their way. The settlers went to work, cut logs, and built their cabin five rounds high, the same day. Sabbath, the 2d, they observed, as far as possible under the circumstances. Monday, the 3d, the building went on, with occasional aid from land-hunters as they passed by. A. Robinson and Mr. Stark's son were in the mean time sent for more provisions, and also with the instruction to bring such female members of the family as might feel willing to brave the perils of the wilderness.

Tuesday, the 4th, Abner Robinson and his wife and sister, Sarah B. Robinson, set out from their temporary shanty for their new home, with a fresh stock of provisions, encamping for the night at the second encampment of the previous trip. Wednesday, the 5th, they arrived at the new home, between one and two o'clock. These were the first white women who settled in the county. Thursday, the 6th, and Friday, the 7th, four men were busy at the cabin, and by the evening of the latter it was inclosed, a chimney started, and a door-way cut out. They found much difficulty in making floor-planks with a broad-ax. Saturday, the 8th, Henry and Coleman Robinson and Mr. Stark left for the settlement, leaving Abner Robinson, wife, and sister at the cabin. On Wednesday, the 12th, the absentees returned, and the members of the two families were all gathered into the new cabin.

Shortly after this, Benjamin D. Angell removed with his family to this neighborhood. Mr. Angell, however, died the ensuing Fall. His was the first adult death in the county. Pretty soon afterward, Aaron Merriman settled on Rock Creek. Aaron Wilds and John Carey made an opening a short distance above, where Mr. Isaac Wilson afterward resided. Some time in February or March, Daniel Baum, with five families in a boat, arrived. About the same time, or a little before, Craig Black commenced an improvement a short distance above, where the dam is now built. During the Summer and Fall, Mr. John Odell and Thomas Stirlin settled on Deer Creek; also a Mr. Kilbreath located on the General Milroy farm, but was taken sick with his family, and soon left.

Early in the season, the Robinsons commenced the improvement of the mill-site, afterward owned by James Roach & Co., above Delphi. It was slow, hard work, for want of proper tools. The nearest blacksmith resided at Crawfordsville, where was also the nearest mill, store, and post-office; and it generally took eight or ten days to make the trip. It was the common practice for some one to go with his ox-team to mill, and to transact business for all the settlement. John R. Ballard and his brother, Jeremiah Ballard, arrived here on the 5th day of May, 1825. This season John Cary was bitten by a rattlesnake, which led to the discovery of their den, and some three or four hundred were killed during that and the following year. There was some considerable sickness during that Summer and Fall. In September or October, Hugh Manary arrived; and pleasant weather concluded the year.

Sabbath, January 1, 1826, the settlers met for the first time for social prayer.

A saw-mill was raised in May or June of this year, near the spot were Roach & Co.'s mill afterward stood. All the residents of the country, from Wild-cat to Rock Creek, were invited, and were at the raising some time during the day, with some that came from beyond those limits, and they made, *all told, twenty-eight men.* It was the first and the last time that all the men, in what is now Carroll County, were together. The saw-mill started some time in September, and about three weeks afterward a pair of small mill-stones were put in motion for grinding corn. There was more rejoicing at that event than even the erection of any subsequent mill. About the same time, the neighborhood received considerable accessions by the arrival of Isam Atkinson, James M'Dowell, John Kuns, and General Milroy.

Lafayette was laid out in 1825, and late in that year, or early in 1826, a post-office was established there, and a Mr. Gay started a small mill. Lafayette was fixed upon for the county-seat, in the early part of this year, 1826. A petition was presented to the Legislature, at the session of 1826–7, for the organization of a new county; but it was not granted.

The citizens endured more than usual hardships the Fall and Winter of 1826. The old stock of provisions, clothing, shoes, tea, coffee, and sugar, was nearly exhausted. As for the latter, the sugar-tree was taxed to supply a part; while sassafras or spice-wood, or milk (when it could be had), supplied the place of coffee and tea. A large emigration into Tippecanoe County took up all the supplies from there, while our first citizens, having settled in the heavy timber, did not raise enough produce to supply their own wants. Mr. Robinson, in his narrative, from which I am quoting so largely, says he "lived six weeks without scarcely tasting bread, coshaw squashes and potatoes being the only substitute; and nothing," he remarked, "ever afterward tasted so good." What little flour they had was brought mostly from Ohio, nor was there any to be had nearer than Terre Haute.

January 1, 1827.—The settlement progressed as fast as could be expected. Two stores were opened; one at Mr. Baum's, by Daniel F. Vandeventer, and the other by the late Isaac Griffith, south of Halsey & Griffith's mills. Still they had no post-office, and all legal business had to be done in Montgomery and Tippecanoe Counties. The settlers, however, had but little legal business; harmony prevailed, and they were living in peace with all around them. Each one was willing to divide his goods with his neighbor. A better feeling prevailed than has ever existed since.

A small settlement was in progress where Logansport now stands; also on the west bank of the Wabash, in Deer-creek Prairie, on lands reserved by the Indians at the treaty of 1826.

In the early part of this season, many of our citizens were taken out near to where Rochester now stands, to build the "Indian Mills." Politics began to run high, but not sufficiently so to disturb social relations. In the Fall and Winter of this year, another petition was presented to the Legislature, asking the organization of a new county, and this time with success. An act passed the General Assembly on the 7th day of January, 1828, for the organization of the county of Carroll, of which the following is a copy:

AN ACT

FOR THE FORMATION OF THE COUNTY OF CARROLL.

Approved January 7, 1828.

SECTION 1. *Be it enacted by the General Assembly of the State of Indiana:* That from and after the first day of May next, all that part of the oounty of Wabash contained within the following boundaries, to wit: beginning at the north-west corner of township numbered twenty-four north, range two west of the second principal meridian; thence south nine miles to the center of township numbered twenty-three; thence east seventeen miles to the western boundary of the great Miami Reservation; thence north with said boundary eighteen miles to the center of township numbered twenty-six; thence west eight miles, to the south-east corner of section sixteen, range one west; thence north three miles to the township line, dividing townships twenty-six and twenty-seven; thence west thirteen miles to the section line, dividing sections four and five, range three west; thence south with said sectional line, twelve miles to the northern boundary of Tippecanoe County; thence east four miles to the place of beginning,--shall form and constitute a county, to be known and designated by the name and title of CARROLL, *in honor of Charles Carroll, of Carrollton, the only surviving signer of the Declaration of Independence;* and the boundary line of the county of Tippecanoe, on the east and north, so far as it divides that county from the county of Carroll, is hereby established and to be deemed and taken as unalterable, unless by common consent of the boards authorized by law to transact county business in the counties of Tippecanoe and Carroll, respectively.

SEC. 2. The said new county shall, from and after the first day of April next, enjoy all the rights, privileges, and jurisdictions which to separate and independent counties pertain.

SEC. 3. That Samuel Jessup, of Hendricks County, Asa B. Strong, of Marion County, Frederick Moore, of Montgomery County, Enos Lowe, of Putnam County, and Josiah Bryant, of Fountain County, are hereby appointed commissioners, for the purpose of fixing the seat of justice in said new county, agreeably to the provisions of an act entitled "an Act for fixing the Seats of Justice in all new counties hereafter to be laid off." The commissioners above named, or a majority of them, shall convene at the house of Henry Robinson, in said new county, on the second Monday in May next, and shall proceed to discharge the duties assigned them by law.

SEC. 4. It shall be the duty of the sheriff of Montgomery County to notify the commissioners herein above named, either in person or by written notification, of their appointment, on or before the tenth day of April next; and for such service the board of justices, or persons doing county business in said new county, shall allow him a reasonable compensation out of the county treasury thereof.

SEC. 5. The Circuit and other courts of said new county, shall be held at the house of Daniel Baum, or at any other place therein to which the said courts may adjourn, until suitable accommodation can be had at the seat of justice thereof, when the courts shall adjourn to meet at said county-seat.

SEC. 6. The agent who shall be appointed to superintend the sale of lots at the county-seat of said new county of Carroll, shall reserve ten per centum out of the proceeds thereof, and also ten per centum out of all donations to said new county, and shall pay the same over to such person or persons as may be appointed, according to law, to receive the same, for the use of a county library for said new county.

SEC. 7. It shall be the duty of the qualified voters of the county of Carroll, at the time of electing a clerk, recorder, and associate judges, to elect three county commissioners, agreeably to the provisions of an act entitled "an Act to establish a Board of County Commissioners," approved January 30, 1824; who, when elected and qualified as prescribed by said act, shall have all the powers, and perform all the duties prescribed by said act; which act is hereby revived, and to be deemed and taken as in full force, as relates to said county of Carroll; and also said board of commissioners shall have all the powers, and perform all the duties prescribed by law, as relates to boards of justices in the several counties. Said commissioners shall have power to hold special sessions, and to do and perform any duties required at any previous regular session.

This act to take effect, and be in force, from and after the first day of April next.

January 1, 1828.—Some considerable excitement commenced with the year in consequence of the organization of the new county, and the proposed election of officers. The first post-office was opened April 3d, Abner Robinson, Postmaster.

The election for county officers was held at the house of William Wilson, on the 28th day of April, 1828. The following is a copy of the list of voters at said election:

1 Benjamin Baxter,
2 John E. Metcalf,
3 William Carey,
4 Moses Tullis,
5 Thomas Burk,
6 William Price,
7 Jeremiah Ballard,
8 William M'Cord,
9 Abner Robinson,
10 Henry Robinson,
11 Joseph Jackson,
12 David Hamilton,
13 Richard Chabert,
14 Thomas Hamilton,
15 Coleman Robinson,
16 Christopher M'Combs,
17 William Hines,
18 Dan'l F. Vandeventer,
19 David M'Combs,
20 Stephen Miller,
21 Henry Baum,
22 Stephen Guile,
23 John Cook,
24 Nathaniel Hamilton,
25 David Baum,
26 John Mitchell,
27 Moses Hicks,
28 John Surface,
29 Manual M'Combs,
30 John Little,
31 Henry B. Milroy,
32 John Carey,
33 John Mixwell,
34 George J. Baum,
35 Elisha Brown,
36 David Lucas,
37 Joshua Whitcher,
38 John Givens,
39 Moses Thompson,
40 Moses Standley,
41 Moses Scott,
42 Eli Cotner,
43 Joseph M'Cain,
44 James M'Dowell,
45 John Adams,
46 Henry Bingaman,
47 Hugh Manary,
48 John Kistler,
49 Isaac Griffith,
50 Daniel M'Cain,
51 John Phillips,
52 Peleg Babcock,
53 William Sieres,
54 Daniel M'Cain,
55 Nathan Rose,
56 William Cummins,
57 Jacob Baum,
58 Aaron Hicks,
59 Jacob Underhill,
60 William Hicks,
61 Graham Roberts,
62 Daniel Baum,
63 Moses Alldridge,
64 Samuel Wells,
65 John M. Ewing,
66 Samuel Milroy,
67 Andrew M'Coy,
68 Thomas Stirlin,
69 Thomas R. M'Cain,
70 John Odell,
71 William Wilson,
72 John Ballard,
73 James Odell,
74 Isam Atkinson,
75 Levi Sagers,
76 Aaron Dewey.

CERTIFICATE OF THE JUDGES AND INSPECTOR OF THE ELECTION HELD ABOVE.

At an election holden in Carroll County, State of Indiana, April 28, 1828, in pursuance of a writ of election, issued by the

Governor of said State for electing two associate judges, one clerk and recorder, and three county commissioners.

JUDGES.		CLERK AND RECORDER.	
Isaac Griffith received . .	65	Daniel F. Vandeventer rec'd	42
Christopher M'Combs . .	43	John M. Ewing	22
Henry Robinson	42	John Carey	9

COMMISSIONERS.

Jacob Baum received	47
Aaron Hicks "	44
Graham Roberts "	40
Thomas Stirlin "	36
Daniel M'Cain "	31

We, the inspector, judges, and clerks of the election above named, holden at William Wilson's, in said county, certify the above to be a true copy of the vote taken at said election. Given under our hands the day and date above mentioned.

JAMES ODELL, *Inspector.*

DANIEL BAUM, } *Judges.*
WILLIAM HICKS, }

AARON DEWEY, } *Clerks.*
JOHN BALLARD, }

The next exciting thing in the new county was the location of the county-seat. Several sites were offered; one by William Wilson, *the one finally selected.* Henry Robinson offered one on the bluff south of the creek. Samuel Wells offered the land which was afterward laid out and named West Delphi, and M'Combs and Bozarth offered the tract of land which was afterward laid out and called Tiptonsport.

The commissioners appointed by the Legislature to make the location, reported to the Board of County Commissioners, on the 15th day of May, 1828:

That we have established the seat of justice of Carroll County on a tract of land of one hundred acres, being a part of the north-west quarter of sec. 29, R. 2 W. of the second principal meridian, T. 25, north; the said one hundred acres having been received by us as a donation from William Wilson, of said county, as will more fully appear by his bond for a title, payable to the county commissioners of said county, by which bond, herewith submitted, it will appear that the said tract of land of one hundred acres is bounded on and is to be taken parallel to the western line of the section aforesaid, the length north and south of said quarter section, and to extend east for quantity; upon which tract of one hundred acres, we, the undersigned commissioners, have, and do hereby establish the seat of justice of said county of Carroll, to be known and designated by the name and style of *Carrollton.*

The condition of said bond, executed by William Wilson, reads as follows:

The above bound William Wilson has this day donated to the county commissioners of Carroll County, for the permanent seat of justice thereof, one hundred acres of land, being part of the north-west quarter of sec. 29, N. of R. 2 W. of second principal meridian, T. 25. The donation to be situated as follows: Beginning at the south-west corner of said quarter-section, thence east one hundred rods, thence north, etc., so as to include one hundred acres, except what shall be found south of the creek; to which lot of ground the said William Wilson is to make a good and sufficient deed in fee simple, etc. The above donation the aforesaid William Wil-on makes without any reservation whatever, except the crop of the present year, now growing on said lot of ground, the rails also excepted. Signed in presence of Isaac Griffith and Samuel Milroy.

At the time the first election was held, and the above donation was made, W. Wilson was living on the quarter-section of land, a part of which was donated for a county-seat—about the spot on which Robert H. Bowen now resides. He did not long survive, but died during the year 1829.

The county commissioners met on the 24th day of May, and decided that the seat of justice should be known and designated by the name of Delphi.

The sale of lots took place on the 11th day of August, 1828; but they did not bring a very high price, and so but a part of them were sold.

During the early part of this year, 1828, a Presbyterian Church was organized, by the name of "Deer-creek Presbyterian Church," and the Rev. James Crawford was employed as a stated supply *one-half* of his time; the other half being employed at Lafayette; the dwelling-house of Henry Robinson (the same afterward owned by Mr. George Bolles), being used as the place of preaching, for about seven months. A large number of emigrants arrived during the latter part of this year.

January 1, 1829. The last Fall and Winter were very dry, and Spring unusually so. The merchants shipped their goods from Cincinnati for the Wabash on steam-boats, which could proceed no farther than the rapids below Vincennes, at Mount Carmel. From that point they were conveyed here by wagons, very much to the injury of the merchants and the disappointment of the people.

Mr. Henry Robinson was busily engaged this season in improving the mill-site now known as the "Delphi Mill," and owned by Messrs. Bulger & Co. Judge Griffith and Samuel Wise each started a saw-mill on Deer Creek, and Samuel Williamson started one on Rock Creek.

Mr. Henry Robinson's saw-mill started early in the year 1830. The Summer was dry and very sickly. The country improved very fast, but unfortunately for Delphi, as it just came into notice this season, the unusual amount of sickness gave it a bad name, from which it did not recover for many years. It has now, however, been conceded for a long time that, in point of health, it will compare favorably with any other city on the Wabash.

CHAPTER II.

OLD SETTLERS' MEETING.

IN the year 1855, an Old Settlers' Society was organized in Carroll County, and the author became its secretary. Its object was to procure a reunion, once a year, of the men who had come here while the country was a wilderness; who had assisted each other in rolling logs and building houses; had given ready and prompt aid in sickness; had assisted in burying the dead; had attended all the early weddings and merry-makings; and who had thus formed strong personal attachments for each other. The Society also had another object in view, which was to collect as many incidents as possible connected with the early settlement. Since the year 1855, these annual meetings have been kept up. The old settlers find them very pleasant, and at the last meeting it was ordered that the permanent time of meeting should be on the second Saturday of August, in each year, and that the permanent *place* of meeting should be on the old General Milroy farm, afterward owned by his son, Mr. Samuel L. Milroy.

The following is a copy of the call for the organization of the Old Settlers' Society, published in the *Weekly Times* and *Dollar Journal:*

OLD SETTLERS' MEETING.

The undersigned hereby request all the citizens of Carroll County, who settled here prior to the year 1831, to meet at the court-house in Delphi, at 10 o'clock A. M., on the 9th day of June next, for the purpose of spending a *social day* in reviewing the scenes of the olden time; and also with a view of forming a society to perpetuate the early history of this county. All persons who have been inhabitants of this county, prior to the time above named, are requested before the day of meeting, to reduce to writing the history, so far as they may remember it, of this county, up to the first of January, 1831, and, particularly, anecdotes of the early settlement, and incidents calculated to throw light upon the early history of the county.

Abner Robinson,	J. R. Ballard,
W. B. Givins,	James Odell,
A. W. Gillam,	C. M. D. Wilson,
James Alldridge,	G. C. Saunderson,
Daniel Baum, Sr.,	H. M. Graham,
Thomas Stirlin,	Joseph Kuns,
Wm. M'Cain,	Enoch Stansel.

The meeting of the old settlers was held at the court-house in Delphi, on the 9th day of June, 1855, in pursuance of the above notice. The Hon. James Odell was called to the chair, and James H. Stewart appointed secretary.

Mr. Odell, upon taking the chair, remarked: That the early history of this county was now known to but comparatively few persons, and no one but a participant was aware of the trials of the early settlers. In many counties, the old pioneers have held meetings, for the purpose of getting up the early history. In order to do this, it was necessary to meet together. The minutes of such meetings should be taken down, and published from time to time. The rising generation would be astonished at what the early settlers endured. For the purpose of perpetuating the incidents connected with the early history of Carroll County, this meeting had been called. He would recommend that a committee be appointed to collect facts, and any person might write down such incidents, as he might be in possession of, and hand the same to the committee. Important facts might thus be collected and recorded.

On motion of James H. Stewart,

Resolved, That the old settlers present give the secretary their names, place of birth, age, and date of arrival in Carroll County.

In accordance with said resolution, the following persons came forward, and communicated the facts sought:

Names.	Where Born.	Age.	Date of Settlement.
Abner Robinson	Kentucky	54	Dec. 31, 1824.
William M'Cord	Virginia	59	February 6, 1827.
James Odell	Indiana	44	February, 1825.
Thomas Gillam, Sr	Pennsylvania	68	April 4, 1829.
John M. Gillam	Pennsylvania	69	March 4, 1829.
Thomas Stirlin	Pennsylvania	54	March 3, 1825.
John Little	North Carolina	66	November, 1826.
John M. Ewing	Pennsylvania	58	April, 1827.
Daniel M'Cain	Ohio	55	April, 1826.
William Hughes	Virginia	68	February, 1829.
Adam Porter	Virginia	50	Nov. 20, 1829.
Aaron Gregg	Ohio	53	October, 1830.
William M'Cain	Ohio	52	Dec. 10, 1828.
John W. Gillam	Indiana	44	April 1, 1829.
Isaac Robbins	Ohio	39	October, 1828.
William B. Givins	Virginia	37	April, 1827.
Henry M. Graham	Indiana	38	January 6, 1829.
John B. Milroy	Indiana	35	December, 1826.
John Archer	Ohio	40	April, 1831.
Joseph Cox	Kentucky	37	April 17, 1829.
John Barr	Ohio	47	September, 1831.
Isaac Jackson	Virginia	40	October, 1827.
James F. Givins	Indiana	28	April, 1827.
George Royster	Indiana	29	June, 1830.
James H. Stewart	Kentucky	46	April 10, 1830.
Andrew Burntrager	Virginia	55	September, 1829.
Enoch Stansel	Ohio	49	November, 1830,
David Baum	Pennsylvania	50	April, 1825.
Noble Conklin	Ohio	48	October, 1830.
James M'Dowell	North Carolina	69	August 14, 1826.
Sam. D. Gresham	Virginia	49	April 30, 1830.

A motion prevailed that a committee of five persons be appointed by the chair, as a permanent committee, to collect historical and other facts connected with the early settlement of Carroll County; whereupon James

H. Stewart, Abner Robinson, James Odell, Thomas Stirlin, and John M. Ewing, were appointed that committee.

On motion of Col. John B. Milroy,

Resolved, That the old settlers here present be requested to make such statements as they may see proper.

Under this resolution, Abner Robinson read the paper to the meeting, from which such copious extracts have been made in the preceding pages.

MR. WILLIAM M'CORD, being called upon, said: That he fully concurred in the remarks of Mr. Robinson, He was here nearly a year before removing his family to this county. In the month of July, 1826, there were only twelve heads of families in the territory now comprised within the limits of Carroll County; in July, 1827, about seventeen heads of families. When he removed to this county, there were not one hundred acres of land under cultivation. New settlers had a hard time in getting along. Corn-bread and fat meat, milk and butter, were about the only articles of food.

MR. JAMES ODELL said: He was only fourteen years of age at the time his father removed to the Wabash. His father (James Odell) was born in South Carolina, and settled in the state of Ohio in the year 1800. In the year 1810, Mr. Odell, Sr., removed to the "new purchase" near Richmond, at which place the speaker was born. He was the first white child born in that part of the country. In the year 1823, his father, and John Odell, his brother, started to explore the Wabash country; came as far as Wild-cat, and returned. In the Spring of 1824, they came to the Wea Plains, and raised a crop. John Hedrick and Mr. M'Mahan were in the neighborhood at the same time. In November, 1824, the Odell family removed to the West. In the Spring of 1825, the families of John Carey, Benjamin

D. Angell, and Aaron Wiles (who were sons-in-law of James Odell, Sr.), removed to the territory now known as Carroll County; also James Odell and family. For the first year or two, the settlers were compelled to go to Crawfordsville to get their corn ground; but afterward a little mill was erected at Lafayette. When they could n't get meal, hominy was substituted. Corn-bread, venison, and pork were the principal articles of living. Coffee was fifty cents per pound, in Crawfordsville. We made our sugar from the sugar-tree. Salt was brought up the Wabash in keel-boats (the Kanawha salt), and cost ten dollars per barrel.

In those early times, the citizens were extremely accommodating. If one man had a bag of meal, they all shared. All assisted in raising cabins and rolling logs. No people who ever settled a new country were more moral than the pioneers of Carroll County. In those days we had no *law*, nor had we need of any. We had no contentions, and the people were universally peaceable.

Mr. Odell spoke of Henry Robinson, and remarked that he had done more for the settlement of this county than any other man. He immediately engaged in the erection of a mill, at a time when he was compelled to go to the state of Ohio to get his turning done! Amid difficulties which would have appalled almost any other man, he persevered, and erected a mill. No other man, it seemed to him, would have displayed the same energy. When the little "corn-cracker" (on the site now occupied by the mill of Roach & Co.), got in operation, the settlers were rejoiced. Sometimes, however, the "corn-cracker" would freeze up. The early settlers were compelled to go to Shawnee (Fountain County), to get their wool-carding done. Mr. Odell himself had gone there.

May 20, 1827, Mr. Odell's mother died. Dr. John

M. Ewing had just then arrived in the settlement, and she was his first patient.

Judge Thomas Gillam, being called upon, stated: That he had an affection of the throat, which made it painful for him to talk, but would say something. He removed to this county on the 4th day of April, 1829. The neighborhood where he located was an unbroken forest. He had but little means, and was compelled to use great exertions to raise enough produce to supply the wants of his family. He, however, resolutely commenced his clearing; but instead of taking the usual method of cutting down, a young man would climb the trees, begin at the top branches, and continue to lop off the limbs until the tree was stripped, while Mr. Gillam would throw the branches on a fire, and burn them.

Nine acres were put under cultivation that year, and they had corn to sell the ensuing Fall. One morning, his children and those of his brother, John M. Gillam, eight in all in number, started to dig ginseng, which was found there in great abundance in the woods. They got lost; night came on, but the children could not be found. The families were dreadfully alarmed, as the nearest houses were William Bishop's and John Briggs's. Three or four started in pursuit. He (Judge Gillam) came to Bridge Creek, and ascended the same. Morning came, but still nothing had been heard of the children. The neighbors were all aroused, and started to the woods with horns and guns. Allen Gillam, son of Mr. G., and one of the lost ones, observed to the other children that they must *pound* on a tree with a club, in order that the persons seeking them might hear. The children followed this advice, and the noise thus made reached the ears of the coming party, and the children were found, after being in the woods all night.

At another time, a child of his brother, David Gillam, got lost, while its mother was getting dinner. The fact of its absence was unnoticed until after dinner. All parties started in pursuit, and hunted till dark; sent runners to Delphi; roamed the woods all night. Next morning at least fifty men were engaged in the search. They formed in a line, with men from fifty to one hundred yards apart; thus the hunters took a sweep, and found the child at noon the day after it was lost. When found, it was asleep. [David Baum here remarked that he had assisted in hunting for that child]. Judge Gillam concluded by remarking that he could recount a great many hunting-scenes, did time permit.

Mr. JOHN M. GILLAM (now a resident of Jasper County) said: That in February, 1820, he started from the eastern part of this state, to remove to the Wabash country. "Moving," then, was quite a different thing from what it is now. Then there were no bridges, and he swam or forded the river with a six-horse team and wagon. One night, having encamped in a low place, it rained during the night, and they were compelled to cut saplings to place beds on. Fountain County then was a wilderness. From Fountain County he removed up into Carroll County. He brought up a wagon-load of corn-meal, and, of course, had meal to lend. The neighbors availed themselves of the opportunity. At the time Mr. G. settled here, union and good fellowship were the order of the day. Then the Christian found it extremely pleasant to worship God. He has frequently walked six miles to attend meeting.

At the first settlement, wolves were very bad; they killed five sheep for him in one night.

Mr. THOMAS STIRLIN said: That the statements made by the "old settlers" had greatly interested him. His family was the eleventh that came to this county. He arrived in July, 1826, and cleared off a turnip-patch, on the place on which he still resided. His family came the following Winter. Provisions were scarce, and at one time he had purchased a *few ears of corn* of Mr. Manary. The times were "hard," but the feeling was good. It is very pleasant to meet the "old settlers." The first "log-rolling" he attended, was on the place now owned by Isaac Wilson's heirs. There were just seventeen hands in the county. We set our stakes that all things should be done without *alcohol*, and I still stand on that same platform. The first temperance society was organized in the year 1828, in the little old log school-house, used as a court-house, in Delphi.

The first school taught in this county, was taught by Miss Sarah B. Robinson, in a cabin, on the farm of her father, Henry Robinson.

Mr. Stirlin remarked, that the *only* enemy he was afraid of was *snakes*. A young hunter, being alone, camped on the ground on which the city of Logansport now stands, was bitten by a rattlesnake one night, and would have died; but some Indians had their tents in the vicinity, to whom he "halloed." They took charge of the white hunter, cured him of the bite, and sent him on his way rejoicing.

John Carey was bitten by a rattlesnake, on the farm now owned by Isaac Wilson's heirs. Four hundred snakes were killed in one day near Griffith's mill.

To return a moment to the young man who was bitten at Logansport (whose name was Alexander): the Indians kept him three days, and when he left them, they told him if he got *wet* he would die. Mr. Alexander told Mr. S. this circumstance himself.

Mr. James Odell here remarked: That, by leave of the audience, he also would relate a snake story. Judge

Carey (brother-in-law to Mr. Odell) was bitten one Sabbath. They were all living together on the Isaac Wilson place. The spot where Carey was bitten, was where the old still-house now stands. Upon examination, they found seven or eight snakes, and became satisfied that a den must be in the immediate vicinity. They searched, and found holes like *ground-hog* holes, with a smell very much like a *menagerie.* The next day they killed sixty-five snakes near this den. Every warm day after that, they hunted snakes, and the practice was followed at that place for some time; but it was eight or ten years before they were all killed.

On motion of Mr. Aaron Gregg,

Resolved, That when this meeting adjourn, it meet again on the first Saturday of August next, at 10 o'clock A. M.

Before parting, it was resolved that at the next gathering each person be requested to bring his family and a basket of provisions. Also, that some person be selected to deliver an address.

Abner Robinson was chosen President of the Society for the ensuing year.

The meeting adjourned, to meet again on the 4th day of August, 1855.

CHAPTER III.

OLD SETTLERS' SECOND MEETING.

August 4, 1855.

THIS being the day appointed for the meeting of the "old settlers," in pursuance of adjournment, the following persons convened at the court-house in Delphi: Abner Robinson, William M'Cord, James Odell, John M. Ewing, William Hughes, John B. Milroy, George Royster, James M'Dowell, and James H. Stewart.

The following persons were received as members:

Names.	Where Born.	Age.	Date of Settlement.
John D. Wilson.............	Virginia...........	26	October, 1829.
Isaac Wilson.................	Carroll County...	24	....

Abner Robinson, President of the Society, took the chair, and James H. Stewart officiated as secretary.

Dr. JOHN M. EWING, being called upon, stated as follows:

"In the year 1827, when I first landed on Deer Creek, there were but forty families living in what now forms Carroll, White, and Cass Counties. Where the town of Delphi now stands, was a hazel and blackberry thicket. Where the town of Logansport stands, every thing was in a state of 'nature,' except a trading-house on the point, occupied by a Mr. M'Cain. What is now the city of Lafayette, had then but six log-cabins, and a one-story hewed log-house, occupied as a tavern.

"There were then no roads, except one that was opened by Father Robinson, in December, 1824, his being the first family that crossed the Wild-cat. Traveling had then to be done in Indian trails and *deer-paths.* The face of the country was then covered with a growth of nettles, which were in the upland as thick as a crop of flax and about as high, and on the river bottom as high as a man's head, on horseback.

"There were then no rabbits, partridges, larks, thrushes, or other variety of birds that follow civilization. *Frogs* were abundant. I have traveled for days without ever getting out of hearing of their croaking music. Snakes were also plenty, especially the large rattlesnake. The settlers watched their dens in the Spring, and killed them when they came out to sun themselves. I have killed as many as five at one time. Wolves were also plenty—the large gray wolf—and, like the Indians, they surrendered their rights to the country with reluctance. I have seen them walk off with a snarl and a growl, looking at me as though they thought me an intruder on their domain.

"Indians were not very numerous in what is now Carroll County. A few came to the settlement occasionally to trade. The principal Indian trade was established at Logansport. It was the Indian trade that made Logansport what it is, by bringing men of capital and enterprise there, and also the 'Indian Agency.'

"The location of the Michigan road, also, gave it a permanent advantage over Delphi. That road would have been located through Delphi, on a much better and nigher route, if any person here had taken the time to show the commissioners the route. They came to this county for the purpose, and were sent to Cass County, where they found men that were willing to spend the time to gain this important thoroughfare.

"Henry Robinson was the first justice of the peace

elected in Carroll County, commissioned by Governor Ray, July 14, 1828.

"The first court held in the county, was at the house of Daniel Baum, Sr. The first post-master in the county was Abner Robinson. The first apples grown from the seed, was on the farm of Henry Robinson (the General R. H. Milroy place).

"The natural advantages of Carroll County in regard to fertility of soil, the facilities for water-power, and good springs, were not surpassed by any county on the river. It was at the head of steam-boat navigation on the Wabash. Boats could always ascend to Delphi, at any time they could come to Lafayette. Nature did all for Carroll County that it has ever done for any place; and the early settlers depended on its natural advantages bringing in an enterprising population, and building them a town. They used no efforts of their own, so that business and capital concentrated at Lafayette and Logansport; and Delphi, with all its natural advantages, was left in the rear.

"There were comparatively few difficulties and privations experienced by the first settlers of Carroll County. Provisions were generally plenty in the lower counties on the river; and the settlers soon raised enough to supply themselves, and a surplus for coming emigrants. They were not molested by the Indians, as is often the case with new settlements. They had nothing to do, but to go to work, open up their farms, and receive a bountiful return for their labor.

"In a small prairie near Delphi (now Manary's addition), Mr. Manary raised one hundred and ten bushels of corn to the acre. The labor of the husbandman was bountifully rewarded in the luxuriant productions of the soil.

"In opening up farms and raising cabins there was a union of effort and harmony of feeling, in which all participated. I have spent as many as four days in the week at log-rollings, and cabin-raisings; have walked at the end of a hand-spike from morning till night, with some of the stoutest men in the county, or 'shoved' up the end of a log, after carrying it on a spike; always trying which end could beat. The 'Hurrah, *our end best!*' or '*Up with your switch end!*' would surely be heard at the pushing up of every log.

"I have experienced more real satisfaction and pleasure at log-rollings and house-raisings, in the first settlement of the county, than I ever have at any social party or gathering, since. The social, friendly feeling which existed, caused the work to appear like play. Then the appetite which it created for the bountiful repast, prepared by the no less industrious matrons and their blooming and rosy-cheeked daughters, was a feast good enough for a king.

"It is union of feeling and harmony of effort that form the basis of all true happiness. Such union and harmony then existed to a far greater extent than it has since; and there was more real happiness then than now. Then there was harmony in schools, harmony in churches, harmony in politics, harmony in all the social and domestic relations of society. But these fond recollections are among the things that were. That *real* friendly feeling which then manifested itself, in being interested in the welfare and prosperity of others, is now concentrated in a spirit of acquisitiveness and selfishness, prevented only from trespassing on the rights of others by legal restraints. Civil laws were then unnecessary; now they are not sufficient to restrain the inordinate selfishness of society. Why this difference in the primary and present condition of society? Are the people any wiser or better now than they were then? Or does the change in their social, civil, and political relations, render them any happier *now* than they were *then*?

"In the Fall of each year, for a number of years, there was considerable sickness. My practice then embraced the whole of the population north of the Wildcat. I have often visited families, in which one was not able to give another a drink. In many instances I have cooked for them, and left their medicine so that each one could get it and take it without disturbing the others.

"I often visited and prescribed for as many as fifty patients in a day, riding day and night. I charged from five to ten dollars. For like services a physician would *now* charge fifty dollars, and get his pay. I never calculated upon getting more than half what I charged, and in one half the cases, I never charged any thing.

"In the first settlement of Carroll County, the people lived as well, and suffered as few privations and hardships, as any new country that has ever been settled. They had all the substantial necessaries and many of the luxuries of life; such as sugar, coffee, tea, etc. Though they were deprived for a few years of apples, peaches, and pears, they had plenty of wild fruit—crab-apples, plums, grapes, gooseberries, blackberries—and these were excellent. I have gathered many a mess of blackberries where the court-house, public square, churches, business houses, and residences now stand, in the town of Delphi.

"The first settlers of Carroll County possessed more intelligence and piety than is usual for new settlements, and the moral tone of their influence and example has left its impress on the present inhabitants. There is no town on the Wabash decorated with more churches and schools, in proportion to the inhabitants, than Delphi.

"In conclusion, I will just say, that no man labored more for Carroll County than Henry Robinson. He put up the first mill, at a time when it required more labor and capital than it would now, and the profits were not sufficient to keep up the repairs. His labor and money were appropriated more for the benefit of others than for himself.

"In establishing Churches and schools, he was ever foremost. In giving a correct tone to moral and religious sentiment, the influence of his example was always on the side of virtue. He was a most indefatigable opponent of idleness and vice of every description, and hesitated not to reprove it whenever and wherever it came under his notice, regardless of the opinions and censures of man. Had all the old settlers labored as much for the benefit of Carroll County as did Father Robinson, Delphi would have been a different town to what it is now."

COLONEL JOHN B. MILROY said: That he had been a scholar of Miss Sarah B. Robinson, and that she whipped him with a goose-quill! He went to school also to Mr. Crawford, Mr. Dewey, Mr. Simon, Mr. Gage, Judge Saunderson, and Mr. Odell.

General Samuel Milroy (the father of Colonel M.) removed with his family to this county late in the Fall of 1826. The succeeding Winter was very cold; they had three head of cattle frozen to death! Upon the first arrival of the *Milroy family*, they settled on the land, one mile above Delphi, now known as the "Milroy farm."

For the first and second Winters, they used hominy for bread, and his brother Robert and himself took turns, and pounded hominy each day, alternately.

When Robinson's mill was frozen up, the neighbors would meet together, and heat water to thaw it loose.

When we first arrived here, the nearest mill was on the Wea Plains.

MR. GEORGE ROYSTER remarked: That his father, Robert D. Royster, and family, including himself, removed from Fayette County, in this state, and settled three and a half miles above Delphi, in June, 1830. Mr. R. remembered that the first Winter was extremely cold.

Mr. JAMES M'DOWELL said: That he removed from Vigo County, in this state, and came here in August, 1826. David Lucas and Alexander Chamberlain came at the same time. The present location of Mr. M'Dowell was the one chosen in that early day.

Very heavy rains visited this section of country shortly after his arrival, and at the house of Mr. Lucas the water came through the roof, and poured upon a bed where a sick boy was lying, causing him great distress.

When Mr. M'Dowell raised his cabin, he was assisted by John Ballard, Jeremiah Ballard, David Lucas, and another young man. The first night after getting into the cabin, Mrs. M'Dowell was taken sick, and was severely afflicted for thirteen weeks. They would gladly have sent for a physician, but there was none in the county, and as yet they had never called one.

The old settlers in this county were in the habit of digging ginseng, and Mr. M'D. made sixty dollars, the second Fall after his arrival, in this way.

Previous to his removal to Carroll County, he resided three years in Vigo County. Before that, lived in Darke County, Ohio. When they left Ohio, they had seven children—three born in Vigo, and five were born in this county. Out of sixteen children, they raised fourteen to be men and women. Never had a doctor prior to nine years ago. My son Alfred then had the "white swelling," and then for the first time they employed a physician.

On the second Fall after coming here, the *blackbirds* destroyed half the corn. Many persons who had made up their minds to remove to this county, abandoned the idea, and were deterred from coming, on account of the *birds!*

In the Summer of 1827, Alexander Chamberlain raised a double log-house, below Logansport, nearly opposite the mouth of Eel River. Persons from this distance went up to assist him.

I was offered eighty acres of land where Delphi now stands, for $125.

After his wife recovered, she gathered a large quantity of nettles, cured or dried them, broke the stalks, leaving a kind of flax, from which she wove and made clothing.

DANIEL BAUM, SR.—Mr. Baum was not present, but sent a paper to be read to the meeting, of which the following is a copy:

"I was born on the 7th day of October, 1780, in Mifflin County, Pennsylvania. Married in the same county, on the 20th day of February, 1801, to Assenath Rotrock. We have had twelve children; six of them are now living.

"I removed from Mifflin County on the 8th day of October, 1805, and settled in Ross County, Ohio. The county was afterward divided, and I fell in Pickaway County. Remained in Pickaway County twenty years. Started to remove to the Wabash on the 7th day of March, 1825, on a *flat-boat*, in company with four other families, consisting of Robert Mitchell, Sr., Robert Mitchell, Jr., John Kestler, and Jacob Baum.

"On the river, sold the flat-boat, and purchased a keel-boat. With this keel-boat the company entered the Wabash River, and cordelled and polled it to the mouth of Deer Creek, without making a stop. The boat was run up Deer Creek about half a mile where it was tied, at a point about one hundred yards below Howlitt's old slaughter-house. The boat lay tied to the shore till the Spring of 1826, at which time the ice-flood sunk it, and doubtless its bottom still lies embedded in the mud and sand of Deer Creek, at the point where it was first landed.

"The five families landed on the 30th day of April, 1825. It was too late in the season to lose any time, and all erected tents on the bank of Deer Creek, near the old Baum buildings, in the bottom, just below the railroad bridge. Immediately broke up some land, and put in four acres of corn. Robert Mitchell, Sr., put up a cabin on the bank of Deer Creek. Pretty soon I built the house, still standing, in which I resided so many years. Mr. Kestler removed to the farm now owned by Spears, Case & Co., adjoining 'Bondis's Reserve.' Robert Mitchell, Jr., returned the ensuing Fall to Ohio. Jacob Baum removed to the land now owned by Peter Toughman. I had visited the Wabash in the Fall of 1824, attended the land-sales at Crawfordsville, and purchased my land. None of the others purchased until after their removal here.

"In October, 1825, we moved into our new house; and from that time till after the location of Delphi, were crowded with travelers, land-hunters, and others, as the old 'Lafayette trail' crossed the creek just below my house.

"Old Robert Mitchell died in the Fall of 1826. He was buried at the foot of *Front Street*, in Delphi, at the section corner. Mr. William Sims, who was a newcomer, living near where Logansport was afterward located, got sick up there, and having no one to take care of him, except his brother-in-law, Mr. Young, he was brought to my house to be cared for. After remaining sick about two weeks, he died, and was buried at the section corner, near the same place where Mr. Mitchell was buried. This was probably in the Fall of 1826.

"Hugh Manary, Sr., settled in the bottom, on what is now known as 'Manary's Addition,' in the Fall of 1825. He sold a mill-seat off from his land to Philip Starr, and removed across the creek, on the hill, above the old slaughter-house.

"In the Spring of 1827, Dr. Daniel F. Vandeventer, who was a partner with Mr. Graham, brought a little stock of goods. I built a log store-house for him in the yard. Dr. V. was elected clerk and recorder in the Spring of 1828, and kept his office in that same store-room; and, until the log school-house was built in Delphi, on the lot adjoining the present residence of William Barnett, the courts were held in the same building. That old store-room, clerk's office, and court-room is still standing. In January, 1828, there was a great flood; the water came into my kitchen. Once since that time, when my son, Daniel, was living in the same house, the flood was about one foot higher than in 1828."

Miss Elizabeth Robinson, daughter of the late Henry Robinson, having kept a register of the deaths, from the first settlement of the county up to 1830, the same was read to the meeting, as follows:

Name.	Date of Death.
James Gilbreth,	September 8, 1825.
Benjamin D. Angell	September 16, 1825.
John Nelson Newman	July 11, 1826.
Robert Mitchell	August 27, 1826.
William Sims	September 5, 1826.
Henry Alex. Robinson	January 20, 1827.
Mrs. Merriman	February, 1827.
Sarah Odell	May 20, 1827.
Elizabeth Odell	June 11, 1827.

Name.	Date of Death.
Mrs. Hamilton	1827.
George Baum	November, 1827.
Mary Baum	December 5, 1827.
T. Hughes	May 20, 1828.
Andrew Forbes	September 11, 1828.
John Bean	September 20, 1828.
Malinda Bozarth	September 23, 1828.
Sarah Clister	October 3, 1828.
Wm. Waugh Griffith	October 5, 1828.
Rebecca Lowther	October 6, 1828.
James M'Cain	January 7, 1829.
Emanuel M'Combs	January 17, 1829.
Infant of Jno. Adams	January 27, 1829.
Benjamin Lowther	March 30, 1829.
Mrs. Metcalf	May 26, 1829.
Margaret Adams	June 12, 1829.
Infant of Mr. Thornberry	June 30, 1829.
Hervey Dewey	August 19, 1829.
Infant of Mr. Bross	August 24, 1829.
James M'Clellan	August 26, 1829.
Mr. Bross	August 31, 1829.
Rebecca George	September 25, 1829.
Margaret Black	October 2, 1829.
Sam'l Wise	October 21, 1829.
Daniel Kuns	November 1, 1829.
James Briggs	December 1, 1829.
William Wilson.	January 22, 1830.
Mrs. Adkison	February 10, 1830.
Hugh Manary	February 16, 1830.
M. Kennon	March, 1830.
Susan Wilson	March 31, 1830.
Mabala Clark	April 5, 1830.
Harrison Blackburn	June 2, 1830.
William Roberts	July 26, 1830.
Elizabeth Pike	August 15, 1830.
John Baum	August 27, 1830.
Infant of Mr. Pike	September 8, 1830.
Martha Humrickhouse	September 2, 1830.
William Seeley	September 10, 1830.
Mr. Silvers	September 12, 1830.
Mrs. Gideon	September —, 1830.
Mr. Clark	September 24, 1830.
Mrs. Long	September 26, 1830.
Mrs. Olinger	September —, 1830.
Mrs. Hulry	September 30, 1830.
Mat. Henry Ewing	October 6, 1830.
Sophia Bricker	October 26, 1830.
Mary M'Combs	1830.
Mr. Merriman	1830.
Two children of Mr. Thomas	1830.
Mrs. Bell	1830.

Mr. Thomas Smith, who settled on the west side of the Wabash River, one or two miles above where Pittsburg, Indiana, now stands, was not at the meeting, but his statement was read as follows: Thomas Smith, Sr., was born in Pennsylvania, July 5, 1776; arrived in Carroll County, April 4, 1830. He lived in a camp some time; broke up twenty acres of land on Deer-creek Prairie, and raised one crop; afterward built a cabin. His family then consisted of James, Thomas, Jr., Catherine (now Mrs. Gibson), and Eliza. His son John (removed to California) was married before coming to Carroll County.

James H. Stewart, the secretary of the Society, said he had started from Clarke County, in this state, to remove to the Wabash, on the 27th day of March, 1830, the day he arrived at the age of twenty-one years; and arrived in Delphi the 10th day of April, 1830.

A few nights after his arrival here, some young men, who had become offended at an old lady residing in the village, took her out, and "*tarred and feathered her!* The occurrence created a great deal of excitement for a long time.

It seems that an old lady by the name of S. had given offense to five or six of the young men who lived in the village, and they determined to have *revenge.* She resided, at the time, on the lot now occupied by the "Knight House." On the night in question, after Mrs. S. had retired to bed, some one knocked at the door, and told Mrs. S. that Mrs. Thornbury, who resided on the lower end of Front Street, was sick, and wanted to see her immediately. She hurried on her clothes, and started across the Public Square in the direction of the residence of Mrs. T., and when she got about one hundred yards from her house, she was seized by the young men, who were lying in ambush, and a coat of tar and feathers applied. I never could ascertain what she had said or done, that offended the young men.

The next morning, upon the facts becoming known, the little community was greatly stirred. The perpetrators were arrested, and taken before Esquire Robinson, who resided on his farm above town (same place now owned and occupied by General R. H. Milroy). Nearly every body attended the trial. The young men were defended by Colonel T. J. Evans, at that time residing in Logansport. Every one was satisfied that the young men arrested were the guilty ones; but very little direct proof could be obtained. Colonel Evans fought hard for his clients; but the justice was so fully satisfied that the defendants were guilty, that he bound them over to court.

When court came on, the prosecuting attorney became satisfied that he would be unable to procure sufficient proof to convict. He therefore dismissed the indictment as to Jesse Fleming (one of the defendants), and made a witness of him against the balance. Fleming, upon being placed on the witness stand, swore *that he did n't know any thing about it!* Of course the boys were cleared.

It was known that Fleming had perjured himself. In fact, I myself *saw the tar on his pantaloons the next morning after the occurrence!*

Poor Jess. Fleming! He was assisting Ex-sheriff Hopkinson a few years afterward to dig a well on his farm below town (the same now owned by Henry Lyon), and lost his life by the caving-in of the walls. It required twenty-four hours to dig his body out.

CHAPTER IV.

OLD SETTLERS' THIRD MEETING.

ON the 14th day of June, 1856, the Society met again in the grove above Delphi. Rev. E. W. Wright addressed the Throne of Grace. The roll was then called, and the following persons answered to their names: Abner Robinson, William M'Cord, James Odell, Thomas Stirlin, Aaron Gregg, William M'Cain, John W. Gillam, Isaac Robbins, Henry M. Graham, John B. Milroy, Joseph Cox, Isaac Jackson, James F. Givins, George Royster, James H. Stewart, Andrew Burntrager, Isaac Wilson.

The following persons then came forward, and enrolled their names as members of the Society:

Names.	Where Born.	Age.	Date of Settlement.
Michael Kite	Tennessee	49	October 1, 1831.
Vine Holt	Kentucky	42	October, 1829.
Samuel Holmes	Ireland	80	1833.
Robert D. Royster	Virginia	68	July 8, 1830.
Enoch Cox	NewJersey	72	April 17, 1829.
Solomon Hoffman	Virginia	38	October, 1830.
John Beckner	Virginia	63	February, 1829.
Daniel Baum, Jr.	Ohio	41	April 30, 1825.
Samuel More	Virginia	56	January, 1832.
William Crooks	Kentucky	...	....
Cornelius Williams	Virginia	68	January 28, 1830.
Dan. F. Vandeventer	New York	59	August, 1827.
Hamilton Thompson	Kentucky	48	November, 1827.
Daniel Baker	Virginia	76	1834,
Amos Ball	Ohio	31	October, 1830.
Christopher Vandeventer	New York	51	December, 1829.
Dan. V. Thayer	New York	36	April, 1831.
Joshua Thayer	Indiana	31	April, 1831.

Names.	Where Born.	Age.	Date of Settlement.
Noah Sandifer	South Carolina	58	September, 1832.
John M. C. Hanna	South Carolina	55	September, 1832,
Jacob Ball	Ohio	36	October, 1830.
James Ball	Ohio	42	October, 1830.
Archibald Slane	Virginia	...	....
William M. Young	Ohio	38	July 13, 1829.
Jonas Elston	Kentucky	55	November, 1832.
William Allen	Ohio	32	October, 1829.
Martha Milroy	Pennsylvania	70	December, 1826.
Nancy Ann Ball	Pennsylvania	66	October, 1830.
Phenia Royster	Kentucky	57	July 1, 1830.
Fanny Stirlin	Ohio	52	February, 1826.
Isam Adkinson	Virginia	77	November, 1826.

The Hon. ANDREW INGRAHAM, of Lafayette, having been appointed by the Executive Committee to address the meeting, was now introduced, and read an excellent address.

The following letter from Judge Milroy was read to the meeting, and ordered to be spread upon our Minutes:

"RENSSELAER, INDIANA, *June* 11, 1856.

"GENTLEMEN OF THE COMMITTEE:

"*Dear Sirs,*—Your kind invitation to be present and address the 'old settlers'' meeting at Delphi, on the 14th inst., came to hand, or rather to this place, during my absence at New York, from which place I returned a short time since. Your letter was unfortunately mislaid, and I did not get it till this morning. I hope, therefore, you will not think me guilty of negligence or disrespect, as nothing is farther from me. It would afford me great pleasure to be present at your meeting to talk of '*auld lang syne*,' and to take by the hand old friends with whom I associated in 'life's morning march, when my bosom was young.'

"I am just forty years old this day. My father moved to the territory now composing the county of Carroll, on the place where he lived and died, in the

Fall of 1826, now more than thirty years ago. How brief that period seems, to look back; and yet what changes have taken place! The 'old settlers' of Carroll of thirty years ago, where are they? A few still remain; but the greater part of them have gone to join that 'old settlers' meeting' which will have no end!

"But business imperiously forbids my absence from home. I must therefore deny myself the honor and the pleasure of accepting your invitation.

"Please accept my sincerest wishes for your health and happiness, and that of all the 'old settlers' of Carroll. R. H. MILROY.

"TO JAMES H. STEWART, JAMES ODELL, ABNER ROBINSON, THOS. STIRLIN, AND I. M. EWING."

The following sketch, written by Mrs. Magdalina M'Cain, the wife of Daniel M'Cain, was read to the meeting:

"*June*, 1855.

"My husband and myself were both born and raised near Lebanon, Warren County, Ohio, our parents having settled there in early times, and stemmed the hardships of a new settlement; and when we turned out to seek our fortunes in the world, we thought it best, while we were young, to emigrate still farther West. My husband having been out, selected and secured a home. We accordingly made preparations, and on the 9th day of November, 1826, we bade adieu to weeping friends and relatives, and to our native country, and, with two ox-teams, slowly wended our way for Indiana, which at that time was almost an unbroken wilderness, where the sound of the white man's ax was seldom heard; but in the place of it the chirping of birds, or the occasional howl of the wolf, the dismal hoot of the owl, or the shrill screaming of the wild-cat. On the 28th day of the same month we landed here on Deer Creek, where we still reside.

"I have not many particular incidents to relate during our journey, except the road, if such it could be called, was very muddy, and difficult to pass in many places, on account of the trees and gulleys. We had some cold, disagreeable weather, and some snow, the night before we reached our forest home. We camped near what is called 'Little Sugar Creek.' Here a dismal night we passed. It had been snowing occasionally for two days, and after dark the wind began to blow, and it blew almost a hurricane. It is now more than twenty-eight years; but the tall trees bending over our heads, are still fresh before my eyes. It appeared as if every tree would be leveled with the ground by the contending elements. And yet, though there were seven of us in number, there was not even a hair on our heads injured; for He who feeds the young ravens, is able to save us through the greatest dangers. So, we being spared through that stormy night, soon arranged every thing in the morning, and started again with fresh vigor for our destination, which we reached about the middle of the day. We then pitched a tent, and having every thing arranged, I prepared dinner, and we ate a hearty meal, for the first time, at our new home. Kings in their palaces, and with all their dainties, never ate with better relish and with more pleasure than we did, with the hind-gate of the wagon for a table, and nothing but the blue heavens over our heads. After we had finished a hearty repast, the men began the work of erecting a cabin—there being five in number—three of them being my brothers-in-law, Joseph, William, and Ramsey M'Cain, and a cousin, John M'Cain, having accompanied us. In just *three days* they had our cabin so that it was barely possible to live in it, the roof being on, a door cut out, and one side and end chunked, which afterward received a partial supply of mortar. It then commenced raining, and we put what little we had into our new abode. Right happy were we to have at last, poor as it was, a shelter from the storms The next morning, two of the men took their guns, and went out to try their luck at shooting deer, and they had the good fortune to bring one in. It required but a few minutes to dress it; and then the men all went about a mile distant, to erect a cabin for William M'Cain; for it was his intention to move out the ensuing Fall. I was left alone with my son, then a little over two years old. We were, of course, very lonely; but being busily engaged, I got along very well, except one little fright. Toward noon, I saw, some distance from the house—for I was continually on the watch—two animals, which I knew could be none other than the hungry wolf, smelling along the trail of the deer that had been brought in. As one would naturally suppose, I was very much frightened, and for a few moments cast in my mind what I should do. But on consideration, I thought if they attempted to come near, or to attack us, I would try to scald them, as I had plenty of hot water. But I suppose they deemed it prudent to keep at a tolerable distance, for women are dangerous; they generally fight with formidable weapons, such as *scalding water* or the *broom*. At length they disappeared, and I saw no more of them. This was on Saturday. The first of the next week, the men finished their cabin, and William and John M'Cain left for their respective homes, in Ohio, leaving the other two with us. The provisions we were unable to bring with us, such as corn and pork, were to be provided for the Winter; and by the time they were hauled up from Wild-cat, for they could not be had any nearer, cold weather set in so severe, that we were forced to live in our house all Winter, just as we first went into it. But we did not suffer; for we kept a good fire in one end of the house, and left an opening in the roof for the smoke to escape. There were no mills in reach of us, except Mr. Robinson's little mill, which answered a very good purpose for grinding corn; but even that, because of the severe cold weather, froze up, and we were obliged to make hominy, and pound corn to make meal for bread. We had brought two barrels of flour with us; but *that* we did not wish to use up immediately. We were blessed with health and good appetites, and we lived happy and contended. Neighbors were very scarce, there being no more than ten or eleven families on Deer Creek, from the Wabash up to where Mr. John Odell lived, a distance of seven or eight miles, and but as many more a few miles north of us, on Rock Creek. The Indians were, for a year or two, more frequent visitors at our cabin than were the whites, but they were always peaceable.

"After a long and tedious Winter, Spring came at last, and brought with it all the comforts and delights that a wild country was capable of affording. My husband cleared five acres for corn, and he soon made our cabin more comfortable. He laid a floor, having hauled logs through the deep snow (for it fell over two feet deep), to Mr. Robinson's saw-mill, who was kind enough to erect a small grist and saw mill, for the accommodation of himself and those who might chance to follow him. We also got a chimney up, and added several comforts that we stood in need of. I believe that I then felt as happy as a queen. Spring brought with it its troubles as well as its beauties; for the rattlesnakes were so numerous, that we were in danger wherever we went. I was continually afraid that our little son, in strolling around, would be bitten by one, or that one might crawl into the house, as they frequently did among the neighbors; but we got along very well in that line. We killed a great many snakes of every description. When I would be out attending to my domestic affairs, working in the garden, and milking, I had no one to take care of my infant, except my eldest child, and he did it well; for he would sit and watch over his little brother, and rock him in a sugar-trough, which was a very good substitute for a cradle. Although many years have passed since those events, yet I can never think of them without a shudder; to think how easily the Indians might have slipped into the house, in my absence, and carried off my little treasures. But they were protected and spared, I hope for better purposes; for our eldest son is now in the far West (Kansas) at a missionary establishment, teaching the young Indians.

"Our family was small when we first came here, having but one child. Our children now number eleven. We came here in high hopes, and our hopes have been in a great measure realized. We have labored and toiled, and been greatly blessed with health and strength, and with all the comforts of life. We have seen the great change from a mere wilderness to a well inhabited country of finely cultivated farms; comfortable buildings, towns, and villages have dotted all over the beautiful land. What astonishing improvements in the roads and travel! For years after we came here, if a man on horseback could ride from here to Lebanon, Ohio, in five or six days, it was considered a *very speedy trip*. And only think of the lazy ox, trudging along for weeks, completely worrying down his driver, who, with uplifted gad, with slow and weary steps, is continually trying to urge him on, but to no purpose. Not so with the fierce and warlike iron horse; he goes thundering along at most fearful speed, and carries you over the same distance in one day. What a contrast! It is perfectly astonishing, and yet it is even so. DANIEL AND MAGDALENA M'CAIN."

"Since the above was written, I have been called to drink deeply of the bitter cup of affliction, which God in his providence saw fit to send to me; and the reason why I now send this to you, is because my husband was anxious that we, with the rest of the early settlers, should give a short account, simple though it might be, of our emigration and hardships, if such they could be called; for I can scarcely realize that I had any hardships, when I remember that I experienced them with a kind and beloved husband.

"MAGDALENA M'CAIN."

Her husband died on the 5th day of September, 1855.

Judge INGRAM, being called on, said:

"It is gratifying to meet so many old friends; I feel peculiarly endeared to the early pioneers.

"I came to the Wabash when I was young. Then we had but few of the comforts of life. The most kindly feelings were felt for all, and by all. *Then there was true friendship!* The cares are much greater *now* than they were then. Perhaps the reason is, that when we are younger, we have fewer cares.

"The 'old settlers' knew each other well. In the settlement of a new country, our mutual *wants* make us dependent on each other.

"I came to Indiana in 1824—saw the Wabash in 1826. I attended the 'house-raisings,' 'log-rollings,' greetings, etc. I experienced much pleasure. Every person was kind and generous; it arose from the goodness of their nature. People were kind, benevolent, and frank.

"Attended the first court in Delphi, in the Spring of 1828; it was held at Mr. Baum's house. Next Fall attended court again; I was then living at Indianapolis. On my way to court, seven or eight miles below Delphi, I got lost; night overtook me; there was no track; nothing but an Indian trail; felt for the path; got into the woods; heard a dog, and at length reached Mr. M'Cord's house, about midnight, where I was received with characteristic hospitality. And yet, these were not hardships; for if the rattlesnakes and wolves kept at a distance, I was satisfied.

"On my first trip to Indiana, I came with my knapsack on my back,—sorry that I did not retain it as a 'relic.' Then, if we were able to be the owners of a horse, we were getting along finely. It is no credit to a man to see him ashamed of work; it is also a bad sign not to know how to work; and it is an excellent idea for young ladies to know how to make coats and pants.

"I was only four years old when my mother died, and eight at the death of my father. I have worked by the month. Work gives us vigor of body, as well as of mind. Idleness leads to bad habits. Let a boy be brought up idle, and he is always idle.

"I remember, on one occasion, to have slept out in the woods, six miles above Logansport; no town there then; was traveling with James Rariden, who was a member of Congress afterward. Rariden had a tin-cup and some venison. Struck a fire, and got some spice-wood. The only fear was of rattlesnakes; but we fell asleep, and slept till morning. I have slept out of doors often.

"Industry was a peculiar characteristic of the first settlers. Much extravagance has been introduced by persons who get their money by stealing. I remember how the early settlers talked of the importance of *good morals*. Their hopes have been realized. People are now prosperous, and are reaping the fruits of industry."

ENOCH STANSEL, Esq., being called upon, said: He had nothing at all interesting. He came to this county the first time in 1825 or '26. Aaron Gregg was with him. It *was* a new country then.

"Left Crawfordsville, and came to Lafayette; they could not take us in, and we lay in the hazel-brush. Then we came up in this section, and camped at night; we had nothing left except hard crackers. My father, Mr. Gregg, and his father, were with us. My father had been a prisoner with the Indians five years. We laid out on a bluff, near Rock Creek. We then returned to Crawfordsville, and entered our land.

"In the Fall of 1831, I removed to this county. One time, when we came to the Wabash, we had our horses stolen, and were compelled to walk home.

"I attended canal land-sales, at Logansport. I took the Indian trail; but when night came on, my horse left the trail, and, after wandering about a long time, I found myself at old man Harness's, on the Michigan road. I was so lost that, next morning, I took the wrong end of the road.

"In the Fall of 1831, started to remove to this county; was twenty-one days on the road. We had to cut brush to make our beds on, as it rained all the time."

Mr. Aaron Gregg said: "Mr. Stansel and myself were together. He has given a correct account. On the last day of December, 1826, I was married. In October, 1828, myself, my wife, and brother left Warren County, Ohio, and came to this county. We camped out every night; had good roads, as the Fall was dry. Built a shanty and cleared off an acre of ground, between Christmas and New-Years; started back to Ohio, and arrived at home January 17th, spending half a month in the journey. In October, 1830, I removed here again."

John Wesley Gillam said: "I was in my twentieth year when I removed to this county. The last of March we crossed on the ice. Four of us started in advance, and arrived four days before the family. When we arrived on the land which my father, Judge Gillam, had purchased, our company camped out. *Then*, but one family resided in the direction of Delphi. I never enjoyed myself better in my life. We went to clearing land, and had a sufficient quantity of acres under cultivation to support the family. It was some time after our arrival at our new home before we saw a 'settler.' "

HENRY M. GRAHAM said: "I came to this county in January, 1829. We had considerable trouble. We had eight boys in the family, and I was next to the oldest. When we arrived at General Milroy's, we removed into a *stable*, and remained in that till we got a cabin up, with a hole in the roof to permit the smoke to escape. The first night after we were in the cabin, it snowed, and the snow continued six weeks; all were bare-footed, except father and myself. My feet were frozen that Winter. We rented some cleared ground of Mr. Odell. Our mill was erected in the house, in the shape of a hominy-mortar."

CHAPTER V.

OLD SETTLERS' FOURTH, FIFTH, SIXTH, AND SEVENTH MEETINGS.

JUNE 13, 1857, being the day fixed for the annual meeting of the old settlers of Carroll County, the following members met in the grove above Delphi: Abner Robinson and family, William M'Cord, James Odell and family, Thomas Stirlin, Adam Porter, Aaron Gregg, Isaac Robbins, Henry M. Graham, John Barr, Isaac Jackson, Andrew Burntrager, Enoch Stansel, Isaac Wilson, Hamilton Thompson, William M. Young, Mrs. Martha Milroy, and James H. Stewart.

After partaking of a bountiful repast, the meeting was called to order by the president; the roll was called, and the Minutes of last meeting read.

Judge ROBERT H. MILROY (then a resident of Rensselaer), being called upon, addressed the meeting, and gave a great many interesting incidents connected with the early settlement of Carroll County. Judge M., at the time of the removal of his father, General Milroy, to this county, was only about ten years old. He spoke of the large number of rattlesnakes; said that more than once he had stepped upon them with his naked feet, but had escaped being bitten. The raccoons were also very plenty; and one year they actually destroyed the *entire* corn-crop of Joseph M'Cain! Judge M. referred to several persons present. William Hughes, he said, was the great deer and "coon" hunter, and if the ghosts of all the deer and "coons" killed by him could be gathered in one place, and be visible to the naked eye, the sight would be a horrible one? The judge described the great interest taken in house-raisings, and how important it was to have good *corner-men*, and that John Ballard, James Odell, and Thomas Stirlin were celebrated in that way.

The judge said he had been taught in the first school ever opened in Carroll County. It was kept on the old farm of Henry Robinson, at the house in which Mr. R. first resided, on the ground now covered by the barn. The school was kept by Miss Sarah Robinson.

He concluded his interesting address by exhorting the early pioneers to prepare for that "old settlers' meeting" beyond the grave, to which we are all hastening.

After the conclusion of the address, the president requested all "old settlers," who had not heretofore enrolled their names as members of this Society, to come forward and do so. The following persons gave in their names:

Names.	Where Born.	Age.	Date of Settlement.
William Hance..................	Kentucky	62	October 25, 1828.
George Merkle................	Pennsylvania...	52	February, 1832.
Joseph H. Newman.........	North Carolina	60	October 6, 1831.
Robert H. Milroy...........	Indiana..........	41	October, 1826.
John R. Ballard..............	New York......	52	May 5, 1825.
Charles Angell...............	Indiana..........	35	February, 1825.
Franklin G. Armstrong...	Indiana..........	34	October 20, 1829.
William A. Barns..........	Ohio..............	46	April, 1831.
Joel H. Dewey...............	Indiana..........	32	March 5, 1827.
Daniel H. Lenon............	Ohio..............	44	October 21, 1829.
John Lenon....................	Ohio..............	36	October 21, 1829.
Martha G. Frazer..........	Delphi...........	26½	....

On motion of Mr. Isaac Jackson, it was

Resolved, That the next meeting of the Society be held on some farm to be selected by the Executive Committee.

Abner Robinson was again unanimously re-elected president of the Society.

OLD SETTLERS' FIFTH MEETING.

August 14, 1858.

In accordance with previous notice, a large number of "old settlers" and others met on the bluff of Deer Creek, above the house of Samuel L. Milroy. After dinner, Abner Robinson, Esq., the president, called the meeting to order, when the following members answered to their names: Abner Robinson, William M'Cord, James Odell, Thomas Stirlin, Adam Porter, Isaac Robbins, John B. Milroy, James H. Stewart, James M'Dowell, John D. Wilson, Isaac Wilson, Hamilton Thompson, William M. Young, Fanny Stirlin, George Merkle, John R. Ballard, and Joel H. Dewey.

The president requested all persons who arrived in Carroll County prior to the 1st day of January, 1835, and who desired to become members of this Society, to come forward and enroll their names, whereupon the following individuals complied with the request, and became members:

Names.	Where Born.	Age.	Date of Settlement.
Sarah Robinson	Ohio	60	January 5, 1825.
William C. Carson	Tennessee	31	November 6, 1834.
James Brown	Tennessee	61	May 1, 1833.
Wm. H. Buford	Kentucky	52	Sept. 30, 1832.
Aston L. Brown	Tennessee	28	May 1, 1833.
Milton R. Graham	Indiana	31	January, 1829.
Sarah Graham	Carroll County	33	....
Ambrose Phelps	New York	58	March, 1834.
Charlotte D. Phelps	New York	46	1827.
Austin Williamson	Ohio	33	October 1, 1830.
John Curtner	Tennessee	37	January 15, 1831.
Lemuel Patterson	Alabama	32	October, 1832.
John Greenup	Kentucky	41	Sept. 30, 1832.
Samuel G. Greenup	Kentucky	39	Sept. 30, 1832.
Samuel Lenon	Ohio	29	October, 1829.
Jane Griffith	Kentucky	63	April 1837.
Israel Rohrbaugh	Virginia	31	October 4, 1828.
Henry H. Greenup	Kentucky	40	Sept. 30, 1832.
Mary Dunkle	Carroll County	30	....

Names.	Where Born.	Age.	Date of Settlement.
Samuel M'Cain	Carroll County	24	
Mirinda Dugan	Ohio	...	
Editha C. Holt	New York	33	August, 1834.
Sarah Odell	Ohio	49	August 1836.
Mary Dale	Parke County	...	1832.
Nancy Ramey	Washington Co	...	September, 1826.
Louisa Greenup	Kentucky	...	Sept. 30, 1832.
Matilda Stauffer	Indiana	35	February, 1826.
James W. Milroy	Carroll County	30	
Emeline Burns	Kentucky	...	1834.
Cassandra Brown	Virginia	53	May 1, 1833.
Sarah E. Robinson	Carroll County	...	
Malinda Patterson	Virginia	32	1832.
George Kuns	Ohio	36	Sept. 18, 1827.

Colonel JOHN B. MILROY spoke of some of the characteristics of many of the "old settlers." He remarked particularly of Judge Isaac Griffith; thought he had done more than any other man for the early settlers; he was against vice in all its forms, and he had many virtues. He built the first saw-mill, and opened the first store. He "pushed business." The colonel also spoke of the many manly virtues of Jonah T. Hopkinson; he was a "first-rate" old man. The colonel remarked, that no citizen born in Carroll County had ever been hanged or sent to the state prison. The speaker also alluded to Hugh Graham, and paid a flattering compliment to his many manly virtues; also of Jacob Baum, one of the first county commissioners; of his willingness to help his neighbors at log-rollings. Colonel M. also named the Greenups, Captain Buford, Daniel M'Cain, George Merkle, Joseph M'Cain; also John Ballard, who made the first shingles in the county. He also referred to Jeremiah Ballard, who married one of Mr. Baum's daughters; it being the second marriage in the county. The first marriage was George I. Baum and Miss Manary. The colonel also referred to Jacob Mitchell.

He described the operation of pounding hominy in those early days; the *coarse* was used for hominy and the *fine* for bread.

He alluded to James M'Dowell in complimentary terms, Solomon Burket, John Bozarth, Sr., and John Robbins, who opened the second or third store ever opened in the county; his dry jokes were very amusing; they were very much like those told by old Joseph Jackson.

Major WM. H. BUFORD said: He was happy to meet so many of his old friends. The major said he arrived in Delphi in 1832, and painted the first house in Delphi; mustered the first company; also, that he was the second cabinet-maker. The first twelve months, he shook with the "ague" *all the time.*

AUSTIN WILLIAMSON next addressed the meeting, and gave an interesting account of the settlement of his father, David Williamson, and his grand-father, Samuel Williamson, on Rock Creek, in this county. He also spoke of the great number of rattlesnakes killed in that locality. Mr. W. said his grandmother still resided on the *old place*, and, although over eighty years of age, could still mount her horse, and ride several miles to church.

It having been stated that Dr. John M. Ewing, a member of the Executive Committee, was absent from the county most of the time, on motion, Colonel John B. Milroy was elected to fill the vacancy.

Colonel MILROY remarked: That his father, General Milroy, succeeded in getting through the Legislature the first act against gambling; had organized the first *temperance society;* and that, by his influence, Delphi was located here.

Abner Robinson, Esq., was re-elected president of the Society.

The Rev. N. L. Brakeman, Pastor of the Methodist Episcopal Church, being present, opened the meeting with prayer, and closed the same with the benediction.

OLD SETTLERS' SIXTH MEETING.

August 20, 1859.

A CONSIDERABEE number of the "old settlers" of Carroll County met on the farm of Mr. Samuel L. Milroy.

On calling the roll, the following members answered to their names: Sarah Robinson, Milton R. Graham, Austin J. Williamson, Lemuel Patterson, Jane Griffith, Mrs. Mirinda Dugan, Mrs. E. C. Holt, Mrs. Sarah Odell, Mrs. Nancy Ramey Coble, Mrs. Martha Beck, George Kuns, Abner Robinson, Wm. M'Cord, James Odell, Thomas Stirlin, Adam Porter, Aaron Gregg, William M'Cain, Isaac Robbins, John B. Milroy, Joseph Cox, Isaac Jackson, James H. Stewart, Andrew Burntrager, Enoch Stansel, James M'Dowell, John D. Wilson, Isaac Wilson, Enoch Cox, Daniel Baum, Jr., Hamilton Thompson, Archibald Slane, John Lenon, Martha G. Frazier Whittaker.

The president of the Society called the meeting to order, and the secretary made a short address, in which he stated what he understood to be the object of the Society: To spend at least one day in the year in renewing old acquaintance among the early pioneers, to throw off labor and care, and thus cultivate social feelings.

The following persons then enrolled their names as members of the Society:

Names.	Where Born.	Age.	Date of Settlement.
Joseph M'Cain	Ohio	62	December 8, 1826.
David Williamson	Pennsylvania	57	October 1, 1830.
Rhoda Phelps	Connecticut	59	August, 1834.
Anna Williamson	Pennsylvania	56	October 1, 1830
Magdalena M'Cain	Ohio	53	Dec. 28, 1826.
Susanna Ballard	Ohio	51	April 30, 1825.
George Malcom	Virginia	69	Dec. 20, 1831.
George Zook	Ohio	37	October, 1828.
Rob't Davidson	Pennsylvania	64	October 28, 1835.
Margaret Davidson	Pennsylvania	62	October 28, 1835.
Thomas Thompson	Kentucky	47	October 15, 1831.
Hugh R. M'Cully	Tennessee	38	February, 1833.
Anna M'Cally	Ohio	33	October 28, 1835.
George S. Fouts	Ohio	54	October 10, 1831.
Elizabeth Gregg	Pennsylvania	55	October, 1830.
Elmira Stansel	Ohio	50	1832.
Elizabeth Berkshire	Ohio	...	....
Mary Burntrager	New Jersey	50	September, 1829.
John F. Evans	Ohio	30	September, 1834.
Ann Caroline Robinson	Carroll County.	23	....
Lydia I. Robinson	Carroll County.	20	....

Mr. George Malcom said: That in early times he was compelled, on several occasions, to swim his horse across the Wabash River, in order to get to Henry Robinson's mill, above Delphi.

Hon. Thomas Thompson compared the present with the olden times; and made a very interesting speech.

Austin J. Williamson made a happy address, and presented to the Society a part of the cloth which composed the bolt in the flouring-mill of his grandfather, Samuel Williamson, on Rock Creek.

On motion of Colonel Milroy, a committee of five, consisting of Samuel L. Milroy, Samuel M'Cain, John Odell, John D. Wilson, and Enoch Stansel, were appointed to prepare tables, and procure music for the next meeting of the Society.

On motion, Abner Robinson, Esq., was elected president of the Society **for life.**

OLD SETTLERS' SEVENTH MEETING.

August 25, 1860.

AGAIN the "old settlers" of Carroll County met on the farm of Samuel L. Milroy. After Heaven's blessing was invoked by Mr. William M'Cord, and a bountiful repast, the meeting was called to order by the president.

The following members answered the roll-call: Abner Robinson, Wm. M'Cord, James Odell, Adam Porter, William M'Cain, Isaac Robbins, John B. Milroy, James H. Stewart, Andrew Burntrager, Enoch Cox, Hamilton Thompson, William M. Young, John R. Ballard, Franklin G. Armstrong, Martha G. Whittaker, Sarah Robinson, William H. Buford, Milton R. Graham, Charlotte D. Phelps, Samuel M'Cain, Sarah Odell, Sarah E. Robinson, Magdalena M'Cain, Susanna Ballard, George S. Fouts, Ann Caroline Robinson, Lydia I. Robinson. The following persons were admitted as members of the Society:

Names.	Where Born.	Age.	Date of Settlement.
Samuel Grimes..............	Maryland	54	June, 1835.
Elizabeth Smith.............	Pennsylvania..	...	1836.
Nancy Hubbard............	Vermont	69	1833
James Griffith	Carroll County	26	....
Geo. Vandeventer...........	Carroll County	...	....
Elizabeth Bragunier.......	Pennsylvania..	65	April, 1836.
Lucretia Sherfey............	Vermont	...	April, 1836.
James Kirkpatrick..........	Indiana	...	July, 1836.
Amanda Kirpatrick.........	Indiana	...	....
Abigail Lyon.................	New York.......	45	1833.
James H. Barns..............	Carroll County	24	....
Matilda A. Milroy...........	Ohio	33	November, 1830.
Mary Ann M'Donald......	Carroll County	24	....
Mary E. Martin..............	Carroll County	...	....
Abigail M'Cain...............	Pennsylvania..	53	December 10, 1828.
Ann Lyon......................	Ohio	34	February 17, 1829.
Mary J. Armstrong.........	Ohio	29	....
John W. Wharton............	Pennsylvania..	48	June, 1837.
Ann Wharton.................	Pennsylvania..	40	June, 1837.
Harvey Wilson	Carroll County	25	....
Edward M. Barns............	Carroll County	22	....

It was ordered that all "old settlers" who came to this county prior to the 1st day of January, 1836, be accepted as members of this Society.

It was ordered that the permanent time for the meeting of this Society be on the FOURTH SATURDAY OF AUGUST IN EACH YEAR, and the farm of Samuel L. Milroy be the permanent place of meeting.

Colonel MILROY addressed the meeting. He spoke of John Ballard, and said that in 1825 Mr. B. did nothing for six weeks but wait upon the sick.

Remarks were also made by J. H. Stewart, Abner Robinson, Esq., William M'Cord, John W. Penn, James Odell, and Dr. F. G. Armstrong.

At this stage of the proceedings, a young man rode up dressed in Indian costume, and rehearsed an excellent Indian speech, portraying the wrongs and outrages inflicted by the white man on the red man.

The meeting then adjourned till the fourth Saturday (24th) of August, 1861.

CHAPTER VI.

OLD SETTLERS' EIGHTH AND NINTH MEETINGS.

A PRELIMINARY meeting of the Executive Committee was held at Dr. James H. Stewart's office, July 27, 1861, and prepared the necessary programme for the coming general gathering. A little scrap of valuable history came in, which we insert here.

Hugh Graham was born on the 12th of March, 1787, in Greenbrier County, Virginia, and moved to Clarke County, Indiana, in September, 1816, and again to Washington County, in 1818. He arrived in Carroll County, January 6, 1829. In 1836, he was elected one of the Carroll County commissioners.

Having lost his wife, July 14, 1838, he returned in May, 1839, to Washington County, where he died on the 18th day of April, 1844. Mr. Graham was married twice, and left two children by his second wife and several by his first, as mourning kindred.

THE MILROY FARM, *August 24, 1861.*

This being the day appointed for the annual meeting of the "Old Settlers'" Society, the following members answered to their names: Abner Robinson, Wm. M'Cord, Thomas Stirlin, William Hughes, Aaron Gregg, John W. Gillam, Isaac Jackson, Isaac Robbins, James H. Stewart, Andrew Burntrager, John Wilson, Isaac Wilson, Fanny Stirlin, John R. Ballard, William A. Barns, Sarah Robinson, Austin Williamson, Samuel M'Cain, Mirinda Dugan, Sarah Odell, Martha Beck, James W. Milroy, Dan. Williamson, Anna Williamson, Magdalena M'Cain, Susanna Ballard, George Malcom, Robert Davidson, George S. Fouts, Elizabeth Gregg, Mary Burntrager, Ann Caroline Robinson, Lydia J. Robinson, Abigail Lyon, James H. Barns, Mary A. M'Donald, Abigail M'Cain, Edward M. Barns.

The meeting was opened with prayer, and Abner Robinson, the president, called for new members, and the following persons recorded as such:

Names.	Where Born.	Age.	Date of Settlement.
John W. Penn	Kentucky	52	Nov. 14, 1833.
Elizabeth Graham	Virginia	39	....
Huldah Penn	Kentucky	48	Nov. 14, 1833.
Abraham Deal	Pennsylvania	57	May 10, 1830.
Elizabeth Deal	Indiana	49	May 10, 1830.
James G. Malcom	Indiana	46	Dec. 30, 1831.
Charles Martin	Tennessee	58	1834.
James H. Johnson	Tennessee	36	October 1, 1834.
George Byers	Ohio	57	October, 1827.
Robert Fisher	Indiana	41	October, 1827.
Abner H. Bennett	Ohio	52	August 11, 1836.
Martin Wagoner	Pennsylvania	62	May, 1832.
Johnson Earnest	Ohio	56	March 1830.
David Harter	Ohio	41	November, 1827.
Thomas Meneaugh	Indiana	42	October, 1835.
Arthur Compton	Ireland	...	Oct. 1829, Clint. co.
Alex. Sanderson	Ohio	51	Sept. 20, 1836.
Adam Rohrbaugh	Virginia	41	October 4, 1828.
Anna Sanderson	....	43	1827.

John W. Penn made some remarks, in which he said that the men who helped to raise his cabin when he settled in Carroll County, were John Shanks, Abner Shanks, Levi Cline, John Lenon, Daniel Lenon, Jacob Slusser, Joseph Neff, and William Armstrong. These men were now nearly all gone. Mr. P. said he had enjoyed himself, and had general good health since his arrival in the county. The people in the early settlement were remarkably clever.

George Byers and Isaac Jackson also made some interesting remarks, and the meeting adjourned, after having spent a very pleasant day.

OLD SETTLERS' NINTH MEETING.

MILROY'S FARM, *August* 23, 1862.

THE Society met at the usual place; Abner Robinson, the president, presiding.

To the roll-call, the following members answered to their names: Abner Robinson, William M'Cord, James Odell, Thomas Stirlin, Isaac Robbins, William Hughes, John B. Milroy, Joseph Cox, Andrew Burntrager, John Wilson, Isaac Wilson, Enoch Cox, Hamilton Thompson, William M. Young, Phenia Royster, Fanny Stirlin, Nancy M. Coble, Magdalena M'Cain, Robert Davidson, Elizabeth Smith, Harvey Wilson, John W. Penn, Huldah Penn, Abraham Deal, Elizabeth Deal.

By request of the president, the following persons came forward, and had their names recorded as members of the Society:

Names.	Where Born.	Age.	Date of Settlement.
Sam. Thompson............	Kentucky	55	October 10, 1826.
Hugh Manary...............	Ohio..............	50	October 4, 1825.

The president stated, with much feeling, that he missed the faces of many. Old Mr. R—— had gone to "that bourne from whence no traveler returns." He referred to the many happy reminiscenses of old times, when the people met together in the log-cabins. He said that there was not a person present who assisted him to build his cabin, but Mr. Stirlin came soon afterward. He referred to some of the trials of the first settlers, among which were, having to go fifty miles to mill, and cut out the road before you; having no neighbors; having to go fifty miles to the nearest post-office, and fifty miles to procure marriage-license, and seventy-five miles to obtain a minister to solemnize the same.

Colonel JOHN B. MILROY said he was glad to see so many people here in good health. We can meet here on a common platform. He looked upon his first years spent in the wilderness of Carroll County as the happiest of his life.

Colonel Milroy referred to the death of Dr. John M. Ewing, one of the early pioneers of the county, and the *first physician.* Dr. Ewing had, for several years past, resided in Illinois. He joined the Ninth Indiana Regiment a short time prior to the battle of *Pittsburg Landing,* and was appointed hospital steward, in which position he died. Dr. Ewing was a true patriot, and died alike honored and respected.

The colonel spoke of the present unhappy condition of the country, and said that Carroll County had no cause to blush. The colonel's old company (A, Ninth Regiment) had been in six fights, and in the last, four were killed and fourteen wounded.

After having spent a few hours very pleasantly, and partaking of a picnic dinner, the meeting adjourned.

On account of the War, no records are found of the years 1863, 1864, and 1865.

CHAPTER VII.

OLD SETTLERS' TENTH, ELEVENTH, TWELFTH, THIRTEENTH, FOURTEENTH, AND FIFTEENTH MEETINGS.

Saturday, August 4, 1866.

ON this day the "old settlers" of Carroll County met at the usual place of meeting ("Milroy Farm"), Abner Robinson, the president, presiding.

All the members of the Committee of Arrangements were also present, to wit: Thomas Stirlin, James Odell, John B. Milroy, Abner Robinson, and James H. Stewart.

Rev. John W. Gillam addressed the Throne of Grace; after which the meeting was opened for business.

The Minutes of the last meeting were read, and adopted.

Rev. Williamson Wright, who had previously been selected by the Committee of Arrangements (Executive Committee), delivered a most excellent address.

After which the venerable JAMES BLAKE, of Indianapolis, aged seventy-four years, proceeded to address the people. Mr. B. gave a history of the first settlement of Indianapolis; of the clearing of the heavy timbers on the town plot; the employment of *niggers* in burning off logs, etc. He detailed his operations in the purchase of ginseng in Carroll County; told a great many anecdotes, particularly about the bear and the man with the jug of whisky. Mr. B. was in Delphi at the first sale of lots, and started the subscription paper for the erection of the *school-house*, and the house for Rev. James Crawford, Presbyterian minister.

Mr. B. spent three months of the year (while curing ginseng) in this county; was always superintendent of Sunday-school while here. He spoke of his intimacy with General Milroy, and eulogized the firmness of his wife. Said that on one occasion (while he, Mr. B., was present), two of the boys, General Robert H., and Colonel John B., were taken with spasms at the same moment; that Mrs. B., calmly as an old physician, tied up their arms and *bled* them, thus saving their lives! Mr. B. continued to interest the audience with incidents connected with the early settlement of this county, and anecdotes connected with his long and eventful life; and when he proposed to close, his old friends, so anxious were they to hear him, would scarcely permit him to do so.

At this stage of the proceeding, it was announced that *soup was ready;* and the crowd, numbering ten or twelve hundred, proceeded by the old Indian trail down the bluff to the bank of Deer Creek, at the mouth of M'Cain Run, where that old settler, Joel H. Dewey, had prepared a soup never surpassed; and besides this, citizens had furnished provisions of every kind, together with the barrel of buttermilk cooled with the running brook and ice; and we must not forget the fixtures for the tea preparation, all constructed and arranged under the management of the inimitable Joel. It is scarcely necessary to add that the *old* and young settlers did ample justice to the soup and other good things. After which the people quietly took their departure for their various homes, after, as was universally said, spending one of the most pleasant days of their whole lives.

And the meeting adjourned.

JAMES H. STEWART, *Secretary.*

OLD SETTLERS' ELEVENTH MEETING.

August 10, 1867.

THE "Old Settlers'" Society met at the farm of Samuel S. Milroy, and organized. Prayer was offered; after which the meeting adjourned for dinner.

At half past one the meeting assembled again at the stand. Rev. A. Jones delivered the regular address; after which General Robert Milroy, Judge Orth, Colonel John B. Milroy, Isaac Jackson, John W. Gillman, and others, addressed the meeting.

The following persons connected themselves with the Society: Jacob Humerickhouse, John Burr, John Clark, John Humerickhouse, Daniel H. Leven, Lewis Martin, Robert Fisher, Isaac H. Lake, Jonathan L. Knight, J. R. Saxton.

The meeting adjourned at 5 P. M., after having spent a delightful day.

The 4th of July, 1868, the Executive Committee held a meeting at the office of Sims & Stewart, and Captain George Bowman was selected to deliver the address at the next meeting of the "old settlers," to be held, August 8, 1868.

OLD SETTLERS' TWELFTH MEETING.

August 8, 1868.

A VERY large meeting of "old settlers," and others assembled on the Milroy farm at the time appointed. Abner Robinson, the president of the Society, being absent on account of sickness, the Hon. James Odell was chosen president *pro tem.* The meeting was opened with prayer by the Rev. Wilson Beckner.

Captain George Bowman came forward and spoke to the audience in a very eloquent manner.

After which, General Robert H. Milroy, Henry C.

Dibble, Austin Williamson, Isaac Jackson, Colonel J. B. Milroy, and others, were called upon for speeches.

Grandmother Baum was present, bringing with her a *coffee-mill* that had been used in the Revolutionary War.

A much larger number than usual were present on this occasion, and the day was spent in a most agreeable manner.

Mr. George Bowman was presented to the audience, and interested those present in a well-timed address of about forty minutes. He showed the difference between the education of the children of our pioneer parents and "Young America" of to-day. His remarks upon the benefit of a correct education were excellent, and if carried out would instill into the minds of children loftier and better ideas than they are in the habit of possessing themselves with, in the fast age in which we live.

General Milroy was called on to relate a few of the incidents that occurred in the early settlement of the county. He told about the early settlers having to haul their grain from this county to Michigan City and Chicago, their nearest market, and they would bring back store-goods in return for the merchants. At that time, the ground upon which stands the Garden City of the West, was a wet, marshy prairie, with but a few small frame buildings. At that time there was a United States fort there; and it was here that the general, for the first time in his life, heard the strains of martial music and saw the first of Uncle Samuel's Boys in Blue,—all of which was a great curiosity to him then. At that time the general little dreamed of the future that awaited him in the service of his country. Where he saw but a handful of the brave soldiery of our country then, he lived to witness the marshaling of a million Boys in Blue to defend the Republic in the hour of danger; and at the head of legions he rode foremost in the fight. The general spoke of Uncle Billy Hughes, who was present, being known as the great hunter among the early settlers; and he believed Mr. Hughes had killed a deer on every fifty feet of square ground for ten miles round and about Delphi. He spoke of Mr. John Ballard, who was present, making the first coffin manufactured in the county, which was made to contain the remains of the father of Dr. Angell, who was the first white man that died in the county. The general recited other incidents of the early settlers, which were interesting and amusing to those who listened.

H. C. Dibble, Esq., formerly of Carroll County, now a resident of New Orleans, being present, was called upon and made a few happy remarks. It gave him great pleasure to be present at the meeting of the "old settlers." Though he, perhaps, was a stranger to many of the "old settlers" present, yet they would remember his father, Milo Dibble, who was one of the early pioneers, and at one time treasurer of the county. Mr. Dibble closed his remarks by promising to come from New Orleans to be present at the next meeting of the pioneers of Carroll County.

Rev. Mr. Beckner was then called on. He showed the march of progress from the first settlement of the county until the present time. Then no railroads, no canals, no modern modes of travel—none of the advantages for farming that are in use to-day. It was hard work then, compared with the means used to do the labor of the farm to-day. Mr. Beckner stated that he was among the first children born in the county, and that his mother was the first white person who died in the county, in the region south of Deer Creek. His entire remarks were very appropriate.

Isaac Jackson was next called on. Though perhaps his appearance would not indicate him to be one of the early pioneers, yet he claimed to be one of that number. He had seen the county an unbroken wilderness, and lived to see it blossom as the rose. He had seen it when the only mode of travel was in wagons and on horseback through the dense forest and along the red man's trail; and he had lived to see it with its canal, yea, with its railroad, along which the iron horse speeds his way as with the wings of lightning. Mr. Jackson, in common with all our pioneer fathers and mothers, can see the change since then and now, and can realize how thankful the late settlers should be for the advantages they now enjoy.

Major John B. Milroy was next called on, and related a number of interesting incidents, among which was the plentifulness of rattlesnakes during early times. He had seen as many as three or four hundred in one gang. His father had an old sow that had a systematic way of killing them; she would motion, and get the snake to strike, then pounce upon it with her fore-feet, and tear it in pieces. He had seen deer kill them in the same manner.

Austin Williamson, of Rock Creek, was called on, and related a few incidents of the "early settlers." He contrasted the difference between boys in his day and "fast young men" of the present age. Then it was considered a happy privilege to ask the permission of parents to go to church, or to any little gathering that might be going on in the neighborhood, even though they had to go bare-footed and without a coat or vest; for they had to dress according to their means at that day. How is it now? No parents' wishes are consulted when "Young America" chooses to go. The patent-leather boots, the broadcloth suit, sleek hat, kid-gloves, fast horse, wine-glass, and giddy ball-room, are a part of the fashionable life of to-day not indulged in by the pioneer parents and children. Mr. W's. remarks were gratifying to those who heard him.

Several other old settlers were called upon; but, there being a high wind blowing, making it difficult to be heard, and not being very well, they declined.

Among ancient relics presented, was an old copper tea-kettle, fifty years old, and an iron coffee-mill, the property of Mrs. Daniel Baum, Sr., which had been used in grinding coffee for Revolutionary soldiers.

The president stated that there were four persons present, whose average ages was about eighty years.

A large frame, containing eighty-four pictures of old settlers, the workmanship of J. P. Eversole, was a rich treat to look upon; and to J. M. Grant, of Delphi, who has been years in acquiring the faces of the pioneer fathers, is due the praise. It was justly said, by an old lady who was looking over the collection, "that it was selfish to have all the pioneer fathers in the frame, to the exclusion of the pioneer mothers." Our sentiments exactly; and this grand collection will never be finished until the pioneer mothers, who, alike with their husbands, underwent the trials and perils that attended the first settlement of our county, are secured for exhibition at the next meeting of the "old settlers."

Dr. Stewart, who is permanent secretary of the organization, stated that at least half of the first signers of the organization had passed from earth to their long home.

All business being done, the meeting adjourned.

After the exercises were over, the young folks repaired to Milroy's barn, where they enjoyed themselves in the delights of the dance.

A match game of base-ball was played between the Delphians and Valleys, resulting in a victory for the former. The game was witnessed by hundreds of delighted admirers.

For want of further room, we must draw the curtain over the scenes of the happiest, largest, and best "old settlers'" meeting ever held in the county, trusting that another year may call the survivors together again.

REMINISCENCES OF AN OLD SETTLER.

THE following paper was handed to the secretary by Mrs. Thomas Stirlin, to be read at the recent "old settlers'" meeting, but was unintentionally overlooked, It portrays Mrs. Stirlin's recollection of the scenes of the first settlers of our county, as follows:

"On the 16th day of February, 1825, I, in company with Mr. Odell's family, left Wayne County, Indiana, to emigrate to the Wabash country. Our journey lasted fourteen days. We had rain every day, except two, during our trip. The men would cut brush on which to lay our beds, to sleep. Our clothes would be wet upon our backs in the morning, sometimes. The country from White River to the Wabash was an unbroken wilderness, uninhabited, with the exception of a few Indians at Thorntown. We got along tolerably well, until we got this side Thorntown, when our wagon broke down; then I got into John Odell's wagon, and rode to Potatoe Creek. There John Little met us, with a horse and a yoke of oxen. My husband went to the south fork of Wild-cat Creek, to old Mr. Odell's, after a wagon. We encamped at Potato Creek that night. The next morning I started with Little for his home, on Flint Creek, twenty-five miles distant. I got on the horse, with my babe in my lap, with Little on foot, in advance. Sometimes it rained, and then it snowed, as fast as it could come down. I was on the horse from sunrise until dark, with a child in my arms, two years old. You may be sure that I was very much fatigued. The next day, March 2d, my husband came with our goods. On the day following he was taken sick, and kept down about six weeks. We thought he would die. We had no doctor, nor any medicine. John Odell came to see us, and brought a dose of tartar emetic and some blister flies. These, with some butternut pills, composed our stock of medicine, with a bottle of Bateman's Drops, which we used as an anodyne. He recovered, and we all kept well until August, when he was attacked again with fever and ague, and was very sick for some time. I was confined the 21st of August, and could procure a nurse but for two days, when I had to get up, and perform my work as best I could. A man named Luce took sick and died, near us. As almost every body was sick, my husband and myself had to see to him. My husband was sick, and my babe was only a week old. We succeeded in getting help to dig his grave, and Mordecai Ellis made his coffin by splitting a bass-wood tree, dressing the boards with a broad-ax and jack-plane, and painting them black. He made quite a decent-looking coffin. Another family came to the neighborhood, who had settled on Deer Creek, on what is now the Milroy farm, who all got sick, and lost a child that is buried near the spot we now occupy. Their name was Galbraith. They wanted me to wash for them, as they had no washing done for six weeks. I told them I would try; and I did try, and performed as large a day's work as ever I did, when my babe was but three weeks old. The next December my husband came up to Deer Creek, and built a cabin. February 15, 1826, we started for our new home. We arrived here on Deer Creek on the 19th. The weather was very cold, and the snow about a foot deep. We stopped at John Carey's, and got some fire—we had no matches those times. We drove up to the cabin; I crawled under the wall, scraped away the snow, and kindled a fire, while the men sawed out a door. The snow was about shoe-top deep in the house. We threw down some clapboards, and on them we placed our beds. We slept inside, and the hogs outside. The next morning the mud was as deep in our cabin as the snow had been the evening before. The weather was cold. We built a log-heap in our cabin, but still we almost froze. My husband would hew puncheons all day, and chink our cabin at night. We were nearly three miles from our nearest neighbor. We brought corn-meal with us, sufficient, as we thought, to last until after planting; but it gave out, and I had to pound corn in an iron pot, with an iron wedge driven into the end of a hand-spike, and sift it through a basket-lid. We used the finest of the meal for breakfast, and the coarse for dinner and supper. We got our corn planted about the first of June, and then went to mill in a pirogue, down the Wabash, to a little corn-cracker, near where Lafayette now stands. I was taken sick about the first of July, and both our children. I shook forty days with the ague, without cessation. We then got some quinine, which stopped it for ten days. I got able to ride on horseback, and while going to see John Ballard, who was sick at Mr. Odell's, my horse became frightened, and threw me off; and that brought on the ague more severely than ever, and it held on to me until Christmas. I never saw a woman, except one (Sarah Odell) for three months. My husband was cook, washer-woman, and milk-maid during that time. In October, my husband had to leave home for three days, and I was left alone with my two children. One night our dog fought some animal near the door, which had no shutter but a quilt. I was very much frightened, and our faithful dog was almost killed. He could not walk the next day. John Ballard stayed at our house after that till my husband returned.

"Forty-two years have passed since those times. I have seen our country rapidly settling and improving. There were but eleven families in Carroll County in 1826. One generation has passed away; another has succeeded. There are but two families left whose united head still live—Abner Robinson and ours. A few of the "old settlers" have emigrated to distant lands; but the greater number have passed to that bourne from whence no traveler returns. We, who are left, expect soon to cross the River, and join them in that better land, where sickness and sorrow, pain and death, are feared and felt no more.

"FRANCES STIRLIN."

OLD SETTLERS' THIRTEENTH MEETING.

Extract from the "Delphi Journal" of the Old Settlers' Meeting, held August 14, 1869.

THE "Old Settlers'" Society of Carroll County met at the grounds on the Milroy farm on last Saturday. The sun rose bright and full in the morning, indicating a clear day for the meeting. The Delphi Silver Cornet Band volunteered their services on the occasion, discoursing some of their sweetest music.

At eleven o'clock, the meeting was called to order by the president, Abner Robinson, Esq. The Rev. Mr. Foxworthy addressed the Throne of Grace.

On motion, the Hon. James Odell was elected permanent vice-president, and Joel H. Dewey permanent assistant secretary, of the Society.

The meeting then adjourned for dinner.

Dinner being over, the meeting reassembled. Upon calling the roll, the following members answered to their names:

Abner Robinson, William M'Cord, James Odell, Thomas Stirlin, William Hughes, Adam Porter, Aaron Gregg, Isaac Robbins, John B. Milroy, John Archer, Isaac Jackson, James H. Stewart, Andrew Burntrager, John Wilson, Daniel Baum, Jr., Hamilton Thompson, Fanny Stirlin, Robert H. Milroy, John R. Ballard, Charles Angell, Joel H. Dewey, Ambrose Phelps, Charlotte Phelps, Austin Williamson, Mary Dunkle, Samuel M'Cain, Mirinda Dugan, Martha Beck, Magdelena M'Cain, Susanna Ballard, George Malcom, Robert Davidson, Elizabeth Gregg, Mary Burntrager, John Burr, Matilda A. Milroy, Ann Wharton, Daniel H. Lenon, Robert Fisher, Isaac H. Lake, J. R. Saxton.

After the calling of the roll, Henry C. Dibble, Esq., a native of Delphi, but a citizen of New Orleans, was called upon, and interested the audience for an hour with one of the most beautiful and appropriate addresses we ever listened to. We very much regret our inability to give the address to our readers.

The Hon. C. B. Lasselle, of Logansport, then addressed the meeting, and stated many interesting events in the first settlement of the county. Among other things, he gave a somewhat detailed history of a battle between a detachment of the army of General Hopkins, in 1812, and the Indians, in Carroll County, near where Morkert's (formerly Featherhoof's) mill, on Wild-cat, now stands.

The Hon. G. S. Orth being present, was called for, and gave a very interesting account of his recent trip to California over the Pacific Railroad, and his interview with Brigham Young.

From Cass County, there were in attendance, Job B. Elldridge and wife, William R. Davis and wife, G. R. Thomas and wife, John M'Millen and wife, Charles B. Lasselle and sister, Mrs. Cornwell, Mrs. Andrew M'Clure, Mrs. M. H. Gridley, Mrs. P. Dunkle, Mrs. B.

Bronson, George Dewey and wife, T. B. Helm and son, and Richard Tyner. There may have been some others, whose names have not been reported to us.

It may be proper in this connection to state some of the incidents attaching to the history of two or three or more of the individuals named.

Job B. Elldridge, of Logansport, was the first contractor for carrying the mails from Fort Wayne, through Logansport and Delphi, to Lafayette. At the first, the mail was carried on horseback, once in two weeks; and, as the increasing population of the valley developed the necessity, it was taken once in a week. The horse service soon gave place to the more improved system of *mud-wagons*, and these, in turn, to the *hack* and *coach*. As a pioneer in this department Mr. Elldridge is remembered by many of those early days for his zeal in furnishing them with news from their friends in the home-land. There are many items of special interest, as mementos of the past, connected with this individual, which we might with propriety reproduce at this time, were it not that our columns are already full. We promise, however, in a short time to favor our readers, as of yore, with further and thrilling reminiscences of the almost forgotten past. In this Mr. E. will figure quite extensively.

Richard Tyner related some of his experiences, as one of the "old settlers" of Delphi in particular, though shortly after, and now, a resident of Cass County. He says that in the Summer or Fall of 1831, the first steam-boat on the Upper Wabash was laden with dry-goods for Robert Gist. The goods were landed at a little "opening" near "Sampson's Ferry," where he, with Hiram Calvert, now, also, of Cass County, stood guard over them some six or seven days. The means of transit from that point to Delphi, the place of their destination, being only a "cart," owned, he says by

Father Dewey, and the bayou, now occupied by the canal, full of water, and so muddy, their removal to the "store" required much time, patience, and perseverance, to consummate the enterprise. These goods constituted one among the first regular stores in Delphi.

Among other things, he stated that, about the same time, a few of the aspiring ones organized a body known as the Delphi Legislature, of which Dr. Stewart and a number of others were prominent members. He referred, as a notable incident, that not one of the members of that venerable body ever reached a seat in the Legislature of the State, notwithstanding their eminent legislative experience at home.

John M'Millen, then quite a young man, participated in the erection of several domicils for the accommodation of the enterprising settlers south and east of Delphi—during the period from 1824 to 1826.

Wm. R. Davis, "old settler," is also entitled to remembrance for his judicious and timely handicraft in providing his fellow-settlers with "deer and squirrel rifles" of long and short range, with other paraphernalia for the hunter and scout.

Charles B. Lasselle, whose energy and perseverance in preserving and bringing to light, for the use of posterity, the memorials of the past, made his own speech, and whose history, also, being well known, needs no further comment from us at this time.

T. B. Helm—who, it will be remembered, some years ago, wrote for the *Journal* a series of articles entitled "Historical Reminiscences of Carroll County"—made his appearance, also, among the "old settlers," and participated in their festivities. He promises erelong to resume the publication of those Reminiscences for the benefit of the numerous readers of the *Journal*.

On account of a heavy rain-storm which occurred about four o'clock, many "old settlers" were prevented from relating their early experience. The crowd in attendance was estimated to be at least three thousand, and the reunion was among the most pleasant events in the history of the county.

OLD SETTLERS' FOURTEENTH MEETING.

August 27, 1870.

ABNER ROBINSON called the meeting to order, and, in the absence of the secretary, on motion, Isaac Jackson was appointed secretary *pro tem.* Prayer was offered by Rev. Mr. Brum, of Indianapolis, followed by singing by the "old settlers," and music by the Delphi Silver Cornet Band. The Minutes of the last meeting were read and approved.

The following persons were admitted members of the Society: L. M. Graham, Delilah Stretch, Sarah A. Davis, Eleanor Jackson, Maria Sampson, Lucinda Baker, Lewis Runkle, Joseph Bridge, Elizabeth Bridge, W. W. Holmes, David Cobb, Anson Ballard, Eli Rohrbaugh, Wm. Adkinson, N. I. Malcom, J. G. Malcom, J. H. Johnson, N. A. Johnson, J. N. Cline, Harriet Cline, J. S. Armitage, Elizabeth Williamson, Wm. M'Cain, George J. Baum, Jane Baum, John Youghman, Elizabeth Cox, Margaret Charles.

The following *deaths* of "old settlers" was announced:

John Tedford, February 12, 1870; Elizabeth Robinson, February 12, 1870; S. B. Robinson, August 17, 1869; Ascinath Baum, March 31, 1870; John Anderson, June 1, 1870; William Andrews; Nancy Ball, August 26, 1870; Aaron Gregg, August 16, 1870; Abraham Deal; John Huntsington; Margaret Davidson, April 17, 1868.

After these soelmn announcements, several of the members made short addresses, and, with music by the Silver Cornet Band and singing by the "old settlers," the meeting adjourned to meet the second Saturday in August, 1871.

OLD SETTLERS' FIFTEENTH MEETING.

August 12, 1871.

PROCEEDINGS OF THE MEETING.

THE "old settlers" of Carroll County assembled at the Milroy grove on Saturday last, the 12th instant.

Present: Abner Robinson, President; James H. Stewart, Secretary; James Odell, John B. Milroy, and Thomas Stirlin, the Executive Committee; and a large number of the members of the "Old Settlers'" Society.

By request, the call published in the *Weekly Times* and *Dollar Journal*, the 1st day of June, 1855, preceding the organization of the Society, was read as follows:

OLD SETTLERS' MEETING.

THE undersigned hereby request all the citizens of Carroll County who settled here prior to the year 1831, to meet at the court-house in Delphi, at 10 A. M., on the 9th day of June next, for the purpose of spending a social day in reviewing scenes of the olden time; and also with a view of forming a society for perpetuating the early history of this county. All persons who have been inhabitants of this county prior to the time above named, are requested, before the day of the meetirg ,to reduce tc writing the history, so far as they may remember it, of this county up to the 1st day of January, 1831, and particularly anecdotes of the early settlement, and incidents calculated to throw light upon the early history of the county. Signed by

ABNER ROBINSON,
W. B. GIVINS,
A. W. GILLAM,
JAMES ALLDRIDGE,
DANIEL BAUM, SR.,
THOMAS STIRLIN,
WILLIAM MCCAIN,
J. R. BALLARD,
JAMES ODELL,
C. M. D. WILSON,
G. C. SANDERSON,
H. M. GRAHAM,
JOSEPH KUNS,
ENOCH STANSEL,
JAMES H. STEWART.

After the reading of the above call, prayer was offered by the Rev. Mr. Rice, of Indianapolis.

Sanford C. Cox, Esq., of Lafayette, was then introduced, and entertained the audience by the relation of many incidents connected with the early settlement of the Wabash. With his father, he emigrated to Crawfordsville, in October, 1824. He remembered the time when only three inhabitants lived north of Crawfordsville, in the whole of what is now Northern Indiana. When a boy, Mr. Cox had his thigh broken, and it became necessary to amputate the leg. A runner was sent a distance of one hundred miles to Dr. Shuler, of Terre Haute, requesting his professional services in performing the operation. The messenger found the doctor in an adjoining county, where he was electioneering for Congress against Ratliff Boone. He suspended the electioneering canvass for a few days, visited Crawfordsville, and amputated the leg. Mr. Cox remembered when people wondered whether the Wild-cat and the Shawnee Prairies would ever be settled up.

At the conclusion of Mr. Cox's address, which was listened to with marked attention, the crowd, numbering three or four thousand, adjourned for dinner.

At a quarter past one o'clock, the audience met at the stand, and the first thing was singing by the "old settlers'" choir, led by Austin J. Williamson, and composed, among others, of Dr. J. C. Todd, James Odell, Robert Holt, Thos. Stirlin, Mrs. E. Holt, and Mrs. Strawbridge.

After the singing, several interesting relics were exhibited by Major Buford, the committee appointed to take charge of such articles as might be placed in his hands. Among other things exhibited, was a powderhorn taken from an Indian who had been killed by Mr. Lucas, the gentleman who was the owner of the horn.

On motion of James H. Stewart, the following preamble and resolutions were unanimously adopted:

Whereas, in view of the fact that this county is not the owner of any public grounds suitable for county fairs or other public meetings; and,

Whereas, the interest and convenience of the whole community demand that suitable land should be purchased for the use of the citizens of this county, in holding county fairs, "old settlers'" meetings, and gatherings on other occasions of general interest; therefore,

Resolved, That the Board of County Commissioners of Carroll County be requested to purchase — acres of land convenient to the county-seat, to be used in the holding of county fairs, "old settlers'" meetings, and meetings on other public occasions.

Resolved, That a committee of three be appointed by the president of this Society to circulate petitions asking the county commissioners to purchase public grounds for the purposes aforesaid; and that said committee be requested to act as a permanent committee until the purposes for which it is appointed shall be accomplished.

Messrs. Vine Holt, Robert Fisher, and M. R. Graham were appointed the committee.

The following resolution was then offered by A. J. Williamson:

Resolved, That the president appoint a committee of five to select a location for holding our annual meetings, as near the geographical center of the county as can be secured, and recommend the same to be purchased by the Board of County Commissioners.

The following gentlemen were appointed as the above committee: A. Williamson, R. Holt, A. Porter, John Milroy, and John Pollard.

The following persons enrolled themselves as members of the "Old Settlers'" Society: E. Segraves, Isaac Watson, John Sidenbender, Eli Wingard, J. C. Todd, Lewis W. Wood, G. W. Sinks, W. M. Wyatt, Benj. Lucas, W. Hornback, M. Bair, Geo. Speece, J. Granthem, Mary F. Buford, L. Speece, S. Mills, D. P. Cline and John Curtner.

The deaths of the following named members of the "Old Settlers'" Society were announced: Wm. Atkinson,

Henry Seibert, Lucinda Greenup, John Hardy, Isaac Lake, R. H. Thompson, and J. Boylan.

The Hon. Godlove S. Orth, of Lafayette, being on the ground, was loudly called for, and made a very interesting little speech.

Also, J. D. Hance, now of Fort Wayne (son of Captain Hance, formerly county commissioner), who was raised in this county, having been called out, entertained the audience greatly to its satisfaction.

The meeting then adjourned until the second Saturday of August, 1872, at a place to be designated by the Executive Committee.

CHAPTER VIII.

"O. P. Q."

IN the Spring of 1849, the author published several communications in the *Weekly Times* (then published by Messrs. Applegate & Graham), over the signature of "O. P. Q."

A few of these are here inserted.

EARLY HISTORY OF CARROLL COUNTY.

Mr. Baum came to this county in the Spring of 1825, having attended the land sales at Crawfordsville, and purchased his land in the Fall of 1824. Robert Mitchell, Sr., Robert Mitchell, Jr., Jacob Baum, and John Kistler, accompanied Mr. B. in his keel-boat; erected shanties, and raised corn, in the bottom adjoining town, the first season. It was there, in the Summer of 1825, the first white child was born in Carroll County, Mrs. Kistler being the mother.

When Mr. Baum came to this county, in the Spring of 1825, the only white persons residing in the county were, Henry Robinson, Mr. Angell, Mr. Black, and Aaron Merriman. Until the Fall of 1826, the first settlers had all of their *grinding* done at a little mill, erected by a Mr. Stansbury, on a little stream a mile or two below Lafayette.

In the Fall of 1826, Henry Robinson built his mill. It was not very prepossessing in appearance, but was of great service to the inhabitants. Just below the mill, in a small cave, which may be seen in the bank of Deer Creek, was a celebrated rattlesnake-den; and the writer recollects that the first time he ever saw that cave, a hunter had just shot a large rattlesnake, a few feet back in the cave, and was dragging it out. A den, from which many rattlesnakes came forth every spring, was formerly to be seen on the bank of the creek just below the late Isaac Wilson's residence, and Mrs. Griffith (wife of the late Judge Griffith) told the writer stories about rattlesnakes in the neighborhood of Griffith's mill, that have made him dream of snakes for many nights. Large rattlesnakes were alarmingly plenty. But as the county became settled, their *snakeships* have disappeared, until now it is a very rare occurrence to see one.

NUMBER III.

On the 7th day of January, 1828, the act for the formation of Carroll County passed the Legislature, and on the 12th day of May, in the same year, the first Board of County Commissioners met at the house of Daniel Baum. The Board consisted of Jacob Baum, Aaron Hicks, and Graham Roberts. At that meeting, Daniel Baum was appointed treasurer of the county; Henry B. Milroy was appointed collector; Joseph M'Cain and David M'Combs were appointed constables; Isaac Griffith and Daniel F. Vandeventer were licensed to keep store. . . . .

Henry B. Milroy was appointed, by the Governor, sheriff, to organize the county, and at the August election, 1828, was elected sheriff, Stephen A. Miller being his opponent.

On the 15th day of May, 1828, Enos Lowe, Frederick Moore, Asa B. Strong, Samuel Jessup, and Josiah Briant, the commissioners appointed by the General Assembly, located the seat of justice at Delphi. Samuel Milroy was appointed the first county agent. On the second Monday in August, 1828, the agent, after giving notice in the *Indiana Journal*, *Terre Haute Register*, and a paper at Dayton, Ohio, proceeded to sell the first lots offered for sale in Delphi.

In the Spring of 1829, Joseph Dunham opened the first *tavern* in a *hewed log house*, on the lot occupied by Henry Gros as a dwelling. The next tavern was opened by a Mr. Hays, in the house since occupied by Robert M. Larimer. Hays sold out and quit the country pretty soon, and Samuel Hulry kept the same house for a year or two.

NUMBER IV.

The Summer of 1828 proved very disastrous to the few citizens then residing in Delphi. Being all *new-comers*, unacclimated, moving into a *new place* in temporary habitations, with but little to eat except *fish* and fresh provisions, the consequences might very easily have been foreseen. They were all taken sick. Such a result, under the circumstances, *only* could have been expected; and so it required many years for the town to recover from the effects of that one Summer's sickness. *Rival towns*, in particular, were determined to vote Delphi a "sickly" place, and emigrants and others, on their way to the Wabash, in search of a home, were sure to be warned to shun Delphi. How little *justice* there was in these oft-repeated assertions, may be gathered from the fact, that in *four years*, from 1830 to 1834, only one adult person, Joseph G. Glass, died in the town.

In the Spring of 1830, Delphi could boast of three stores: Gavin Black, who kept where Anthony Foust has since held forth in the blacksmith line; Judge Griffith, in a little frame, across from the market house; and Isaac Martin, on the lot occupied by Dewey and C. E. Balles, in a one-story frame, afterward removed down Franklin Street, and turned into a pottery, and since owned by the red-headed Dutchman, Kaufman. About the 1st of July, 1830, M'Carty & Morris opened a stock of goods in the house now owned by Spears, Dugan & Co., and formerly occupied by Captain Gist. In the Spring of 1831, Robert C. Gist, opened a store in the house on the corner above Bowen's brick, formerly occupied by Daniel B. Doggatt as a cooper-shop.

In the Summer of 1830, most of the citizens had the "ague," and the town improved but little. Joe Dunham moved into his new tavern, above Ewing's store, on Main Street, but was burned down, together with the whole block, in the memorable fire of February, 1839. About the 1st of July, in the same year, the first *lawyer*, Henry Chase, made his location in the town. In April, the logs were rolled on the Public Square. Courts were held in a log school-house adjoining William Barnett's lot (the same on which he has since erected his brick house), and the clerk's office was kept in a little frame in the center of the Public Square. That little frame, after traveling to various points of the town, was at length wedged in between C. E. Bolles's and Lewis Martin's store. Dr. Vandeventer was the clerk, recorder, and post-master, all kept in that house, together with the County Library, Dr. White's shop, and Chase's law-office; William George, Justice of the Peace and County Treasurer. Enoch Cox kept a boarding-house in the *Indiana House*, lately owned by Dr. Williams. Henry B. Milroy resigned the office of sheriff, in 1829, and James Miller succeeded him, and served until the August election, 1830, at which time John M. Pinkston was elected. The vote stood: Pinkston, 55; Miller, 50; Hopkinson, 50; Bozarth, 36.

NUMBER V.

It is not the intention, in preparing these papers, to follow any particular *arrangement* of facts, but to speak of matters and things as they may occur to my mind.

All the "old settlers" will recollect James Odell Sr., (father of our county clerk.) As Mr. Odell was one of the first citizens of Carroll County, it may not be uninteresting to know something of his history, inasmuch as a portion of that history is identified with that of the county. He was born in South Carolina, in the year 1765, and although young, served a short time as a volunteer, during the Revolutionary War. In the year 1800, he moved to the state of Ohio, and in 1810, he came to Wayne County, in this state. In the Fall of 1824, Odell, together with his whole family, including three sons-in-law, Benjamin D. Angell, John Carey, and Aaron Wiles, started to the Wabash, with the intention of making Carroll County their permanent home. The Odell family, together with that of Henry Robinson, who started about the same time from Montgomery County, Ohio, were the first pioneers.

. . . Robinsons came up, a few weeks previous to the other. Aaron Merriman moved in, the same Spring; and about the first of May, in the same year, Daniel Baum, and the families who accompanied him in his keel-boat, settled in the bottom below town, as related in previous numbers. Mr. Odell at first settled on the land, afterward purchased by Isaac Wilson. He died in 1845, universally beloved. Under a rough exterior he possessed a heart ever alive to the kindliest sensibilities; and the writer of this will never forget that, a few months after his settlement in Delphi, when taken sick among strangers, unknown, unfriended, and uncared for, the old gentleman took him home with him, attended to his wants, and nursed him as if he had been his son. *He was one of nature's noblemen—"an honest man."*

It may be seen that the county increased in population very slowly from 1825 to 1828. The reason was, the land in this section of the country was offered for sale in the Fall of 1824; but being far in the wilderness, but little of it was purchased at the first sale. As the General Government had donated each alternate section of land, for five miles on each side, for the purpose of constructing the Wabash and Erie Canal, the land east of Tippecanoe River was withheld from sale until the canal lands were selected by the agents of the State. The land in this section of the country was not open for purchase from 1826 until the Spring of 1830, at which time it was again offered for public sale at Crawfordsville.

NUMBER VI.

HENRY ROBINSON was born near Gettysburg, in Pennsylvania, in the year 1778. At a very early age, Mr. Robinson's parents removed with their family, to Washington County, in that state, at a time when the best house in that whole region of country was a *log-cabin*. When Mr. R. was seventeen years of age, the family removed to Scott County, Kentucky, where he lived until the Spring of 1806. He was married in Kentucky, in the Spring of 1799. In the Spring of 1806, he settled in Miami County, Ohio, where he resided five years; and in 1811, he located on Mad River, in Montgomery County, Ohio, where he rebuilt a mill in 1818. He remained at that place until the Fall of 1824, at which time he removed to this county.

Mr. Robinson died in July, 1845, universally respected. As a mechanic, he had few equals, as the mill now owned by Bulger & Co., built mostly by himself and sons, bears ample proof. As a member of the Church and of the community, he was always straightforward and upright; and although sometimes giving offense by his rigid adherence to what he thought right, every one, upon reflection, was bound to give him credit for honesty and strict integrity.

In the Spring of 1827, Aaron Dewey came, with his family, to this place. He built a log-cabin on the hill, near the house since occupied by John Marsh and Miss Sallie Robinson. He resided in that house until the Spring of 1829, at which time he built and removed into the house now owned by Joseph Assion. In 1828, Mr. Dewey made brick over on the hill, and the same year built the first brick house erected in the county; or, rather, the first *two* brick houses. These houses still stand as monuments of the architecture of that day. They belong to Vine Holt, and are located on the south-west corner of the Public Square.

The first house built in Delphi was a little frame, in the corner lately occupied by George W. Pigman. This was in the Fall of 1828. The same day the little frame was put up, the log part of the house, now owned by S. D. M'Intosh, was erected for the Rev. James Crawford; and in the ensuing Winter, the log school-house, on the lot adjoining William Barnett's, was built. For many years that school-house was used for every imaginable purpose,—courts, schools, singing-schools, church, mock legislature, debating society, shows, political speeches, and many other things, "too tedious to mention."

Mr. Dewey was the first school-master. He taught school in a cabin adjoining the one in which he resided, in 1827.

The Rev. Mr. Crawford came to this county in the Fall of 1827, and remained here in charge of the Presbyterian Church until the year 1835.

NUMBER VIII.

JAMES ALLDRIDGE came from Knox County, Tennessee, to Carroll County, in November, 1828. At that time,

General Milroy, Daniel M'Cain, John Carey, George Diffendaffer, John Little, Thomas Stirlin, Samuel Wise, and John Odell, were residing on the road between the points now known as *Delphi* and *Camden.* At that time, Elisha Brown, Moses Alldridge, Jeremiah and John Ballard, were all residing on the land they had previously purchased, on the south side of Deer Creek; and being all of them *unmarried*, they were "going it alone," or, in other words, keeping "bachelors' hall." It was this circumstance that gave the name to that beautiful little creek which empties into Deer Creek at Wise's saw-mill, "Bachelors' Run." It was not long after that, that all the bachelors took wives; but the creek still retained its name notwithstanding. Jerry Ballard married a daughter of Daniel Baum; John Ballard, a daughter of John Robbins; Moses Alldridge, a daughter of Mr. Hewitt. Elisha Brown resisted the charms of the fair sex much the longest; but he, too, finally laid down the weapons of rebellion, and married one of the daughters of Mr. John Wingart.

James Alldridge *camped*, on his first arrival in this county, *against a big log*, on the land now owned by Joseph M'Cain.

Captain Hance came to this county in the Winter of 1828–29, and located on the farm since owned by John E. Snoeberger.

In one of my former numbers I stated that Aaron Dewey was the first "school-master." So he was, but he was not the first "school-teacher." Miss Sarah Robinson taught the first school, in her father's old log house, now torn down. This was in the Summer and Fall of 1827. General Robert H. Milroy, John and Samuel Milroy, Baum's, Manary's, Angell's, Dewey's, and Odell's children made up her school. Miss Sally would scarcely recognize, in the strapping *six-footers* of some of her scholars, the urchins of that day.

In the month of March, 1831, the writer of this was at the pains of taking the census of Delphi. The following shows the names of the heads of families, with the *number* of persons comprising the same: William M'Crery, 5; William George, 2; Enoch Cox, 14; landlord, Isaac Martin, 7; Isaac Griffith, 11; —— Birkit, 3; John M. Pinkston, 6; Samuel Carpenter, 3; Aaron Dewey, 8; Andrew Wood, 3; J. Mills, 3; Jacob Humerickhouse, 7; Jacob Watson, 4; Henry Sidenbender, 6; Francis Ludlow, 8; Silas H. Seeley, 3; Widow Wilson, 5; Jacob Bross, 5; Thomas Pike, 5; Martin Thornberry, 3; William Craig, 5; Jacob Starr, 6; Samuel Thompson, 4; James Crawford, 4. Whole number, 130. Single males over twenty-one, 17; single ladies over fourteen, 6; number of voters, 41.

THE "DELPHI ORACLE."

THE *Delphi Oracle* newspaper was established in the Summer of 1835, by Mr. Robert C. Green, and was the first paper ever published in the county, although Dr. Robert R. Webber and W. Clymer began the publication of the *Banner* within a very few days after the appearance of the *Oracle*. The author has been unable to procure any copies of that paper prior to Vol. III, No. 9, September 15, 1838, at which date Henry B. Milroy was the editor. The copy of the date named contains a communication on the subject of shade-trees—another giving a description of the emigration of the Pottawatomie Indians, the tribe having passed down on the west side of the Wabash River a few days prior, on their way to their new home west of the Mississippi. He describes the procession as being "very imposing, occupying a distance of perhaps *three miles*, accompanied by some thirty or forty troops; the whole (for the present) under the direction of General Tipton, who intended to place them under the care of Judge

Polke after they leave the state line." The writer concludes as follows: "While speaking on this subject, permit me to remark, that to General Tipton belongs the greatest praise for his efforts to quell the feeling of insubordination lately manifested by the Indians on the subject of emigration. It is my firm belief that no other individual in the world could have got them off without great trouble and perhaps bloodshed."

The paper also gives a list of seminary trustees, appointed by the county commissioners. The following is the list: For the town of Delphi—James H. Stewart, James P. Dugan, Henry B. Milroy; for Deercreek Township—George C. Saunderson; Tippecanoe—Frederick Dosch; Jefferson—James M'Cully; Adams—John Grantham; Rock Creek—Enoch Stansel; Jackson—Jonathan Martin; Washington—John Shanks; Carrollton—John Irwin; Burlington—John Calvert; Democrat—William Dawson; Clay—Joshua Simpson; Madison—Michael Kite.

A year or two after the establishment of the *Oracle*, H. B. Milroy carried it on for some time; but, the latter part of 1838, R. C. Green again appeared as the editor, and continued to conduct the same until toward the close of 1839, at which time he finally ceased his connection with it.

In 1840, Mr. Green commenced the *Express*, in Delphi, and warmly advocated the election of General Harrison. A few years afterward, he removed to Cincinnati. In May, 1846, in company with his wife and three children, he started for the Wabash on the steamer *Pink*, and on the 25th day of that month, the *Pink* came in collision with a large boat, and sunk in a very short time, drowning Mr. Green and his whole family, and several others. This was the fate of the man who started the first paper in Delphi. A very melancholy one indeed.

On the 4th day of September, 1841, Mr. James Coleman started a paper, which he also called the *Delphi Oracle;* but that paper, however, had no connection with the paper established by Mr. Green.

THE DELPHI HOUSE.

THE old frame building at the foot of Main Street was, some twenty-five years since, a notable tavern-stand, and was kept at one time by Mr. Guyger. It was built by Chevalier Richardson, elected recorder of the county in 1834. I have an advertisement before me signed, "A. Richardson, C. Richardson his agent, Delphi, Indiana," which gives notice that said stand was for rent, and going on to speak of it thus: "This large and splendid tavern-stand in Delphi will be completed by the 4th of July next, and will be for rent. This house contains forty-five rooms, which will be finished off in the most convenient and elegant style; and a cellar the entire length of the house (one hundred and twenty feet). The stable is sufficiently commodious to receive horses without inconvenience; and the other buildings attached to the establishment will be well fitted up. The house is situated at the lower end of Main Street, in Delphi, in the most eligible location, as it commands a view of the river, the canal, and the town. It is presumed to be unnecessary here to speak of the advantages and prosperity of Delphi, as both must be too well known to require commendation. I will barely remark that it is the opinion of men well qualified to judge, that the day is not distant when *Delphi will be the largest town on the Wabash River.* In the nature of things, this must be the case." (April 28, 1838.)

When we look at the above "puff," and then at the dilapidated building at the "lower end of Main Street," an involuntary smile comes over the countenance, and we conclude that human wisdom is not very far-sighted!

CHAPTER IX.

RECOLLECTIONS OF EARLY SETTLERS.

JAMES BLAKE.

THE "old settlers" of Carroll County look upon James Blake as a public benefactor. Although never a citizen of the county, he lived here for several months, during each year, for several years. He had an establishment for curing *ginseng* on General Milroy's farm, and purchased a large quantity of that root, for which he paid out thousands of dollars annually; and it is a well-known fact that many of the early pioneers raised from this source *alone* a sufficient amount of money to enable them to purchase their land from Government.

Mr. B. was a man of marked influence with the first settlers, and they had the most unbounded confidence in his integrity. Strictly pious, honorable and straightforward in all his dealings, he made a decided and most favorable impression upon the people. He attended the first sale of lots in Delphi; and on the day of the sale, he headed a subscription for the erection of the old log school-house. The contract for the building was made on the spot, and in about ten days the house was up and completed. He immediately organized a Sunday-school, of which he took the supervision on all occasions, during his stay in the county. The weight of his character and influence was felt most sensibly on the side of religion, morality, and virtue. He assisted the good men who first came here, to give the young community a start in the right direction, and that influence is seen up to the present day.

Mr. Blake was born in the county of York, Pennsylvania, on the 3d day of March, 1791. In his early years, at the time when nearly all the goods that were consumed in the valley of the Ohio, were brought by wagon across the mountains, he drove a six-horse team from Philadelphia to Pittsburg. He continued thus occupied from 1812 to 1818. During the War, at the time the British army was threatening Baltimore, he volunteered in the company of Captain Bishler, and marched to that city. He remained in the army until the danger was over, a period of about three months, till the troops were disbanded. He proceeded to Washington with his team, and hauled a cannon from that city to Perth Amboy, New Jersey, the trip occupying about three weeks.

In the Summer of 1818, such was the financial embarrassment of the county, and its effects on all branches of business, that teaming became quite dull, and Mr. B. accordingly sold out.

In the Fall of 1818, he set out for an extensive tour through the Western country, on horseback. He passed through Pittsburg, Beaver, Canton, New Philadelphia, and at Springfield, Ohio, spent a week or ten days with some old friends; thence by way of Xenia and Lebanon to Cincinnati. The Queen City, at that time, was nothing but a small village. He then proceeded to Louisville, Ky., by way of Lawrenceburg, Vevay, Madison, and Charleston. From Louisville he went to Corydon, Indiana, at which place he arrived between Christmas and New-Year. The Legislature of the new State was then in session, and Mr. B. made many acquaintances and friends, which have lasted through life.

From Corydon the traveler went to Vincennes, and on the way made the acquaintance of Judge Blackford and Thomas H. Blake. The country was a wilderness, the road nothing but an *Indian trace*, and for a considerable distance the party carried their pistols in their hands, looking out for robbers, by whom they expected to be attacked, judging from the awful reports they had heard respecting that part of the country.

He remained at Vincennes two or three days. At that time the *Old Post*, as Vincennes was generally designated, was much the most flourishing town in Indiana. It contained between thirty and forty stores, and an immense business was done, particularly by the Ewings.

From Vincennes he went to Terre Haute; found a rude court-house, and the clerk's office in a cabin, but no tavern; and he had to ride up to Fort Harrison, about three or four miles above the little village, to procure lodging for the night. Major Churn, and several other United States officers, were there at the time. He crossed the Wabash River at Terre Haute, and returned by way of Palestine to Vincennes. He then went to St. Louis, which at that time did not contain a single public house, and nothing in the shape of one, except a boarding-house. After remaining one day, he went to Kaskaskia, and found the Illinois Legislature in session, being its first. He was very much disgusted with things about Kaskaskia. From the Governor down to the lowest official, all were playing cards and drinking whisky. He remained about twenty-four hours, and set out again for Vincennes—nothing but a dim trail for a road, and in some places from forty to sixty miles between cabins. Mr. B. then returned to his home in Pennsylvania, by way of New Albany, Louisville, Frankfort, Lexington, Maysville, Chillicothe, Lancaster, Wheeling, Washington and Pittsburg. He arrived at home on the 4th day of April, 1819, having started on his journey the 21st day of the preceding November.

While at Corydon, Indiana, he had heard of the *new purchase*, and then determined that whenever the seat of Government should be located, he would emigrate there. Having learned that Indianapolis had been selected, he left Pennsylvania with a view of making that place his home, on the 25th day of May, 1821. At Pittsburg he took the steamer *Henry Baldwin* for Louisville, at which place the boat arrived in *nine days!* He crossed over to New Albany on the 9th of June and remained there until the middle of July. Having purchased a horse, in company with his friend West, who was the owner of a wagon, the two set out for Indianapolis, at which place they arrived on the 25th day of July, 1821. The sale of land was then progressing at Brookville; and the lots in Indianapolis were sold the ensuing October. Mr. B. followed surveying until the Fall of 1823, at which time he entered into partnership with Samuel Henderson, in the hotel business, and the two kept the "Washington Hall." He pursued this business two or three years, at the end of which time a Dr. Helin visited Indianapolis and formed a partnership with him in the purchase and cure of ginseng. Their first location was in Putnam County, at a place which took the name of Blakesburg. They carried on that establishment four or five years; and at that time, by paying Major Isaac Elston, who then had a little store in Crawfordsville, the cash for ginseng, he was enabled to give that enterprising gentleman a start, which, many think, laid the foundation for the fortune afterward acquired by him.

The ginseng-root becoming scarce in the region of country around Blakesburg, Mr. B. started persons out to look for a place where it could be found in greater quantity. These persons reported that the article was found in great abundance above Wild-cat (north of Lafayette). In fact, such quantities were then in that location, that wagon-loads were brought to Blakesburg from there.

In May, 1827, Mr. B. took a tour to the Upper Wabash. Longley (a French trader, married to an Indian woman, about three miles above Lafayette) informed him as to the best places to find ginseng, and particularly spoke of the Deer Creek country. Mr. B. came up to Mr. Daniel Baum's, who kept tavern in the bottom below, where Delphi was afterward located. He visited General Milroy, and remained in the neighborhood a week. He leased a tract of a few acres of land from General M., and entered into a contract with Joseph M'Cain for the erection of the necessary buildings. The ensuing Winter, General M. went to Indianapolis, with the view of urging the passage of an act for the organization of the new county. In this matter he received the active co-operation of Mr. Blake; and the two blocked out the counties in the Upper Wabash, so that the county-seats would necessarily be located on the river. This wise arrangement was subsequently adopted by the Legislature with the most beneficial results.

In August, 1827, he commenced the purchase and cure of ginseng at his factory, on General Milroy's farm, and remained there until late in the Fall, his brother Jesse, in the mean time, overseeing the Blakesburg establishment. In August, 1828, he was again at his post. He attended the first sale of lots in Delphi, and not only inaugurated the building of the school-house, as heretofore named, but also the erection of a house for the Rev. James Crawford, a Presbyterian minister, recently located in the settlement; the school-house being the *first*, and Mr. Crawford's the *second*, house built on the new town-plot.

Mr. B. carried on the ginseng business at his establishment above Delphi, until the close of 1830—four years—at which time his lease on General Milroy's land expired. After closing his Carroll County factory, he established one near Logansport, which he carried on two years. In 1832, he set one in operation at Frankfort; in 1833, another at Marion; and in 1834, another at Leesburg, Kosciusko County. He finally discontinued that trade in 1835.

Mr. B. always laughed heartily when relating a circumstance which occurred, perhaps the first season he was located above Delphi. One of the men employed by him represented, one morning, that he felt very badly, and must have some whisky. Mr. B. told him to mount the horse, and go down to Father Baum's and procure some, he taking a jug along. On his return, a bear came cantering along pretty close to the horse, which so frightened the animal that he ran away. The men at the factory, upon looking down the road, saw man and horse coming toward them, Gilpin-like, with the fleetness of a deer. But the most amusing part was to witness the superhuman efforts made by the rider *to save the jug.* His efforts were successful, and the "O be joyful" came, without the loss of a drop!

It is proper to add, before closing this brief sketch, that Mr. Blake was married on the 29th day of March, 1831, to Miss Eliza Sprole, of Baltimore, Maryland, by whom he had four sons.

Mr. B. discontinued the ginseng business in 1835; and his work was principally confined to the city of Indianapolis. He was universally acknowledged to be one of the most useful, energetic, and public-spirited citizens during his day. He led the van in every improvement. His name was always found at the head of the list in every benevolent enterprise. It may be truly said that his name is identified with the prosperity of the city of his residence. His heart was the home of benevolence, and the poor and friendless were sure to find in him a ready ear and willing hand.

Such is but a very imperfect account of a man whose life has been made up of noble, unselfish, and benevolent *works*.

COLONEL ZIBA HOLT.

ZIBA HOLT was born August 25, 1769, in the town of Hampton, county of Windham, state of Connecticut. He had four brothers and six sisters. His birth-place was about seven miles from the residence of General Israel Putnam. He remembered many incidents of the Revolutionary War, and particularly that soldiers were quartered in the neighborhood. When he was nineteen or twenty years of age, he assisted to bury General Putnam; the general having selected the men who were to take charge of his funeral prior to his decease, the subject of this sketch being one of them. He was buried with the honors of war.

Colonel H. remembered many anecdotes of General Putnam. Among others was the following: One day he met a poor boy, who had on a very ragged shirt, of whom he asked, *how much he would take for it.* The boy replied, "*A new one,*" and the general immediately answered, "*You shall have two;*" and they were presented accordingly.

When Colonel H. was about sixteen years of age, he went to learn the blacksmith trade, in the neighborhood of his birth, and continued in his apprenticeship until he arrived at the age of twenty-one years. Afterward he worked as a journeyman till he was twenty-five years old. He then went to the city of New York, and remained, working at his trade about a year and a half; after which he pursued the same avocation in Mount Pleasant, Morris County, New Jersey.

On the 16th day of February, 1800, in company

with three others, he started for the then wilderness of Kentucky—the party commencing the journey in two sleighs. Upon arriving in Washington County, Pennsylvania, they purchased a flat-bottomed boat, and floated down the Ohio River to a point eight or ten miles below the mouth of the Kentucky River (on the Kentucky side, in Gallatin County), where they arrived some time in April, 1800. The village of Milton was afterward laid out at the point where the party landed. Colonel H. purchased one hundred acres of land on the hill opposite Madison, Indiana, where he made a "deadening," worked at his trade; and himself and a man by the name of Hoagland were the first to cut a stick of timber on the river-bottom at that point.

He remained there nearly one year; then hired as a hand on a flat-bottomed boat from the neighborhood of Frankfort, and started for New Orleans. His wages amounted to sixty dollars. Remained at New Orleans two or three weeks; then took a sailing-vessel called the *Herald*, and sailed for New York, at which place he arrived after a tedious voyage, having been becalmed for a long time in sight of the island of Cuba. He arrived in New York in the month of June or July, and after remaining about ten days, went to his father's house in Connecticut.

About the 1st of June, 1802, he returned to his land in Kentucky. He put up a blacksmith-shop near his land, and worked at his trade the same time he was improving his farm. He carried on his trade very extensively for a new country—working three fires. At one time his shop and every thing contained therein was burned up; but such was his energy that in sixteen days he had his shop rebuilt and was at work again.

Colonel H. was married to his first wife, Miss Penelope King, in the year 1805. His wife lived but four or five years, at the end of which time she died of consumption, leaving three children. About one year after the death of his first wife, he married Miss Lucinda Wood, by whom he had eight children. His second wife died on the 15th day of March, 1825.

Colonel H. was in the battle of New Orleans, on the right bank of the river. He left Kentucky as captain of a company, in the Fall of 1814. The troops floated to New Orleans on flat-bottomed boats. The boats contained no arms, the troops expecting to draw them upon arriving at the end of their journey; but the arms were not received until some time after the battle. The Kentucky troops reached New Orleans on the 4th day of January; but having no arms, they could be of but little service. On the night before the battle, that portion of the Kentucky troops to which Captain Holt belonged, was ordered to cross the river. Upon their arrival, about daylight, on the 8th of January, in the vicinity of the camp of General Morgan, they were ordered to repair immediately to the river to prevent the British from landing. Colonel Davis was the superior officer. They soon saw the British approaching, and the troops sent to oppose them not numbering more than one hundred, the little force retreated to some old saw-mills, at which place a stand was made; but upon the approach of the enemy in large numbers, the Kentuckians were again compelled to fall back. They recrossed the river on the 9th. During the action on the right bank of the river, Colonel H. never saw General Morgan, the commanding officer, and he always entertained the opinion that General M. acted cowardly and badly. The order "to prevent the British from landing," was given them by Morgan's aid.

The Kentuckians remained on the battle-field until the 18th of March, at which time they were marched to Camp Washington, seven miles in the rear of Natchez. Colonel H. was ordered to remain at that place and take charge of the sick, and give them assistance in their homeward march. Finally, after his arduous duties in taking care of the sick at Camp Washington, he returned home, where he arrived in July, 1815. During his stay in the lower country he was breveted major.

Upon his return, he found that the Governor of Kentucky had appointed him a major in the State militia. He was afterward appointed a lieutenant-colonel, then colonel, and afterward a brigadier-general; but this last commission he refused to accept. He commanded the Fifty-first Regiment of Kentucky Militia for a great many years; and for more than *thirty* years he was an officer of the militia of that State. He first commenced his military life as orderly-sergeant in a company in the city of New York.

In August, 1828, in company with Captain Andrew Wood, Colonel H. came to Carroll County, and selected three or four lots of land. While in the neighborhood, they remained with Elisha Brown. He employed Daniel M'Cain to *deaden* sixty acres of his land, build a cabin, and put a fence around the same. After remaining about one week, they returned home. In August, 1829, he removed one load of his goods to his new home in Carroll County, and about the 20th day of October, 1829, with his family, he arrived at his cabin. His neighbors were Elisha Brown, Daniel E. M'Cain, John and Jeremiah Ballard, and James M'Cain.

Colonel H. departed this life at the residence of his son, Vine Holt, in Delphi, on the 6th day of May, 1860. For many years prior to his decease, on account of his extreme old age, Colonel H. mingled but little with the world. The earlier residents remember him as a remarkably energetic and public-spirited citizen. In the section of the county were he resided (about six miles east of Delphi, on the Burlington road), he was ever first on the list in pushing forward and encouraging those improvements so necessary in a new country. By thus taking a leading part, by his influence and example, he was the means of doing much good.

Colonel H. exhibited in his life the sterling qualities and virtues of the *past age.* Honest and candid himself, he was above dissembling. He honored *truth;* indeed he never swerved from truth *for any thing.* He was honest and upright in all his dealings; and no man, living or dead, could say that Ziba Holt ever wronged him out of a farthing. He ever acted on the principle *to ask nothing but what was clearly right; to deal honestly with all men, and promptly and punctually to pay all his obligations.*

In the language of the obituary notice published soon after his decease: "And thus the long life of Colonel Holt is brought to a close. He had looked death in the face for many years, and for a long time has been anxious to depart. His funeral was attended yesterday by a large number of our citizens; Rev. N. R. High officiating. He died as he had lived, an honest, honorable, upright man; his word always as good as his bond. He was faithful to his country; he was fraternal to his fellow-man. He was an affectionate husband, a devoted and indulgent father."

ABNER ROBINSON.

THE following sketch of the present chairman of the "old settlers'" convention, has some facts and incidents worthy of record:

His father was of Irish descent and lived in several places in three or four of the Western States. An incident runs thus, which beats modern spiritualism, inasmuch as it had a reforming tendency: In their quiet neighborhood they were annoyed by a family where, from father to child, they drank, quarreled, and fought

ABNER ROBINSON,

(President of the Old Settlers' Meeting.)

furiously. The Messrs. Downey were very large, strong men, one of whom stood six and a half feet high, and was equal to any emergency. He, with others, determined to break up the continual "rumpus" over the way, and so blacked his face, arranged some horns on the sides of his head, and looked, when equipped, as much like the devil as the most vivid imagination could depict. The rest of the party, variously disguised, followed their leader, who carried an old brass kettle, and in it several trace-chains.

At the usual time in the evening the row commenced, and soon the cry of "murder" was heard. It was just the evening for hobgoblins. A drizzling rain had set in, and the fearful shrieks from the house made night hideous.

In the midst of the uproar, Mr. Apollyon stepped in the door without knocking, and with a deep, sepulchral voice said, "I am come to take you to my infernal den, where you belong." Suiting the action to the word, he drew a chain over the edge of the kettle, and commanded two of his servants to bind the father hand and foot, and cast him into outer darkness.

The family were just intoxicated enough to be really superstitious, and began to beg for dear life. After all were chained, the leader called his servants one side and held a "gibberish confab;" and then, returning, informed the family that their prayers had taken them out of his power for the present, but that he hoped some day they would have another quarrel, and then he would have them sure.

From that time the family became exceedingly temperate, and always believed that they had received a personal visit from his Satanic Majesty.

In October, 1824, Mr. Robinson left Dayton, Ohio, came to Crawfordsville, and finally "squatted" on a piece of land about four miles south-east of Lafayette.

He came to Deer Creek settlement several times, in company with other land-hunters, and finally built a cabin, in December, 1824, and in the following January brought his family here.

Abner Robinson was born August 1, 1801, near Cynthiana, Kentucky. In 1811, his father settled near Dayton, Ohio; but such were the surroundings that young Abner had no school privileges whatever. His father and uncle finally hired an old tyrant of a master; but the few children under his galling rule did not learn much. Mr. R. says:

"My second quarter of schooling was in a house of my own building—what but few others, I presume, can say. All the schooling I ever got put together was eighteen months.

"On the 18th of January, 1824, I was married to Miss Sarah Barns. Shortly after this, father sold out, and moved to the Wabash, and finally to Deer Creek. I was in very poor health during the years 1832–34. Early in 1835, having somewhat recovered my health, I drafted the Delphi Mills, and superintended the work until it started, on the 4th of July, 1837, and then I acted as foreman till 1840.

"Early in 1840, I went to New Orleans with a boat-load of flour; but was taken sick when I came home, and was laid aside for the balance of the year. Early in 1845, I went a second time to New Orleans, this time with part of a boat-load of lumber; but it was a financial failure. I arrived at home, July 4th, just in time to see my father die.

"And here began my troubles. While father was alive, we understood business matters, and had things in common; but after his death, advantage was taken of this state of affairs to my great detriment. Two of the heirs would not settle according to the agreement of my father. Alas, that there is no more democracy in the settlement of estates!

"Early in the year 1848, I bought a small tract of land on the north-west side of the Wabash, and removed to it, February 24. For the first year every thing appeared to prosper with me, but 1849 brought clouds and darkness."

He speaks of the death of several members of his family in touching words, and of his love for those gone before.

Mr. R. is a valuable member of the "old settlers'" meeting; and when he is gone from among us, his name will live in the sweet memories of the past.

CHAPTER X.

GREAT FIRE OF 1839.

WE copy the following account of the fire which occurred in Delphi, on the 29th day of January, 1839, from the *Delphi Oracle:*

"DELPHI, *Tuesday, January* 29, 1839.

"This morning, about half-past five o'clock, we were awakened by the cry of *fire* proceeding from the chamber below, and, instantly rising, discovered that the store of Mr. M'Crery, next door, with the upper part of the drug-store of Dr. Phelps, was enveloped in flames. The fire spread with alarming rapidity, and in less than one hour the entire block of buildings, from the corner of Washington Street to the alley, was in ashes. We annex a list of the sufferers, as near as can now be ascertained. This calamity falls heavily upon some of our most industrious and worthy citizens, who are now turned out of house and home.

"Mr. J. P. Dugan's dry-goods store, on the corner of Main and Washington Streets; storehouse entirely consumed, with a large portion of the goods; loss about $8,000; insurance, $7,000. Green & Lipper, shoe-store; loss about $2,000; no insurance. A. L. Holmes's law-office; loss, including library, $600; no insurance. Wm. M'Crery's dry-goods store; loss about $3,000; no insurance. Lasselle & Polke, storehouse; loss about $2,000; insurance $660. Calvert & Henry, tailoring establishment; loss about $1,700; no insurance. Doctor Phelps's drug-store and dwelling burnt to the ground;

loss $3,000; insurance $900. 'Washington Hall' tavern, belonging to John Kuns; loss probably $3,000; no insurance. This house was occupied by several families, and the above estimate falls far short of the amount of property destroyed.

"ON WASHINGTON STREET.

"J. P. Dugan's warehouse; loss about $1,800; no insurance. In this house was a large lot of pork, flour, and salt. Loss in the aggregate about $6,000; no insurance.

"R. T. Brandon's dwelling-house, in which were several offices. The total loss of books, etc., can not be less than $2,000; no insurance.

"In the upper rooms of Dr. Phelps's drug-store, we may name the loss of a large quantity of furniture, etc., about $300 of which is a loss to R. C. Green.

"The flames soon reached the dry-goods store of Charles W. Kendall, which was partly destroyed by the dashing of water through the roof and windows. The house was saved, but the goods were much damaged.

"The office of the *Delphi Oracle* is in the same block, and at the moment of the greatest danger, the entire establishment was thrown into the street in a confused heap. The presses and type have been brought in, and we are arranging for business. We can not tell when we shall be able to issue another paper.

"The grocery establishment of Mr. Clover was dashed into the street. His loss is trifling.

"That of Mr. Hoyman shared the same fate."

FIRE OF 1844.

On Sunday morning, November 24, 1844, a fire broke out in the store-room of Mr. A. F. Martin, in Delphi. Before it could be arrested, it entirely destroyed the shop of Mr. Klepser, with the whole of his saddlery, harness, and stock on hand, valued at five hundred dollars. The tailor-shop of Mr. Mastaw, and the storehouse of N. W. & A. H. Bowen, together with a considerable portion of their goods, were also destroyed.

FIRE OF 1850.

On Thursday morning, October 10th, 1850, a fire broke out in the shoe-shop of M'Dannell & Ruffing, and was supposed to be the work of an incendiary. The wind blew a brisk breeze from the south; and had it not been for the rain that set in just after the fire commenced, and the new brick buildings, erected a short time previous by Messrs. Wm. Bolles and James H. Stewart, which confined it somewhat in bounds, one-half of the town would have been laid in ashes.

The following persons were sufferers: J. D. & M. Simpson, grocery and provision merchants, $650, no insurance; James H. Stewart, $1000, insured; Smith & Sherm, $100, no insurance; L. D. M'Intosh, $250, $100 insured; J. E. Gridley, $200, insured; J. Klepser, $50, insured; N. Smith, $250, insured; Jacob Spence, $700, insured; Ruffing & M'Dannell, $1,000, insured; Wm. Bolles, $12,000, $11,000 insured; T. C. Reyburn, $50, no insurance; J. M'Carthy, $300, insured; Thomas Weakly, $160, insured; J. C. Applegate, $50, insured. A little ready cash in those days was very valuable.

DELPHI IN 1838.

A Delphi newspaper, printed in 1838, contains numerous advertisements, which will give an idea of the business and business men of the place, and will be interesting to "old settlers." W. H. Calvert informed the public that he carried on the tailoring business, and that he had taken J. R. Henry into partnership. Finch & Niles had formed a partnership in the practice of the law. M'Curdy & Cleaver were selling goods. Irwin & Bradshaw, merchants, notified customers that accounts were left with William George, Esq., for collection. S. L. & J. Broadwell had just received a lot of splendid saddlery. Martin & Crooks, various kinds of books for sale. N. W. & A. H. Bowen, merchants. A. L. Robinson & Hiram Allen, law partnership. Lasselle & Polke, merchants. John Phelps, drugs and medicines. Tweed & Pigman, merchants. "Washington Hall" tavern-stand for sale, inquire of M. C. Dougherty. J. P. Dugan & Co., just received 1,300 barrels of salt. "Exchange Hotel," kept by R. V. Jones. Cutlery, T. P. Emerson. Bondie Land for sale; address John E. Hunt or O. Williams & Co., Maumee City, O. R. T. Brandon, agent of the *Ladies' Monthly Magazine of Fashion*. Public sale of lots in the town of Franklin. Jacob R. Newman; (Mr. Newman concludes, "From what has been said in relation to this beautiful town-site, it is very readily to be seen that there are but few towns in the Wabash country that can surpass it for advantages.") Merkle, Kendall & Co., merchants. Horse taken up by John Eikenberry, certified by William Alldridge, J. P. Administrator's notice; Parker Lucas, administrator of Sam'l J. Moore. Domestic attachment before Reuben G. Munday, J. P., against Nathaniel R. Stephenson. Public sale. F. Dosch, administrator of Samuel Williams. Administrator's notice; John M. Evans, administrator of Philo H. Scovill. Baptist ministerial meeting. To the members of the Delphi Reading-room Association. Taken up; an estray, by Lewis Ewing. Elisha W. Luke, J. P. Partnership between James Crumley & John Brown dissolved. James Carney's notice to settle up. Wood for the court-house, and proposals for placing railings around court-house square. Administrator's notice; James H. Boylan, administrator of Brigham Hubbard. Sale of land belonging to the estate of Thomas M'Grew; George Bear, administrator. R. J. Adams's notice to customers (saddling business). Thomas Barns, administrator of Nathan Spry. Samuel Grimes, giving timber and stone to burn lime or coal, on land between Delphi and the river. Henry B. Milroy, administrator of James B. Larimer. Joseph Granthem, administrator of David Loucks. Horatio J. Harris, attorney and counselor-at-law, had formed an association with White & Lockwood, of Lafayette. Thomas Brown against Elizabeth Brown; notice. More new goods, Enoch Bowen.

DELPHI MOOT (MOCK) LEGISLATURE.

THE Delphi Moot Legislature was quite an institution in its day. It commenced its first session January 1, 1831, and its last meeting took place February 7, 1834. Nothing of the kind has ever been organized since, that created so great an interest in the community. It met at the public school-room in Delphi, on the 1st day of January, 1831. Daniel F. Vandeventer was called to the chair. The society then elected the following officers: Henry Chase, Governor and Speaker; James H. Stewart, Clerk; Aaron Dewey, Treasurer; and Theophilus Hardman, Door-keeper. James H. Stewart, Rev. James Crawford, Daniel F. Vandeventer, and Henry Chase were appointed a committee to draft a Constitution. The following is a list of the members who subscribed to the first Constitution: Henry Chase, James H. Stewart, Daniel F. Vandeventer, James Crawford, Thompson Calvert, Aaron Dewey, Milo Dibble, Joseph G. Glass, William George, Jacob Humerickhouse, Francis Ludlow, Milton M. Morris, Benjamin Millspaugh, Isaac Martin, J. M. Pinkston, Christopher Vandeventer, Nathaniel Wilson, Ralph P. Wilson, Thomas Hight, John Carey, William M'Crery, James Carney, James Miller, Stephen A. Miller, Oliver D. Butler, A.

G. Coleman, Isaac Griffith, Gavin Black, Joshua Lindsey, Andrew Wood, John Mills, James B. Larimer.

At the second meeting, held January 8th, the following committees were appointed:

On the Judiciary—Messrs. Stewart, Vandeventer, and Crawford.

On Internal Improvements—Messrs. Dewey, Glass, and Calvert.

On Ways and Means—Messrs. Dibble, George, Humerickhouse, and N. Wilson.

On Education—Messrs. Ludlow, Morris, and Hight.

On Affairs of Town of Delphi—Messrs. Millspaugh, Martin, Pinkston, and Butler.

On Military Affairs—Messrs. Nath. Wilson, John Carey, and C. M'Crery.

According to the Constitution, the length of each session was four weeks. At the beginning of each session, the governor delivered a message. The following gentlemen filled the executive chair during the time the society existed: Henry Chase, Isaac Griffith, Jacob Humerickhouse, Andrew Wood, James H. Stewart, Oliver D. Butler, Levi S. Dale.

The society celebrated the 22d of February, 1832. The Preparatory Committee reported. The members were requested to meet at the house of Mr. Cox, at twelve o'clock. Members and citizens were desired to "meet at Mr. Hardman's shop, with guns, at daylight, on the morning of the 22d, for the purpose of firing a salute, under the direction of the marshal." The Committee further reported, that it had "spoken to individuals who can perform on the *violin and drum*, and requested them to assist in the celebration." The Committee concluded with an expression of the hope that a unanimous attendance would be given by the members, "and that no discord of any description would be permitted to mar the good feeling that always should prevail on such occasions, and particularly on the birthday of him, to whom more than to any other mortal, we are indebted for our liberty."

THE BLACK-HAWK WAR.

ALL the "old settlers" remember the terror and alarm that spread over the Upper Wabash country on the breaking out of the Black-Hawk War. Reports constantly arrived that the Indians were making rapid advances toward the settlements of this section of Indiana, and marking their track with blood. The settlers on the west side of the Tippecanoe and Wabash deserted their homes, and took refuge on the east side of the river.

The writer remembers that one night, during the excitement, the town of Delphi was guarded, and the next day, about twenty of the citizens, under the command of Captain Andrew Wood, started up the Tippecanoe River, on a scouting expedition. We found that the inhabitants along the borders of the Grand Prairie had all *vamosed the ranche.* Our company proceeded to the mouth of the Monon, and, after leaving a guard at the house of Malachi Gray, and not seeing any Indian signs, we returned home.

The following is an extract of a letter written by the author, dated June 10th, 1832: "The people of the Wabash have been alarmed very considerably lately, on account of the Indians, so much so, that the inhabitants fled from the west side of the Wabash River over to the more populous parts of the country. In this place there was no alarm, with the exception of one night, and that was caused by information, received by a gentleman, that the Indians were burning the houses in a grove on the Grand Prairie, some ten or fifteen miles from this place. I suppose, during that evening and night, a person could have formed a very good idea of how people act in time of danger. The men stood about in groups conversing solemnly; the women running from one house to another, telling each other the woful tidings of Indian outrage and savage murder! It was concluded that a company should march out the next morning, to reconnoiter the country, and repel the invaders. At sunrise we marched, leaving anxious countenances behind us. After proceeding ten or fifteen miles into the Grand Prairie, we ascertained that the fires which caused the alarm were nothing but grass burning. After traveling about twenty-five miles up Tippecanoe River, we returned home, where we arrived about midnight. Thus ended the first Indian campaign.

"The truth is, the inhabitants of the Wabash had no more cause for alarm than the people of Louisville, Kentucky. The Sac Indians and some Winnebagoes have embodied themselves near Rock Island, some two or three hundred miles from here, across the state of Illinois. They will have enough to do to protect their own women and children, without molesting us, now that General Atcheson and Governor Reynolds are upon their trail.

"If I was going to fight the Indians, I would as soon risk the citizens of Indiana as any in the world. They are a hardy, bold, intrepid set of fellows; and almost universally acquainted with the use of the gun. Tranquillity is restored, and the people of the west side of the river have returned to their homes, ashamed of the false alarm and uncalled-for panic."

CHAPTER XI.

CHURCHES.

THE METHODIST CHURCH.

THE first Church was a Methodist Society, organized in November, 1826, and was composed of eight members, to wit: John Odell, Sarah Odell, his wife; Elizabeth Angell; John Carey, Ruth Carey, his wife; Thomas Stirlin, and Frances Stirlin, his wife. Henry P. Buell was the first preacher, and filled the appointment about once in four weeks. It was called the "Crawfordsville Mission."

He organized the *first* regular *society* in what is now known as Carroll County, consisting of nine members, namely: John and Ruth Carey, Sarah Odell, Sr., John and Sarah Odell, Thomas and Francis Stirlin, Elizabeth Angell, and Rebecca Bishop. Buell was succeeded by Stephen R. Beggs, in October, 1828. In 1829, Eli P. Farmer, was the circuit-rider, and in 1830, '31, and '32, Hackaliah Vredenburgh. Mr. V. was a pioneer in the Wabash Valley, and has done much for the cause of Christianity in the wilderness.

The Annual Conference, in 1832, laid off the Upper Wabash Mission, which extended from Wild-cat Creek up the Wabash to the mouth of Salamonia River, and north to the Pottawatomie Mills (near Rochester now), and embraced all the intervening settlements. The first conference, for the Upper Wabash Mission, was held at Gillam's Meeting-house, December 22, 1832.

Members present: S. C. Cooper, Missionary; Thomas

Gillam, Elder; Thomas Stirlin, Thomas Stoops, Leaders; the superintendent of Missionary District, James Armstrong, not being present. In 1833, Carroll Circuit was laid off, it being a part of Upper Wabash Mission. Enoch Wood, Circuit Preacher; James Armstrong, Presiding Elder. The second Indiana Methodist Conference adopted the following resolutions, namely:

This Conference resolves itself into a Temperance Society, upon the principle of total abstinence. 2d. We will use our best endeavours to prevent the use of ardent spirits in our families and neighborhood. Members voting: Enoch Wood, R. H. Hanna, Thomas Gillam, John Briggs, Benjamin Underwood, John Carey, J. W. Gillam, Charles Smith, Thomas Stirlin, Henry Stair; all voting *aye*.

The next Indiana Methodist Conference furnished the preacher-in-charge with a copy of the foregoing resolutions, and requested him to use his best endeavors to have them adopted in each class. Here he met with some opposition. A few good brethren did not like to *sign away their liberty*. In 1834, Thomas Bartlett succeeded Enoch Wood; J. L. Thompson, Presiding Elder. In 1835, Eli Rogers, Circuit Preacher; the presiding elder the same as last year.

At the Annual Conference in 1836, the name of Carroll Circuit was changed to Delphi Circuit, Jared B. Mirshon appointed preacher-in-charge; J. L. Thompson, Presiding Elder. 1837, J. B. Mirshon reappointed; Allen Wiley, Presiding Elder. Mirshon being sick, his place was filled the three last quarters by William Campbell. October, 1838, J. J. Cooper, Circuit Preacher; G. M. Beswick, Presiding Elder. October, 1839, A. Beach, Circuit Preacher; G. M. Beswick, Presiding Elder. October, 1840, Joseph White and Samuel Reed, preachers; the same presiding elder. October, 1841, William M. Fraley and James Newland, preachers; C. M.

Holliday, Presiding Elder. October, 1842, D. Chipman and J. Casad, Preachers; the same presiding elder.

October, 1843, Delphi Circuit was organized with Delphi Station. F. Taylor was appointed to Delphi Circuit; A. Wood, Presiding Elder: and C. Swank for Delphi and society at Odell's. H. B. Milroy was elected recording steward at the first quarterly-meeting held in Delphi, January 13, 1844. Swank left at the end of third quarter.

In 1844 and '45, Delphi Station and Delphi Circuit were united as Delphi Circuit. In 1844–45, Allen Skillman, Circuit Preacher; S. C. Cooper, Presiding Elder. The following notice appears in the Minutes:

"On the —— day of May, 1845, our highly esteemed brother, H. B. Milroy, was called to leave us. His disease, though painful, was borne with patience and Christian fortitude. He was enabled in the last conflict to cast all his care in the blessed Savior, and has left a lasting-testimony to the truth of our holy religion. He had been a member of our Church in Delphi for more than two years, and filled the offices of steward and leader, and promised much usefulness to the Church. He was in his fortieth year, and had buried the companion of his youth several years before. We lament his loss, in expectation of meeting our brother again."

1845–46, Rufus J. Blowers was appointed to Delphi Circuit, and S. C. Cooper, Presiding Elder. 1846–47, Jacob Casad was appointed to Delphi Circuit; J. M. Stallard, Presiding Elder. 1847–48, J. Colclazer, Circuit Preacher; J. M. Stallard, Presiding Elder. 1848–49, J. W. Parritt, was appointed to Delphi Circuit; J. M. Stallard, Presiding Elder.

Delphi and Pittsburg were organized as a separate charge, in 1849 and 1850.

For many years Delphi has now been a station, and enjoyed the services of some excellent Methodist pastors:

Professor Philander Wiley, J. A. Reed, D. D., John Eddy, N. L. Brackman, A. M., James Green, W. O. Wyant and others, whose names are green in the memories of the old settlers.

THE PRESBYTERIAN CHURCH.

The Presbyterian Church of Delphi was organized on the 23d day of May, 1828, by the Rev. James Crawford and the Rev. James Thompson, who were appointed a committee by the Presbytery of Crawfordsville for that purpose. It was the first organization of a Presbyterian Church on the Upper Wabash, and was called "The Presbyterian Church of Deer Creek," which title it retained until the 22d day of January, 1833, when, by the unanimous consent of the members, it was made to correspond with the name of the *town* in which it was located.

The following persons gave in their names at the first meeting: Henry Robinson and his wife, Elizabeth Robinson; Abner Robinson and his wife, Sarah Robinson; William M'Cord, John M. Ewing, Jane Waugh, Aaron Dewey and Charlotte Dewey, his wife; William Wilson and his wife, Ann Wilson. This number was increased at the same meeting by the addition of Sarah Robinson, Sophronia Robinson, Lydia Ann Robinson, Mrs. Rebecca M'Cord, and Hugh Manary, making in all *sixteen*.

Henry Robinson and William M'Cord were chosen ruling elders. Mr. Crawford was immediately engaged as a stated supply to preach to the congregation, and he continued in this relation until early in the year 1834. During this period twenty-five members additional had been received to the Church; two had died, and four dismissed to other Churches, leaving a membership of thirty-five at the time of Mr. Crawford's resignation.

Mr. Crawford purchased a lot, and erected a log

house upon it, one of the first dwellings built in Delphi, upon a lot which was then a thicket of hazel-grubs. This house has only lately been demolished to make room for one of far superior style and pretensions, erected by Mr. Samuel D. M'Intosh.

The meetings of the congregation were held in the old log school-house which stood on the corner lot now occupied by the handsome residence of Mr. William Burnett. This school-house served for many years as a house of worship for all the different congregations in Delphi. Previous to the time of Mr. Crawford's leaving, there was talk of securing a site, and erecting a suitable house of worship, but nothing definite was done for some years afterward.

In February, 1836, the congregation employed Rev. John Stocker as a stated supply, and he continued to preach to them until the first of April, 1837.

About the first of the year 1839, Rev. Leander Cobb was employed as stated supply, and remained with the church until after the division into the "Old" and "New School," which occurred in the Fall of the year 1839. Since that time the "Old School" branch of the Church have enjoyed the labors of Rev. Jesse Edwards, who preached here a part of his time, from October, 1844, until the Spring of 1846. Rev. E. W. Wright became its pastor in May, 1846, and still continues to officiate in that relation. The number of members when he commenced his ministrations here, was 24; it is now 95; the Church of Camden having been organized from it in the mean time, which has tended to diminish its members.

The "New School" branch of the Church have enjoyed the labors of Rev. George Plummer, Rev. Mr. Steele, Rev. Mr. Thomson, Rev. B. J. Relyia, Rev. R. B. Belmont, Rev. Mr. Bacon, Rev. James A. Carnahan, and Rev. A. Jones. This body now comprises sixty members.

In 1843, a portion of the Church was detached from it, to aid in forming a separate organization on the opposite side of the river, at Pittsburg. Some years ago, in connection with the "Cumberland Presbyterians," they erected a house of worship between Delphi and Camden, so that in an area of five miles in extent, there are three kindred congregations that come under the supervision of the same pastor.

"OLD SCHOOL."

On the 18th day of April, 1834, a new Church was organized on the hill, on the south side of Deer Creek, called the "Church of Lebanon." This little Church, in the Fall of 1838, employed Rev. Alexander Williamson, whom many of our citizens remember as a man of eminent piety and worth. He continued to serve them for a few years; but becoming subject to a deep religious melancholy, he at length removed to Corydon, where, after a lingering illness, he died. After the division of the Church, the Lebanon branch was dissolved, and its members attached to the "Old School" Church of Delphi.

On the 2d day of May, 1835, fifteen members of the Delphi Church, were organized into a new Church, at Odell's school-house, called "Deer-creek Church." This Church was afterward, about the year 1839, divided, and two Churches organized out of it; one on Bachelors' Run, which has since become extinct, and one on Rock Creek, which now has a membership of seventy, and a large and elegant house of worship.

The first house of worship (the old house near the residence of E. Rinehart, Esq.,) was commenced in the year 1837. This house was retained by the "New School" branch of the Church, and occupied by them until the year 1859, when they erected a handsome brick house, which they now occupy.

In the year 1846, the "Old School" branch of the

Church commenced the house of worship now occupied by them, and was dedicated to the service of God in February, 1848. In the year 1837, the Rev. E. W. Wright for the first time attended a meeting of the Logansport Presbytery, which held its session at Delphi. There being at that time no house of worship, the meetings were held in a new house which was being built by Mr. James Witherow, for many years a prominent member, and afterward a ruling elder in the Church. A ludicrous circumstance occurred at that meeting, which fixed the remembrance of it indelibly upon my mind. Some chickens had been accustomed to seek a lodging for the night on the upper joists of the building, and while the Rev. Mr. Hummer (then of Lafayette) was preaching, the chickens were disturbed by the light of the candles and the unaccustomed sounds, and commenced uttering their protests in subdued "*quawks*," which would probably have soon ceased, had they been let alone; but there was an officious member of the presbytery, who seemed to feel that such unearthly sounds were unbecoming the sanctity of the place, and seizing a long pole, he commenced an unmerciful attack on the defenseless chickens. They came flying over the heads and into the faces of the audience. The preacher paused in unutterable dismay; the ladies were terribly frightened; and for a few moments the scene was one of indescribable confusion. Such was the first religious meeting Mr. Wright ever attended in Delphi. At *that* time the entire membership of the Presbyterian Church in Carroll County was considerably less than one hundred. It is nearly five times as large. There was then no house of worship belonging to the Presbyterian Church. The Old and the New School have lately blended together, like two drops of water, and their interests, spiritual and temporal, are shared in common.

EPISCOPAL CHURCH.

On the 21st day of May, 1845, St. Mary's Church, Delphi, was consecrated, under the ministrations of the Rev. Samuel R. Johnson, then located at Lafayette, Indiana. Mr. J. had occasionally visited Delphi, and held services for several years prior to the consecration of the church. The first baptisms into the Episcopal Church were by the Rev. Benjamin Halsted, on the 16th day of March, 1844. John Burr, Susan Burr, Mrs. Mary Daubeny, Newton H. Gist, Amelia Ann Gist, Caroline Robinson, Jane Howlitt Wilson, Sarah Stewart, John Phelps, Rhoda Phelps, Christopher Stuzaker, Sarah Garrett, Sarah Ann Bladen, and Zerua Amelia Green, were added to the Church, under the pastoral care of the Rev. W. Johnson, of Lafayette, and the Rev. Anson Clark, of Logansport, in the years of 1844 and 1845. Rev. Anson Clark was the first minister who had the regular charge of the parish.

On the 26th day of July, Messrs. Newton H. Gist, James Spears, John Burr, Christopher Stuzaker, and John Phelps, the vestrymen of the parish, invited the Rev. Dr. Bryan B. Killikelly, then of Vincennes, to officiate, and Dr. K. accepted the invitation, and removed to Delphi in October, 1846.

At a meeting of the vestry, held on the 26th day of December, 1846, the treasurer reported that he had received one hundred and twenty-five dollars from Rev. S. R. Johnson, of Lafayette, for the purchase of the lot of ground adjoining the church lot, whereon to build a parsonage-house, whenever it might be convenient. It was unanimously resolved "that the thanks of this vestry be tendered to the Rev. S. R. Johnson for this new evidence of his continued interest in the welfare of the parish of St. Mary's Church; and the vestry avail themselves of this opportunity to express further the great indebtedness of the parish to the said reverend gentleman for his ministerial services, *gratuitously rendered* for a long period from the first organization; for the munificent donation of six hundred dollars, *from himself*, and one hundred dollars procured through his agency, without which the vestry would not have felt justified in proceeding with the erection of their church edifice, now erecting; and, it is hoped, long to remain a proud monument of the untiring zeal and Christian liberality of the Rev. Samuel R. Johnson."

On the 27th day of May, 1848, the Rev. Dr. Killikelly resigned his charge of St. Mary's Church, to take effect on the first day of the following July. After the resignation of Dr. K., the Rev. Edward Magee took the ministerial charge of the parish, and continued his services until 1850, at which time Rev. Josiah Phelps became the minister, and resigned about the first of June, 1851.

October 29, 1852, Rev. Walter E. Franklin accepted the charge, and gave one-half of his time to the parish at Logansport, and the other half to this parish. On the 6th day of July, 1854, Mr. F. also resigned.

July 25, 1854, Rev. Alonzo J. M. Hudson was invited to give the parish his ministerial services *each alternate Sunday*. Mr. H. accepted, and continued in charge until the first day of August, 1858.

August 28, 1858, Rev. Elias Birdsall was called to the charge of the Church, who continued until the beginning of 1860. In February, 1860, the Rev. Nathaniel R. High commenced the care of the Church, giving it one-half of his time, the other half being devoted to the parish at Logansport.

Several gentlemen have been in charge of this Church since 1860, and a part of the time the parish has been without a minister.

CHAPTER XII.

LETTERS FROM EMINENT MEN.

HON. GEORGE L. KINNARD,

MEMBER OF CONGRESS FROM THE INDIANAPOLIS DISTRICT,

Who was burned to death on a steam-boat, on the Ohio River, while on one of his trips to Washington, D. C.

HOUSE OF REPRESENTATIVES, 12*th March*, 1836.

DEAR SIR,—I have the honor to acknowledge the receipt of your letter of the 26th February, 1836, recommending Mr. Finch for commissioner to treat with the Indians, and requesting my aid in obtaining the appointment.

Some time since a similar request was made in favor of another gentleman, which I referred to the proper department, as I shall do the present case, with my recommendation in his favor.

I entertain little expectation that any new commissioner will be appointed to this service, since it has been but a very short time since General Marshall was so employed.

The Government has been in the habit of sending Mr. Schermerhorn among the Indians to treat with them, and I think it probable that he will be sent to the Miamies, which I shall not advise. This is, however, a mere conjecture of my own.

I have no doubt the mail-route proposed by you will be adopted.

So far as my information extends, the Democratic party will prevail in a majority of the states in the ensuing Presidental election.

The narrow limits of a letter will not allow me to give you a detail of Congressional proceedings, which I presume you see in the papers.

I have the honor to be, your friend,

GEO. L. KINNARD.

HON. WILLIAM HENDRICKS,

UNITED STATES SENATOR.

SENATE CHAMBER, *February* 4, 1835.

DEAR SIR,—I have just received yours of the 15th, on the subject of a post-route from Judge Kirk's, by way of Frankfort and Delphi to Monticello, and then to Michigan City. On this subject, I think, General Tipton has already introduced a resolution. It shall not, however, be forgotton, should a law pass establishing mail-routes at the present session; but I am sorry to inform you that so much is the post-office department laboring under its difficulties, that there is no prospect of any such bill passing. It is not the least of the evils which the present condition of the department exhibits, that the necessary facilities can not at this time be afforded to the people; particularly the people of the new states, who require additional mail accommodations every day, so rapid is the progress of our settlements. There is, however, an existing law authorizing the department to supply Monticello with a mail, it being a county-seat; and if it has not one from your place to Lafayette, it must have.

I was anxious to have seen you as an old acquaintance, last Fall, when in Delphi; but, arriving late, and starting early, had no opportunity of doing so. Mr. George, poor fellow, was in a hurry, and I did not wish to lose his company. I send you Mr. Adams's oration on the life and character of Lafayette, and will always be glad to hear from you.

FROM THE SAME.

SENATE CHAMBER, *April* 7, 1836.

DEAR SIR,—I have received yours, covering a petition of the people of Delphi, representing that place as the head of steam-boat navigation, and praying that a port of entry may be established there. This I have presented to the Senate, and it is referred to the Committee on Commerce. I hope that, for the safety of the Wabash Improvement Bill, a port of entry may be established on the Wabash. This bill has passed the Senate, and I am told will also pass the House. It is important, then, to avoid the veto. I have mentioned the petition to Mr. Hannegan, whose wishes will probably be to some extent consulted, it being in his district. He spoke favorably of Delphi, but did not say conclusively any thing on the subject, nor did I mention it for a final answer. Your mail-route petition has been presented by General Tipton, and the route will, I think, be established.

FROM THE SAME.

May 9, 1836.

I HAVE received yours of the 25th, and hope for the prospects of the Wabash Appropriation Bill, which having passed the Senate, and is now before the House, that a port of entry or port of delivery will be established on the Wabash; and there is much force in the reason you give for considering Delphi as the head of steam-boat navigation. It is a measure which will, in all probability, originate in the House, and I will, with much pleasure, give Delphi my support, should it be selected as the place.

The mail-route mentioned in the same letter shall not be forgotten.

Yours sincerely, WILLIAM HENDRICKS.

FROM GENERAL JOHN TIPTON.

AT HOME, *July* 23, 1830.

DEAR SIR,—Your note of yesterday has been received, and in reply I have to inform you that I would greatly prefer remaining in the situation I now hold, as Indian Agent, to any other that could be given me. I have many letters on this same subject, and am of opinion we should weigh well this matter before we act. If, after the election, it is found best to use a name, and mine is best (strongest), I will go with my friends for the cause and for our country; but believe me, that I am not seeking office, and will esteem it a sacrifice of peace and property to do this. My talent is not of the kind that I wish to see in the United States Senate.

FROM THE SAME.

WASHINGTON, *April* 14, 1836.

DEAR SIR,—By the accompanying letter from the secretary, you will perceive that your recommendation of Mr. Finch, for commissioner to negotiate, was presented by me, and you will learn that about the time this reaches you, Mr. Ellsworth will make an attempt to modify the Miami Treaty, made by Marshall. Now for the explanation: Every body wants the Miami Treaty altered and ratified. The interest of the Upper Wabash demands it. The delegation in Congress could not all agree on who should be appointed to effect the alteration. General M'Carty, I am told, wanted Marshall to make another, which would be a *fourth* trial. Mr. Kinnard had a brother here, who wanted the appointment. I thought that *neither* could do the business, and a very large majority of our delegation thought with me, and we requested the President to send a man that he confided in, to submit propositions. He is not paid as a commissioner; it is not to make a *treaty*, but to alter a paper, that he is sent.

Boone, Hannegan, and myself have agreed to have Finch appointed to negotiate, as soon as we can get an appropriation for that object. I have been thus particular, that you may understand our real situation. Let Finch see this.

Your obedient servant, JOHN TIPTON.

FROM HON. ALBERT S. WHITE.

INDIANAPOLIS *December* 23, 1832.

DEAR SIR,—I snatch a few moments from my duties to-day, to acknowledge your favor of the 18th. I duly appreciate (and participate) the anxiety of the people of Carroll to have the survey of the canal-route, below Logansport, settled. Some of our friends, however, think that, for the present, we had better interpose on ground of local division, and that when a survey is made, it ought to be carefully and definitely made, which would be attended with some considerable expense, and that all our resources ought now to be devoted to *digging*. Not surrendering entirely to this policy, I shall endeavor to impress upon our friends and other members the necessity of an early settlement of the question, and assume it at all times as a postulate that the canal *must* run on the south side of the Wabash. The Canal Committee have as yet made no report. A joint resolution has passed, directing the governor to institute an immediate correspondence with the Governor of Ohio, upon the continuation of the canal through their territory. Their Dayton canal and ours will unite at the mouth of the Auglaize, and as this is their last session, when they can accept the grant (of land) made them by Congress, it is hoped we may come upon some terms with them. I am unapprised what provision the canal-men will ask for operations the coming season, but I incline to think there will be no violent opposition to a liberal canal policy. Some of our Wabash people fear that the State will exhaust her credit if the bank project succeeds, as that will require the loan of $800,000. Present appearances, however, do not indicate success to the bank charter.

The only vexed question which has yet been up, is the subject of the public lands, the governor, as you will have perceived, having recommended the plan reported by Mr. Clay to the Senate of the United States. The topic has been much discussed, and has produced reports and counter-reports of ominous length. Mr. Lane's report, which favors a cession and graduation, you have seen in the papers; the counter-report of Mr. Dunn, advocating the distribution system, I will send you when printed. For myself, I have yet to decide which plan is my favorite. Mr. Clay's plan, to please me, must be well provided with checks and salvos. Indeed, sir, there is no question in the future history of our politics so momentous as the distribution of the public revenues. The public lands (though only an inconsiderable source of these revenues) seem first to have attracted the attention of the West. Gold in the coffers of a nation yields to the people no benefit, and corrupts the rulers. A liberal and enlightened system of internal improvements affords a ready antidote, and *who can predict the great strength that this nation will attain, if blessed with the genial sunshine of peace?* Then she will well apply the ten thousand resources springing from her boundless commerce and her fertile fields.

There will be a new judicial circuit in the north, including Carroll. Messrs. Ewing, Jenners, Everts, and Anthony are candidates for judge. Your Congressional district will be Parke, Vermilion, Montgomery, Warren, Tippecanoe, Clinton, Carroll, Laporte, St. Joseph, and Elkhart. Cass will come to the Indianapolis District.

The lowering clouds are gathering over the plains of South Carolina. To-night's mail informs us that several regiments and pieces of artillery have been ordered by the President to Charleston. The proclamation of the President is received here with enthusiasm by all parties, showing that in the utmost need of the Union we can all be one. It is a semi-official paper, the propriety of which the occasion warranted, as the demonstrations of the past must convince all that General Jackson could wield an overwhelming influence, for good or evil, over the destinies of the nation. He has stamped the indelible impress of his patriotism, by this act, upon the records of the country. I consider it a popular appeal which would have done no discredit to the tongue of Demosthenes.

There is nothing to detain the Legislature beyond five weeks longer—not half the local business there was last session. Your representative, General Wilson, is considerably indisposed, but convalescing.

We learn to-night that Dr. Canby is removed—his successor is not known—conjecture fixes upon Mr. Pollock, or Mr. Palmer.

A committee of the House has been directed to prepare a memorial to Congress for land to aid in building the Lafayette and Deschemens Railroad; but we have multiplied memorials to Washington until, I fear, they are not in very good odor there.

FROM THE SAME.

WASHINGTON, *September* 12, 1837.

DEAR STEWART,—Will you be kind enough to send me a list of names of reading persons who receive their communications at Delphi, without respect to party, as full as your convenience will allow. I request also, as the shortest way of learning the fact, that you will inform me of the names and location of the post-offices in Carroll.

By votes in each House, taken yesterday, it was resolved to confine the business of the special session to the *single* subject in the message, even including *private* business. The session, will, therefore, it is thought, close in four weeks. The Committee on Finance, in the Senate, introduced a bill to postpone, until further provision by law, the payment of the fourth installment of the surplus revenue to the States. Whether it will pass the Senate, I know not, but feel confident it can not pass the House. However it may be with other deposit banks, ours in Indiana can pay the State in funds at par, by which they will nearly relieve themselves from the balance of debt due the treasury. We have therefore every motive to desire that the payment of the fourth installment may not be interrupted. The Committee of Ways and Means, in the House, will, it is understood, present their measures promptly. Some of the *Whig* leaders, however, say that they will only propose *temporary* relief, and dare not present their sub-treasury schemes as a matter of permanent policy. On the other hand, Mr. Cambrelling challenges the opposition to avow their plan. It is rather unsettled whether any direct issue will be made up. I am looking on coolly, content to gather wisdom from the wise, determined to follow no leader where the glory of that leader is the only aim.

We hope to have a favorable decision on our claim for lands for our extended line of canal to Terre Haute.

Let me hear from you occasionally.

FROM THE SAME.

WASHINGTON, *March* 3, 1838.

A COMMITTEE of investigation has been appointed in relation to the late duel. It is not supposed they will bring out any new facts which are material. Mr. Graves has resumed his seat as usual. It was truly an unfortunate affair; said to be the first of the kind which has ever occurred during a session of Congress.

A man with a "ten-foot pole" can scarcely reach any practical business in our House, so much do we deal in episodes, parentheses, abstractions, etc., not to speak of idle and long-winded debate. The "old ones" say we shall adjourn about the 4th of July. I should like to stir my blood a little with the argument of a demurrer, or the trial of a jury cause.

It is thought there may be a tie in the Senate upon the Sub-treasury (I beg pardon, Independent Treasury) Bill. I think it will go by the board in our House; but what succedaneum may spring from its disintegrated elements, I do not know.

D. V. Cully has been appointed to the land-office in Indianapolis, and General Milroy has been nominated to the Senate, to supersede Mr. Pollock, at Crawfordsville. No other land-office appointments have yet been made in Indiana. Dire war is waging between Mr. Reed, of Wayne, and Mr. Rockhill, of Allen, for the Fort Wayne Land-office. It is doubtless suspended between them; and (but mum's the word when *great* men are concerned) John Law and John W. Davis, (both here) are tugging for the same office at Vincennes. "The devil take the hindmost." I suppose the people care but little who gets the spoils, so he be but "honest and capable." Do you think these Jeffersonian requisites are often to be met with now-a-days?

Let me hear from you, and particularly after court, how you like your new judge. Will thank you to state whether the new post-offices at Pittsburg and Carrollton are in operation, and supplied with the mails.

What are your prospects for business this Summer on the Wabash? Will improvements advance? Will your public works be vigorously prosecuted? I perceive there is to be an expenditure on that part of the Madison and Lafayette Railroad lying between Crawfordsville and Lafayette, lately transferred, etc.

Mr. Whitcomb is now writing his opinion upon the claim of our State for additional selections of land for the extended line of canal from Tippecanoe to Terre Haute. I feel very solicitous on this subject, but fear the mad-dog cry against donations of land to the new States. I think the decision of the department will be favorable.

We have had a Winter of unusual mildness, and generally good health, in which blessing I participate. General Tipton was quite sick a few days back, but is convalescing.

FROM THE SAME.

WASHINGTON, *April* 13, 1840.

DEAR SIR,—I have received your letter of the 2d inst., covering petition for post-road from Prince William via Lexington to Burlington, and for the establishment of a post-office at Lexington, and appointment of Adam Clark, Esq., as postmaster.

I will immediately present the memorial, and if any law is passed this session for new routes, will see that this is included.

It will be proper to await awhile the issue of such a bill, before taking steps to comply with your request to remove the present office from Xenia to Prince William, which, I understand you, is asked with the consent of the people and postmaster at Xenia.

The subject of a former petition for a route from Frankfort via Delphi, Monticello, and Buncombe, to Ottowa, is still borne in mind, and as well for these routes, as others in my charge. I have pressed the

Committee to report a bill for the new states, if they can do no more. They are embarrassed only by the want of funds in the department, and have not yet determined what report to make.

Political matters have been so much transferred from Washington to the different sections of the Union, where the Presidential struggle is going on, that we look to the interior for news with more eagerness than you can expect any thing from the center.

The month of May will be the great gathering-time in Baltimore, when I shall expect to see many of my Indiana friends of both parties who will doubtless extend their visits to Washington, and should be gratified if you were one of the number. The honorable designation of my townsman, Dr. Jackson, as a State delegate, will doubtless compel his attendance.

Most heartily I congratulate you upon the decisive measures adopted by Ohio for the completion of the Wabash and Erie Canal. That work accomplished, we shall soon look for better times in our beautiful valley; yea, doubtless under the auspices of Mr. Van Buren's administration, or under those of General Harrison.

General Howard's circular, announcing his intention to resign at the end of the session, has, I presume, been read by you. The filling of his vacancy will add a spice of interest to the August election in the Seventh District.

Mr. Smith, from the Ripley district, who has been very ill, is rapidly recovering.

The offices of the *Madisonian* and the *Democratic Review* were burnt down on Friday night, with almost a total loss to both. Allen's loss, about $5,000, without any insurance; Langton & O'Sullivan's losses are equally or a larger amount beyond their insurance.

After considerable debility, during a great part of

the Winter, I am at length reinstated in good health. I hope you are in the same condition.

With sincere respect, I remain your friend and servant, ALBERT S. WHITE.

HON. EDWARD A. HANNEGAN.

INDIANAPOLIS, *January* 21, 1833.

DEAR DOCTOR,— . . . In the way of legislative business, the most important is the passage of the Bank Bill through the Lower House, on Friday last, by a vote of 41 to 28. There was a most bitter and inveterate opposition displayed to the measure throughout. Notwithstanding all, however, the bill was carried in a shape that, I think, will be every way safe and satisfactory. Its fate is somewhat uncertain in the Senate.

A bill appropriating fifteen thousand dollars for the improvement of the Wabash River, at the Rapids, has passed the Senate, and is now before the House. This sum is intended to meet a similar appropriation on the part of the State of Illinois, and there is no doubt, should we succeed in carrying it through our House, but the aggregate of the sums will be sufficient to remove the main obstructions to the navigation of the stream at that important point.

A change will be made in the manner of electing the canal commissioners, so that one shall be elected every year. This is done for fear that at some time the whole Board may be turned out at once, and, having all new men, might for a time retard the work. I think the change every way salutary.

We have no news of any consequence from the East. Congress is engaged in discussing the tariff. The late treaty with the Pottawatomie Indians has been ratified in every particular.

FROM THE SAME.

HOUSE OF REPRESENTATIVES, *June* 9, 1834.

DEAR STEWART,—I received your letter last night, and may proceed as per direction to return an immediate answer; but what interest I can lend to the letter by the news I have to give, must depend on your love of reading, not the matter that will be written.

You have doubtless heard of the resignation of Stevenson as speaker, the election of Bell, etc., and our determination, with the consent of the Senate, to adjourn on the 30th of the present month.

Tyler has been nominated by the President to the Senate; but that body, however, has not as yet acted on the nomination. I sometimes fear he will be confirmed. I drew up a protest against him, and sent it to the Senate, signed by myself, Boone, and Kinnard.

I have not as yet received an answer to my application, founded on your letter, for future transportation of the mail, as you desire.

The bank has finally blown herself out of the water. Her refusal to permit an investigation by the Committee, has produced a reaction in the public mind beyond what you would believe, even in the large cities; the excrescenses, as I consider them, of the body politic. I fear much, however, that the opposition will not suffer us do any business for the country at the present session. They are determined to spend even the little time now left us in useless and idle debate. Let the responsibility, however, rest where it should, though, no doubt, there are those who, even removed from the corrupt atmosphere of the bank, will still justify the course of the leaders of that party. . . .

The weather has grown outrageously hot, and, you may rely upon it, I am anxious to return home. Present my respects to Mrs. S.

FROM THE SAME.

WASHINGTON, *April* 3, 1836.

MY DEAR STEWART,—I have delayed answering you for some days, until the department should determine upon the course to pursue in relation to the Indian lands. There being no appropriation for the purpose by Congress, of course, no regular commissioner could be appointed, and Mr. Ellsworth offered his services without compensation, to go to Indiana and submit Marshall's treaty (so modified as to suit the President's views) to Richardville. He has accordingly gone, and if he is successful, commissioners will be appointed to purchase the remainder; one of whom will be Aaron Finch. The other man I am not at liberty to name, as his friends wish nothing said about it at present; but on this you may rely, Finch will be one, as I have a promise to that effect. But you must not make it known, nor, indeed, any thing about the transaction, as it would only be the means of sending on some fifty applicants, thereby involving us all in trouble.

. . . . On last evening, the bill to admit Michigan into the Union passed the Senate, after a desperate struggle of two days. It contains stipulations on the subject of boundary, confirming Indiana, and extending Indiana to the point she contended for, which must be acceded to by Michigan in convention, after which the President is authorized to declare her a member of the Confederacy by proclamation. The bill to admit Arkansas was also ordered to be engrossed, last night, for a third reading. The debate in the Senate during the two days was in the highest degree interesting; a deal of excitement existed, and every speaking member of the body was called out. The North Carolina election, which, first and last, gave us a good deal of trouble, was decided during the week, by sending the election back to the people. For this I voted, as I would do in all cases of contested elections, where the merits were not clear and palpable. Some time during the coming week, I will have an interview with Kendall, and endeavor, if possible, to have a general arrangement of stage-routes in my district. I have been put off from time to time, but it is now necessary that something should be done, if at all. The Senate have set the —— day of May for adjournment, but whether our House will agree, is more than I can say; in fact, I do not believe they will. We have too many talking members, and too little disposition for business. Benton gave them a most glorious lecture in the Senate on this subject yesterday. After all, Stewart, he is the great man of our party, the great man of the country, whom no selfish considerations can warp or bias. The more I see of him, the more I admire him.

My respects to Mrs. S. and all friends.

FROM THE SAME.

WASHINGTON, *March* 20, 1836.

DEAR STEWART,— . . . Your mail-routes are all before the committee, and will pass in the general bill, if that passes.

You will doubtless have seen the confirmation of Taney, Barbour, Kendall, Stevenson, etc. This is at last a glorious triumph; but Judge White has astonished us wonderfully by voting against every one of them. On yesterday Benton called up his expunging resolution, and occupied the Senate for three hours, in a speech of unsurpassed force and vigor. He has not yet concluded, but will probably occupy Monday, as the Senate does not sit to-day. His speech will produce a tremendous effect throughout the country, as it has on all who heard it. I will send you a copy so soon as it is published.

Cass will be sent out as Minister to France, and King, of Alabama, instead of Polk, will be appointed Secretary of War. Polk does not desire to leave his present station. Some time back, I thought we would adjourn by the 1st of June, but I entertain no such hopes now; there is such a disposition to speak in this house, that the people at the polls must interfere to check it. I have some hope that the Graduation Bill may pass, more especially if Clay should resign, as is it confidently stated he will do in a short time. . . .

WASHINGTON, *March* 1, 1844.

DEAR STEWART,— . . . I send you a copy of my Oregon speech. I hope you will like it. I believe it is better received here than any speech I ever made in Congress. Robinson, for the present, must consider this an answer to his favor also.

The horrible occurrence on the Princeton, you will see in the papers. I was standing with General Jessup at the main-mast, some twenty-five or thirty feet from the explosion, and was the first person who pressed forward to the place. Colonel Benton had been prostrated by the awful concussion, having been standing immediately behind the breach of the gun. When I reached his side, he was lifting a poor sailor in his arms, whose left arm was shot off; *thoughtless of himself*, he thought only of the poor suffering man. But I need not comment on it: you will see at once the noble heart it betrays. He was cool and collected. I asked him if he was wounded "No, Hannegan," was his reply; "but look at this poor fellow. Bring a surgeon to him quick." Judge Phelps, of Vermont, was standing near Benton at the time of the explosion, who acted likewise with great coolness and courage; has declared publicly that injustice shall no longer be done to Benton's generous and noble heart; that he will seek an occasion in the Senate to pay him a tribute. He is, as you know, a warm Whig. Benton and Phelps were standing immediately by the bulwarks, which were swept entirely away, and their hats were also carried overboard, with the bonnet of a lady who stood between them. Benton is out of danger, but not able to sit up. The force of the concussion struck his breast; had it struck his head, he must have been instantly killed.

Yours truly, ED. A. HANNEGAN.

FROM GENERAL T. A. HOWARD.

ROCKVILLE, INDIANA, *January* 15, 1839.

SIR,—The letter of yourself and others, members of the Lafayette Convention, dated the 9th inst., has been received.

In regard to my visiting the northern counties, I take great pleasure in assuring you that I shall do so as early as the circumstances connected with the canvass will justify. Should I do so before the adjournment of the Legislature, it might seem that I desired to forestall public opinion in the absence of a gentleman who is already announced as a candidate for Congress. I shall visit every part of the district, during the Spring and Summer, and publicly address the citizens on the various topics involved in a canvass for the Congress of the United States.

FROM THE SAME.

ROCKVILLE, INDIANA, *September* 5, 1839.

DEAR STEWART,—I make no apology for troubling you, and challange you to write me frequently in return. I want you to do me the favor to furnish me a list, embracing the names, at length, of your sheriff, coroner, judges, clerk, lawyers, doctors, merchants, tavern-keepers, ministers, contractors, who reside in Delphi; and the names of your townships, with the justices in each, of both parties, the names of all the other towns in the county, and some of the citizens in each. Send me the names of all the school-masters in the county, and their residences.

Give my respects, most gratefully tendered, to my friends in "old Carroll," and to my friends in Delphi, including those ladies with whom I had the pleasure of becoming acquainted when I was there.

FROM THE SAME.

WASHINGTON CITY, *December* 17, 1839.

DEAR SIR,—The opposition, this morning, again brought up the New Jersey case, and it has been discussed throughout the day. When we will be done with it, I know not. It will, however, I hope have one good effect; it will open the eyes of the people to the dangers which may attend the rights of suffrage, even after they have deposited their will in the ballot-box.

Your friend, T. A. HOWARD.

FROM GOVERNOR WHITCOMB.

JAMESTOWN, N. Y., *July*, 21, 1849.

MY DEAR FRIEND,—Yesterday was three long months since I was so violently attacked by sickness at Buffalo, while on my way home, as to make it impracticable to proceed any further; and since that time, I have been under medical treatment. My disease is, essentially, great debility or prostration of the nervous system, of a chronic or complicated character, hastened and aggravated, if not produced, by mental labor of a severe and unremitting character. Few are apprised of the severity of my labors while in the General Land-office, the labor of two canvasses for the office of governor, and the solicitude and anxiety incident to that position, especially in arranging the State debt with advantage to the best interests of the people who had honored me with their confidence. All this was only calculated to accelerate the silent but sure progress of disease. Above all, the great domestic bereavement with which I was struck, as with the arrow of death, two years ago, on the 17th inst., worked fearfully on my health and spirits. And, although, after some three or four weeks, I flattered myself with making some progress toward the restoration of my health, yet I continued to have so many "back-sets" and new symptoms, requiring an altered treatment, that I am greatly discouraged. Eleven days ago, however, at my suggestion, my physician, a prudent and cautious man, but not a dogmatist, assented to my use of the cold-water bath. I have already taken eleven of these baths, in as many successive days, in water of the temperature of 62°, and latterly fresh from the well, and as low as 52°. The effect on my feelings and symptoms for the better has been wonderful, and I thank God that I now begin to feel a strong confidence that by His mercy, through this instrumentality, I shall again see in this life my own Indiana. And the moment I think of Indiana, there is indissolubly associated in my mind, and intertwined in every fiber of my heart, the noble-hearted of her sons who have favored me with their friendship, in the very *first rank* of whom my heart instinctively places you. Being sufficiently recovered to write, it is natural, therefore, that I should address you. It is not yet deemed prudent for me to travel, and I shall scarcely get home in time to see Delphi before another session of Congress, but if my life continues to be spared by the Divine mercy, I yet count on the great gratification of again taking you by the hand, as well as seeing you. Pray write me (at this place) soon, as to all the news, the progress of the cholera, etc., etc. If you see your late worthy representative, give him my most grateful thanks and respects.

I desire my most respectful compliments to your lady, and accept my best wishes for your prosperity, from,

Faithfully, your friend, JAS. WHITCOMB.

FROM GENERAL LEWIS CASS.

DETRIOT, *February* 21, 1834.

DEAR SIR,—I have received your obliging favor, and thank you heartily for your friendly feelings.

Duty and inclination equally prompt me to be a silent spectator of passing events. My name has been placed before the country, without any action of my own, and the result gives me as little trouble as almost any other man. I have sat still since my return, and have not been out of the place, except during the short trip I made to Fort Wayne.

I am not, however, the less grateful to my friends, who have espoused my cause, and I am under a deep debt of gratitude to the State of Indiana, for the manifestations of favor which have been exhibited there. It is obvious that the most active politicians through the country have determined upon Mr. Van Buren, as the candidate of the "Republican" party. Whether this decision will be confirmed by the people, remains to be seen. It may be that at the Baltimore Convention, such doubts respecting the result may prevail as to lead to the selection of some other person. Indications of dissatisfaction, as you say, are exhibiting themselves, and it is difficult to foresee the extent to which they will reach. But under no circumstances ought the Democratic party to suffer itself to be broken up by divisions. After the nomination, I hope we shall all take hold and support the candidate agreed upon. This I shall do, and I shall recommend my friends to act in the same manner. With great regard,

I am, dear sir, yours truly, LEW. CASS.

JOHN DUMONT,

AND THE ELECTION OF 1837.

ONE of the most exciting and interesting election canvasses ever witnessed in this state, was the race for governor, in 1837, between Governor Wallace and the Hon. John Dumont. These gentlemen both belonged to the same political party, and the sole issue between them was the classification of the *Public Works.* Governor Wallace and his friends favored a simultaneous carrying on of all the works embraced in the mammoth Internal Improvement Bill; while the friends of Dumont favored a *classification*, contending that by prosecuting one or two works to completion at a time, the whole might ultimately be finished, and the State saved from bankruptcy. In the early part of the race, Judge Gamaliel Taylor, a Democrat, of Madison, was on the track, but the great interests at stake, in the all-absorbing subject of Internal Improvement, produced an overwhelming desire to ignore old party lines and fight the battle on the new issue. Judge Taylor, perceiving this feeling, declined the race, thus leaving the contest between Wallace and Dumont. Although Governor W. was the successful aspirant, Mr. Dumont made a most brilliant canvass, and the author remembers very well the effect his speeches produced in Carroll County. Like Whitcomb, he made no effort at the "spread-eagle style," but he presented his points so ingeniously, his illustrations were so plain, and his manner so candid and honest, that he produced a powerful effect. In fact, few men in the state were better calculated to *make votes* on the stump, than John Dumont. . . . . Being a warm advocate of the classification of the Public Works, the author supported him.

FROM JOHN DUMONT,

CANDIDATE FOR GOVERNOR IN 1837.

SCIPIO, JENNINGS CO., INDIANA, *July* 2, 1837.

DEAR SIR,—I have progressed so far, and made a speech here this evening. Since I left Indianapolis, I passed through Johnson, Morgan, Owen, Monroe, and Bartholomew Counties, and have no doubt of a strong impression in my favor in Owen, Monroe, and Bartholomew. As to the others, I have no certain intelligence, but do not doubt of getting a respectable number of votes in each of these counties. I have been on, and will be on, all the *battle-ground of the railroad from Indianapolis to Madison.* I call it the *battle-ground*, because it is the ground to be contested; but even along this line there is a great division of the people. If Taylor has any force in any county that I have passed through, it has entirely escaped my observation. Will you be so good as to notice favorable articles in the prints, and have them republished in the Delphi *Oracle?* I have, from the journals, made the following abstracts, which you could weave into an article for the *Oracle.* It is from a report to the Board made by Mr. Blake, and it shows, what is not generally known, that the corps of officers belonging to the present system, cost more than the whole State Government! It was some labor to extract it, but you may rely on its being a true expose of that which Mr. Blake reported in such a way as not to lead the mind to the expense of this almost sinecure Board.

These are:

1	Principal Engineer on Canals		$3,500
1	" " on Roads and Railways		4,000
11	Resident Engineers	$1,500	16,500
5	Senior Assistants	920	4,600
7	Assistants	696	5,072

11 Junior Assistants	$556	$6,116
6 Senior Roadmen	456	2,736
16 Roadmen	396	6,336
2 Junor Roadmen	348	696
15 Axmen	315	4,725
		$54,271

Besides the Board of Internal Improvement, their secretary, and other contingencies. A *classification* would tend to disband two thirds of this eating corps.

Has my speech in favor of opening the Wabash and Erie Canal been published in the *Oracle*. It was to have been published in the *Mercury*, of Lafayette, and in the Logansport papers, from one of which it may be copied. If it be copied in the *Oracle*, can a paper with a mark for publication be sent to the *Miami Chief* and to the Fort Wayne paper?

Please write me a line about matters and things, to Vincennes, Knox County, and,

Believe me yours, truly, JOHN DUMONT.

FROM THE SAME.

MIDDLETON, VIGO COUNTY, *July* 22, 1837.

DEAR SIR,—I received your favor at Vincennes, for which I am greatly obliged to you. I at the time received a letter from the north, speaking of my prospects being good in the northern counties, excepting Michigan City. Also, a letter from General Burnett, of New Albany, stating that I could obtain very large majorities in Clarke and Harrison, and a respectable vote in Floyd County. The latter I had not expected. I have also had a confirmation of good news from Parke, Vermilion, Monroe, and Owen. I was advised to spend no more time in my own Congressional district; good judges thought I would get a majority of three thousand in it. I have traversed the Pocket, and am not much elated with the prospect that it affords. You know I must be beaten in Vanderburg. In Posey I will get a heavy majority. In the rest of the river counties, below Crawford, though I will get majorities, they will not be large, because my notices could not get on in time. My own opinion is, that I will do well in Knox, Davis, and Gibson, but as yet have had no certain information since I left them. In Sullivan my vote must be very heavy, and in Vigo I must be beaten. I have labored indefatigably. I spoke in Madison, July 4th, to a large and delighted audience. I go to Terre Haute to-morrow; thence to Clay, Greene, Lawrence, Orange, Crawford, Harrison, and Floyd, to speak in New Albany again; thence up to Washington, Jackson, Scott, and am to speak again at Madison, on the 5th of August. I will then take a steam-boat, and speak at Lawrenceburg, on Monday morning, August 7th.

As I travel, it is so difficult and impossible to have a full view of the state, or to have the news, that it baffles conjecture as to the result. I shall, however, believe that on my own part I have done as much as almost any other person would have done in the same time, and I have a well-grounded confidence that I have active and efficient friends in every county, among whom I consider you as one of the most zealous.

With sentiments of high regard, I remain yours,

JOHN DUMONT.

HORATIO J. HARRIS.

THIS gentleman was born, if we mistake not, in Newark, Ohio, and was the son of Dr. Harris, a prominent physician of that place. He graduated at Miami University; soon after which he came to Indianapolis, and resided for a short time in the family of Nicholas M'Carty, who was an old friend of his father. Not long afterward he procured the appointment of assistant engineer on the Wabash and Erie Canal, and in that capacity came to the Wabash. Some of the young men of this place having made the personal acquaintance of Mr. H., through their influence he was selected to deliver the Fourth of July oration, at the celebration of the National Anniversary, in 1837. Being a small man, and presenting nothing very intellectual in his appearance, public expectation was by no means high. The surprise was very great, therefore, when the day came, and he pronounced the finest address ever listened to in the county.

Not many months afterward, he entered the office of Messrs. White & Lockwood, attorneys-at-law in Lafayette, and commenced the study of that profession.

In June, 1838, he returned to Delphi, and commenced the practice of law.

In 1840, he was nominated by the Democratic party and elected, from the counties of Carroll and Clinton, to the State Senate, having been elected principal clerk of the House of Representatives the preceding Winter. At the expiration of his term as senator, in the Winter of 1843–4, he was elected Auditor of State. Having served out his term as State Auditor, Mr. H. spent a few months in the city of New York, assisting the Agent of State in carrying the Butler bill into operation.

Having, in 1847, married an adopted daughter of Joseph E. Davis, of Mississippi (brother of Jefferson Davis), Mr. Harris removed to Jackson, Mississippi, and after remaining there about two years, he removed to Vicksburg. Through the influence of Jeff. Davis, who was a son-in-law of General Taylor, Mr. Harris, although a Democrat, received from President Taylor the appointment of District Attorney for Mississippi, which office he continued to hold for several years, and perhaps up to the time of his death.

The author has a large bundle of letters from Mr.

Harris, many of which would be interesting to the public; but he regrets that he can find room but for a few of them. The first one was written from Lafayette, while he was reading law. The following is a copy:

LAFAYETTE, *October* 8, 1837.

MY DEAR FRIEND STEWART,—Writing to you thus early in reply to yours of yesterday, will indicate a determination to be a punctual correspondent, whether I have any other good quality as such or not. For the expression of your good-will toward me, I can only, at *present*, make you the return of my sincerest gratitude; but I trust that the time *may* come when I shall be able to afford you a more substantial and valuable recompense. Wherever my future lot may be cast, whether in the rich valley of my native West, or in the sunny climes of the palmy South, I shall ever make it a matter of pride that the reports that may reach your ears of my conduct, will convey the gratification of knowing that your counsel and your friendship have not been without their effect in molding my character to all that is honored and honorable in human nature. And I shall look to it also, that under no circumstances of life the charge may be brought against me of having undervalued the kindness of those who were my friends at a time when most I needed them, and when their friendship for me could be liable to no imputation of insincerity, no suspicion of cold-hearted and scheming selfishness. "Sweet are the uses of adversity," says the great poet; but in my estimation it has nothing *more* sweet than its power to test the purity of feeling and the strength of principle—a power equally efficient, whether it be brought to bear upon social, religious, or political life. Clouded and convulsed as my short life has been, I should, in all probability, long since have given myself up to dark and gloomy thoughts, if not to despair, had I not in some way or other, God only knows how, been successful in securing the smiles and the approbation of a host of friends to brighten my pathway and cheer me in my onward and upward progress. Among these, be assured, that you stand like Saul among his brethren, head and shoulders above them *all*. Perhaps I ought to except two or three, but I have not time at present to analyze my feeling accurately enough to determine whether I *should* do so or not. But I shall grow tedious by writing any thing further of this description.

You are not the first one of my acquaintance who has given me the reputation of possessing ambition in a predominating degree. In fact, I have heard it objected to me more than once, that I have carried that passion to excess, and consequently to criminality; but I have never thought so myself, and probably never shall. My own persuasion remains now, what it has long been, that the evils arising from an ambition like mine, will be only a personal inconvenience, while the good that may result from its exercise may be lasting and general: and, looking upon it in this light, I can certainly feel myself under no obligations to check, to repress, or destroy it. I trust I shall ever be found seeking to attain *honorable ends* by *honorable means*—bowing in submission to the dictum of no one without the exercise first of my own judgment, and conceding not one iota of my principles, until my own observation, reason, or experience convinces me that *I* am *wrong*, and that those who oppose me are right. In this way I hope that if, in the end, I shall have but little to congratulate myself upon, I shall at least have nothing to regret; that if I should not be so fortunate as to sit in high places, among the wealthy, the influential, and the honored, I shall nevertheless, within an appropriate sphere, be useful, respected, and respectable. Your advice with reference to the subject to which I alluded in my last, has determined me to follow out what was my own inclination before I wrote. If we can only get C. to aid, even indirectly, in tomahawking the measures, and scalping the principles of some of our great little men, we can then probably induce him to be of some use to the party to which he nominally belongs. Otherwise, I am afraid he will be of no more consequence than the salt about Jerusalem that has lost its savor.

I hardly know how to defend myself against the charge of having written poetry, as this is the first time it was ever brought, and consequently startles me much by its novelty. A general denial of the fact, I suppose, is all that is left me. I know of no young lady in Delphi whose eyes could induce me to make so great a blunder, except our friend Julia's, and begging her pardon a thousand times, I do not think that even hers, bright, beautiful, and witching as they are, could accomplish so great a victory. God knows that there are enough miserable ingredients in my composition already, without being cursed with a desire to scribble poetry. It is, however, a matter of but little consequence at any rate, and rather than the verses should go out into the world like penniless orphans, at the next meeting of the probate court of the Muses, I will sue out letters of administration, and have myself appointed guardian.

Our friend, the colonel, is here yet, and looks as hale and smiling as if he had fifty Democratic victories inside of him. Present the assurance of my high regard to Mrs. Stewart, and my compliments to all other friends, should I be so fortunate as to have any besides her. You must please consider this letter as an off-hand, random one, and wait till next time, with the expectation of receiving a better. In the mean time think of me as

Your sincere friend, HORATIO J. HARRIS.

P. S.—I have just got the *Oracle*, and read the poetry of which you speak. E'hew! a mixture of ice and salt would not cool that fellow off. If you should hear of any one dying of spontaneous combustion, my word on it, he is the man who wrote the poetry.

FROM THE SAME.

LAFAYETTE, *November* 7, 1837.

FRIEND STEWART,—I have not had time to answer your letter of the 5th as soon as you wished, and indeed, have not, even now, leisure enough to compose any thing that may be worthy of a perusal. I mention this fact in advance, in order that your indulgence may be extended toward me, should you find me even duller than is usual with me (which is dull enough, God knows), and feel inclined, after having waded through the mud and mire of my thoughts, to throw my letter aside with a hearty curse on my hapless head for troubling you with such trash. So much for an apology—a thing that I hate in my very soul, but which I feel sometimes obliged to make.

I read the last *Oracle* with some attention, and was much pleased with the tone in which a number of the editorials were written. The editor seems, in my judgment, to have taken the proper course with reference to those soulless things called "Banks;" and as a member of the Democratic party, I should be gratified to see all the papers that profess to advocate our principles take the same bold and fearless stand. In these days of political apostasy, when a man's friends are too often like Job's comforters, the duty devolves the more imperiously upon the *truly faithful* to make the stronger and more untiring exertions to rescue the cause of Republican freedom from the perils that surround it. The great question, whether the Bank shall triumph over the Government, or the Government over the

Bank, should be presented before the people, and always kept in their view. That is, indeed, the true issue, and the one which must ultimately be joined. Any other would only delay the determination of the case, and be productive of fresh and greater evils. I look upon a total separation of the Government from the banks as an event that must sooner or later occur; and why may it not as well be now as at some future day, when the poison shall have penetrated deeper and spread wider, and when the strength of the patient is less able to bear the necessary and unavoidable pain of the remedy? Why should we not as well calk the constitutional ship, while her bottom discloses only a single leak-hole, as to wait in blind recklessness until the worms have gnawed her timbers to dust, and she begins, as the waters gush in from every side, to settle down to a fathomless grave? Shall we advise our physician to defer his prescriptions until the death-rattle is in our throats, the eyes are wild, the cheeks pallid, the frame nerveless, and the pulse gone? Shall we wait until the impetuous current is dashing us against the rocks, and sweeping us irresistibly onward to the brink of the precipice, before we shall begin to think about the means of escape? Shall we fold our arms and close our eyes, until the conflagration has gained its mightiest power, and the wealth of years of toil is perishing in a moment, and then begin to stir ourselves to check the progress of desolation? Surely not. In a madman, such a course might be expected, but never could it be deemed the dictate of wisdom or the admonition of prudence. Now is the accepted time, and now is the day of salvation for the country, from the destructive power of grasping, moneyed monopolies. Let the occasion be embraced as it ought, and the people will be free; let it be deferred, and their chains are forged.

. . . . I know not when I shall come to

Delphi, not for a week or two at least. My engagements with Mr. Lockwood will not permit me to stay with you any length of time. Pray tell me when the Thespians again astonish the natives? It may be that I can make it convenient to attend, and *laugh* at their *tragedies* and *weep* at their *comedies*. Are you one of them? If so, I beg pardon for the last remark. . . .

FROM THE SAME.

LAFAYETTE, *May* 8, 1868.

DEAR STEWART,—On next Sunday morning I shall start for Indianapolis to procure me a law library. After staying there long enough to get heartily tired of that sink-hole of political iniquity and corruption, which will take but a short time, I shall return here, and from here take up the line of march to Delphi, to commence practising as an attorney and counselor-at-law. I am *resolved* on this, and trust it will be for the best. I am aware that there will be many difficulties in my way, but you know I am not one of those who will venture nothing for fear there may be a "lion in the street." Lockwood goes in with me for that county; but this between ourselves. Pray write me by return mail, and tell me whether I can have a comfortable office and a good boarding-house. I shall have my shingle nailed up by the 10th of June at farthest.

I heard, with much sorrow, of the death of your boy. There, indeed, would seem something like a fatality hanging over your children. Aware, as I am, how deeply your affections were centered in that child, I can readily conceive that the blow must have been more than an ordinarily severe one, both to you and to your wife. The dispensations of Providence are often dark and inscrutable, but should be bowed to in submission, both as a dictate of reason, as well as religion. Remember me kindly to your wife, and assure her how much of happiness I anticipate from the continued manifestations of her friendship for me.

FROM THE SAME.

INDIANAPOLIS, *December* 12, 1839.

DEAR STEWART,—The Eastern mail this evening brings the news that Harrison has received the nomination for President, and Tyler, of Virginia, for Vice-President. What think you of that? Can we muster sufficient force in Indiana to give her vote for Matty? I think we can, though the leading Whigs here think we can not.

. . . Poor Tallmadge is laid on the shelf, to sleep unhonored and unknown. His fate I pity not; he has met a traitor's reward; his treason was a grievous fault, and grievously hath Cæsar answered it.

It can not be concealed that the nomination of Harrison will operate more injuriously upon the interests of our party, as far as this State is concerned, than the nomination of either Clay or Scott. The contest here will be a severe one, but if things are properly managed, if we bring out the proper man for governor on the 8th, and organize our party well, we are sure of success. Should we make a misstep on that day, or should our Legislature, in its action during the present session, give the Whigs any ground for objection, we may lose the State. I learn, by letter from Delphi, that probably no one will attend our Convention as a delegate from Carroll. We must be represented, however, and should Henry Bruce, Milroy, and myself, or either of us, be authorized to represent our county, I wish you would write me fully what you think are the wishes of our county, and generally, what you think the Convention should do. The probability at present is, that Ewing, of Cass, will receive the nomination for governor, and some one from the south, Mr. Tuley, for instance, that of lieutenant-governor. Would that be a strong team? How would Ewing go off in our county? Dr. —— has written me a letter, in which he states that, although he had no intention, when first spoken of, to present his name to the Convention, he has finally determined to do so, and requests that I should stand his friend. This places me, or rather *would* place me, in a delicate situation, should I be appointed a delegate. Should I not vote for him, I incur, *of course*, his eternal displeasure, and to vote for him would be doing a very foolish thing. Every man knows that he can not be elected if nominated.

. . . No organization of the House of Representatives in Congress up to the 6th inst. The probability of a row—a real Harrisburg affair—brightens every day. God only knows in what it will end. . . . Write me immediately, and believe me your sincere friend.

FROM THE SAME.

INDIANAPOLIS, *January* 1, 1840.

DEAR STEWART,—Your letter of the 26th was duly received. Whitcomb absolutely refuses to be presented to the Convention, and Read will probably do the same; so your instructions are of no avail. I am satisfied, from what I have heard in the last three or four days, that General Howard will receive the nomination. Every part of the State is uniting upon him, and calling upon him to run. Tuley, of Floyd, will perhaps be the candidate for lieutenant-governor. In my opinion, this will be a strong ticket; it can not and will not be beaten. Should Howard accept the nomination, there will be a vacancy in my Congressional district, which it will be hard to fill with one of our party. Lane will be the Whig candidate, and will be a strong one, too. Hannegan could beat him, but no other man of our party could. . . .

FROM THE SAME.

SENATE CHAMBER, *January* 8, 1841.

DEAR STEWART,—Your books have been forwarded to you *via* Logansport. The delay was occasioned by the absence of Mr. Slater.

I received your letter inclosing two petitions, one on the subject of procuring the location of a bank at Delphi, and the other, praying that the members of the Carroll Light Infantry may be exempted from poll-tax and working on the roads. It is perfectly idle to think of getting a bank at our town, as there are two branches already authorized which can not be put in operation for the want of funds. The State has no money to take stock with. But even if that insurmountable objection were not in the way, I doubt very much the propriety of having any such institution in our place. The corrupting influence of banks is well known, and I never wish to live near one, much less to have any connection with them.

We have passed the law repealing our mode of doing township business. It takes effect from the time of filing a certified copy thereof in your office. I will have it forwarded to you for publication immediately. We have no news of any consequence. Legislation is progressing slowly, and without much excitement.

FROM THE SAME.

INDIANAPOLIS, *January* 9, 1840.

DEAR STEWART,—We had the greatest convention, it is acknowledged on all hands, that ever assembled in the state of Indiana. Men who do not generally take part in political contests of the day, but content themselves with silently casting their votes, have flocked here by thousands, and such excitement, such confidence of success, such enthusiasm, I never saw, and perhaps the like was never seen here, or elsewhere. Nathaniel West, of this town, was appointed president; two old Revolutionary soldiers, one of whom had fought under General Harrison, and two or three other distinguished gentlemen were chosen vice-presidents; and Hutchins, Glenn, Ellis, and Carlton (of Fountain), appointed secretaries. An address to the people of the state was presented by Robert Dale Owen, and unanimously adopted. It is, indeed and in truth, one of the most able documents that has ever been issued from our conventions. Fifty thousand copies were ordered to be printed.

Who shall we run against Henry S. Lane, to supply Howard's vacancy? Chamberlain and Hannegan are talked of, and no doubt Bryce and Jackson will wish to take the track. We will have hard times in the Seventh. A false step, and all is gone.

Dr. Grimes handed me your letter this morning. . . . . I write this while a debate is going on in the House, and have not time to add more.

FROM THE SAME.

JACKSON, MISS., *April* 14, 1848.

DEAR STEWART,—The mail of Sunday last brought me your acceptable letter, for which you have my hearty thanks. You can hardly imagine with what interest I read your narrative of the events which have taken place in my own town since I heard from it last, which is now more than a year ago. Death, it seems, has made sad havoc among our old acquaintances, and I infer from what you say, that the character of our portion of the Wabash country has not much improved as respects salubrity. Many of those whom you inform me are now "moldering cold and low," were the very pictures of good health when I saw them last;

they have been stricken down, while such lean-visaged and weakly fellows as you and I are still the spared monuments of God's mercy. I was truly sorry to hear of our old friends, Wilson's and Milford's decease.

. . . About a week ago, my wife and boy (now just a year old) came up from her friends', and we have got regularly to housekeeping. We have a nice little home, about a mile from Jackson, consisting of fifty acres of land with a comfortable dwelling-house and out-houses. I walk to town every morning, return in the afternoon, and spend the cool of the evening at work in the garden. This will have a salutary effect upon my health. In reference to business matters, I have nothing new to write. My prospects seem flattering, and so far, I am well pleased with the South. . . I hope you will keep me advised of such matters and things in Carroll and other parts of the state, as you may think would interest me. Please remember me to Mrs. Stewart, and to Dr. Elliott, when you write to, or see, him. Give, also, my compliments to my old and valued friends, Mr. and Mrs. Buford, and Lucinda Greenup, and Captain Gist and lady.

With sentiments as in the olden time, yours truly, in F. L. and T., HORATIO J. HARRIS.

ALBERT S. WHITE.

WASHINGTON, *July* 15, 1861.

DR. J. H. STEWART—*Dear Sir*,—At your request I subjoin a personal memoir, which you may put through your sieve as often as you please, and if you act wisely, will perhaps reject the whole, since probably neither my "name nor station" will add to the interest of your history.

I was born in Blooming Grove, Orange County, N. Y., on the 24th of October, 1803. My paternal ancestors (English) settled at Weymouth, Massachusetts, in 1636. Captain Thomas White, my first American ancestor, was a member of the Legislature of Massachuchetts Bay Colony, as early as 1638. His grandson, Ebenezer (my ancestor in the fifth degree), emigrated to Southhampton, on Long Island, near the close of the seventeenth century. He and his son, Silvanus, both graduates of Cambridge, were Presbyterian ministers. One settled at Southhampton, the other at Bridgehampton, where he preached fifty-five years to one congregation. My grandfather, Silvanus, who was a farmer and son of the Rev. Silvanus, emigrated to Blooming Grove about 1755, and built the house, still standing, wherein both my father and myself were born. My father, Nathan H. White, graduated at Columbia College in 1791, being contemporary there with the father of the Rev. Samuel R. Johnson, D. D., late of Lafayette.

I was educated at Union College, where I graduated in 1822, under Dr. Nott; was licensed as an attorney in the Supreme Court of New York, in 1825, and immediately emigrated to the West. Having practiced intermediately, first at Rushville and next at Paoli, I came to Lafayette in March, 1829. During the session of 1828–29, I reported the Legislative Debates for the *Indiana Journal*, which was the first session the current debates were reported in Indiana. From 1830 to 1835, I was clerk to the Indiana House of Representatives, two years assistant and three years principal. This was the period of the prosecution of our canal policy, which induced me thus to prolong my service as clerk, though adverse to my professional business at home. I attended all the earlier courts in Carroll, from the time of their inauguration in Mr. Baum's log house.

In 1833, I was an unsuccessful candidate against Edward A. Hannegan for Congress; was elected in 1837, and served in the House of Representatives during the memorable Twenty-fifth Congress. The Calhoun policy, already adumbrated, of annexing Texas and expanding the area of the empire of slavery, produced a reaction, especially in New England, flooding Congress with petitions, most of which took extreme ground on the other side, and have not since been adopted in the platforms of any of the great political parties.

During my term in the House of Representatives, and afterward in the Senate, where I served from 1839 to 1845, I voted and acted with the conservative Whigs, steering, if possible, between the Scylla and Charybdis of this dangerous Mediterranean, adhering to every social obligation in our constitutional compact, but persistently voting against the policy of Texas annexation in all its forms.

It was my fortune, while in Congress, to assist in obtaining the land grants for the extension of our canal, first to Terre Haute and afterward to Evansville. Leaving Congress in 1845, I resumed, for a short time, my profession, but soon renounced it entirely, and have since, with but little intermission (until 1860), been engaged in helping to pioneer and build the railroads penetrating the Upper Wabash Valley. I was president of the Lafayette and Indianapolis Railroad Co., from its organization until 1856, and, during three years of that period, served also as president of the (now) Toledo, Wabash, and Western Railroad Co., having, at the commencement of the last-named enterprise, negotiated with Eastern capitalists to become the principal proprietors, and to build the road. Its accomplishment, so useful to the country, has been attended with great loss to its proprietors.

Since December, 1859, I have resided at Stockwell, being one of six proprietors who are attempting to build an academic village there. From that retirement my fellow-citizens of the Eighth District called me to serve another term in Congress, a duty which I assumed with great diffidence, and, in common with my sober and patriotic countrymen who are still loyal to the Union, pray that Providence may evolve light from the surrounding darkness, and save our country alike from the desolation of anarchy and the withering embrace of tyranny. It may be that we are to be co-workers with destiny to purge our institutions of all antagonistic elements, and that this desolating Civil War will be school-master to those sections which are at once the cause and the chief sufferers in this ruin, persuading them voluntarily to inaugurate such a change in their system as will make us a homogeneous nation—a result, which if it requires three generations to accomplish, posterity will arise and call them and us blessed.

I was married in January, 1843, to Harriet, daughter of Thomas Mann Randolph, of Virginia, and hope that my children may never see a divided Union, or be unable to look with equal pride and affection upon both Virginia and New York.

Most truly, your friend, ALB. S. WHITE.

CHAPTER XIII.

BIOGRAPHY.

GENERAL SAMUEL MILROY.

ONE among the early and most prominent of the pioneers of the territory, out of which Carroll County was organized, was General Samuel Milroy, who was born August 14, 1780, in Kishakoquillas Valley, in Mifflin County, in the state of Pennsylvania. His grandfather, John M'Elroy, was the Earl of Annandale, in Scotland, a lineal descendant of Robert Bruce. He engaged heart and soul in the attempted revolution in Scotland, in 1744, in which Charles Stuart, the last heir to the throne of Scotland, sought to regain the kingdom of his ancestors from the English, but was terribly defeated by the Duke of Cumberland, at the battle of Culloden. His followers were proscribed and pursued without mercy. John M'Elroy, with his young wife, escaped to Ireland, and changed his name to Milroy, and, after a few years, emigrated to the American Colonies, and settled near Carlisle, Pennsylvania, and became a prosperous farmer. He had a family of two boys and three girls, and afterward was, with his eldest son, killed by the Indians. Henry, the surviving son, after arriving at maturity, married, and settled in Kishakoquillas Valley, Mifflin County. He had a family of four boys and two girls. Samuel, the subject of this sketch, was the third son, and when eleven years old, his father died. He was soon afterward apprenticed to learn the trade of carpenter and joiner.

After the completion of his apprenticeship, in 1800,

he set out the next year, in company with his elder brother John, to *seek their fortunes.* They came northwest to Lake Erie, where, by an act of the Legislature of Pennsylvania, land was to be donated to actual settlers, upon certain conditions. They located upon a claim of four hundred acres, near where the city of Erie now stands. After working on and improving their claim three years, keeping "bachelor's hall," and undergoing much hardship and privation, on account of the newness of the country, by some kind of legislation and *skulduggery* among speculators, they lost their claim, which was taken from them, with all their labor and improvement.

After the loss of their land, in 1803, Samuel returned to Mifflin County. The same year he married Frances Alexander, and settled in Center County, Pennsylvania, following his trade until 1806, in which year his wife died, leaving two children, a daughter and a son. The daughter was the first wife of John Adams, who built the "Adams Mill," in Wild-cat, in this county. The son was Henry Bruce Milroy, who was the first sheriff of Carroll County, and well known to all our old citizens.

Soon after the death of his wife, Samuel left his two children in the care of his mother, and again set out with his brother John, to try their fortunes in the great West—then an almost unbroken wilderness. They came across the Alleghany Mountains on foot, carrying their knapsacks to Pittsburg—then a small town with a few hundred inhabitants, besides the soldiers in the fort. From Pittsburg, they descended the Ohio River on a flat-boat, partly paying and partly working their passage to Cincinnati—then a trading-post, probably as large as Camden, in this county. They remained in Cincinnati a few weeks, to recruit their finances. Samuel obtained work at his trade, and was very successful;

but John tried in vain to procure employment at his business, that of surveyor; and having previously acquired expensive habits, in an attempt to play merchant for a year or two, and also having served as lieutenant, for a few years, in the idle standing army of the elder Adams, which was disbanded by the Administration of Jefferson, he proved rather an unprofitable companion to Samuel, whose earnings were spent nearly as fast as received, to relieve John from difficulties and prosecutions.

They left Cincinnati, with the intention of going to St. Louis, to which point they had intended directing their steps from the time of leaving Pennsylvania. The country through Indiana Territory being almost uninhabited, except in places along the Ohio River and on the Lower Wabash, they crossed over into Kentucky, and traveled by land down the Ohio River, intending to recross again somewhere below Louisville, and thence, by way of Vincennes, to St. Louis. But when opposite Bardstown, in Nelson County, Kentucky, in which county a large number of their old neighbors, acquaintances, and some relatives from Pennsylvania resided, John wished to turn south and go to Bardstown, about twenty-five miles distant, and enjoy themselves among their old friends and relatives awhile, and argued that perhaps they could get into some good business; but Samuel insisted on proceeding to St. Louis. Upon examining into their finances, they found that they had but *one dollar between them.* John argued that this was insufficient to go on with, but Samuel, although strongly tempted to drop in among their old acquaintances for a while, urged that it would be best to push on to St. Louis, relying upon the known hospitality of the early settlers, and his ability to earn money by a few days' work, to help them through; and when once there he felt certain that they could each get into a lucrative business that would enable them to visit friends in much better style than they were then able to. This argument took place at the forks of a road; one fork running south to Bardstown, and the other running west, down the Ohio. John, being a little inclined to superstition, proposed that they should decide the matter by setting up a stick, and which ever way it fell, that that would be the way to proceed. Samuel, not being very strenuous, consented to this. John accordingly balanced his walking stick on its end very nicely, and let it fall, when lo! it fell to the south. So they proceeded to Nelson County, and found plenty of warm friends; and both went to work, Samuel at his trade, and John to surveying; and after surveying about a year, he was married to Miss Isabella Huston, by whom he had ten children, the eldest of whom, Dr. Henry A. Milroy, resided for some years in Delphi, and will be remembered by many of our citizens.

Samuel, after working at his trade for some months, still had dreams of making a fortune in St. Louis, and in the Fall of 1807, in company with George Wilson, a distant relative, of the same trade with himself, traveled on foot, by way of Vincennes, to St. Louis, where they worked at their trade very successfully for about ten months, when both were taken down with bilious fever, from which Samuel recovered after an illness of about six weeks, and Wilson about the same time. As soon as they were sufficiently able to travel, they set out on their return to Nelson County, Kentucky. They struck the Ohio River at Evansville, and were there offered wages as hands on a keel-boat (the only kind of a boat in those days, besides a pirogue and canoe, that could be taken up stream), loaded with goods for Louisville. They accepted the offer, and on the way up, an incident occurred that proved the sincerity of Wilson's friendship.

While passing a large drift, one day, Samuel, being on the side next the drift, saw a log sticking out at the upper edge, and supposing from its appearance it was solid and stationary, placed the end of his setting-pole on it, and threw his weight on the pole for the purpose of propelling the boat; but the log suddenly turned, and he went into the river head foremost, and sunk down. All the men on board of the boat were greatly alarmed. Wilson rushed to the place where his friend had gone down, and plunged in after him without a moment's hesitation, knowing that he could not swim. Samuel kept his presence of mind as he was going down, and thought it would be best to let himself go down to the bottom without resistance, and that he could then by a vigorous spring send himself to the surface; but finding the water very deep, and that he did not reach the bottom after sinking some fifteen or twenty feet, he commenced working for the surface, and, upon reaching it, Wilson came to the rescue. He called to the men on the boat to throw out a rope to him, which was done, and they seized hold of it when within a foot or two of the upper edge of the drift, under which the water was sweeping with a strong current. They were taken on board just in time to save their lives.

Upon his arrival in Nelson County, he again resumed his trade with his usual energy, and in 1809 purchased a tract of land, and commenced improving it. In 1810, he married Miss Martha Huston, a young sister of his brother John's wife, by whom he had ten children, seven sons and three daughters. Three of the boys died young. The eldest, Colonel Robert H. Milroy, after having served a campaign in Mexico, and having been a member from this county of the Constitutional Convention of 1850, and after having served a few months as president judge of this judicial circuit, finally located at Rensselaer, Jasper County, engaged in the practice of the law. In April, 1861, Colonel Milroy raised a company at the call of President Lincoln, and was one of the first to reach Indianapolis. Upon the election of officers, he was elected colonel of the Ninth Regiment. Naturally a military man, and brave as a lion, he gave a good account of himself.

John B. Milroy, the second son, resided in Carroll County. He has served one year as representative to the State Legislature, and one term as county auditor.

Samuel, the third son, remained on the old home-place, and James resided at Galveston, in Cass County.

The eldest daughter became the wife of Mr. Valentine Coble, and resided in Adams Township, in this county. The second daughter was the wife of Dr. Samuel Grimes, of Delphi, and died in 1850. The third daughter is the wife of Dr. E. W. H. Berk, of Delphi.

But to return. In September of the year 1812, the Indians attacked and destroyed a settlement in Scott County, Indiana Territory, killing three men, five women, and sixteen children. The news of the massacre spread through the territory, and into the state of Kentucky, creating intense excitement. Mounted volunteer companies were hastily raised in several of the border counties of Kentucky. Samuel Milroy raised one of these companies in Nelson County, and reached the scene of the massacre with his company, near a hundred miles distant, in just four days after its occurrence. The other volunteer companies that arrived from Kentucky, swelled the number of volunteers from that state to about three hundred and fifty men, which, with the militia companies of the surrounding counties, constituted a little army of near five hundred men. They found the ruins of the houses still smoking, and the bloody, mangled corpses of the victims scattered in ghastly array around them, some of them partly burned. These sights created feelings of the most intense desire for revenge upon the bloody monsters who had perpetrated the horrid deed. A council of war was called, to determine what to do. There were several colonels and majors present, all wishing to be commanders-in-chief, several of them claiming it by virtue of rank, so that the council finally broke up in a row, and the companies separated. Some of them disbanded, and some of them returned home at once. Captain Milroy, with what volunteers he could raise, determined to follow the Indians. They accordingly set out on the trail and followed it several days; but a fall of snow covering the foot-prints, they were compelled to give up the pursuit. After ranging the woods for some time, in hope of finding the trail, made after the fall of the snow, their provisions giving out, they reluctantly returned. During this scout, he had a good opportunity for observing the country, and formed a very favorable opinion of a portion of Washington County. After his return home, he continued the improvement of his farm, and built a horse-mill; but becoming disgusted with the institution of slavery, he determined to emigrate to Indiana Territory, from which slavery was excluded by the Ordinance of 1787. He effected a sale of his property in Kentucky in 1814, and in the Fall of that year, in company with his youngest brother, James, then unmarried, and a blacksmith by trade, came out to Washington County, and purchased a tract of one hundred and sixty acres of land in partnership, on a branch of Blue River, about five miles east of Salem. They built a house, and made some improvement, and in the Spring of 1815, he (Samuel) removed his family to their new home. They went to work with great energy to clear off the heavy forest and make a farm. They erected a blacksmith-shop, and afterward a grist-mill, on the creek that ran through the land.

On the 19th day of April, 1816, the Congress of the United States passed an act to enable the people of Indiana Territory to form a Constitution and State Government. This act required an election to be held in the several counties of the territory, on the second Monday of the following May, for delegates to a Constitutional Convention. Samuel Milroy was elected one of the delegates from Washington County. The Convention met at Corydon, Harrison County, the old seat of Government, on the 10th day of June, in the same year, and finished their work in nineteen days, and adjourned on the 29th of June. By reference to pages 557 and 558 of "Dillon's History of Indiana," it will be seen that Milroy was a member of three of the most important committees of the Convention—the Committee on the Legislative Department of Government, the Committee on the Judicial Department, and the Committee on Prisons.

The election for members of the first Legislature under the Constitution was held on the first Monday of August, 1816. At this election, Samuel Milroy was elected one of the representatives from Washington County. This Legislature met at Corydon, on the first Monday of December of the same year, which was the day of the meeting of the Legislature under the old Constitution.

He was commissioned a major by Governor Posey, in 1816; a colonel by Governor Jennings, in 1817; and a brigadier-general by the same governor, in 1819.

He was re-elected a member of the Legislature from Washington County for nine years successively, and was speaker of the House at the session of 1821. His name was on the Jackson electoral ticket of this State in 1824, and the author, when a boy, remembers being present in the old stone court-house, in Corydon, and witnessing the casting of the five electoral votes of Indiana for "Old Hickory." He continued a warm supporter, admirer, and friend of General Jackson while he lived. In the Winter of 1824–5, he built a large flat-boat on the Muscatatuck, a branch of White River, which forms the boundary between Washington and Jackson Counties, and loaded the same with staves for the New Orleans market. In the Spring, when the waters were high, he successfully ran his boat down the Muscatatuck, White River, Wabash, Ohio, and Mississippi, to New Orleans. The experiment was a new one, and had never been tried before from that part of the State, but it opened a new branch of commerce that numbers profited by afterward.

He sold his farm in Washington County in the beginning of 1826, and in the Spring of that year, in company with his son, Henry Bruce, he came out to the Wabash; and after looking over the country, then new and mostly uninhabited, he finally located, and entered eighty acres on Deer Creek, one mile above where Delphi now stands, and adjoining the old homestead. After renting a piece of land of Mr. Page, on Wild-cat Prairie (near where the town of Dayton, in Tippecanoe County, now stands), the nearest point where farming land could be rented, and planting it in corn, he commenced improving his land, which was heavily timbered. Having erected a temporary shanty, in which to cook and lodge, they cleared and fenced ten acres of land, and planted it mostly in potatoes and turnips, which proved a wise and fortunate provision for the family, the next Winter. Through the Summer of 1826, they cultivated their corn, on Wild-cat Prairie, and cut and hewed house-logs, and made clap-boards for a dwelling-house, which they "raised" with some difficulty, with the assistance of all the settlers within ten miles, about a dozen in all. After the house was raised and covered, they returned to Washington County, and removed the family out here about the 1st of October, 1826.

Having been appointed one of the commissioners to locate the county-seat of Tippecanoe County, he met with the other commissioners, and attended to that duty by locating the seat of justice at Lafayette. This he did while his family were on their way. After arriving at home, with his family, in the woods, he determined to have ground cleared, and a sufficient quantity of wheat sown to furnish bread the ensuing year. Considering the lateness of the season, the density and heavy growth of the forest; corn to be hauled from Wild-cat Prairie, where it had to be gathered; doors and windows to be cut out, and a door to be made; puncheons to be hewed out; floor laid; house to be chinked and daubed; fire-place to be cut out, and chimney built, etc., etc.,—this seemed a gigantic undertaking. But he went at it with his indomitable energy, and working all day and by the light of burning brush-heaps at night, and being remarkably favored that season with fine weather, which was so warm that the ground was not frozen before Christmas, he succeeded in clearing and fencing six acres. He commenced breaking up, harrowing, and sowing, about the 18th of December, and continued until Christmas morning, at which time he found the ground was frozen too hard for plowing. He had succeeded in putting in four acres, which produced about fifty bushels of wheat the next year. As soon as seeding was suspended by the cold weather, the general, with his whole disposable force—consisting of his sons, Bruce, then about twenty-one years of age; Robert, about ten; John, about six; a young hired hand by the name of Samuel Thompson, who resides in this county, on Rock Creek—commenced clearing his land, in the Deer Creek bottom. By the last of May, he had succeeded in getting twenty acres grubbed, cleared, rolled, and burned, rails made, fenced, broken up, and planted. He thus, in a few years, surrounded his family with comfort. In the Fall of 1827, a petition to the Legislature was circulated among the inhabitants of the territory, now composing the county of Carroll, asking the organization of a new county out of said territory. General Milroy proceeded to Indianapolis with this petition, at the session of 1827–8. He appeared before the committee to whom the petition was referred, and suggested the present boundaries of the county, and the name. He was requested by the committee to draw up a bill, which he did. The original draft of the same is still among his old papers. Having a personal acquaintance with the commissioners appointed to locate the county-seat of Carroll County, they were the guests of the general most of the time they were engaged in making the location. A number of points were offered, and urged as good locations by their respective owners, but principally through the influence and management of General M., the present site (Delphi) was selected. It was the site he had picked out for a county-seat when he first came to the county. It was more particularly his influence and skillful management that procured the liberal donation of *one hundred acres* for the county-seat from William Wilson.

The name "Delphi"* was suggested to the commissioners by General M. One day, when they were

* The following short abstract of the leading incidents in the early history of ancient Delphi, will, we believe, possess considerable attractions for the people of this community.

The original Delphi was a small but important city of Phocis in Greece, situated on the southern slope of Mount Parnassus, and built in the form of an amphitheater. It is said to have had a circuit of sixteen stadia. Some say it was not walled, according

discussing what name should be given to the new county-seat, he handed them a slip of paper, on which several names were written, Delphi among others, and that was the name selected. After the location of the town, he (with his compass and chain), assisted by Wilson, and some of his boys and neighbors, laid out and located the streets and Public Square of the new town. He was appointed the first agent to sell lots in the town, and after advertising six weeks in the *Salem Annotator* and *Terre Haute Register*, he held the first sale of lots,

to the custom of those days, its precipices forming a natural defense. In its earlier days, probably, it was defended, like Olympia, by the sanctity of its oracle, and the presence of its god. This defense not being sufficient protection against the predatory Phocians, perhaps it was regularly fortified after some of their incursions; or the walls may have been coeval with the foundations of the city itself. Whence the name of Delphi itself was derived we have no information. Some say it was named after Delphus, a son of Apollo. Others that Apollo leaped into the sea in the form of a large dolphin (hence he is called *Delphin*), took possession of a merchant-vessel, and forced it to pass Pylo and enter the harbor of Crissa. After the Cretans had landed, Apollo appeared as a beautiful youth, and told them that they must not return to their country, but they should serve him as priests in his temple. The Cretans were discouraged when they saw the sterility of the country, which surrounded the sanctuary, on the rocky declivity of Parnassus; but, being reassured by Apollo, they built the city of Delphi, calling it at first *Pytho*, from the monstrous serpent, Python, which was said to have been slain by Apollo. There are several other etymological theories in regard to its derivation. One makes it *Tel Phi* "the oracle of the sun." Another says it is probably derived from the ancient names of the sun; as the Greek word *Delas*, the Latin *Sol*, and the term *Bel*, the Oriental Baal; hence Delphi is the city of the sun. The oracles were delivered from a cave called *Pythium*. Its discovery has been attributed to many different parties. One is, that a shepherd was pasturing his flocks at the foot of Parnassus, and was filled with prophetic inspiration by the intoxicating vapor which arose from it. The sacred tripod was placed over the cave whence the exha-

on the 11th day of August, 1828. He continued to act as agent until some time in 1829, when he resigned; refusing to receive any compensation for his services, merely requiring a trifle to cover expenses.

Near the close of the year 1827, he was appointed, by the Administration of John Quincy Adams, to examine the land-offices of Illinois. This appointment, not having been sought by him, came very unexpectedly. Having warmly opposed the election of Mr. Adams, and being strongly opposed to the principles of

lation proceeded, on which sat the Pythia (the Priestess), who, having caught the inspiration, pronounced her oracles, in extempore prose or verse; if in prose, it was immediately versified by the poet kept for that purpose. The most remarkable of the Pythian responses were those given to the Athenians, before the invasion of Xerxes, to Crœsus,* to Lycurgus, to Glaucus the Spartan, and one relating to Agesilaus. There seems, however, to have been as little difficulty in influencing the responses of the ancient propthees as there is said to be in bribing a modern politician. The fame of the Delphic shrine was established at a very early period, from the mention made of it by Homer, and other historians of the earliest times. The Amphictonic Council held an assembly at Delphi every Spring, which gave it still greater celebrity. As none dared approach or ask counsel of the god without gifts, hence the temple possessed immense treasures, and numerous works of art and offerings of gratitude. The rich also deposited their treasures in Delphi, under the protection of Apollo, though this did not prevent it from being frequently plundered by Greeks and barbarians. Upon a portion of the ruins of Delphi stands the present village of Castri. At the present day no trace of the sacred aperture has been discovered, though it is said to have been of great depth.

* As a sample of the responses, we give the answer to the messengers of Crœsus. He sent to different oracles, and instructed his messengers to inquire of the various oracles what he, Crœsus, was doing at a certain hour of a certain day. The Delphic oracle gave the following response:

"I number the sands, I measure the sea;
What 's hidden to others is known to me.
The lamb and the tortoise are simmering slow,
With brass above them and brass below."

Crœsus, it is said, was boiling the flesh of a tortoise and a lamb, at the time this was given, in a brass vessel, covered with a brass lid.

his Administration, he always supposed that this appointment was given him for the purpose of influencing his political action in the approaching Presidential campaign of 1828. Very much needing the emoluments of the office, he accepted it, and discharged the duties required by it, during the Spring of 1828; but he did not swerve from an energetic support of General Jackson, at the Presidential election that year. In August, 1829, he was elected a representative to the Legislature from the district composed of the counties of Montgomery, Fountain, Warren, Tippecanoe, and Carroll, and shortly after the election, he again, unexpectedly, received the appointment to examine the land-offices of Illinois, from President Jackson. Soon afterward, and before he had time to discharge the duties of the office, he received from the same President the appointment of Register of the Land-office at Crawfordsville, an office then worth three thousand dollars per annum. He thus held three offices at one time, and it was with him a matter of deep solicitude, about which he was undecided for some time, which office should be retained, and which resigned. On the one hand, the emoluments of the land-office, which he might hold for years, offered pecuniary inducements to himself and family, which, to a man in his circumstances, were of the most tempting character. On the other hand, the people of his district had selected him, by a large majority, to represent them in the Legislature, and he felt that he ought not to disappoint them, though the office would expire in two or three months, and its emoluments were worth nothing. He could have held on to the appointment to examine the land-offices in Illinois, before the time for the meeting of the Legislature, and by so doing could have realized five or six hundred dollars over expenses. Finally, by the advice and urgent solicitation of his friends, he concluded to accept the Registership of the

Land-office at Crawfordsville, and resign the other two offices. He held the office of register about four years, the duties of which were faithfully attended to by his son Bruce; and he finally gave up the office rather than remove from his farm, with his family, to Crawfordsville, which he was required to do.

He was a delegate to the first Democratic National Convention ever held in the United States, which met at Baltimore, in May, 1832, and which nominated General Jackson for his second term. He was a delegate, and attended every succeeding Democratic National Convention from that time up to 1844, at which time James K. Polk was nominated. This was the last convention held prior to his death.

In 1835, he was appointed by President Jackson, as one of the Board of Visitors to the United States Military Academy, at West Point, and nobly discharged that duty. In 1837, and again in 1838, he was elected a representative to the Legislature from Carroll. In 1836, he was elected a State Senator from the counties of Carroll and Clinton, and drew the short term. While serving in the Legislature, he, in the most determined manner, opposed the gigantic Internal Improvement folly, which has been an incubus upon the prosperity of the State ever since, entailing a debt of fifteen millions of dollars. Finding that the current of interest was too strong in favor of the bill to be resisted, he made a strong effort to have the various works classified, that one might be begun and completed at a time. If this plan had been adopted, the finished works would have yielded some revenue from tolls, and the works would have been of some benefit to the State, and would have saved, in a great measure, the great debt. But in the effort, though tried in various ways, he was unsuccessful, for the reason that a majority of the members had become personally interested in the system, and expected to make fortunes out of it. The utopian idea was held up, that the State could borrow $10,000,000, and complete the Public Works all over the state at once; and that the works, when completed, would bring in such a vast revenue, that in a few years the loan could be paid off, and the revenue continue ample to pay all state, county, and township expenses, and forever relieve the people from all taxation! It was also contended that in addition to refunding the principal and interest of the ten million loan, the revenue would support a system of *free schools*, in which the children of the state could be educated, up to the highest point, through all coming time! General Milroy told them, in his last speech against borrowing the ten millions, and in favor of classification, that their great system would be a gigantic failure, which would entail a ruinous debt on the State, under which the people would be ground down by taxation for generations to come; and that the men who voted for and were instrumental in fastening this curse upon the people, would soon become so unpopular, odious, and hateful, that the very dogs would not lick their blood. Time has proved his wisdom and foresight in relation to this *Internal Improvement System.* In 1839, he was appointed agent for the Miami and Pottawatomie Indians, and in 1840, he succeeded in purchasing from the Miami tribe their great reservation, which the Government had previously, for many years, through different agents and special commissioners, tried in vain to purchase. He was removed from the office of Indian Agent, in 1841, by President Harrison, whose election he had opposed; he was reappointed to the same office in 1845, by President Polk, and held it up to the time of his death, which occurred on the 26th day of May, 1845. His death was occasioned by erysipelas, of which disease his son Bruce had died two weeks before. Though a strong believer in the truths of Christianity, he never belonged to any Church. He estimated men by their acts and conduct, never by their professions.

General Milroy never sued a man in his life, and was never sued for a debt of his own contracting. His house was the home of hospitality, where friends and strangers found a ready welcome; for he never, in the whole course of his life, charged any one for a night's lodging or a meal's victuals.

He was one of the warmest friends of the interests of Delphi. He struggled against her enemies; and had it not been for his never-ceasing exertions, on one or two occasions, the county-seat would have no doubt been removed.

Such is a very brief outline of the most prominent events in the life of General Samuel Milroy, who, in his day, was not only one of the most prominent citizens of Carroll County, but of the state of Indiana.

General Milroy is buried in the old Delphi graveyard. His children have erected a monument over his grave. The following is the inscription on the west side:

This Monument
IS ERECTED AS
A TRIBUTE OF WORTH AND AFFECTION TO THE MEMORY OF
General Samuel Milroy,
BY HIS CHILDREN.

BENEATH THIS STONE REST THE MORTAL REMAINS
OF
GENERAL SAMUEL MILROY.
BORN AUGUST 14, 1780.
DIED MAY 26, 1845.
Aged 64 *years,* 9 *months, and* 12 *days.*

"Then shall the dust return to the earth as it was, and the spirit go back to God, who gave it."

(*On the east side.*)

ONE OF THE PIONEERS OF THE WEST; ONE OF THE SIGNERS OF THE CONSTITUTION OF INDIANA; AND ONE OF THE FRAMERS OF HER LAWS AND INSTITUTIONS.

Morality, justice, and truth were his guide;
His honor, his friends, and his country, his pride.

(*On the south, Masonic emblems.*)

Before closing this sketch of the life of General Milroy, the author desires to give extracts from letters received from him while a member of the Legislature. He speaks of many things now well-nigh forgotten.

INDIANAPOLIS, *Jan.* 10, 1837.

DEAR SIR,—Inclosed is a paper which will be interesting no doubt; it will show the politics, etc., of members of the General Assembly.

For news, I must refer you to the papers, and to a long letter I have written to Mr. Green. I think I will succeed in obtaining the location of the river lock, that is to be erected for the benefit of the river navigation in the bayou, so that the river navigation will pass through the bayou.

Delphi is indebted for what has been done for her this Winter, $500,000. She will be benefited to that amount.

We will get a road, but can get no appropriation.

Respectfully yours, etc.,

DR. STEWART. SAMUEL MILROY.

INDIANAPOLIS, *Dec.* 9, 1837.

DEAR SIR,—We are at this moment progressing with the election of circuit judges, and have elected Isaac Naylor, judge of the first judicial circuit; the vote stood, for Bryant, sixty-nine, and Naylor, seventy-five. The vote was as near a party vote as any perhaps, that will be had this Winter, in our Legislature.

. . . I. H. Thompson was elected in the second circuit without opposition, notwithstanding there were twenty-four scattering votes. Miles C. Eggleston was elected; he had seventy-five votes, and Andrew Davidson (Van Buren) had sixty-six votes—two scattering. The election for prosecutor in our circuit resulted in the election of Joseph A. Wright, who, on the first ballot, had sixty-nine; Mace, forty; Wilson, nineteen; Lockwood, fifteen; no choice being made. On the second ballot, Joseph A. Wright received seventy-eight votes; Mace, sixty-one; and Lockwood, four. John Dumont was elected prosecutor in the Third, by a large majority over all competitors.

Monday, December 11.—This day, at two o'clock, the two Houses met for the purpose of electing Treasurer of State and Auditor, which resulted in the election of the present incumbents. This was done by a kind of informal understanding, that if the Whigs would not turn out Palmer, the Democrats would not turn out Morris. Strange as it may appear, I believe the parties could have effected these things, if the attempt had been made. It was a leading object to save Palmer, and to do this, we were willing to yield something. The vote stood: Palmer, seventy-seven; William Sheets, sixty-one; and five scattering. For Morris, eighty-three; Mahne, thirty-one; Fingle, twenty-six.

The elections are now over, and we will go to work at legislation. We have had a meeting this evening, to determine as to the most advisable method of *remodeling*, *revising*, or *classifying* the Public Works. The meeting consisted of all those favorable to those objects. Our strength in the House of Representatives is upward of forty, and if a proper system of remodeling the Public Works is proposed, I flatter myself we will be able to carry it. *All* admit the necessity of doing something to insure the system of internal improvements, and at the same time prevent the necessity of oppressive taxation.

You will have seen that the Whigs have had a meeting, and *speechification* on the subject of the New York election. The Democracy have also had a meeting for consultation as to the propriety of a meeting and celebration in support of our principles, which are as fixed as the eternal hills, and can not be disturbed for a moment by such puffs of wind across the political horizon as the New York election. We will have our meeting for the object on the 8th of January—a day always auspicious to the Democracy.

The President's message has arrived. I have not yet seen it. It is said to reiterate the former recommendations of the Executive in his message at the special session. Mr. Van Buren is not to be driven from his purposes by the alarms of party. The New York election appears to be perfectly understood by him.

Can not some of our Carroll County friends be here on the 8th of January?

I shall be wide awake as to any contemplated change of our county boundaries, and as to the desired alteration in the mode of doing township business. I would like to see petitions, though I will attempt the proposed change, whether I receive them or not.

I should like much to hear from you often during the session. Never had better health in my life. When you read this, have the goodness to hand it over to my son, H. B. Milroy.

REPRESENTATIVE CHAMBER, *February* 3, 1838.

DEAR SIR,—I have to inform you that on yesterday a bill passed the House of Representatives, changing the character of the Madison and Lafayette Railroad into a macadamized road, from Indianapolis to Lafayette, and limiting the road south of Indianapolis to a single-track railroad. If this bill becomes a law, of which I have no doubt, we may say that we have reduced the *system* at least $7,000,000 the present session, in dispensing with the railroads; and there is not much doubt but that further curtailments will be made. I think that the anti-system men have, in some measure, the control of the fortunes of Indiana. We have this moment concurred in a resolution of the Senate, fixing the 19th as the day of adjournment of the two Houses. I have not a doubt but the day is too early to enable the Legislature to go through the vast amount of important business before us. A bill is now pending in both Houses, fixing the compensation of the different officers connected with our Internal Improvement system, and there is a general feeling in favor of retrenchment in this department.

I have seen that I have been very liberally abused by letter-writers from Delphi, published in the Logansport papers, on the subject of the steam-boat lock at Delphi. No one need be at a loss as to the writer of these letters; and in answer to the whole matter, I have only to say, that I have taken no measures whatever to prevent the erection of this lock; but will take all honorable and proper means to prevent *timber or other materials* for the construction of this *useless structure*, to be taken from the lands of citizens of Carroll County. In this, I doubt not, I will be sustained by the good sense of the people. If the State, or State Board of Internal Improvement, should build this *useless lock*, which can only benefit a few, and these few having a personal interest only, I am unwilling that the timber of our citizens shall be taken for such purpose. Another objection is, that if the river is to be kept open for steam-boats, then it becomes necessary to change the whole plan of the Public Works, as it will be impracticable to cross the river with canal-boats, on the proposed towing-path bridge at Carrollton. This matter is perfectly understood here, and all the interests connected will be duly explained to the people at a proper time.

There never was such a mass of business before the two Houses at one time as at the present; and much, I fear, must be left undone, or unacted on, if we adjourn on the 19th.

Have the goodness to let my son read this after you have looked it over.

INDIANAPOLIS, *Representative Chamber, February* 12, 1838.

DEAR SIR,—I have this day received a communication from General John Tipton, inclosing notice from the Post-office Department of the establishment of a post-office at Pittsburg, and the appointment of Nelson Blakslee post-master, and the removal of Pleasant Run Post-office to Pittsburg. Also, the establishment of a post-office at Carrollton, and the appointment of Israel Steel post-master. I have written to Messrs. Tipton and White on the subject of a tri-weekly mail from Frankfort via Delphi to Monticello; the daily mail from Indianapolis to Lafayette passes Frankfort and if we could have a branch route from that place through Delphi to Monticello, it would be to us an accommodation. I have also written to Mr. White to obtain, if practicable, for the contractors on the mail-route from Lafayette to Logansport, the privilege of carrying the mail on horseback; the trip they are bound to go on the west side of the run, as I had been informed it was a great inconvenience to cross the stage and horses over the river once a week. If you think further explanation is necessary to obtain the accommodation to those contractors, you will please write to Mr. White, as he desires information on the subject.

Both Houses have resolved to adjourn on the 19th, and there must be near one-half of the business of the session untouched. The revision is hardly commenced. The exciting questions of the bank and internal improvements have consumed nearly one-half the time we have been here. The *system* has been curtailed in some respects; that is, the New Albany and Crawfordsville Railroad has been changed to a macadamized road, at a saving of $5,000,000. The Madison Railroad has also been changed to a macadamized road from Indianapolis to Lafayette, at a saving of $2,500,000. We have in these two cases saved within $2,500,000 of the original estimated cost of the system, and it is yet believed to be equal to $20,000,000. So much for the estimates of engineers and canal commissioners.

A most animated debate has continued from day to day on the subject of the bank; and it can yet hardly be determined what will be done. The general wish was to restore the supposed forfeiture of the charter with amendments, and at the same time increase the bank capital for the benefit of internal improvement. There is a party, however, who are disposed to restore the charter unconditionally, and not even to require resumption of specie payments, as a condition of an increase of State stock in the bank; to this I can never agree. To borrow $3,500,000 on the credit of the State, and place it in the vaults of a bank that refuses to redeem its notes or liabilities of any description, and having at the same time evidence of gross mismanagement on the part of the bank, those who could sanction an increase of capital under such circumstances, can do more than I am willing to do. Notwishstanding, I am positively in favor of an increase of bank capital, with a view to the payment of interest on an internal improvement loan.

There perhaps never has, nor never may be again, so

many exciting subjects to engage the attention of our Legislature. The consequence has been that many of the most interesting subjects remain unacted on. For instance, the *Militia Law, the Road Law, the bill incorporating townships*, though long since reported, can not be reached, and I think will not, until the session closes. This whole day has been spent in an angry contest about the bank. In the evening a joint resolution instructing our delegation in Congress to use their exertions to cause all bank paper that pays specie for the notes, to be received in payment of public dues,—this was the fire-brand of party. The Whigs had a majority, and had therefore the power to pass it; *but the Democrats took their hats in their hands and walked out*, and left them without a quorum. We left them "alone in their glory." After several calls of the House, they at length obtained a quorum, and the Whigs passed a resolution to instruct Colonel Boone. No other needed it; all the balance would do their bidding, without instruction. This is a specimen to show how uselessly the time of the Legislature is wasted.

On Saturday last we had a Democratic-Republican meeting of the members and citizens favorable to the present Administration, and had a most splendid address delivered by Robert Dale Owen, a copy of which I will send you as soon as printed, which will be in the course of a week. We have certainly used up the Whigs and System men in many cases, and we have succeeded over them, though in an acknowledged minority.

I will conclude by saying that our principles will soon be triumphant in Indiana, as they will be throughout the Union.

REPRESENTATIVE CHAMBER, *January* 23, 1839.

DEAR SIR,—I have to inform you that, within the hour, the Modification Bill passed the House of Representatives. It is but little changed from the printed bill, except that the fifteenth section is stricken out. The bill is not what I could have wished, but it is as good as could be had; the Senate has yet to pass on it; and perhaps, with the alterations that body will make in it, it may be improved. I consider the passage of this bill, by the Modification Party, as the complete prostration of the System men. They fought it at every stage, and in all forms, but finally had to yield to superior numbers. Some of the System men had to call in Whiggery to their aid, to sustain them, begging them not to let Democrats take the System from them. All this would not do; we triumphed. If, now, we can secure the passage of the Valuation Law, we will have effected all that I had expected to attempt. There is a bill pending, doing away with imprisonment for debt, which will no doubt pass. The Revenue Bill will be reported to-morrow, and the people may make up their minds to pay fifty cents on the hundred dollars' worth of property; either that, or the credit of the State must fail; and in that case we can procure no more loans. Nothing is yet said as to the time of adjournment.

REPRESENTATIVE CHAMBER, *February* 7, 1839.

DEAR SIR,— . . . . The Modification Bill has finally passed both Houses, and needs but the signature of the governor to become a law. The bill is not materially changed from its original form, as it came from the committee, of which I had the honor to be chairman. This is the measure for which I have contended for three years, and it has finally succeeded.

On this morning, a bill passed this House, increasing the bank capital $5,000,000, and I doubt not it will pass the Senate. This bill is not all that I could have wished; but the main point was to secure additional bank facilities to the people, and if we had coupled with the proposed increase, propositions to amend the charter, we would have endangered the whole measure, as the bank has the power, under the charter, to accept the proposed increase of capital; and if we had imposed conditions, they might not think it for their interest to accept. I therefore voted for the proposed increase on the terms contained in the bill, and depend on other times for an opportunity to amend the bank charter.

One of the conditions of the capital is, that it must be discounted on, and the discounts extended to the several counties in proportion to the State tax paid by each; doing away with the system of favoritism practiced by the bank.

Much remains yet to be acted on in the two Houses, and we propose to adjourn on the 18th. I think we can not adjourn so soon, if we take a correct view of the interests of the State. The Revenue Bill is not yet acted on, and many others equally important.

I regret extremely to hear of the disastrous burning in Delphi.

Yours, etc.,

DR. STEWART. SAMUEL MILROY.

AARON HICKS,

ONE OF THE FIRST COUNTY COMMISSIONERS.

AARON HICKS was born in Cumberland County, Pennsylvania, March 1, 1800. His father soon afterward emigrated to the western part of Pennsylvania, and, in the year 1807, to the vicinity of Marietta, Ohio. After residing in various counties in that state, he died in Shelby County, in 1822. In the Autumn of 1825, in company with three neighbors, and his brother William, Mr. Hicks came on an exploring tour to Indiana. They took the route down White River, and thence across to the Wabash, in Tippecanoe County. The settlement in that county had but just commenced.

Lafayette contained but one comfortable house, and although this part of the state was then a wilderness, the party were so well pleased with its beautiful and extensive prairies, its rich and heavily timbered woodlands, and its abundant springs of clear cold water, that they returned home and made immediate arrangements for emigration. In the Spring of 1836, Mr. Hicks, in company with his brother (who had a small family), left the state of Ohio for Indiana. The party assisted Messrs. Odell & Ridenhour to build a boat on the Mississinewa, which was loaded with bacon and apple-trees, on which boat the party took passage, and landed at the mouth of Rock Creek (now in Carroll County), on the 24th day of April. From the point at which they took the boat in Randolph County, to the mouth of Deer Creek, except a few trading-posts along the river, the country was entirely unsettled by the whites. A few families, in the Spring of 1825, landed at the mouth of Deer Creek, in a keel-boat which they had brought down the Scioto and Ohio Rivers to the mouth of the Wabash, and up the Wabash to this place. In the same Spring, Aaron Merriman (then unmarried) made an improvement on the bluff, a short distance from the mouth of Rock Creek (being a part of the farm afterward owned by Jacob Kuns), and having no family, the Hicks family removed into the cabin of Merriman. At that time the settlers had neither mills, roads, or teams. By canoe they sought a little mill below Lafayette, where their corn was ground. In the ensuing Fall, Mr. Hicks built a cabin on the bank of the river, on land which he afterward purchased. On that same place he resided while he remained a citizen of the county. The same Fall Mr. H's mother and family arrived. He then had raised plenty of corn and potatoes; but in order to supply himself with meat, he took a pirogue and went to the mouth of Sugar

Creek. During the trip he came very near being frozen up in the river. Mr. Robinson was then building a small mill just above where Delphi was afterward located. The Rock Creek settlers expected to procure grinding at this mill, but it had only been in operation a few days before it was frozen up, and was not thawed out again before the latter part of Winter. The people in Mr. H's neighborhood subsisted on potatoes, meat, and hominy, until the mild weather of Spring unlocked the mill.

In the Spring of 1827, Mr. Hicks married a daughter of Mr. William Price.

At the first election held in the county, Mr. Hicks was elected one of the county commissioners, Jacob Baum and Graham Roberts being his colleagues. He discharged his official duties honestly and faithfully, and to the satisfaction of the people.

After a residence of about seven years in the bounds of what is now Carroll County, having witnessed its progress from almost a wilderness to an organized county, rapidly increasing in population, improvements, and wealth, he sold his property, and removed about eight miles north, into the territory out of which the county of White has since been made. In that county Mr. H. still resides, one of its most respected and worthy citizens. He is the only survivor of the first Board of County Commissioners.

CHAPTER XIV.

DEPARTED VETERANS.

JACOB OLINGER.

ALL the early settlers remember "Father Olinger," who removed here at an early day from the state of Tennessee. He had been a soldier of the "Revolution," and like most of the men who fought in '76, was fond, when he came to town, of indulging in a social glass. When asked "if he would take something," his invariable reply always was, "Would a duck swim?" Of course a duck would swim, and just as naturally would "Father O." take a "nipper."

He was a kind-hearted, honest old man as ever lived, and one who loved the country he had fought for, with his whole heart. It was his custom, on election days, to take his place on the court-house steps, and about every half hour shout at the top of his voice: "*Whoop'e! Whoop'e more votes! More votes! Our end best.*" This speech would never fail to put the crowd in a good-humor, and raise a laugh.

SAMUEL WELLS.

SAMUEL WELLS purchased the land on which was afterward located the town of West Delphi, east of the Wabash River. Wells had the name of being "awfully avaricious;" a "fip," in his eyes, looked as big as the full moon. A short time after the location of Delphi, a Yankee peddler came along, vending his "wall-sweepers." After remaining over night at Joseph Dunham's tavern, when about to depart in the morning for a trip to the sparse settlements on the west side of the river, he inquired of the landlord, if any one resided between the town and the Wabash. He was informed that a man by the name of Wells lived on the river bank, but that he was "awfully stingy," and it would be wasting time to attempt to sell him a clock. The peddler started out, hitched his horse at Wells's door, and was informed that W. was plowing in a field at some distance. He took up his line of march, and after finding his man, saluted him as follows: "Is your name Wells?"

W.—"Yes, sir."

P.—"I presume I have come upon a fool's errand. I am engaged in selling clocks. I inquired about you at the little village the other side of the bayou, and they informed me that you were so close, that it was all nonsense to think of trading with you."

W. (Very indignant)—"The rascals over at that hole have always been abusing me."

Thereupon he proceeded to the house with the peddler, and to prove to him how outrageously he had been slandered, he purchased a "sweeper" for forty-five dollars, and paid for the same with Mexican dollars, which he resurrected out of an old chest!

At one time, Wells, after having built a hewed log house, the one that stood just below the dam, undertook to saw off the ends of the logs, which were projecting six or eight feet from the corner. He commenced with the upper log, but unfortunately was seated on the outer end of the same! The consequence was, the log fell, and so did Wells! He was pretty nearly killed by the fall, and was compelled to send for a doctor to do up his bruises!

The author has another anecdote of Wells, told him by Robert Cade. Wells and Tom Burk met one day at Cade's. A quarrel arose and they proposed to fight; Wells was at least twice as large as Burk, but was generally thought to be a great coward. The moment Burk commenced to pull off his coat, W. sat down and commenced taking off his shoes and stockings! At this moment Cade interposed, and the fuss was compromised. After Burk left for home, Cade had the curiosity to ask W. "why he had pulled off his shoes and stockings?" W. replied that he "was afraid if he got into a fight, he would kick Burk's guts out!"

Cade believed, until his dying day, that the true reason was, to enable W. to do some "tall running."

JOHN ROBBINS.

Mr. Robbins was a decided "character," quite eccentric, and celebrated for his dry humor. His acts were those of kindness, although his manner would be sometimes quite the reverse. He must have his fun, even if his best friend was at the point of death.

Mr. R. was not a member of any religious denomination, although his wife was a member of the Baptist Church. On one occasion a minister of that persuasion rode up to Mr. R's. door, about sunset, and found the man of the house busily engaged in chopping wood for the next morning's fire, when the following colloquy ensued:

Preacher—"Is your name Robbins?"

R. (Without stopping his work)—"Yes, sir."

P. (Still sitting on his horse)—"Any news, Mr. Robbins?"

R.—"No, sir; none that I know of."

P.—"I believe, Mr. Robbins, that your wife is a member of our Church?"

R.—"I generally carry my members in my pocket when I leave home."

P. (After a long pause, R. still chopping)—"Mr. R., can I stay all night with you?"

R.—"Certainly, with great pleasure. Why did'nt you name the matter at first?"

THE CONSTABLE.

An anecdote is told of one of the first constables elected in the county. Pretty soon after he had received his commission, an execution was placed in his hands for a small amount against Bob Scott, who resided on the Forsythe land, on Deer-creek Prairie. The constable proceeded to Scott's, and demanded the money or property. Scott, who was fond of fun, and something of a wag, told him that he might levy on that calf, pointing at the same time to one on the other side of the fence. At that time there were no cross-fences on Deer-creek Prairie, and a field would contain from four to six hundred acres. "But," said Scott, "the law requires that you must put your hand on the calf before you can make a legal levy." So, stripping off his coat and vest, and tying his suspenders around him, he jumped the fence and started after the calf. The animal, frightened of course, started off with the swiftness of an antelope. Around and across that six-hundred-acre field went the calf, and close upon his heels pursued the constable. After a hard run of three hours, he caught the calf by the tail, and satisfied the law by exclaiming at the top of his voice, "Now, mister calf, I levy on you."

Scott described the race as one of the most amusing ones he ever witnessed.

CAPTAIN WILLIAM HANCE.

For many years Captain William Hance was one of the county commissioners of this county. He died on his farm, a short distance above Camden, on the 20th day of June, 1859, in the sixty-fourth year of his age.

Captain Hance emigrated to Carroll County, from

the county of Miami, Ohio, in the year 1828. He was a consistent and influential member of the Baptist Church for forty years.

As a county commissioner, Captain H. was distinguished for the fidelity with which he discharged the various duties connected with that office. To sum up, he was one of that honest, incorruptible class of men, too little appreciated, we fear, in this degenerate age. *His word was as good as his bond.*

As a husband, father, friend, neighbor, and Christian, he was always true and consistent. He was a zealous follower of the meek and lowly Redeemer.

JUDGE SANDERSON.

George C. Sanderson was born in England, but came to the United States when quite a young man, and settled near Dayton, Ohio, where he married. He emigrated to this county in the year 1829, and engaged in the occupation of teaching school, which he followed most of the time during life. He was a successful and popular teacher, and in that vocation did a great deal of good.

In 1834, Mr. Sanderson was elected one of the associate judges of the Carroll Circuit Court, which position he continued to hold under repeated elections until the adoption of the new Constitution. He was a man of stern integrity, an upright and honest judge.

He died at his residence, six miles east of Delphi, on the 25th day of October, 1859.

WILLIAM HUGHES.

One of the first settlers was William Hughes, who was born in Winchester, Virginia, on the 28th day of April, 1790. When William was a boy, his father removed to Clarke County, Kentucky; thence to Highland County, Ohio; thence again to Clarke County,

Kentucky, and thence to Adams County, Ohio. In that county, at about the age of twenty, he was married to his first wife.

In 1814, he volunteered, and served six months in the war with Great Britain, was stationed at Upper Sandusky, and was there at the time Colonel Croghan fought the battle of Lower Sandusky. While in the army, he had a pitched battle with the "*bully*" of another regiment ("*fist and skull*"), and whipped him.

About the year 1820, he removed to the Indian territory of Indiana, in what was afterward organized into Madison County. He purchased a tract of improved land from a Delaware Indian, and remained on it about two years; sold out, and removed to Henry County. Resided in Henry at the time Sawyer, Bridges, and others, killed the friendly Indians, and saw Hudson, Bridges, and Sawyer hung, and young Bridges reprieved.

About the year 1825, Mr. Hughes went to Texas, induced to do so by the promises made by Colonel Austin. First located about one hundred miles up the Colorado. He returned home to Henry County, having been absent nearly two years.

He was married to his second wife about the year 1823. After his return from Texas, he came to this part of the Wabash twice, on a peddling tour. He started with his family to remove here, in January, 1827, and arrived the last of February. He came down the Mississinewa; had a pretty hard time in coming; could procure scarcely any thing to eat, until he arrived at Aleck Chamberlain's, who kept tavern on the river, a mile below where Logansport was afterward located.

When Mr. Hughes arrived in Carroll County, he settled near where Eli Wingard now resides, in the Burntrager neighborhood. One of his near neighbors was Moses Standley. He afterward bought thirty-six acres in the same neighborhood, which he improved. He made his living principally by hunting.

In 1828, in company with Moses Standley and John Mitchell, he got on board a "*bitter-head*" boat, and went down to the mouth of the the Big Vermilion River, with beeswax, etc., purchased corn and meal, and then pushed the boat all the way up, and landed at the "Elm Ford," on the Wabash, just below the mouth of the bayou, near the paper-mills. They were absent about one month.

Mr. Hughes was at the first sale of lots in Delphi; bought the corner lot, on which the wigwam was erected in 1860. He gave seventy dollars for the lot, but soon sold out to old Billy Wilson.

Mr. Hughes has killed deer near where the present court-house in Delphi stands, and he found a "bee-tree" just below where the jail is located.

The Delphi town-plat, before it was cleared off, was open woods of oak, walnut, elm, plum-bushes, and hazel. A favorite Indian camping-ground was on Deer Creek.

Mr. Hughes is residing about three miles south-west of Delphi.

ENOCH COX.

Enoch Cox was born August 28, 1784, in the state of New Jersey, and in 1789 his father removed to Mason County, Kentucky, where Mr. C. continued to reside thirty-six years. In 1825 he removed to Montgomery County, Ohio, and resided there until the 2d day of April, 1829, on which day he started to Delphi, in company with his family, and arrived at the house of John Robbins, on the 17th day of April, 1829. After remaining at the house of Mr. Robbins three or four days, he removed into the town of Delphi, and lived in a log house belonging to Joe Dunham, on the lot afterward occupied by Robertson, Wood, and Eichhold. He resided in Delphi until February, 1830, and then removed about five miles below town, on the farm owned by the Waller's family; here he remained ten months, and about Christmas, 1830, returned to Delphi, and moved into a house he had erected on the "Wigwam Lot." He remained in that location two or three years, and then removed to his farm, about two miles below Delphi, on the railroad.

Mr. Cox was married on the 28th day of August, 1810, in Mason County, Kentucky, to Isabella Logan.

At the time Mr. Cox came to Delphi, in 1829, he remembers that the following families were residing here: Aaron Dewey, William George, Joseph Dunham, Rev. James Crawford, Dr. Anthony, and William Wilson.

SAMUEL WAGONER.

Samuel Wagoner settled in Clay Township, in this county, in October, 1828. He came from Montgomery County, Ohio. He was a member of the "*German Baptist Church*," *or* "*Dunkers*." This Church was organized in Clay Township in the latter part of 1828, and meetings were held at the houses of the different members. Mr. Imon (Eyman) was the first preacher. John Shively and Samuel Ullery were next, and David Ullery visiting minister. John Shively also officiated.

The following families composed the first Church: David Ullery, John Wagoner, Joel Fouts, John Shivley, Samuel Ullery, Christian Replogel, Lawrence Fouts, and Samuel Wagoner.

ADAM PORTER.

Adam Porter was born in Bath County, Virginia, in the year 1805. In October, 1815, his father and his family started from Virginia for Indiana, and settled in Franklin County (now Fayette), near Connersville, on the 15th day of December, 1815.

In March, 1825, in company with Moses and Aaron Alldridge, Adam came to Indianapolis, then a small village. He worked there between one and two years, at eight dollars per month, and cleared off a tract of land for James Blake, for nine dollars an acre. He purchased eighty acres of land near Indianapolis, made a "deadening" on it, and afterward sold out.

In April, 1827, he came to Carroll County, and purchased eighty acres of Government land, a part of his present farm, worked a few months in the neighborhood, made another "deadening" on his land, and boarded with Thomas Stirlin and John Odell. At that time, John Little, Thomas Stirlin, and John Odell were the only persons who resided above Henry Robinson's, on Deer Creek.

It so happened that five single men had purchased land in Mr. Porter's neighborhood, and were making improvements on the same, to-wit: Elisha Brown, John Ballard, Jeremiah Ballard, Moses Alldridge, and Adam Porter. One day John Little remarked that they ought to give the name of "*Bachelor's Run*" to the little creek near which these *bachelors* had settled, and pretty soon the Register of the Land-office wrote the name on his plats, and thus that stream will be known in all coming time as "*Bachelor's Run.*"

About the 1st of June, 1837, he returned to Indianapolis, and thence to Rush County. The same Fall, he visited Virginia, and remained there until January, 1828; returned on horseback to Rush County, and from there he walked to this county, and purchased another eighty-acre lot of land, adjoining the first track. On this trip he came near perishing in the woods between Crawfordsville and Indianapolis; he and his companion lost their way, and were compelled to walk the whole night to keep themselves from freezing. During this visit he made some more "deadenings" on his land, and again returned to Rush County, where he remained until after the Presidential election in 1828. He then started to Tennssee, where he remained all Winter, with a half-brother. In March, 1829, he went to Lebanon, Ohio, remained there till October, 1829, and then returned here—driving a six-horse team for Cornelius Williams. Enoch Alldridge and family accompanied them.

About the 10th day of November, 1829, he again settled on his land, boarding with James Alldridge. He "worked around," and the following Winter cleared land for John Odell. He married Catharine Holeman on the 1st day of April, 1830.

Rattlesnakes were very plenty. Mr. Porter stated that, at one time, Moses Alldridge and the two Ballards killed twenty-two at a den on the land lately owned by William Halsey, then belonging to Isaac Griffith.

Mr. Porter resides on his farm, about seven miles from Delphi, and is known as one of the most energetic of the citizens. He owns a fine flouring-mill on Deer Creek, about one mile below Camden.

He is the father of a numerous family, fifteen having been born under his roof. He accumulated a large property, and affords a striking proof of what may be accomplished by industry and perseverance.

JOHN R. BALLARD.

John R. Ballard was born in Cayuga County, New York, on the 30th day of April, 1805. When six years of age, his father removed to the West, and arrived at Cincinnati in the Fall of 1810, and settled eight miles from that village on Mill Creek. The family resided in Hamilton and Butler Counties, until about the year 1814, at which time his mother died with the "cold plague." The family then (nine children) broke up, and scattered among relatives. John and a younger brother were taken to a married sister's in Wayne County,

Indiana. He was then about eight years old. At the end of two years, his father married again, in Wabash County, Illinois, and the younger children were gathered under the paternal roof. He resided with his father until he arrived at about the age of nineteen, near which time his father died. He then returned to Wayne County, where he remained about eighteen months.

In March, 1825, in company with his brother, Jeremiah Ballard, he came to Wea, Tippecanoe County, and remained there until the 5th day of May, on which day the two brothers came to this territory, afterward organized into Carroll County. On the 6th day of May, John commenced work for Benjamin D. Angell, at ten dollars per month, and continued with him four months, Angell having departed this life on the 16th day of September, 1825. He took a fifty-dollar job from the widow of clearing land.

Mr. Ballard, having worked around by the job and month, finally accumulated enough money to purchase eighty acres of land, lately owned by the Hon. Thomas Thompson, and he was one of the young men who gave the name "Bachelor" to the little creek. He boarded with Jediah Johnson three years.

Seven years after his arrival here, he married Lucinda, daughter of John Robbins, who survived the marriage about ten years, leaving four children. He removed to the west side of the Wabash River, about three miles above Pittsburg, in August, 1832.

Mr. Ballard's second wife was Miss Nancy Jane Hamilton, by whom he had four children. He was married to his third wife, Mrs. Terese Wolf, about the year 1848.

The first wedding Mr. B. attended after his arrival here was that of Geo. I. Baum and Miss Manary. One of the first weddings was his brother Jeremiah, to a daughter of Daniel Baum. The first sermon he heard preached was by Rev. James Crawford, at the house of Henry Robinson.

The first Winter after his arrival here, his brother Jeremiah and himself built a wolf-den, near Angell's house, in which they caught six wolves.

James Odell, Sr., James Odell, Jr., John and Jeremiah Ballard, watched the snake-den below Odell's house, and killed one hundred and ninety-four rattlesnakes.

JOSEPH COX.

JOSEPH COX is the son of Enoch Cox, a short sketch of whom is given on a preceding page. Joseph was nine or ten years old at the time his father settled in Delphi, April, 1829. His father kept a little store on the ground on which the drug-store of W. H. Calvert was located. Mr. Cox remembers that Dr. Anthony was in the habit of getting on his mare (being a Marylander, he pronounced the word "mar"), and riding up to Wilson's spring, near A. H. Bowen's house, with a little tin bucket, for water for his family, five or six times a day. Dr. A. became disgusted with the place, and soon left.

Mr. Cox long resided on his farm, two miles below Delphi. He was one of the active and prominent men in the fraternity of Odd-fellows, and a member of the Grand Lodge of that Order. He was an honest man, without guile, and above reproach. Every one spoke well of him, and if the whole world was made up of such men, hatred, envy, strife, revenge, wars, malice, and evil-speaking, would be banished from human society.

JOSEPH JACKSON.

MR. JACKSON was born on the 4th day of June, 1782, in the state of Pennsylvania. At the age of three or four years, his father, Isaac Jackson, removed to Franklin County, Virginia. Upon arriving at the age of twenty-one years, he apprenticed himself to a stonemason, and learned that trade. On the 15th of June, 1814, he married Rebecca Burk; he then resided in Giles County, Virginia. In the Fall of 1823, he emigrated to the West, and settled in Union County, Indiana. He remained there (except one year in Preble County, Ohio,) until October, 1827, at which time he came to the Deer Creek settlement, arriving here in November. He settled in the woods, having secured a lease on the school section above Delphi, on which land he opened up a small farm. He remained on this farm until March, 1831, when he again broke up, and settled on his own land in the green woods, two and a half miles south of Delphi.

He died on his farm, on the 24th day of January, 1851, leaving a numerous and respectable family.

JAMES M'DOWELL.

On Satuday, the 16th day of February, 1861, the writer was called upon to visit his old friend, James M'Dowell, on what proved to be his death-bed. Mr. M'D. said at the time that he would never get up again. He was suffering so much that the writer declined entering into any extended conversation, and therefore failed to elicit from him many particulars of his life.

He was born in March, 1789, in the town of Newbern, North Carolina; left that state in his tenth year, and removed to Bourbon County, Kentucky. He afterward lived in Nicholas County. At the age of eighteen, he left Kentucky, and settled in Preble County, Ohio, in which county he married. He came to Vigo County, Indiana, where he resided three years near Terre Haute, and, in 1826, removed to this territory.

From a statement made by Mr. M'Dowell at the "old settlers'" meeting, in August, 1855, we learn that he came here in August, 1826. David Lucas, and Alexander Chamberlain, also with him, the former locating in this county, and the latter a mile below the mouth of Eel River (Logansport).

He died on the 13th day of March, 1861.

As a husband, father, neighbor, and citizen, our old friend has left a character without blemish. A more correctly honest man never lived than James M'Dowell. He was literally a man without guile.

WILLIAM M'CAIN.

THIS gentleman was born in Warren County, Ohio, on the 27th day of January, 1804. He was married to Abigail Little, on the 4th day of February, 1825. In November, 1826, in company with his brother Daniel and family, and his brothers Joseph and Thomas Ramsey, he started for the Deer Creek settlement on the Wabash. Daniel was the only one of the brothers who brought his family along. Joseph and Thomas Ramsey already owned land in the settlement, and both went to work on their land, neither being then married.

The brothers arrived on the *Daniel M'Cain* land on the 28th day of November, 1826 (see the interesting statement of Mrs. Magdalena M'Cain), and camped west of the hollow, back of the present orchard. The male part of the emigrants immediately commenced cutting logs for a house; some cut down the timber, others split boards for a roof. This was on Wednesday. The cabin was up and covered by Friday night, and a hard, cold rain set in very soon afterward.

Mr. M'C. then cut logs, and erected a cabin on his own land. As soon as his cabin was completed, he started back to Ohio, on the 10th day of December, 1826.

While M'C. was building his cabin, an Indian came along, and it required the whole party to keep their dog from biting the son of the forest. A funny circumstance occurred during his stay. One day he started from his brother Daniel's to his own new cabin; a deep snow was on the ground; he got lost, and wandered around the whole afternoon. He passed his own cabin, and did n't know it!

He arrived at home, in Ohio, on the 28th day of December, 1826, where he remained until the 19th day of November, 1828, when he started with his family to remove, and in the company were his youngest brother, Harry M'Cain, and his wife's sister, Sarah Little. He had one team, two yoke of oxen. Came through Strawtown, Kirklin, and Dayton, and arrived at his brother Daniel's on the 10th day of December, 1828, all well and happy.

DAVID HARTER, Sr.

David Harter, Sr., removed from Montgomery County, Ohio, and settled on Bachelor's Run, in this county, in the Fall of 1827. He built his first mill in 1831. At the time he settled there, Samuel Wise, on Deer Creek, was his nearest neighbor, and no one lived east of him this side of the "Miami Reservation." The Michigan road was not then cut out. The deer would come within twenty steps of the house. They had no gun then. The Indians were plenty, but they gave no trouble. They frequently came to trade for corn, meal, etc.

Mr. Harter died June 12, 1840, leaving a large family. He was a good citizen, and very much respected.

JOHN KUNS.

John Kuns, son of George Kuns, emigrated to this county from Montgomery County, Ohio. Daniel and Jacob Kuns, sons of George, were also residents of this county. Daniel, however, survived but a few years, and died on Rock Creek.

John Kuns was born April 14, 1795, in Huntington County, Pennsylvania. When he was seven years of age, his father removed to Montgomery County, Ohio. John married the daughter of Leonard Wolf, in 1817. In 1824, he attended the land sales at Crawfordsville, and purchased land, and on the 11th day of October, 1826, arrived with his family, and settled on his land. Aaron Merriman, James M'Dowell, and David Lucas were then the only settlers in the Rock Creek settlement.

The "Dunker" Church was organized in the Fall of 1827, by Peter Eyman, who was the first preacher. Having no meeting-house, he preached at John Kuns's, Samuel Wise's, and also at the houses of other brethren.

It was Mr. K. who first erected the flouring-mill near Delphi, afterward owned by Roach & Co. He also carried on a tannery on his farm quite extensively for a new country. He was a very energetic business man and a shrewd trader.

In April, 1859, having lost his wife, he removed to Piatt County, Illinois. The last time the writer saw him was on the 8th day of May, 1861, when he was on his way to Wild-cat, with the view of returning to Illinois with a buxom widow, the future second Mrs. Kuns.

JONAH T. HOPKINSON.

Jonah T. Hopkinson, the fourth sheriff of Carroll County, was born in Connecticut, on the 15th day of October, 1789, and was brought up in New York, probably in Onondaga County. He removed west to Switzerland County, Indiana, in the year 1818, and was married to Miss Lydia Powers, of that county, on the 19th day of February, 1819. After residing in that county one year, he removed to Kentucky, then returned to Switzerland County, from which place he removed to Rush County, where he lived five years.

In the year 1829, a neighbor by the name of Hays came to this county, and took a contract from Judge Isaac Griffith, to frame his saw-mill, on Deer Creek, three miles above Delphi. Hays was no carpenter; but he returned home, and induced Mr. Hopkinson (who was a carpenter by trade) to finish the job for him. Accordingly, in July, 1829, Mr. Hopkinson came here, in company with Hays and Randall, another neighbor, bringing with him his apprentice, William M. Young (since a resident of Delphi), and finished the Griffith saw-mill frame. He was so well pleased with the country, that he returned to Rush County, sold his farm, and removed to this county, arriving here about the 20th day of October, 1829. At Lafayette he became acquainted with Colonel Holt, who was then coming to this county, and the two families came together from Lafayette to Delphi.

From the time of Mr. Hopkinson's arrival here, he diligently followed his trade until he purchased a tract of land, which he improved with his usual energy. It was on this farm (since owned by Henry T. Lyon) that a man by the name of Jesse Fleming was buried in a well. The writer was on the spot the succeeding morning, and well remembers the thrill of horror that shot through the community, at an accident so dreadful. Mr. H. was digging a well; had dug down some fifteen or twenty feet, when he discovered that they were in a bed of *quicksand*, and perceiving the danger, concluded to go no further without curbing. Fleming was sent down for the bucket and tools, and, when in the act of being drawn up, the well caved in up to his neck, covering his face, in fact; at which moment Archibald Slane, at the risk of his own life, jumped down and scraped the sand from his nose and mouth. In an instant, another avalanche of sand fell upon Slane, almost burying him up also, and he was rescued with difficulty. Poor Fleming was not dug out until the next day. He was then dead. The sand was packed so tightly about him, that he could not be removed until they removed it down to his ankles.

Mr. Hopkinson was a member of the Methodist Church, and it was owing, alone, to his zeal and perseverance that the lot was purchased in Delphi, and the frame church edifice was erected. And, notwithstanding this undeniable fact, so rapid is the flight of time, and so very soon are the most important occurrences of life forgotten, that nine-tenths of the members who now worship in the new brick building have never *heard his name.* Is this either just or right?

In 1832, Mr. Hopkinson was elected sheriff of Carroll County. In 1834, a man by the name of Thompson, having been convicted of stealing an overcoat from Levi S. Dale (then a young school-teacher), was sentenced to the State-prison. The author, having some business in Louisville, Kentucky, agreed to accompany Sheriff Hopkinson, as assistant, to convey the aforesaid Thompson to his quarters at Jeffersonville. The trio started on horseback, the feet of the prisoner being connected together by a chain under the belly of the horse. The first night we reached Frankfort, the second Indianapolis, and the third Columbus, at each of which places the prisoner was secured in the county jail. The fourth night we put up at a cabin on the roadside. The prisoner being a very large, athletic man, the question as to the best method of keeping him secure for the night, became quite an important one. Finally, a straw bed was placed on the floor; the prisoner being in the middle, one of his arms was chained to one of the sheriff's, the chain locked, and the key given to the man of the house. The author placed himself on the other side, with a pistol under his head.

But the whole party being very much fatigued, we

soon fell asleep, and neither awoke till broad daylight. The next night we reached Jeffersonville, and delivered Mr. Thompson into the care of the warden of the penitentiary.

After residing on the Lyon farm for several years, Mr. Hopkinson sold out, and purchased the farm above Burt's spring, since owned by John Sidenbender. On this place he died. The author has before him a number of the old *Delphi Oracle*, of March 16, 1839, containing the following obituary notice: "Died at his residence, in this neighborhood, on the 11th instant, Mr. Jonah T. Hopkinson. Mr. H. was one of the earliest settlers of this place, and has ever been an industrious and enterprising citizen. His loss will be deeply deplored by the community in which he has so long resided; but, to a helpless family, his loss will be irreparable. To *them*, the ordinary form of condolence is *mockery*. May the God of the widow and fatherless have them in his special keeping!"

Mr. H. was kind, affectionate, and warm-hearted in his disposition. His attachments were disinterested, and no man loved his friend with a truer devotion than he.

Several years after the death of Mr. H., his family moved to Clinton County, and his youngest daughter became the wife of David P. Barner, clerk of the Clinton Circuit Court.

HUGH GRAHAM,

THE father of Levi M., Henry M., Hugh M., Amos M., and Milton R. Graham, was born in Greenbrier County, Virginia, on the 12th day of March, 1787, and removed to Clarke County, Indiana, in September, 1816. In 1818, he removed to Washington County, Indiana.

He started for Carroll County about the middle of December, 1828, and arrived here on the 6th day of January, 1829.

In 1836, Mr. Graham was elected a county commissioner, which office he held for three years. He was a man of strict integrity, high-minded and honorable; a kind neighbor, a devoted husband and father.

Having lost his wife on the 14th day of July, 1838, he went, in May, 1839, to Washington County, where he married the second time. He died on the 18th day of April, 1844, leaving surviving, his wife and two children, and several by his first wife, some of whom still remain, highly respectable residents of this county.

To many persons the following chapters may not appear interesting as reading matter; but a history of the county would not be complete without these tables and facts. Many of the records are found nowhere else, save as they are collected here.

CHAPTER XV.

Town of Delphi in Official Acts.

ON the 15th day of September, 1835, the citizens of Delphi met in pursuance of previous notices, in accordance with "*an act providing for the incorporation of towns*," and "*an act amendatory to said act.*" William George was appointed president, and Henry B. Milroy clerk. The meeting then proceeded to district the town, after which the following trustees were elected: District No. 1, William George; No. 2, David Henderson; No. 3, Henry B. Milroy; No. 4, Samuel Grimes; No. 5, Andrew Wood.

The trustees met on the 14th day of October, 1835, and organized by the election of Samuel Grimes, President, and Michael C. Dougherty, Clerk.

William George and Henry B. Milroy were appointed a committee to draft rules and regulations for the government of the Board. On the 17th of the same month, the trustees met at the house of David Henderson, adopted the rules, etc., reported by the Committee.

At a meeting held January 23, 1836, a large number of *ordinances* were passed. Samuel D. Gresham was appointed assessor, Robert Adams and Thomas Cole, assistants; James P. Dugan was appointed treasurer.

April 23, 1836.—Samuel D. Gresham was appointed collector; William M'Crery, superintendent of Public Works; Samuel D. Gresham, marshal.

May 14.—Mr. John Armstrong was employed to resurvey the town.

July 9, 1836.—Colonel Crooks appointed to superintend the improvement of the streets.

July 15.—Aaron Finch, Esq., employed to prosecute the suit for violation of ordinance against James Harris.

August 11.—The clerk, M. C. Dougherty, resigned.

October 21.—The second Board of Trustees met, to wit: C. Richardson, W. H. Buford, J. T. Hopkinson, A. Sproul, S. Sherfey, and organized by the election of the following officers: President, Chevalier Richardson; Michael C. Dougherty, Clerk; Samuel D. Gresham, Assessor and Collector; Simeon Sherfey, Treasurer; and Jonah T. Hopkinson, Marshal.

February 13, 1837.—Aaron Dewey was appointed to superintend the burying-ground and to locate the graves; John Carey, elected assessor and collector.

February 16.—James H. Stewart and J. B. Larimer were appointed to assist the assessor.

May 5.—William H. Buford, Andrew Sproul, and James H. Stewart, present. John F. Taylor was appointed to draw off the duplicate. Curtis Keener was appointed collector.

May 13.—A. D. E. Tweed was elected trustee of the Fifth Ward, to fill the vacancy of J. T. Hopkinson, resigned. Curtis Keener appointed marshal. Andrew Davis appointed to level Main and Washington Streets, and William H. Buford to superintend the placing of curb-timbers.

July 1.—A. D. E. Tweed was elected president, and James H. Stewart, clerk of the corporation.

November 13.—The Board met, consisting of William Crooks, Aaron Dewey, Andrew Wood, and Charles E. Sturgis. William Crooks elected president, and Charles E. Sturgis clerk. The following appointments were made: Curtis Keener, Collector, and Aaron Dewey, Treasurer. An election was ordered to be held on the 23d, to fill the vacancies in First and Second Wards.

November 28, 1837.—The Board met. Present, William Crooks, Aaron Dewey, Alfred Ramey, and James Crumly. Alfred Ramey was appointed clerk in the place of C. E. Sturgis, resigned. Curtis Keener was appointed assessor and marshal. Grocery license was fixed at the sum of thirty-five dollars within the corporation.

February 10, 1838.—Mr. Dewey was appointed a committee to ascertain from Mr. Vail, or Apsey, the terms on which they will take the subscription papers, etc., in payment for building the market-house.

February 12.—Contract closed with Mr. Vail for building the market-house.

March 30.—George Sherburn was appointed collector and marshal, in the place of Keener, removed.

May 18.—William Crooks produced his commission as mayor, and the Board organized under the new charter. Aaron Dewey, James Crumly, and Ambrose Phelps sworn as common councilmen. Henry Orwig was elected marshal, assessor, and collector.

November 19.—Samuel Grimes, Mayor, and Samuel Grimes, Simeon L. Broadwell, John Bradshaw, and David W. Bowen, Councilmen.

November 20.—Hiram Allen and Jesse R. Henry sworn as common councilmen. David W. Bowen appointed clerk; William M'Crery, treasurer; Edwin R. Davis, marshal; Hiram Allen, corporation attorney.

February 25, 1839.—Philip A. Clover, appointed marshal; R. C. Green, corporation printer; and Hiram Allen, clerk.

April 20.—Joseph Lafleur, having paid thirty-five dollars, was licensed to keep a grocery, and George W. Goodlander to sell goods at auction.

June 13.—William Brewster appointed surveyor.

All persons were prohibited from selling fresh beef or pork, except at the market-house, on regular market days.

February 15, 1840.—William Simpson was appointed mayor, and Henry Orwig, John M'Curdy, and William Dunkle were appointed councilmen, to fill vacancies.

May 11.—Board met. William Simpson, Mayor, John M'Curdy, David W. Bowen, Henry Orwig, Wm. Dunkle, and Jesse R. Henry, Councilmen, present.

May 25.—Lewis Martin appointed marshal and assessor.

June 22.—H. Tuttle was appointed clerk.

At the corporation election, September 7, 1840, the following persons were elected: George M. Maxwell, Mayor, Henry R. Glazier, Jesse Osbourn, David W. Bowen, and William Dunkle, Councilmen. Jesse R. Henry held over.

November 12.—H. Tuttle was appointed clerk. Messrs. David W. Bowen, Newton H. Gist, and Wm. Dunkle, were appointed a committee to examine chimnies and stove-pipes. Thomas C. Hughes, appointed marshal. The *Carroll Express* appointed corporation printer.

December 26.—Councilman Jesse R. Henry resigned, and William Bolles appointed in his place.

January 29, 1841.—John M'Curdy was appointed treasurer, in place of William M'Crery.

March 19.—H. Tuttle, Clerk, resigned.

May 1.—Levi S. Dale appointed clerk; Thomas C. Hughes, assessor and collector.

December 20.—James Witherow appointed treasurer. Henry R. Glazier, Collector, made report.

February 6, 1843.—Present, George M. Maxwell, Mayor. William Burnett and Robert C. Green, new members, appeared.

February 7.—Present, George M. Maxwell, Mayor,

and Messrs. William Barnett, John Burr, Henry R. Glazier, Robert C. Green, and William Dunkle, Councilmen. R. C. Green was appointed clerk.

April 1, 1843.—O. D. Butler was appointed marshal and collector.

April 16, 1845.—Present, William Dunkle, John Burr, William Barnett. The office of mayor was declared vacant, by reason of the removal of George M. Maxwell from the limits of the corporation. James R. Blanchard was appointed mayor, "until the next annual election."

April 24.—Present, J. R. Blanchard, Mayor, and Messrs Dunkle, Burr, and Barnett, Councilmen.

Messrs. Charles Marquess and Newton H. Gist were appointed to fill vacancies in First and Second Wards. Levi S. Dale, appointed clerk.

March 10, 1847.—Present, Levi S. Dale, Mayor, and Messrs. John Boggs, Samuel D. Gresham, Joseph Evans, Jesse R. Henry, and Nathaniel W. Bowen, Councilmen. E. W. Hubbard was appointed clerk; Edwin R. Davis, marshal; and Enoch Rinehart, treasurer. The copy of the notice for the election for mayor and common council, was ordered to be spread upon the Minutes. The notice reads as follows: "An election for mayor and councilmen of the town of Delphi, will be holden at the usual place of holding elections in each ward in said town, on the third Saturday of January next." Dated December 31, 1846. Signed by Enoch Rinehart, W. H. Buford, L. A. Gaylord, M. Simpson, D. R. Harley, N. B. Dewey, A. G. Leadbetter, John Phelps, V. Holt, H. Foreman, W. H. Calvert, Charles Ruffing, James H. Stewart, J. A. Reed, L. S. Dale, Hiram Allen, William Simpson, William Rees, William Potter, N. G. Gist.

September 1.—Present, Levi S. Dale, Mayor, and Messrs. Samuel D. Gresham, John Boggs, Nathaniel W. Bowen, Jesse R. Henry, and Levi M. Graham.

June 7, 1848.—Present, Levi S. Dale, Mayor; Messrs. J. R. Henry, William Barnett, S. D. Gresham, Levi M. Graham, and John Boggs, Councilmen. R. H. Gordon was appointed marshal.

January 16, 1849.—Present as above. Aquila Jones was appointed marshal, and Messrs. John J. Gibson, James R. Blanchard, and Thomas C. Hughes were appointed a Board of Health.

April 6.—An election was ordered for mayor, to fill the vacancy occasioned by the resignation of Levi S. Dale.

At the election for mayor, on the 17th day of April, 1849, the following was the result: N. G. Gillam, 97; J. H. Boylan, 50; Samuel Rinehart, 4.

July 25.—Officers all present except Nathan G. Gillam, the mayor; and, in his absence, L. M. Graham was called to the chair. The following resolution was adopted:

Resolved, That the proprietors of the hotels in this place be earnestly requested to refuse entertainment to all persons passing or traveling from places infected with the cholera for any length of time—say, time to *get a meal of victuals.*

Ordered, That the marshal be empowered to prevent canal-boats from putting off emigrants, or transient persons, to remain among us; and that the Board co-operate with him in carrying out said order.

August 1.—The celebrated

CHOLERA ORDINANCE PASSED.

"*Be it ordained by the Mayor and Common Council of the Town of Delphi*, That all persons passing or traveling from places infected with the cholera, be prohibited from staying in our midst more than time sufficient to procure a meal of victuals; that all places of public entertainment be required to prohibit the stay of all such persons for a longer time; and that our own citizens, except physicians, be hereafter prohibited from going to, or visiting places, near or distant, where the cholera is prevailing, unless there is absolute necessity for so doing; and that any person or persons offending against or violating any of the provisions of this ordinance, be fined in any sum not less than three nor more than ten dollars, for each offense. This ordinance to take effect from its passage."

[NOTE.—The cholera was prevailing at Lafayette at the time of the passage of the above law, and the citizens of that city were very indignant at the mayor and council of Delphi, on account of the prohibitory ordinance. We understand that one of the citizens of the "Star City" was at the expense of *framing* the ordinance, and the subject was one of jest and ridicule there for a long time.]

CORPORATION ELECTION, *September* 3, 1849.—Jonathan C. Applegate was elected mayor, and Messrs. Charles Marquess, Archibald Slane, John Burr, Nicholas Smith, and J. H. Boylan, Councilmen.

October 15.—The mayor and common council met.

Augustus Linville was elected clerk, Matthew Simpson treasurer, and John J. Gibson marshal.

November 27.—William Potter was elected clerk.

January 16, 1850.—Board met. Present, Jonathan C. Applegate, Mayor; Archibald Slane, James H. Boylan, John Burr, Nicholas Smith, and Charles Marquess, Councilmen; William Potter, Clerk; and John J. Gibson, Marshal.

Archibald Slane and the clerk were ordered to report what alterations were necessary in the by-laws, etc.

The bond of Matthew Simpson, Treasurer, approved.

March 13.—John J. Gibson, the marshal, resigned; and Enoch Rinehart was elected to fill the place.

March 26.—Enoch Rinehart having declined to serve as marshal, William B. Givins was appointed.

July 3.—James Armstrong appointed sexton for the old grave-yard.

August 14, 1850.—The following places were appointed for holding elections: First Ward, Marquess's shop; Second Ward, the recorder's office; Third Ward, the Court-house; Fourth Ward, Arthur G. Connelly's shop; Fifth Ward, Dunkle & Kilgore's shop. M. Simpson was appointed inspector in the First Ward; John J. Gibson, Second Ward; Jesse R. Henry, Third Ward; Arthur G. Connelly, Fourth Ward; and William Dunkle, Fifth Ward.

Tuesdays, Thursdays, and Saturdays were established as *market* days, and all persons prohibited from selling during certain hours, except at the market-house.

September 5.—Councilman Nicholas Smith resigned, and David W. Bowen appointed in his place. E. W. Hubbard was appointed clerk.

September 11.—Councilman John Burr resigned, and Jesse R. Henry was appointed to fill the vacancy.

September 24.—James Armstrong removed as sexton, and Mr. Rinehart appointed in his place.

October 21.—William B. Givins resigned as marshal, and Samuel D. Gresham was appointed.

November 14.—Henry P. Tedford was appointed marshal.

January 7, 1851.—John M'Carthy was appointed treasurer.

May 15.—William Riley appointed marshal.

June 14.—The mayor, Jonathan C. Applegate, tendered his resignation, and Samuel D. Gresham was appointed to fill the unexpired term of said office.

July 24.—Samuel D. Gresham was appointed marshal; Henry M. Graham, collector; and William Barnett, mayor, to fill out balance of unexpired term.

August 9.—The clerk was ordered to give notice, in the *Weekly Times*, of an election, on the first of September next, for mayor and common council. The following persons were appointed inspectors:

First Ward.—John Boggs, polls at his office.

Second Ward.—A. Slane, polls at Gillam's office.

Third Ward.—J. C. Applegate, polls at the Courthouse.

Fourth Ward.—A. G. Connelly, polls at his wareroom.

Fifth Ward.—William Dunkle, polls at his shop.

At the said election, William Barnett was elected mayor, and Messrs. John Finley, Archibald Slane, Anthony Foust, Robert H. Milroy, and Levi M. Graham, councilmen.

October 25, 1851.—E. W. Hubbard was appointed clerk, and John M'Carthy treasurer.

June 2, 1852.—D. I. Jackson accepted appointment for councilman for First Ward, in place of John Finley.

March 19, 1853.—Frazer Duff was appointed councilman for the Fourth Ward, to fill the vacancy occasioned by the removal from the ward of R. H. Milroy.

April 9.—James H. Dunlap, James H. Boylan, and D. I. Jackson were appointed school trustees.

April 16.—Henry M. Graham was appointed marshal.

ELECTION, *September* 5, 1853.—Ebenezer W. Bolles was elected mayor; and Messrs. George Robertson, Christian Brolyer, Anthony Foust, James Kilgore, and John Culler, Sr., councilmen.

October 29.—E. W. Hubbard appointed clerk; Noah B. Dewey, treasurer; and Henry M. Graham, marshal and collector.

November 19.—Lewis B. Sims was appointed attorney for the corporation.

December 24.—John Rinehart was removed from the office of sexton, and John Culler, Sr., appointed in his place.

March 11, 1854.—The old charter was surrendered, and the town was incorporated under the act of the Legislature of June 11, 1852.

May 3.—James H. Dunlap resigned his appointment as school trustee; James H. Stewart appointed to fill the vacancy, and Noah B. Dewey was appointed in the place of D. I. Jackson.

The following is the result of the election held May 1, 1854: Messrs. George Robertson, Enoch Rinehart, Washington L. Black, Nicholas Smith, and James H. Stewart were elected councilmen; John D. Simpson, clerk and treasurer; Henry M. Graham, marshal and assessor.

May 31, 1854.—J. C. Applegate was appointed councilman in place of Washington L. Black, deceased.

ELECTION, May 7, 1855, resulted as follows: James F. Givins, Enoch Rinehart, Andrew H. Evans, James H. Dunlap, and William M'Cain were elected councilmen; Henry M. Graham, marshal and assessor; Erastus W. Hubbard, clerk and treasurer.

May 31, 1855.—James H. Boylan was appointed school trustee; James P. Dugan, school treasurer; and Andrew H. Evans, school clerk.

September 6, 1855.—Rev. E. W. Wright and Vine Holt were elected school trustees; in the place of James H. Stewart and James H. Boylan, resigned.

January 2, 1856.—Noah B. Dewey resigned as school trustee, and J. C. Applegate was appointed in his place.

May 9, 1856.—Board met. Present, Messrs Abner H. Bowen, George Robertson, Thomas Weakly, and James P. Dugan, Trustees, and James H. Stewart, Clerk.

Enoch Rinehart was appointed trustee, in place of George W. Pigman, declined.

Abner H. Bowen was appointed president of the Board.

May 28, 1856.—James P. Dugan was appointed school treasurer, and A. H. Evans school clerk.

August 2, 1856.—Thomas Haugh was appointed sexton, and Thomas C. Hughes fire-warden.

December 16, 1856.—David Leonard was appointed school trustee, in place of J. C. Applegate, resigned.

March 28, 1857.—John B. York was appointed street commissioner.

May 6, 1857.—At an election held on the first Monday of the present month, the following persons were elected: Messrs. Enoch Rinehart, Jesse R. Henry, James P. Dugan, and Abner H. Bowen, Trustees; Daniel L. Richard, Marshal and Assessor; Artemas Merritt, Clerk.

May 23, 1857.—George Robertson was appointed trustee for the First Ward.

April 3, 1858.—Pat Bowes appointed sexton.

ELECTION held May 3, 1858: Messrs. Abner H. Bowen, Enoch Rinehart, James P. Dugan, George Robertson, and Jesse R. Henry, Trustees; Nathaniel M. Crawford, Marshal and Assessor; Clerk and Treasurer, Nathaniel Black; John S. Case, B. F. Schermerhorn, and A. Merritt, School Trustees.

Geo. W. Pigman was appointed school trustee, in the place of John S. Case, declined.

June 3, 1858.—Edwin R. Davis, marshal and street commissioner.

July 7, 1858.—David Leonard, school trustee, *vice* G. W. Pigman.

September 7, 1858.—John M. Bowman was appointed clerk and treasurer, in the place of Nathaniel Black, resigned.

The following is the result of the election held May 2, 1859: Messrs. Anthony Garrett, Enoch Rinehart, Joseph Assion, James P. Dugan, and Milton R. Graham were elected trustees; Reed Case, treasurer; and Robert Shealy, clerk and assessor.

May 16, 1859.—James Shealy was appointed street commissioner.

June 16, 1859.—Robert Shealy, treasurer.

November 4, 1859.—E. R. Davis resigned as marshal, and James Shealy was appointed in his place.

May 14, 1860.—M. R. Graham elected president of the Board; Wm. W. Schermerhorn appointed clerk and assessor, in the place of Robert Shealy, resigned; Andrew Robertson appointed trustee, in the place of Anthony Garrett, resigned.

November 26, 1861.—Wm. W. Schermerhorn appointed marshal. The result of the corporation election, May 6, 1861: Messrs. John Sonenfelt, Enoch Rinehart, Wm. H. Buford, James W. Kilgore, and Erastus W. Hubbard were elected trustees; James P. Dugan, treasurer; Wm. M'Neil, marshal; Bernard B. Daily, clerk; William Barnett, George W. Pigman, and John M. Grant, school trustees.

CHAPTER XVI.

BOARD OF COUNTY COMMISSIONERS.

JACOB BAUM, Aaron Hick, and Graham Roberts, the first Board of Commissioners of Carroll County, met pursuant to an act of the Legislature, for the formation of the county of Carroll, "approved January 7, 1828," at the house of Daniel Baum, on the 12th of May, 1828.

The first duty performed by the Board was to lay off Tippecanoe, Deer creek, Rock-creek, and Eel Townships. Elections to be held in Tippecanoe, at Thomas Hamilton's; in Rock-creek, at Aaron Merriman's; in Deer-creek, at Daniel M'Cain's; and in Eel, at Alex. Chamberlain's.

INSPECTORS.—Nathaniel Hamilton was appointed inspector of elections for Tippecanoe; William G. Bishop, for Deer-creek; Isam Atkinson, for Rock-creek; and Daniel Bell, for Eel.

Elections were ordered to be held in each township on the 7th day of June, 1828, for the election of justices of the peace.

Daniel Baum was appointed treasurer, and Jacob Baum and William G. Bishop appeared as his securities. Aaron Dewey was appointed assessor; Henry B. Milroy, collector; and Samuel Milroy and Aaron Dewey, securities.

CONSTABLES.—Thomas Robb. for Eel; Adrew M'Coy, Tippecanoe; Joseph M'Cain, Deer-creek; and David M'Combs, Rock-creek.

OVERSEERS OF THE POOR.—Daniel Bell and John

Hall, Eel; David Hamilton and Nathan Rose, Tippecanoe; Samuel Wells and James Odell, Deer-creek; James M'Dowell and John Crook, Rock-creek.

FENCE-VIEWERS.—William M'Cord, John Givins, and Thomas Stirlin, Deer-creek; James Hamilton, Benjamin Baxter, and John E. Metcalf, Tippecanoe; William Cummins, Henry Bingaman, and David Lucas, Rock-creek; Alexander Chamberlain, William Scott, and Marsh, Eel.

Isaac Griffith and Daniel F. Vandeventer were licensed to "vend foreign merchandise."

SPECIAL SESSION—COUNTY-SEAT.

THE Board met on the 15th day of May, 1828, at the same place, for the purpose of receiving the report of the commissioners appointed to locate the seat of justice. The locating commissioners reported the same day.

SPECIAL SESSION, MAY 24, 1828.

SAMUEL MILROY was appointed county agent, Isaac Griffith and David Baum his sureties.

Ordered, that three streets in Delphi, on the south side, running east and west, and two streets on the east, the other on the west side of the Public Square, running north and south, be ninety feet in width, and all the other streets eighty feet; alleys, twelve feet; each lot to contain one-fourth of an acre.

Sale of lots ordered to take place second Monday in August next; the agent authorized to give notice in the *Indiana Journal*, *Terre Haute Register*, and a paper at Dayton, Ohio. Conditions of sale: one-fourth in hand, and the residue in three equal annual installments. The agent was authorized "to give any mechanics, who will become actual settlers in the town of Delphi, and build a comfortable dwelling-house thereon, not less than eighteen feet wide, and twenty feet long, one and a half stories high, of hewed logs, frame or brick, with a brick or stone chimney, and a shingled roof, within one year from the sale of lots, *one lot in any part of the town they may choose*, except on Front Street, or around the Public Square."

SPECIAL SESSION, JUNE 14, 1828.

AARON DEWEY was allowed, for assessing the revenue of Carroll County, *eleven dollars*.

Cyrus Taber was licensed to sell goods. The place of holding elections for Rock-creek, changed from Merriman's to the house of Jacob Sager.

SESSION, AUGUST 11, 1828.

SAMUEL M'CLURE, Hugh B. M'Keen, and Walker, Carter & Co., licensed to sell "foreign goods."

Alexander Chamberlain, William Scott, and William G. Bishop were appointed to view and locate a public road from Delphi to Logansport.

Daniel Bell, Samuel M'Clure, and Samuel Taber were appointed to view road from Logansport via John M'Gregor's to Champion Helvey's.

Hugh Manary, William Wilson, and Aaron Dewey, appointed to view two roads, one from Delphi to Benjamin Baxter's, and the other from Delphi to Nathaniel Hamilton's.

Hugh B. M'Keen was licensed to keep a ferry across the Wabash, at Logansport.

Moses Standley, Robert Cade, and John Adams, appointed to view a road from Delphi to intersect a road from Lafayette to the Carroll County line.

Daniel Baum, William M'Cord, and Samuel Wells were appointed to view two roads: one from Delphi to where the meridian-line crosses Deer Creek; the other from Delphi to Elisha Brown's, on "Bachelor's Run."

SESSION, NOVEMBER 11, 1828.

ALEXANDER CHAMBERLAIN, William G. Bishop, and Thomas Stirlin were appointed to view road from Delphi to Logansport.

The Board "ordered that William Wilson receive off the north-east corner of the donation for the town of Delphi, four acres, two quarters, and twenty-two rods of ground, the west line running parallel with the town plat, in exchange for the like quantity of ground, for a public grave-yard, in the north-east corner of the land the said Wilson bought of Henry Robinson in the north-east quarter of sec. 29, T. 25, R. 2 W., to lie in a square form."

Aaron Dewey was allowed ten dollars for laying off the town-plat of Delphi. A permanent corner was ordered to be made at south-west corner of lot No. 1, and at north-east corner of lot No. 63.

William G. Bishop, John Carey, and James Odell were appointed trustees of school section 16, T. 25 R. 2 W.

SESSION, FEBRUARY, 1829.

Rock-creek Township.—David M'Combs was appointed constable; Daniel Kuns and James Cummins, overseers of the poor; Jacob Sager and Lewis Neff, fence-viewers.

Tippecanoe Township.—Benjamin Baxter was elected constable; David Hamilton and Jacob Clister, fence-viewers; Nathaniel Hamilton, inspector.

Deer-creek Township.—Samuel Wells and James Odell, overseers of the poor; David Baum, Robert Cade, fence-viewers; William George, inspector.

Daniel Baum, reappointed country treasurer, and Jacob Baum and Moses Standley his sureties.

Elections for Deer-creek Township ordered to be held at the school-house in Delphi.

Moses Standley was appointed constable for Deer-creek.

Robert Cade was appointed assessor.

Daniel M'Cain, Moses Alldridge, and Elisha Brown were appointed to view a road from Delphi to where the meridian-line crosses Deer Creek.

Hugh Manary, William Wilson, and Aaron Dewey were appointed to locate a road from Delphi to Nathaniel Hamilton's.

Daniel Baum, Samuel Wells, and Joseph Dunham were appointed to view road from Delphi to the Wabash River, the nearest and best route to intersect a road leading from Delphi to Logansport, at a point known by the name of the "Old Trading-house."

The Board ordered a frame building to be erected in Delphi, for a clerk and recorder's office, twenty-two feet wide, and twenty-eight feet long, "the clerk to occupy the front room in said building for a store-room, by paying a reasonable rent."

The road leading from Delphi to Logansport was divided into *four* districts. William M'Crery appointed supervisor of one of the districts, and ordered to work the following hands: William George, William Wilson, Joseph Dunham, Abner Robinson, Coleman Robinson, —— Graham, Samuel Milroy, Henry B. Milroy, Joseph M'Cain, Thomas R. M'Cain, Moses Thompson, Joseph Jackson, Thomas Burk, John Givins, Joseph Patterson, John Robbins, James M'Dowell, and Dr. J. M. Ewing.

The Second District assigned to John Kuns, who was ordered to work the following hands: John Mikesel, Isam Adkinson, William Adkinson, Jacob Kuns, Ephraim Denison, David Moyer, Jacob Sager, Aaron Merriman, William Sieres, Alexander Sieres, Solomon Burket, Eli Cotner.

The Third District was assigned to Henry Bingaman, with the following hands: John Scott, David Kuns, James Cummins, William Cummins, Joshua Merriman, John Cummins, Thomas Martindale, William Hicks, Jacob Bingaman.

The Fourth was assigned to General John Tipton and "all the hands below the mouth of Eel River, to the north line of Carroll County," were assigned to him.

SPECIAL SESSION, FEBRUARY 21, 1829.

THE order for building a clerk and recorder's office was revoked. This was about all that was accomplished at this session.

MAY SESSION, 1829.

JOHN ODELL, John Carey, and Daniel M'Cain were appointed to view a road from Delphi to Daniel M'Cain's north-east corner, thence to the corner of secs. 33–4, on township line, between townships 24–5, 1 W.

John Briggs, John Knight, and William G. Bishop, were appointed to view a road from the house of Thomas Gillam to Delphi.

Jeremiah Ballard, Jacob Zook, and Thomas Gillam were appointed to view a road from Delphi to the meridian-line, where it crosses Deer Creek.

Lewis Neff, Isam Adkinson, and Christopher M'Combs were appointed to view a proposed change of the Logansport road, on the land of Daniel Kuns.

Samuel Wells was appointed supervisor of road from Delphi to Nathaniel Hamilton's, and ordered to work George J. Baum and Jesse Jackson.

The road leading from Delphi to the "Old Trading-house," was divided into two districts. The First was assigned to William Hughes. His hands were Isaac Griffith, James Laughlin, Snelsam Anthony, —— Butler, Laren Shafer, William Craig, Jacob Baum, Robert Cade, John Adams, John Kistler, Elias Sowther, Thomas

Berry, Jacob Mitchell, Philip Rohrbaugh, John Rohrbaugh, Isaac Bozarth, Thomas King, James King, —— Justice.

Second District, Christopher M'Combs, Supervisor, to work the following hands: James Clark, John Mitchell, John Lemuel Marsh, John Swalls, Joseph Swalls, Lewis Neff, Aaron Hicks, Moses Scott, John Moyer, David Glasscock, David M'Combs, John Crook, William Sieres, Isam Adkinson, George Byers, Peter Black, Eli Cotner, Richard M'Griff, William Adkinson.

The road leading from Delphi to Logansport was divided this time into *three* districts. In the First, Joseph Dunham was appointed supervisor, to work the following hands: Enoch Cox, Aaron Dewey, William Wilson, John M'Millin, Joseph Holiday, George M'Millin, Thomas M'Millin, James Cannon, Isaac Jones, William M'Crery, Joseph M'Cain, Thomas R. M'Cain, Moses Thompson, Joseph Jackson, John Givins, Thomas Burk, Thomas Strain, and Ralph Wilson.

Second District, to James M'Dowell, with the following hands: John Mikesel, John Robins, Jacob Kuns, Ephraim Denison, John Kuns, David Myers, Aaron Merriman, Solomon Burket, Lewis Dubois, and —— Harmon.

Third District, to Daniel Kuns, with the following hands: Jacob Sager, Alexander Sieres, Henry Bingaman, John Scott, James Cummins, John Cummins, Alexander Cummins, William Hicks, Thomas Martindale, and Jacob Bingaman.

William George was appointed supervisor from Delphi to Tippecanoe County, to work the following hands: Daniel Baum, David Baum, Martin Thornberry, Jabob Stair, John M. Ewing, William M'Cord, Daniel F. Vandeventer, —— Lamb, Henry Sidenbender.

The bounty on a "full-grown" wolf-scalp, was fixed at fifty cents; under six months old, twenty-five cents.

Election for justice of the peace, ordered on first Monday of August, in Deer-creek.

Contract made with Aaron Dewey. The county sold him a brick-yard on the bank of Deer Creek, for which he was to pay twenty-five dollars a lot, in material for county building.

Isaac Griffith, John Robins, and Enoch Cox were licensed to vend foreign merchandise.

AUGUST SESSION, 1829.

Thomas Gillam, appointed supervisor of the road from Delphi to Gillam's; John Carey, of First District, of Bachelor's Run road; John Odell, of Second District, road from Delphi to forks of Deer Creek; Daniel M'Cain, Sr., of road from crossing of Deer Creek to Bachelor's Run.

William M'Crery was appointed agent of Carroll County; his bond was five thousand dollars; Isaac Griffith, security.

Permanent corners were ordered to be established as follows: At south-west corner of Public Square, also at south-east corner of Public Square. The former order was revoked.

The agent was ordered to perfect the contract made with William Wilson for exchange of ground for grave-yard; also to let out the contract for building the jail, the same to be let to contract October 1, 1829; the jail to be placed on lot No. 101, thirty feet from the front of said lot. The agent was directed to inspect donated lots and buildings thereon, and ascertain if those who have received donations have complied with the terms. The order donating lots to mechanics was revoked.

SPECIAL SESSION, SEPTEMBER 26, 1829.

Present, Jacob Baum, Thomas Stirlin. Mr. Stirlin was elected county commissioner at the August election, 1829, in place of Graham Roberts. The order for the erection of a jail was *partly* revoked.

SPECIAL SESSION, NOVEMBER 9, 1829.

PRESENT, Messrs. Baum, Hicks, and Stirlin.

William Hance, John Little, and David Baum were appointed to view a road from Delphi via south-east corner sec. 28, T. 25, R. 2 W.; thence to Odell's land, and to county line.

John M. Pinkston, Joseph Dunham, and John Gillam were appointed to view a road from one-half-mile stake, on State line, sec. 13, T. 24, R. 2 W.; thence to Wild-cat, between R. 1 and 2 W., "so as to intersect Milroy's '*blazes*,' leading from Delphi to Kirk's;" thence with said "*blazes*" to the county line.

J. H. and I. Martin were licensed to sell goods.

Thomas Martindale was appointed supervisor of the road leading from Delphi to Logansport, in the place of Daniel Kuns, deceased.

The clerk and recorder's office ordered to be built eighteen feet long by sixteen feet wide. The county agent was ordered to give notice of the letting of said building, to take place on the 21st of November, 1829.

Jonah T. Hopkinson was appointed constable of Deer-creek Township, and Isaac Griffith, Wm. George, Aaron Dewey, and Joseph Dunham, approved of as his sureties.

FEBRUARY SESSION, 1830.

PRESENT, Messrs. Baum, Stirlin, and Hicks.

Jonah T. Hopkinson appointed constable of Deer-creek, and John Knight and William M'Crery approved as his sureties.

Daniel Baum was reappointed treasurer; Gavin Black and Isaac Griffith, his sureties.

The following overseers of the poor were appointed: *Rock-creek*—Jacob Kuns, Eli Cotner; *Deer-creek*—John Knight, James Odell; *Tippecanoe*—Alexander Smith, Nathaniel Hamilton.

INSPECTORS.—*Deer-creek*—William George; *Rock-creek*—John Bozarth; *Tippecanoe*—Joshua Lindsey.

FENCE-VIEWERS.—*Deer-creek*—Joseph Dunham, John Knight, David Baum; *Rock-creek*—William Hicks, Thomas Martindale, David M'Combs; *Tippecanoe*—John E. Metcalf, Friend Johnson, Thomas Hamilton.

Moses Scott was appointed constable of Rock-creek.

On petition of Emanuel Flora, John Bozarth, Samuel Marsh, and Solomon Burket were appointed to view change of Logansport road, on land of petitioner.

Jesse Jackson, John Kistler, and William Hughes were appointed to view a road from Delphi via Forsythe's cabins, to the Tippecanoe County line, in the direction of Tippecanoe battle-ground.

William M'Crery was appointed county assessor.

Scott & M'Allister were allowed to establish a ferry across Wabash River, opposite Forsythe's cabins.

MAY SESSION, 1830.

PRESENT, Messrs. Baum, Hicks, and Stirlin.

J. H. & I. Martin and Isaac Griffith licensed to vend foreign merchandise.

Peter Harter asked a change in the road from Delphi to Wild-cat, on his land; and Samuel Wise, Peter Replogle, and Peter Imon were appointed to view the same.

John Bozarth was allowed, for crying the sales of lots in Delphi, three dollars.

John Lenon, George Julian, and William Hance were appointed to view road from Delphi to Michigan road.

Gavin Black appointed trustee of county seminary.

William George, Justice of the Peace, reported that he had assessed and collected the following fines: James Quick, profane swearing, $1; Thomas Ivers, assault, $1; Ephraim Denison, profane swearing, $1; William Craig, Sabbath-breaking, $1; Martin Thornberry, Sabbath-breaking, $1.

The following persons were appointed supervisors: Moses Alldridge, John Carey, William G. Bishop, Jeremiah Ballard, Thomas M'Millin, Isaac Martin, John Robbins, Aaron Merriman, Emanuel Flora, John Rohrbaugh, Lewis Neff, Sam'l Wells, John Odell, Wm. Hance.

Samuel D. Gresham was licensed to sell foreign and domestic groceries, and Robert Scott, Joseph Dunham, James H. Stewart, James Miller, and David Loucks were approved as his sureties.

William George was appointed to superintend the digging of a public well, fifty feet south of the center of the Public Square.

The county agent was ordered to have the lots that were sold to Aaron Dewey and Ralph Wilson, surveyed.

William M'Crery was allowed, for assessing the state and county revenue, ten dollars.

The clerk produced a set of scales and weights, which the Board established as the standard for the county.

William M'Crery was appointed collector for the county, and James Odell and Isaac Griffith approved as his sureties.

SPECIAL SESSION JULY, 13, 1830.

Present, Messrs. Baum and Stirlin.

Thomas Gillam was appointed commissioner to locate a state road from the point of intersection of the Newcastle and Michigan roads to Delphi, in the county of Carroll, to fill the vacancy occasioned by the resignation of Samuel Milroy.

AUGUST SESSION, 1830.

Present, Messrs. Baum and Stirlin.

Jackson Township was organized, and the place of holding elections fixed at the house of Enoch Alldridge. Election was ordered for a justice of the peace on the third Monday of October, and Moses Alldridge appointed inspector.

SPECIAL SESSION, SEPTEMBER 28, 1830.

Present, Jacob Baum and Alexander Smith.

Jacob Humerickhouse was appointed constable of Deer-creek Township.

NOVEMBER SESSION, 1830.

Present, Jacob Baum and Thomas Stirlin.

Morris & M'Carty licensed to vend foreign merchandise.

The following fines reported by justices: By Henry Robinson, against Lewis Dubois, for Sabbath-breaking, $1; by Isam Adkinson, against Stephen Wright, for assault and battery, $3; by William George, against Ephraim Denison, for assault and battery, $3; and John Dukes, for contempt, $1.

William Olinger was appointed constable of Rock-creek, and Christopher M'Combs approved as his surety.

The half-bushel measure made by William George, and branding-iron by Elias Lowther, were adopted, and one dollar paid for each.

The allowance of fifty cents for a wolf scalp was *revoked.*

Moses Standley was ordered to work all the hands from Alexander Sieres's up Rock Creek, and along the road to the county line.

The state road from Delphi to Frankfort was divided into two districts; Samuel Bugher was appointed supervisor of one, and Thomas Gillam of the other; to work all the hands in the Gillam settlement.

Christopher M'Combs, Aaron Hicks, and Lewis Neff were appointed trustees of school sec. 16, T. 26, R. 2 W.

James Alldridge was appointed constable of Jackson Township; Moses Alldridge and Elisha Brown, his sureties.

Oliver D. Butler appointed constable of Deer-creek; Jacob Humerickhouse and Thomas Pike, sureties.

The county agent was ordered to "lay off lots on the north side of the lots already laid off in the donation for the seat of justice for Carroll County, not to exceed in size one block of those already laid off, and make sale of the same at his discretion, with condition to the purchaser to clear off the lot or lots he may purchase, within six months.

A road was ordered to be located from Main Street, in Delphi, to the upper ford of the Wabash River through the lands of Samuel Milroy and James H. Stewart.

William George was appointed county treasurer, in the place of Daniel Baum, resigned; Samuel Milroy and James Odell approved of as his sureties.

"Ordered, that the jail built by Henry Robinson be received as finished, agreeably to contract."

FEBRUARY SESSION, 1831.

PRESENT, Thomas Stirlin, Thomas Hight, Samuel Williamson.

James H. Stewart, James Mark, and William M'Crery were appointed to view a road from John Wagoner's new saw-mill, on the north fork of Wild-cat, to Delphi.

The same viewers were appointed to view a road from the lane of the Widow Wagoner, by the way of Alexander Murphy's, to the Delphi and Frankfort state road, on the north side of Wild-cat Creek.

William Hopkins, Samuel Williams, and George Hornback were appointed trustees of schools, sec. 16, T. 25, R. 3 W.

John R. Merritt was licensed to keep a grocery in Tiptonsport.

James Alldridge, John Wagoner, and Alexander Murphy were appointed to view and locate a road from Wise's new saw-mill at the mouth of Bachelor's Run, thence the nearest and best route to John Wagoner's mill, on the north fork of Wild-cat.

James Alldridge was appointed Constable of Jackson Township; Moses Alldridge and Elisha Brown, sureties.

Robert D. Royster, Stephen A. Miller, and Robert Miller were appointed to alter the road from Delphi to Bachelor's Run.

Nathaniel Wilson was appointed to assess the revenue of Carroll County, "for the sum of eighteen dollars." Isaac Griffith and D. F. Vandeventer became his sureties.

John Carey, Stephen A. Miller, and Isaac Wilson were appointed to alter the road leading from Delphi to the second principal meridian.

Edward Cooley, appointed supervisor, District No 2, Frankfort road.

Clay Township was organized, and the place of holding elections fixed at the house of Jonathan Gillam; Albert G. Hanna, Inspector. Election ordered for second Monday in April.

William M'Crery was allowed, for taking the enumeration of the county, six dollars.

Election ordered in Tippecanoe Township for third Monday in March, for justice of the peace; John P. Smith, Inspector.

John M. Pinkston was allowed for six month's extra

services as sheriff, ten dollars, and James Miller, former sheriff, allowed three dollars.

Deer-creek Township.—James H. Stewart and Milton M. Morris were appointed fence-viewers; John Knight and James Odell, overseers of the poor; Oliver D. Butler, constable; and William M'Crevy, inspectors of elections.

Rock-creek Township.—William Olinger was appointed constable; Isam Adkinson, Aaron Hicks, overseers of the poor; Emanuel Flora, Lewis Neff, fence-viewers; Christopher M'Comb, inspector.

Jackson Township.—Moses Alldridge was appointed inspector; John Lenon and John Odell, overseers of the poor; George Julian and William Hance, fence-viewers.

Clay Township.—Thomas Gillam and Edward Cooley were appointed as overseers of the poor; John Wagoner and Jacob Sheagley, fence-viewers.

Tippecanoe Township.—Nathaniel Hamilton and Thomas Hamilton, overseers of the poor; D. F. Vandeventer and John E. Metcalf, fence-viewers.

William George was reappointed county treasurer; Samuel Milroy, James Odell, sureties.

SPECIAL SESSION, FEBRUARY 25, 1831.

PRESENT, Thomas Stirlin and Thomas Hight.

The county treasurer was enjoined not to pay any orders made for the payment of cost incurred in consequence of a special session of the Circuit Court, called on the 24th day of February, 1831, by John M. Pinkston, Sheriff of said County, for the trial of one James Clark.

MAY SESSION, 1831.

PRESENT, Messrs. Stirlin, Hight, and Williamson.

Aaron Dewey, Thomas Pike, and John E. Metcalf were appointed viewers to locate a road from north-west bank of the Wabash River, thence via Chabert's and Dunham's to the Tippecanoe County line.

Robert C. Gist licensed to vend foreign goods and merchandise.

Nathaniel Hamilton, John E. Metcalf, and Samuel A. Tomb were appointed to locate a road from Nathaniel Hamilton's to the Cass County line.

Eli Cotner, Solomon Burket, and Lewis Neff were appointed to view a cart-way from Samuel Williamson's mill via George Kuns's lane, to the Widow M'Combs's, on the Wabash River.

John Odell, Adam Porter, and William Armstrong were appointed to view road from sec. 16 (now Camden) to the Michigan road.

Aaron Gregg, John Robbins, and Joseph M'Cain, appointed to view change in Logansport road on the land of Jacob Kuns.

James H. Stewart and William M'Crery reported that they had located the two county roads ordered to be viewed by them, and the Board ordered said roads to be opened.

Nathaniel Wilson was appointed collector of the state and county revenue, and Ralph Wilson, Daniel F. Vandeventer, and Thomas Stirlin were approved as his sureties.

Commissioners' Districts.—All the territory north-west of the Wabash River, District No. 1. All territory lying south of the following line: beginning at the Wabash on section line, between 24 and 25, running east on said line to south-east of sec. 23, R. 2 W., thence north with the section line one mile, thence east to the county line, District No. 2. All territory lying north of above line, and east of the Wabash river, District No. 3.

Adams Township was organized.

Contract for the first Court-house let. Ordered that

the bid of Theophilus Hardman for the building of a new Court-house in the center of the Public Square in Delphi, be received, and that a contract be entered into for the completion of the same, agreeably to the exhibit marked "A," and the bond made by the said Hardman, Samuel Milroy, Thomas Pike, and James H. Stewart, and filed in the clerk's office, and the bond made by the said commissioners to the said Hardman and marked "Exhibit B."

AUGUST SESSION, 1831.

PRESENT, Thos. Stirlin, John P. Smith, John Lenon.

Elections in Rock-creek were ordered to be held at the house of John R. Merritt, in Tiptonsport; in Prairie Township, at the house of John Thompson.

Peter Dunkin was appointed supervisor of the road from John Carey's to Wise's. Elisha Brown was made supervisor in Jackson Township.

Isam Adkinson, James M'Dowell, and Jacob Baum, appointed viewers, to view and locate road from Delphi to intersect the road from Delphi to Logansport, below Tiptonsport.

David Motter was appointed supervisor of District No. 5, in Clay.

George Julian, John Armstrong, and John Kuns were appointed viewers, to run a road from Tiptonsport, thence via the settlement of Tindall, Brown, and Alldridge, on Robinson branch; thence to Wm. Hance's; thence to Levi Cline's; thence to the county road leading up Deer Creek.

Thomas Martindale and Samuel A. Tomb were appointed supervisors in Adams Township.

SEPTEMBER SESSION, 1831.

PRESENT, Messrs. Stirlin, Smith, and Lenon.

An election for justice of the peace was ordered in Rock-creek Township, on the first Saturday of October.

Charles Wright, George A. Spencer, and Samuel Alkire were appointed to view a road commencing at the south-east corner of south-west quarter, sec. 35, T. 25, R. 4 W.; thence to strike the old Indian trail at or near the north-east corner of T. 26, R. 4 W.

Thomas Stirlin, John Lenon, and Alexander Sieres, appointed to view road from James Young's, thence to the Cass County line.

John Dollason is recognized as the contractor for building the Court-house; he was allowed $275 out of the Donation Fund, and the county agent was ordered to make John Dollason a deed "for all the lots appraised in 'Exhibit E,' except lot 87, which was ordered to be made to Theophilus Hardman."

Isam Adkinson, James M'Dowell, and Cornelius Williams were appointed to view a road from Tiptonsport to Isaac Griffith's saw-mill.

Election ordered in T. 25, R. 1 W., at the house of George Julian, to ascertain the will of the majority as to selling the school section.

Election ordered at the house of Jacob Reigel in Adams Township, for election of justice of the peace.

John Dollason's bond, for building Court-house, accepted, and Hardman's securities released.

NOVEMBER SESSION, 1831.

PRESENT, Thos. Stirlin, John P. Smith, John Lenon.

Election ordered to be held at the house of John Berry, T. 25, R. 3 W., on the first Monday of December, to ascertain the sense of the qualified voters as to the sale of school section. Also, for T. 24, R. 2 W., at the house of Jonathan Gillam. Also, for T. 25, R. 2 W., at the house of Jacob Watson.

Philip Pollard licensed to sell foreign goods in Tiptonsport.

Samuel Alkire and Benjamin Reynolds appointed

supervisors of the road running from section thirty-five to the old Indian trail.

Thomas Smith, Matthew Borland, and Nathaniel Hamilton, appointed to locate a road from Tippecanoe County line, thence to intersect the Logansport state road, near the house of Thomas Smith.

Richard Chabert appointed constable of Tippecanoe Township; Samuel Williams and Daniel F. Vandeventer approved as his sureties.

John Ballard, William Hicks, and Daniel Neff, appointed to locate road from the point where the Logansport road leaves the line of Carroll County, thence to Conner's reserve.

James B. Larimer appointed constable of Deer-creek Township; Isaac Griffith and Aaron Dewey, sureties.

LIST OF COUNTY COMMISSIONERS,

GIVING THE SESSIONS THEY RESPECTIVELY SERVED.

May	Session,	1828...	Jacob Baum,	Aaron Hicks,	Graham Roberts.
May 15,		" ...	"	"	"
" 24,		" ...	"	"	"
June 14,		" ...	"	"	"
Aug. 11,		" ...	"	"	"
Nov.	Session,	" ...	Jacob Baum,	Aaron Hicks.	
Feb.	"	1829...	Jacob Baum,	Aaron Hicks,	Graham Roberts.
May	"	" ...	"	"	"
Aug.	"	" ...	Jacob Baum,	Aaron Hicks,	Thomas Stirlin.
Nov.	"	" ...	"	"	"
Feb.	"	1830...	"	"	"
May	"	" ...	"	"	"
Aug.	"	" ...	Jacob Baum,	Thomas Stirlin.	
Nov.	"	" ...	"	"	
Feb.	"	1831...	Thos. Stirlin,	Thos. Hight,	Sam. Williamson.
May	"	" ...	"	"	"
Aug.	"	" ...	Thos. Stirlin,	John P. Smith,	John Lenon.
Sept.	"	" ...	"	"	"
Nov.	"	" ...	"	"	"
Jan.	"	1832...	"	"	"
March	"	" ...	Thomas Stirlin,	John P. Smith.	
May	"	" ...	Thos. Stirlin,	John P. Smith,	John Lenon.
Sept.	"	" ...	"	"	"
Nov.	"	" ...	"	"	"
Jan.	"	1833...	"	"	"

March Session, 1833...Thos. Stirlin, John P. Smith, John Lenon.
May “ “ ... “ “ “
Sept. “ “ ... “ “ “
Nov. “ “ ...Thomas Stirlin, John P. Smith.
Jan. “ 1834...Thos. Stirlin, John P. Smith, John Lenon.
March “ “ ... “ “ “
May “ “ ... “ “ “
Sept. “ “ ...Thos. Stirlin, John Shanks, James M'Cully.
Nov. “ “ ... “ “ “
Jan. “ 1835...Thomas Stirlin, James M'Cully.
March “ “ ...Thos. Stirlin, John Shanks, James M'Cully.
May “ “ ... “ “ “
Sept. “ “ ...James M'Cully, Hugh Graham.
Nov. “ “ ...Jas. M'Cully, John Shanks, Hugh Graham.
Jan. “ 1836... “ “ “
March “ “ ... “ “ “
May “ “ ... “ “ “
June “ “ ... “ “ “
Sept. “ “ ...Hugh Graham, Wm. Hance, Jas. M'Cully.
Nov. “ “ ... “ “ “
Jan. “ 1837... “ “ “
March “ “ ... “ “ “
May “ “ ... “ “ “
Sept. “ “ ... “ “ “
Nov. “ “ ... “ “ “
Jan. “ 1838... “ “ “
March “ “ ... “ “ “
Sept. “ “ ... “ “ “
Oct. “ “ ...William Hance, James M'Cully.
Nov. “ “ ...Jas. M'Cully, Hugh Graham, Wm. Hance.
Jan. “ 1839... “ “ “
March “ “ ...James M'Cully, William Hance.
May “ “ ...Jas. M'Cully, Wm. Hance, Hugh Graham.
June “ “ ...James M'Cully, William Hance.
“ “ “ ... “ “
Sept. “ “ ...Jas. M'Cully, John Calvert, David Martin.
Nov. “ “ ... “ “ “
Jan. “ 1840... “ “ “
March “ “ ... “ “ “
May “ “ ... “ “ “
Sept. “ “ ...David Martin, John Calvert, Barney Davis.
Nov. “ “ ... “ “ “
Jan. “ 1841... “ “ “
March “ “ ... “ “ “
May “ “ ...David Martin, Barney Davis.
June “ “ ... “ “
Sept. “ “ ... “ “
March “ 1842... “ “
June “ “ ... “ “
Sept. “ “ ... “ “
Dec. “ “ ... “ “
March “ 1843... “ “

July	Session,	1843...	David Martin, Barney Davis.
Sept.	"	" ...	" "
Oct.	"	" ...	" "
Dec.	"	" ...	David Martin, Barney Davis, John Calvert.
Feb.	"	1844...	" "
March	"	" ...	David Martin, Barney Davis.
June	"	" ...	David Martin, Barney Davis, John Calvert.
July	"	" ...	David Martin, John Calvert.
Sept.	"	" ...	David Martin, Barney Davis, James Odell.
Dec.	"	" ...	" " "
March	"	1845...	" " "
June	"	" ...	" " "
Sept.	"	" ...	Barney Davis, James Odell, Wm. Hance.
Dec.	"	" ...	" " "
Jan.	"	1846...	" " "
March	"	" ...	" " "
June	"	" ...	William Hance, Miles F. Austin.
Sept.	"	" ...	James Odell, William Hance, John Crowel.
"	"	" ...	William Hance, John Crowel.
Oct.	"	" ...	James Odell, William Hance.
Nov.	"	" ...	Wm. Hance, James Odell, John Crowel.
Dec.	"	" ...	" " "
March	"	1847...	" " "
June	"	" ...	" " "
Sept.	"	" ...	Wm. Hance, John Crowel, Matthew Brown.
Nov.	"	" ...	" " "
Dec.	"	" ...	" " "
March	"	1848...	" " "
June	"	" ...	" " "
Sept.	"	" ...	" " "
Dec.	"	" ...	William Hance, Matthew Brown.
March	"	1849...	Wm. Hance, John Crowel, Matthew Brown.
June	"	" ...	" " "
Aug.	"	" ...	" " "
Sept.	"	" ...	" " "
Dec.	"	" ...	" " "
March	"	1850...	" " "
June	"	" ...	" " "
Sept.	"	" ...	Wm. Hance, John Crowel, David Crocket.
March	"	1851...	William Hance, John Crowel.
June	"	" ...	John Crowel, David Crocket.
"	"	" ...	William Hance, John Crôwel.
Sept.	"	" ...	John Crowel, David Crocket, Aaron Gregg.
"	"	" ...	" " "
Dec.	"	" ...	" " "
Feb.	"	1852...	John Crowel, Aaron Gregg.
June	"	" ...	John Crowel, Aaron Gregg, David Crocket.
Sept.	"	" ...	" " "
"	"	" ...	John Crowel, Aaron Gregg.
Dec.	"	" ...	" "
March	"	1853...	John Crowel, James Odell, Aaron Gregg.
June	"	" ...	" " "

Sept. Session, 1853...John Crowel, James Odell, Aaron Gregg.
Dec. " " ...John Crowel, Aaron Gregg, Theo. Smoyer.
March " 1854... " " "
June " " ... " " "
Sept. " " ... " " "
Dec. " " ...Jno. Crowel, Theo. Smoyer, Thos. C. Hughes.
Feb. " 1855... " " "
March " " ... " " "
June " " ... " " "
Sept. " " ... " " "
Dec. " " ... " " "
March " 1856... " " "
April " " ... " " "
June " " ... " " "
Aug. " " ... " " "
Sept. " " ... " " "
Dec. " " ...John Crowel, Thos. C. Hughes, Uriah Blue.
March " 1857... " " "
June " " ... " " "
July " " ...John Crowell, Thomas C. Hughes.
Sept. " " ...John Crowel, Thos. C. Hughes, UriahBlue.
Dec. " " ...John Crowel, Uriah Blue, William Crooks.
Jan. " 1858... " " "
March " " ... " " "
June " " ... " " "
Sept. " " ... " " "
Nov. " " ...Uriah Blue, Wm. Crooks, Wm. Love.
Dec. " " ... " " "
Jan. " 1859... " " "
March " " ... " " "

CHAPTER XVII.

CIRCUIT COURT.

ON the 8th day of May, 1828, a term of the *Carroll Circuit Court* was held at the house of Daniel Baum. The president judge, Bethuel F. Morris, presented his commission as judge of the Fifth Judicial Circuit, dated January 20, 1825, signed by William Hendricks, Governor; William W. Wick, Secretary of State. Oath of office administered by Isaac Blackford.

Henry B. Milroy produced his commission as sheriff, signed by Governor "J. Brown Ray." Oath of office administered by Reuben Kelsey, a justice of the peace of Tippecanoe County.

Daniel F. Vandeventer produced his commission as clerk of the Circuit Court, for the term of seven years, from the date of said commission. Dated May 8, 1828. Oath of office administered by Judge Morris.

The clerk filed his bond in the penalty of twenty-five hundred dollars. Daniel Baum and George I. Baum, sureties; Aaron Dewey and William Wilson, witnesses.

Isaac Griffith and Christopher M'Combs produced their commissions as associate judges, dated May 8, 1828. Oath of office administered, May 9th, by Judge Morris. Messrs. Griffith and M'Combs took their seats as associate judges.

James Rariden, Septimius Smith, William Quarles, and Andrew Ingram, were admitted to practice as attorneys.

Jacob Kuns, by James Rariden, his attorney, filed petition to be appointed guardian of Rosanna Heistand,

CARROLL COUNTY COURT-HOUSE,

DELPHI, INDIANA.

also his bond, signed by Samuel Milroy, William Wilson, and Daniel Baum.

After adopting a seal, which was ordered to be a "*circular scroll with the words 'Carroll County seal' inserted therein*," the Court adjourned until regular Court term.

At the May session, 1828, of the Board of Commissioners, the following persons were chosen as grand jurors for the November term, 1828, of the Circuit Court: Benjamin Baxter, Robert Cade, John Ballard, Moses Thompson, Joseph M'Cain, Thomas Stirlin, David Harter, James Clark, Jacob Baum, Christian Simons, Alexander Sieres, William Cummins, John Mitchell, David Hamilton, John Scott, Richard Chabert, Jacob Sager, William Sieres.

And at the same time the following grand jurors were selected for the May term, 1829, of the Circuit Court: John Mitchell, Daniel Kuns, Stephen Miller, Daniel M'Cain; 2d, Ira Bacon, Joseph Beckner, Lewis Neff, John Bozarth, John E. Metcalf, Daniel M'Cain, Hugh B. M'Keen, John Odell, John Carey, John Little, George I. Baum, Thomas Burk, George Moyer, John Moyer.

The following persons were selected as petit jurors for the November term, 1828: Alexander Scott, Eli Cotner, Isaac Martin, William M'Cord, Thomas R. M'Cain, John Hall, Nathaniel Hamilton, Moses Alldridge, Samuel Wells, James Odell, David Baum, Jeremiah Ballard, Manuel M'Combs, Joseph Jackson, David Lucas, Moses Standley, James Miller, Daniel Bell, Graham Roberts, William Hughes, Aaron Dewey, Jacob Cluster, Daniel Baum, Henry Bingaman.

The following persons were at the same time chosen as petit jurors for the May term, 1829: John Phillips, James Cummins, Samuel Wise, John Adams, John Chilson, John Kistler, Samuel Milroy, Martin Kee, Elisha

Brown, James Hood, Jacob Kuns, Jacob Woodcock, Lemuel Marsh, Aaron Hicks, James M'Cain, William Wilson, John Kuns, Nathan Rose, Frederick Hoover, William G. Bishop, Alexander Chamberlain, John Givins, Aaron Merriman, James M'Dowell.

NOVEMBER TERM, 1828.

A TERM of the Circuit Court was commenced at the house of Daniel Baum, on the 6th day of November, 1828.

Two judgments for debt were entered.

There appearing no business for the grand jury, it was discharged.

Joseph Tatman was admitted to practice law.

Court adjourned on the same day.

MAY TERM, 1829.

COURT met at the house of Daniel Baum, on the 18th day of May, 1829. Judge Morris, President Judge, and Isaac Griffith and Christopher M'Combs, present.

Grand jury impaneled; John Carey, Foreman. All the grand jurors not appearing, the following bystanders were selected to fill up the jury: Thomas M'Millin, William Hughes, and John Knight.

Andrew Ingram was appointed and sworn as prosecuting attorney.

Moses Cox was admitted to practice law.

One judgment for debt entered.

Court adjourned after morning session, "to meet at the school-house in the town of Delphi, at 4 o'clock P. M."

Afternoon session met at the school-house in Delphi.

Albert S. White and Cyrus Ball were admitted as attorneys-at-law.

Second day.—The grand jury returned six indictments for affray, six for assault and battery, and two for fornication. Court adjourned.

Selection of Jurors.—The Board of Commissioners at the May session, 1829, chose the following grand jurors for the November term, 1829: William G. Bishop, Joseph Beckner, Joseph M'Cain, Robert Cade, Samuel Wells, John Givins, John Odell, Samuel Wise, James Laughlin, Nath. Hamilton, John Little, James M'Dowell, John Phillips, Philip Hewitt, Samuel Milroy, Jacob Cluster, Jacob Baum, Aaron Merriman.

The Board selected grand jurors for May term, 1830, as follows: Daniel M'Cain, 2d, Jacob Kuns, James M'Cain, Moses Standley, Thomas R. M'Cain, Lewis Neff, John Mikesel, William M'Cord, Thomas Gillam, Benjamin Baxter, Thomas Stirlin, William Hance, John Bozarth, Eli Cotner, James Odell, Simon Marsh.

Petit Jurors for November Term, 1829.—James Hamilton, Joseph Dunham, John Mitchell, Daniel Lenon, John Moyer, Daniel M'Cain, James Cummins, William Sieres, William Hughes, John Rieul, John Gillam, John E. Metcalf, Elisha Brown, Henry Bingaman, John Crook, John Briggs, Aaron Dewey, Jesse Jackson, Samuel Williams, George I. Baum, Stephen Miller, William Hicks, Joseph Jackson.

Petit Jurors for May Term, 1830.—David Harter, John Robbins, Thomas Hamilton, William M'Cain, William George, Henry Baum, Martin Thornberry, John M'Millin, Jacob Zook, William Odell, William Wilson, Henry Sidenbender, John Carey, James Miller, Graham Roberts, Moses Alldridge, Jeremiah Ballard, David Motter, Alexander Smith, James Hood, David Baum, Moses Scott, Coleman Robinson, John Kuns.

NOVEMBER TERM, 1829.

PRESENT, Hon. B. F. Morris, President Judge, and Isaac Griffith and Christopher M'Combs, Associate Judges.

Calvin Fletcher, William W. Wick, Benjamin Hurst,

Aaron Finch, John B. Chapman, and Thomas J. Evans were admitted to practice law.

William W. Wick produced his commission as prosecuting attorney.

The various indictments found at last term were tried.

In the case of James Burnet against John Davis and Nancy, his wife, and Rebecca Burnet, for partition of land—Evans, attorney for plaintiff—the Court appointed Samuel Milroy, Aaron Dewey, and Daniel F. Vandeventer as commissioners to make partition.

The grand jury returned four indictments for assault and battery, and two for affray.

After allowing Jonah T. Hopkinson $1.50 for services as bailiff, the Court adjourned, after a session of two days.

APRIL TERM, 1830.

John R. Porter, President Judge; the same associates as last term.

Thomas Stirlin, Foreman of the Grand Jury.

William M. Jenners and Thomas B. Brown admitted as attorneys.

Edward A. Hannegan, Prosecuting Attorney.

Jurors.—At the May session, 1830, the Board of Commissioners selected the jurors as follows:

Grand Jurors, October Term, 1830.—Isaac Martin, Emanuel Flora, Joseph Pogue, David Harter, David Hamilton, Samuel Williamson, George Julian, Robert Gillam, Aaron Hicks, Ziba Holt, Andrew Burntrager, Jacob Stair, Jacob Humerickhouse, Jonathan Gillam, John M. Ewing, James B. Larimer, Jedediah Johnson, and Thomas Martindale.

Grand Jurors, April Term, 1831.—William Cox, Eleazer Gray, John Huff, James Hamilton, John Adams, William G. Bishop, Frederick Hoover, Anthony Gamlin, Jacob Kuns, Isaac Bozarth, Edward Cooley, Elisha Brown, Hugh Graham, Andrew Wood, Benjamin Greathouse, Abner Reed, Solomon Burkit, William Davis.

Petit Jurors for October Term, 1830.—Samuel Key, William Cannon, Nicholas Garst, Moses Standley, John Kistler, Joshua Whitcher, Jonathan Justice, William Craig, William Olinger, Alexander Branderman, Nathan Tindall, John Smith, Jr., David Loucks, Thomas Hight, Aaron Dewey, Thomas M'Millin, John Beckner, Christian Olinger, Ralph P. Wilson, Samuel E. Carpenter, Abraham Deel, Levi Dix, William Hughes, William Wilkinson.

Petit Jurors for April Term, 1831.—William Bugher, Joseph James, James King, Daniel Leslie, Enoch Alldridge, Joseph A. Williamson, Joel M'Clelland, John Dollason, John S. Williamson, Elias Dorning, Jonas Hatfield, Simon Moyers, George C. Sanderson, John Flora, David Motter, John Allen, Samuel T. Williamson, Reuben G. Munday, Abraham Hornback, Peter Repplogel, James M'Dowell, Titus B. Willard, Jacob Wilkinson, Richard M'Griff.

OCTOBER TERM, 1830.

PRESENT, Hon. John R. Porter, President Judge, and the same associates.

John M. Pinkston, Sheriff; Elisha Warden, Bailiff; Ziba Holt, Foreman of the Grand Jury.

But two indictments found, one of which was against Presley Dollason, Samuel Motter, Jesse Fleming, Lewis Dubois, and Ralph Wilson, for riot.

Adjourned after a session of three days.

SPECIAL TERM, DECEMBER 1, 1830.

PRESENT, Judges Griffith and M'Combs.

The Court, having learned that there were two vacancies in the Board of Commissioners, appointed Samuel Williamson and Thomas Hight to fill said vacancies.

APRIL TERM, 1839.

PRESENT, John R. Porter, President Judge, and the same associates.

John M. Pinkston, Sheriff; James H. Stewart, Foreman of the Grand Jury; and Jacob Humerickhouse, Bailiff.

E. A. Hannegan, Prosecuting Attorney.

Henry Cooper, admitted as attorney-at-law.

Daniel Baum, Thomas Hight, and Samuel Williamson, appointed to review a proposed change in the road from Delphi to the Michigan road, near Kirk's.

SELECTION OF JURORS.—At the May session, 1831, the Board of Commissioners made the following selection of jurors:

Grand Jurors for October Term, 1831.—John P. Smith, James Brown, Amos Ball, Harvey Ward, Joshua Lister, Samuel Milroy, Thomas M. Curry, Uriah Bell, William Lowe, Joseph Beckner, Samuel Daniels, Enoch Cox, John Berry, Mahlon Frasier, John Adair, Elijah Wolf, Gavin Black, William Adkinson.

Petit Jurors for October Term, 1831.—Joseph Alldridge, Jacob Sheagley, Jacob Bross, Christ Vandeventer, Joseph Neff, Joseph Wood, Samuel Hulry, Enos Isaacs, John Enoch, John Stowell, Michael Burkit, Robert Dunlap, Malachi Prevo, Isam Adkinson, William Conklin, Reuben Thayer, Joseph G. Glass, Joel Fouts, John Armstrong, James Alldridge, Jacob Watson, Friend Johnson, —— Bantney, John Wagoner.

Grand Jurors for April Term, 1832.—Milton M. Morris, Robert Scott, Thomas Martindale, Lewis Johnson, Albert G. Hanna, John M. Gillam, Levi Cline, Aaron Merriman, Aaron Gregg, William Hicks, John Rohrbaugh, John Verneman, David Baum, Robert Larimer, Nathaniel Hamilton, John Lynch, David M'Combs, John Flora.

Petit Jurors for April Term, 1832.—Thomas Pike, Absalom Carney, John Mills, James Young, William Armstrong, Samuel Earnest, Jacob Reigel, John E. Metcalf, Jonah T. Hopkinson, Alexander Galloway, John Shanks, John Givins, Buckner Southworth, George Cline, Robert Newell, John B. Olinger, Taylor Sturgeon, Moses M'Elheny, Abner Robinson, Richard Chabert, William Smith, Elisha Nichols, Chas. Berkshire, Joseph Studybaker.

OCTOBER TERM, 1831.

PRESENT, John R. Porter, President Judge, and Griffith and M'Combs, Associates.

John M. Pinkston, Sheriff; Reuben Thayer, Foreman of the Grand Jury; and John Dollason, Bailiff.

John Pettit, on motion of A. S. White, was admitted to practice as an attorney-at-law.

The first bastardy case (State *vs.* Andrew Motter) was tried this term. The defendant was ordered to pay one hundred and fifty dollars.

LIST OF JUDGES

Who have presided in the Carroll Circuit Court from the organization of the county until the year 1860.

May Term, 1828...B. F. Morris, Presiding Judge; Isaac Griffith, C. M'Combs, Associate Judges.
Nov. " " ...Isaac Griffith, C. M Combs, Associate Judges.
May " 1829...B. F. Morris, Presiding Judge; Isaac Griffith, C. M'Combs, Associate Judges.
Nov. " " ...B. F. Morris, Presiding Judge; Isaac Griffith, C. M'Combs, Associate Judges.
April " 1830...John R. Porter, Presiding Judge; Isaac Griffith, C. M'Combs, Associate Judges.
Oct. " " ...John R. Porter, Presiding Judge; Isaac Griffith, C. M'Combs, Associate Judges.
April " 1831...John R. Porter, Presiding Judge; Isaac Griffith, C. M'Combs, Associate Judges.
Oct. " " ...John R. Porter, Presiding Judge; Isaac Griffith, C. M'Combs, Associate Judges.
April " 1832...John R. Porter, Presiding Judge; Isaac Griffith, C. M'Combs, Associate Judges.

Oct. Term, 1832....John R. Porter, Presiding Judge; Isaac Griffith, C. M'Combs, Associate Judges.

April " 1833...Gustavus A. Everts, Presiding Judge; Isaac Griffith, C. M'Combs, Associate Judges.

Oct. " " ....Gustavus A. Everts, Presiding Judge; Isaac Griffith, C. M'Combs, Associate Judges.

April " 1834...Isaac Griffith, C. M'Combs, Associate Judges.

Oct. " " ....Isaac Griffith, C. M'Combs, Associate Judges.

April " 1835...John R. Porter, Presiding Judge.

June " " ...George C. Sanderson, Lewis Johnson, Associate Judges.

Oct. " " ...George C. Sanderson, Lewis Johnson, Associate Judges.

April " 1836....John R. Porter, Presiding Judge; George C. Sanderson, Lewis Johnson, Associate Judges.

Oct. " " ...John R. Porter, Presiding Judge; George C. Sanderson, Lewis Johnson, Associate Judges.

April " 1837...John R. Porter, Presiding Judge; George C. Sanderson, Lewis Johnson, Associate Judges.

Oct. " " ...John R. Porter, Presiding Judge; George C. Sanderson, John Irwin, Associate Judges.

April " 1838...Isaac Naylor, Presiding Judge; George C. Sanderson, John Irwin, Associate Judges.

Nov. " " ....Isaac Naylor, Presiding Judge; George C. Sanderson, John Irwin, Associate Judges.

April " 1839...Isaac Naylor, Presiding Judge; George C. Sanderson, John Irwin, Associate Judges.

Oct. " " ...Isaac Naylor, Presiding Judge; George C. Sanderson, John Irwin, Associate Judges.

June " 1840...John W. Wright, Presiding Judge; George C. Sanderson, John Irwin, Associate Judges.

Dec. " " ...John W. Wright, Presiding Judge; George C. Sanderson, John Irwin, Associate Judges.

April " 1841....Isaac Naylor, Presiding Judge; George C. Sanderson, John Irwin, Associate Judges.

Oct. " " ....Isaac Naylor, Presiding Judge; George C. Sanderson, John Irwin, Associate Judges.

May " 1842...John W. Wright, Presiding Judge; George C. Sanderson, John Irwin, Associate Judges.

Oct. " " ....John W. Wright, Presiding Judge; John Irwin, Associate Judge.

April " 1843...John W. Wright, Presiding Judge; George C. Sanderson, John Irwin, Associate Judges.

Oct. " " ...John W. Wright, Presiding Judge; George C. Sanderson, John Irwin, Associate Judges.

April " 1844...John W. Wright, Presiding Judge; George C. Sanderson, John Irwin, Associate Judges.

Oct. " " ...John W. Wright, Presiding Judge; George C. Sanderson, John Irwin, Associate Judges.

April Term, 1845...John W. Wright, Presiding Judge; George C. Sanderson, John Irwin, Associate Judges.

Oct. " " ...John W. Wright, Presiding Judge; George C. Sanderson, John Irwin, Associate Judges.

April " 1846...John W. Wright, Presiding Judge; George C. Sanderson, John Irwin, Associate Judges.

Sept. " " ...John W. Wright, Presiding Judge; George C. Sanderson, John Irwin, Associate Judges.

Oct. " " .. John W. Wright, Presiding Judge; George C. Sanderson, John Irwin, Associate Judges.

April " 1847...Horace P. Biddle, Presiding Judge; George C. Sanderson, John Irwin, Associate Judges.

Oct. " " ...Horace P. Biddle, Presiding Judge; George C. Sanderson, John Irwin, Associate Judges.

April " 1848...Horace P. Biddle, Presiding Judge; George C. Sanderson, John Irwin, Associate Judges.

Oct. " " ...Horace P. Biddle, Presiding Judge; George C. Sanderson, John Irwin, Associate Judges.

April " 1849...Horace P. Biddle, Presiding Judge; George C. Sanderson, John Irwin, Associate Judges.

Oct. " " ...Horace P. Biddle, Presiding Judge; George C. Sanderson, David Martin, Associate Judges.

April " 1850...Horace P. Biddle, Presiding Judge; George C. Sanderson, David Martin, Associate Judges.

Oct. " " ...George C. Sanderson, David Martin, Associate Judges.

May " 1851...Horace P. Biddle, Presiding Judge; George C. Sanderson, David Martin, Associate Judges.

Nov. " " Horace P. Biddle, Presiding Judge, new Constitution.

Feb. " 1852...Horace P. Biddle, Presiding Judge.

Aug. " " ...Robert H. Milroy, "

May " 1853.. John Upfold Pettit, "

Oct. " " ... " "

May " 1854... " "

Oct. " " ...John M. Wallace, "

May " 1855... " "

Nov. " " ... " "

May " 1856... " "

Nov. " " ... " "

May " 1857... " "

Nov. " " ... " "

May " 1858... " "

Nov. " " ...Jonathan C. Applegate, Judge P. T.

May " 1859...John M. Wallace, Presiding Judge.

Nov. " " ... " "

Feb. " 1860... " "

May " " ...Henry S. Kelly, Judge P. T.

Nov. " " ...Horace P. Biddle, Presiding Judge.

Probate Court.

MAY TERM, 1829.

Probate Court, for the settlement of decedent estates, met on the 11th day of May, 1829, at the house of Daniel Baum.

Present, Isaac Griffith and Christopher M'Combs.

The Court approved of the grant of letters of administration to Francis Godfrey, on the estate of Francis La Fountain. Also, of letters to Elizabeth M'Combs, on the estate of Manuel M'Combs.

John Odell was appointed guardian of the minor children of Benjamin D. Angell.

NOVEMBER TERM, 1829.

The Court met in the public-school room in Delphi. John Carey produced his commission as judge of the Probate Court, signed by Governor Ray, to serve seven years, dated August 13, 1829. Oath of office administered by Isaac Griffith, Associate Judge.

The probate seal was adopted.

Samuel Hulry was appointed administrator of Jacob Bross, deceased.

JANUARY TERM, 1830.

John Carey, Presiding Judge, present.

William M'Crery, John Knight, and Jonah T. Hopkinson were appointed "to value a certain part of the real estate of Benjamin D. Angell, deceased."

John Kuns was appointed executor of the estate of Daniel Kuns, deceased.

Samuel Hulry was appointed guardian of the minor children of Jacob Bross, deceased.

MARCH TERM, 1830.

John Carey, Presiding Judge, present.

William M'Crery, and Thomas Stirlin were appointed executors of the last will and testament of William Wilson, deceased.

William M'Cord and William George were appointed administrators of the estate of Hugh Manary.

John Odell was appointed commissioner to make deeds to Samuel Milroy and Henry Robinson for part of the land belonging to the estate of Benjamin D. Angell, deceased.

MAY TERM, 1830.

JUDGE CAREY present. No business transacted.

SEPTEMBER TERM, 1830.

JUDGE CAREY present. No business transacted.

NOVEMBER TERM, 1830.

JUDGE CAREY present. Met at the clerk's office.

James M'Dowell was appointed guardian of George Atkins.

The executors of William Wilson were ordered to make a deed to Andrew Dye for the property purchased of Joseph Dunham. Also to make a deed to the agent of the town of Delphi for the grave-yard lot.

Catherine Silvers was appointed executrix of the estate of Ephraim Silvers, deceased.

JANUARY TERM, 1831.

JUDGE CAREY present.

Mrs. Elizabeth M'Combs, administratrix of Manuel M'Combs, made final settlement.

Ralph Wilson, of Vermilion County, was appointed guardian of the minor heirs of William Wilson.

Christopher M'Combs was appointed guardian of the minor heirs of Manuel M'Combs.

Elizabeth Manary was appointed guardian of the

minor heirs of Hugh Manary, deceased, to wit: Hugh, Cynthia, Charlotte, Richard, Eleanor, and Charles.

Alexander Coen was appointed guardian of Willis Gideon.

Letters granted in vacation to David Harter and Margaret Hewitt, on the estate of Philip Hewitt, approved.

MARCH TERM 1831.

JUDGE CAREY present.

John Kuns, executor of the estate of Daniel Kuns, made final settlement. Also Samuel Hulry, administrator of the estate of Jacob Bross.

Aaron Dewey, Thomas Gillam, and John Armstrong, were appointed commissioners to make partition of the real estate of Manuel M'Combs.

MAY TERM, 1831.

JUDGE CAREY present.

The executors of the estate of William Wilson were ordered to make a deed for twenty acres of land off the south-west side of E. $\frac{1}{2}$ of N. W. qr. of sec. 29, T. 25, R. 2 W., to William M'Crery, agent of Carroll County, "in consideration of the county-seat of said county being placed thereon."

John Dubois was appointed guardian of Walter Wright.

JULY TERM, 1831.

JUDGE CAREY present.

A citation ordered against a guardian, was all the business transacted.

SEPTEMBER TERM, 1831.

JUDGE CAREY present.

The letters of administration issued to James H. Stewart and Robert C. Gist, in the estate of Joseph G. Glass, confirmed.

William M'Crery and Thomas Stirlin, executors of the estate of William Wilson, were discharged.

William George and William M'Cord, administrators of the estate of Hugh Manary, were discharged.

NOVEMBER TERM, 1831.

JUDGE CAREY present.

Joshua Lindsey was appointed guardian of John and Graham J. Roberts, minor sons of Graham Roberts, deceased.

The administrators of the estate of Joseph G. Glass, were ordered to give notice to creditors in the *Cass County Times*.

PROBATE AND COMMON PLEAS JUDGES.

JOHN CAREY served as probate judge from the November term, 1829, until the end of the August term, 1836.

JOHN GRANTHAM was elected probate judge at the August election, 1836, and served until the end of the August term, 1850.

THOMAS GILLAM served from the November term, 1850, until the August term, 1852.

JOHN W. BLAKE served as common pleas judge from the January term, 1853, until the end of June term, 1856.

ROBERT P. DAVIDSON served September term, 1856.

JONATHAN C. APPLEGATE served as common pleas judge from the December term, 1856, until the end of September term, 1860.

GUSTAVUS A. WOOD commenced his services at the January term, 1861, as common pleas judge.

CHAPTER XVIII.

Benevolent Institutions.

MOUNT OLIVE LODGE, NO. 48, FREE AND ACCEPTED MASONS.

ON the 17th day of May, 1842, a meeting was held at the sheriff's office, to take the initiatory steps to open a lodge. Samuel Milroy, Daniel L. Shoup, Daniel F. Vandeventer, Alexander M. Berry, and Richard Richardson were present. A petition was prepared and signed by the above brethren, and William Sill and Hiram Allen asked for a charter from the Grand Lodge of Indiana. Alexander M. Berry was recommended for W. M., Samuel Milroy, S. W., and Daniel L. Shoup, J. W.

The petition was indorsed, May 21, 1842, by Tipton Lodge, No. 33, Logansport, A dispensation was granted by the Grand Lodge, which is signed by Philip Mason, Grand Master, attested by William H. Martin, Grand Secretary, dated May 24, 1842; the new Lodge to be designated "St. John's Lodge."

June 13, 1842.—The following brethren were elected officers of the Lodge: Alexander M. Berry, W. M.; Samuel Milroy, S. W.; Daniel L. Shoup, J. W.; Hiram Allen, S.; George M. Maxwell, Treasurer; Richard Richardson, S. D.; David W. Bowen, J. D.; Francis G. Kendall, Tyler.

On the 10th day of November, 1842, the following officers were installed: Alexander M. Berry, W. M.; Henry B. Milroy, S. W.; Daniel L. Shoup, J. W.; James Witherow, Treasurer; Robert C. Green, S.; George M.

Maxwell, S. D.; David W. Bowen, J. D.; William H. Buford, Tyler.

May 25, 1843, the Grand Lodge granted a charter for said Lodge, under the name of "Mount Olive Lodge, No. 48."

June 8, 1843.—The following officers were elected: George M. Maxwell, W. M.; Henry B. Milroy, S. W.; Enoch Rinehart, J. W.; Robert C. Green, S.; James Witherow, Treasurer; Alexander M. Berry, S. D.; David W. Bowen, J. D.; William H. Buford, Tyler; Jacob Linkhauer, A. H. Bowen, Stewards.

November 30, 1843.—Officers elected: James Witherow, W. M.; Henry B. Milroy, S. W.; Abner H. Bowen, J. W.; Robert C. Green, S.; Henry R. Glazier, Treasurer; William H. Buford, S. D.; Benjamin Barnhiser, J. D.; Thomas C. Hughes, Tyler; George M. Maxwell, A. M. Berry, Stewards.

May 30, 1844.—George M. Maxwell, W. M.; Alexander M. Berry, S. W.; A. H. Bowen, J. W.; James Witherow, Treasurer; Enoch Rinehart, S.; William H. Buford, S. D.; Thomas C. Hughes, J. D.; Theodore Armitage, Tyler.

The following have held the office of W. M.:

December, 1844......................Daniel L. Shoup, W. M.
June, 1845..............................Daniel L. Shoup, W. M.
December, 1845......................Hiram Allen, W. M.
June, 1846..............................Abner H. Bowen, W. M.
November, 1846......................Abner H. Bowen, W. M.
May, 1847..............................Abner H. Bowen, W. M.
December, 1847......................Abner H. Bowen, W. M.
May, 1848..............................Abner H. Bowen, W. M.
December, 1848......................Abner H. Bowen, W. M.
May, 1849..............................Miles M. Nichols, W. M.
November, 1849......................Miles M. Nichols, W. M.
June, 1850..............................Abner H. Bowen, W. M.
December, 1850......................Miles M. Nichols, W. M.
June, 1851..............................Enoch Stansel, W. M.
May, 1852..............................David I. Jackson, W. M.
May, 1853..............................Abner H. Bowen, W. M.
June, 1854..............................Thomas C. Hughes, W. M.
May, 1855..............................David Leonard, W. M.

June, 1856..........................John M. Bowman, W. M.
June, 1857..........................Jonathan C. Applegate, W. M.
May, 1858..........................Abner H. Bowen, W. M.
June, 1859..........................Abner H. Bowen, W. M.
May, 1860..........................Milton R. Graham, W. M.
May, 1861..........................Abner H. Bowen, W. M.
June, 1862..........................Edward Walker, W. M.
June, 1863..........................John A. Cartwright, W. M.
June, 1864..........................John A. Cartwright, W. M.
June, 1865..........................John T. Richardson, W. M.
June, 1866..........................John T. Richardson, W. M.
June, 1867..........................Abner H. Bowen, W. M.
June, 1868..........................Milton R. Graham, W. M.
June, 1869..........................Jehu C. Hannam, W. M.
December, 1870....................Jehu C. Hannam, W. M.
December, 1871....................John T. Richardson, W. M.

ADVANCE LODGE, NO. 220, F. AND A. M.

On the 7th day of January, 1858, Solomon D. Bayliss, Master of the M. W. Grand Lodge of Indiana, granted a dispensation for "Advance Lodge, No. 220," and appointed Bernard F. Schermerhorn, W. M.; Anthony Garrett, S. W.; and George Robertson, J. W.

On the 9th day of January, 1858, the Lodge met. The following appointments were made: James P. Dugan, Treasurer; Enoch Rinehart, Secretary; A. L. Benham, S. D.; Henry M. Wright, J. D.; David Wingard, Tyler.

June 11, 1858.—Officers elected: B. F. Schermerhorn, W. M.; Anthony Garrett, S. W.; George Robertson, J. W.; Attalas L. Benham, S. D.; Richard L. Higgenbotham, J. D.; Enoch Rinehart, Secretary; James P. Dugan, Treasurer; D. W. C. Frisbie and Hiram Allen, Stewards.

June 10, 1859.—Officers elected: Bernard F. Schermerhorn, W. M.; Anthony Garrett, S. W.; George Robertson, J. W.; Richard L. Higgenbotham, S. D.; Wm. Kelly, J. D.; A. L. Benham, Secretary; James P. Dugan, Treasurer; Walter Beach and Henry M. Wright, Stewards; John M. Grant, Tyler.

June 22, 1860.—Officers elected: Bernard F. Schermerhorn, W. M.; Henry M. Wright, S. W.; Walter Beach, J. W.; James P. Dugan, Treasurer; Attalas L. Benham, Secretary; Richard L. Higgenbotham, S. D.; George Robertson, J. D.; Nathaniel Black and James H. Stewart, Stewards.

June 21, 1861.—Officers elected: Bernard F. Schermerhorn, W. M.; Enoch Rinehart, S. W.; D. W. C. Frisbie, J. W.; Richard L. Higgenbotham, S. D.; George Robertson, J. D.; James P. Dugan, Treasurer; James H. Stewart, Secretary; Hugh Shields and Oliver Guthrie, Stewards; Jonathan L. Knight, Tyler.

April 25, 1862, Richard L. Higgenbotham was elected W. M. June 3, 1865, B. F. Schermerhorn elected W. M. June 23, 1866, Walter Beach elected W. M.; resigned July, 1866. June 14, 1867, Charles T. Higgenbotham elected W. M. June 12, 1868, C. A. M'Clure elected W. M. 1869, William M. Hazen elected W. M. December 23, 1870, Robert J. Barnett elected W. M.

DELPHI CHAPTER, NO. 21, F. AND A. M.

A CONVOCATION of Royal Arch Masons was held at Masonic Hall, Delphi, on the 15th day of April, 1851, at which was present Companions H. Peters and H. Lawrence, of Lafayette Chapter, No. 3, A. H. Bowen, Daniel F. Vandeventer, Hiram Allen, William H. Buford, Moses Colton, Henry Foreman, and Rudolph Foreman. A dispensation was read from Isaac D. Bartlett, D. G. H. P., dated March 7, 1851, appointing the following officers: Abner H. Bowen, H. P.; Daniel F. Vandeventer, K.

On the 24th day of May, 1851, a charter was granted, signed by Colby A. Foster, G. H. P., Isaac Bartlett, D. G. H. P., Caleb Schmedlapp, G. K., Richard Sopris, G. S. P. N., Francis King, Grand Secretary.

Abner H. Bowen has held the office of H. P. from the organization of the Chapter until May, 1866.

May 29, 1866, Dr. E. Walker was elected H. P. 1868, A. H. Bowen was elected H. P. 1871, J. T. Richardson was elected H. P.

DELPHI LODGE, NO. 28, I. O. O. F.

David W. Bowen, William H. Buford, James H. Stewart, Newton H. Gist, and James P. Dugan, were the petitioners for a charter for Delphi Lodge, No. 28, of the "Independent Order of Odd-fellows." The charter was granted on the 20th day of January, 1846, signed by John H. Taylor, G. M.; Stuart W. Cayce, Grand Secretary; Oliver Defour, R. W. G. C.; P. B. Drown, Jacob Walker, B. Saunders, F. E. Goodsell, L. Noble, A. M. Higgins, Dalby Merritt, and other P. G.'s.

The Lodge was constituted on the 13th day of February, 1846, by D. D. G. M., P. B. Brown, from Friendship Lodge, No. 22, Lafayette. The following officers were elected: David W. Bowen, N. G.; William H. Buford, V. G.; James H. Stewart, Secretary; and Newton H. Gist, Treasurer.

The following officers were appointed at the same time: Levi S. Dale, Chap.; Matthew Simpson, S. W.; Wm. H. Gist, J. W.; L. S. Dale, Con.; Newton, H. Gist, R. S. N. G.; C. M. D. Wilson, L. S. N. G.; Alexander M. Berry, O. G.; Jesse R. Henry, I. G.; Nathaniel W. Bowen, R. S. V. G.; William H. Gist, L. S. V. G.

March 30, 1846.—Officers elected: William H. Buford, N. G.; James H. Stewart, V. G.; William H. Gist, Secretary; Nathaniel W. Bowen, Treasurer.

June 15, 1846.—Officers elected: James H. Stewart, N. G.; William H. Gist, V. G.; Milton H. Milford, Secretary; David R. Harley, Treasurer.

September 21, 1846.—Officers elected: William H. Gist, N. G.; Milton H. Milford, V. G.; Levi S. Dale, Secretary; John Barr, Treasurer.

December 14, 1846.—Officers elected: Milton H. Milford, N. G.; Levi S. Dale, V. G.; Lewis A. Gaylord, Secretary; John Barr, Treasurer.

June 28, 1847........................Levi S. Dale, N. G.
December 27, 1847..................Lewis A. Gaylord, N. G.
June 26, 1848........................Jesse R. Henry, N. G.
December 25, 1848..................Matthew Simpson, N. G.
June 25, 1849........................Noah B. Dewey, N. G.
December 31, 1849..................James R. Blanchard, N. G.
June 24, 1850........................George W. Pigman, N. G.
December 30, 1850..................William Dunkle, N. G.
June 29, 1851........................Erastus W. Hubbard, N. G.
December 29, 1851..................Levi S. Dale, N. G.
June 28, 1852........................Lewis B. Sims, N. G.
December 27, 1852..................James H. Boylan, N. G.
June 27, 1853........................Aquila Jones, N. G.
December 26, 1853..................David R. Harley, N. G.
June 26, 1854........................Lewis B. Sims, N. G.
December 25, 1854..................Henry M. Graham, N. G.
June 25, 1855........................Edward Walker, N. G.
December 31, 1855..................John S. Case, N. G.
June 30, 1856........................Jonathan Barnett, N. G.
December 29, 1856..................Jonathan C. Applegate, N. G.
June 29, 1857........................Joseph Cox, N. G.
December 28, 1857..................Sylvester Berry, N. G.
June 28, 1858........................Nathaniel Black, N. G.
December 27, 1858..................R. L. Higgenbotham, N. G.
June 27, 1859........................Corbley M'Knight, N. G.
December 26, 1859..................Nathaniel Black, N. G.
June 25, 1860........................Daniel M'Cain, N. G.
December 31, 1860..................Joseph Cox, N. G.
June 24, 1861........................John L. Baum, N. G.
January 6, 1862......................John G. Kessler, N. G.
July 7, 1862...........................Joel Peffley, N. G.
January 5, 1863......................Joseph Cox, N. G.
July 6, 1863...........................Daniel M'Cain, N. G.
January 4, 1864......................Henderson Dunkle, N. G.
October 3, 1864......................John L. Baum, N. G.
April 3, 1865...........................John G. Kessler, N. G.
October 2, 1865......................John A. Bachman, N. G.
April 2, 1866...........................Thomas Williams, N. G.
October 1, 1866......................Daniel M'Cain, N. G.
April 1, 1867...........................John R. Copeland, N. G.
October 7, 1867......................Frank Schilling, N. G.
April 6, 1868...........................P. L. Lauglois, N. G.
October 5, 1868......................John G. Kessler, N. G.
April 5, 1869...........................Michael Ottmar, N. G.
October 4, 1869......................John W. Fawcett, N. G.
April 4, 1870...........................James H. Stewart, N. G.
October 3, 1870......................Henderson Dunkle, N. G.
April 3, 1871...........................John W. Fawcett, N. G.

October 2, 1871........................Charles Gros, N. G.
April 1, 1872...........................Joseph Dillinger, N. G.

Present number of contributing members, 68. Resources of the Lodge, including Orphan's Fund, $3,-032.66.

CARROLL LODGE, NO. 174, I. O. O. F.

ON the petition of Matthew Simpson, Henry E. Olds, George W. Pigman, Joseph Potter, David D. Duke, Anthony Foust, Jehu C. Hannam, William B. Givins, Thomas Givins, Erastus W. Hubbard, and Joel H. Dewey, Grand Master James H. Stewart granted a dispensation for Carroll Lodge, No. 174, and appointed January 9, 1857, for its constitution. On that evening Grand Master Stewart presided in person, the following being his appointed officers: J. C. Applegate, R. W. G. Secretary; Charles Angell, R. W. G. P. S.; Christian Herman, R. W. G. Treas.; William Johnson, R. W. G. W.; Edward Walker, R. W. G. Marshal.

The Lodge elected the following officers: E. W. Hubbard, N. G.; Joseph Potter, V. G., Jehu C. Hannam, R. S.; Matthew Simpson, P. S.; Henry E. Olds, Treasurer.

The N. G. made the following appointments: Wm. B. Givins, W.; H. E. Olds, Con.; George W. Pigman, Chaplain; Thomas Givins, I. G.; D. D. Duke, L. H. S. The V. G. appointed Joel H. Dewey R. H. S.; and Anthony Foust, L. H. S.

June 25, 1857.—Officers elected: Joseph Potter, N. G.; Jehu C. Hannam, V. G.; W. B. Givins, R. S.; H. E. Olds, Treasurer.

December 31, 1857.—The following officers elected: Jehu C. Hannam, N. G.; Andrew H. Evans, R. S.; Henry E. Olds, Treasurer; W. B. Givins, V. G.

June 24, 1858..........................William B. Givins, N. G.
December 30, 1858...................Andrew H. Evans, N. G.
June 30, 1859..........................William Draper, N. G.

December 29, 1859..................Andrew H. Evans, N. G.
June 28, 1860..........................Robert Mitchell, N. G.
December 27, 1860..................Thomas A. Doggett, N. G.
June 27, 1861..........................Henry Kuhn, N. G.
January 2, 1862......................William Bradshaw, N. G.
July 7, 1862.............................William Carson, N. G.
January 5, 1863......................J. B. Fisher, N. G.
January 2, 1863......................Henry Kuhn, N. G.
January 14, 1864....................N. C. Pettit, N. G.
October 14, 1864....................W. H. Whittaker, N. G.
April 3, 1865...........................George Stemler, N. G.
October 2, 1865.......................James W. Griffith, N. G.
April 5, 1866............................John C. Bell, N. G.
October 11, 1866.....................Erastus W. Hubbard, N. G.
April 4, 1867............................S. P. Eversole, N. G.
October 10, 1867.....................Louis Gustavel, N. G.
April 9, 1868............................Thomas A. Doggett, N. G.
October 1, 1868.......................Joseph Miller, N. G.
April 8, 1869............................James M. Ramey, N. G.
October 7, 1869.......................J. J. Bragunier, N. G.
April 7, 1870............................A. E. Pierce, N. G.
October 3, 1870.......................Henry E. Olds, N. G.
January 19, 1871....................Joseph Potter, N. G.
April 6, 1871............................William Bradshaw, N. G.
October 5, 1871.......................Alfred Armstrong, N. G,
April 4, 1872............................Joseph Potter, N. G.

The charter for this Lodge is dated May 19, 1857, and is signed by James H. Stewart, G. M.; John H. Staily, D. G. M.; John Kyle, G. H.; George B. Roberts, R. W. G. W.; Schuyler Colfax, P. G. Rep.; Willis W. Wright, R. W. G. Secretary.

This Lodge meets every Thursday evening.

CARROLL ENCAMPMENT, NO. 22, I. O. O. F.

Levi S. Dale, William H. Watson, William H. Buford, Jesse R. Henry, Demas Robinson, James H. Stewart, and John Barr were the petitioners for a charter for an encampment at Delphi. The charter was granted by the G. E. of the State, and is dated 8th day of January, 1850, signed by Isaac H. Taylor, M. W. G. P.; James Gibson, R. W. G. S. W.; John Lilly, R. W. G. J. W.; E. Hedderly, R. W. G. Treasurer; Schuyler Colfax, R. W. G. Rep.; Willis W. Wright, R. W. G. Scribe.

On the 23d day of April, 1850, James M. Warren, D. D. G. P., of Logansport, assisted by Reuben Staily, Lawrence B. Stockton, and John Lilly, of Lafayette, instituted "Carroll Encampment, No. 22," Levi S. Dale was elected C. P.; Jesse R. Henry, H. P.; William H. Buford, S. W.; William H. Watson, J. W.; James H. Stewart, Scribe; and John Barr, Treasurer.

December 20, 1850.—Officers elected: Jas. H. Stewart, C. P.; John M'Carthy, S. W.; Erastus W. Hubbard, J. W.; Lewis B. Sims, Scribe; James R. Blanchard, H. P.; Milo Dibble, Treasurer. Appointed officers: John Tutwiler, S.; George W. Pigman, Guide; Isaac H. Elldridge, 1st W.; Noah B. Dewey, 2d W.; William Halsey, 3d W.; Levi D. Osborn, 4th W.; Henderson Dunkle, Host; James H. Boylan and John Barr, G. of T.

June 20, 1851.—Officers elected: George W. Pigman, C. P.; John M'Carthy, H. P.; Erastus W. Hubbard, S. W.; William J. Sayre, J. W.; Noah B. Dewey, Scribe; William Dunkle, Treasurer; James R. Blanchard and Levi S. Dale were elected representatives to the G. E.

Dec. 19, 1851...Erastus W. Hubbard, C. P.; N. B. Dewey, H. P.
June 18, 1852...Lewis B. Sims, C. P.; Vine Holt, H. P.
Dec. 17, 1852...Jesse R. Henry, C. P.; William J. Sayer, H. P.
June 17, 1853...Jas. R. Blanchard, C. P.; Geo. W. Pigman, H. P.
Dec. 16, 1853...William Dunkle, C. P.; David R. Harley, H. P.
June 10, 1854...Christian Herman, C. P.; J. C. Applegate, H. P.
Dec. 15, 1854...Jesse R. Henry, C. P.; David R. Harley, H. P.
June 15, 1855...J. C. Applegate, C. P.; Henry E. Olds, H. P.
Dec. 21, 1855...Geo. W. Pigman, C. P.; Same.
June 20, 1856...George A. Merritt, C. P.; Henderson Dunkle, H. P.
Dec. 19, 1856...John G. Kessler, C. P.; Jesse R. Henry, H. P.
July 4, 1857...Henderson Dunkle, C. P.; Joseph Cox, H. P.
Dec. 19, 1857...Geo. A. Merritt, C. P.; Matthew Simpson, H. P.
June 19, 1858...R. L. Higgenbotham, C. P.; A B. Robertson, H. P.
Dec. 18, 1858...Sylvester Berry, C. P.; John S. Case, H. P.
June 18, 1859...Joseph Potter, C. P.; R. L. Higgenbotham, H. P.
Dec. 17, 1859...William Crooks, Jr., C. P.; T. A. Doggett, H. P.
June 16, 1860...A. B. Robertson, C. P.; R. L. Higgenbotham, H. P.
Dec. 15, 1860...Henry E. Olds, C. P.; John G. Kessler, H. P.
June 21, 1861...Thos. A. Doggett, C. P.; Jas. H. Stewart, H. P.
Dec. 18, 1861...George Stemler, C. P.; J. B. Fisher, H. P.
June 20, 1862...Henry Kuhn, C. P.; William Curson, H. P.

Dec. 19, 1862...Daniel M'Cain, C. P.; Henderson Dunkle, H. P.
June 19, 1863...Henderson Dunkle, C. P.; George Stemler, H. P.
Dec. 18, 1863...George Stemler, C. P.; J. B. Fisher, H. P.
Sept. 16, 1864...J. B. Fisher, C. P.; R. L. Higgenbotham, H. P.
Mar. 17, 1865...Joseph Cox, C. P.; Thos. A. Doggett, H. P.
Sept. 1, 1865...John G. Kessler, C. P; Jas. W. Griffith, H. P.
Mar. 2, 1866....Jas. W. Griffith, C. P.; E. W. Hubbard, H. P.
Sept. 21, 1866...W. H. Whitaker, C. P.; Lewis Gustavel, H. P.
Mar. 15, 1867...S. P. Eversole, C. P.; Joseph Miller, H. P.
Sept. 20, 1867...Joseph Miller, C. P.; Isaac Farniman, H. P.
Mar. 20, 1868...Isaac Farniman, C. P.; David Kuhn, H. P.
Sept. 18, 1868...Lewis Gustavel, C. P., Samuel Lenon, H. P.
Mar. 19, 1869...Geo. M'Cormick, C. P.; Daniel M'Cain, H. P.
Sept. 17, 1869...Henderson Dunkle, C. P.; W. M. Munday, H. P.
Mar. 18, 1870...A. M. Eldridge, C. P.; John G. Kessler, H. P.
Oct. 7, 1870...James Brown, C.P.; John G. Kessler, H. P.
Mar. 17, 1871...Thos. A. Doggett, C. P.; James H. Stewart, H. P.
Sept. 15, 1871...James H. Stewart, C. P.; Charles Angell, H. P.
Mar. 16, 1872...Charles Angell, C. P.; John J. Bragunier, H. P.

The Encampment meets on the first and third Friday evenings of each month.

Resources of the camp, $1,476.86.

CHAPTER XIX.

OFFICIAL VOTES OF THE COUNTY,

Showing the vote for President since the organization of the county in 1828 to 1860.

1828.		1832.		1836.		1840.		1844.			1848.			1852		1856.			1860.	
Jackson....	Adams......	Jackson....	Clay.........	Van Buren.	Harrison...	Van Buren.	Harrison...	Polk.........	Clay.........	Birney......	Cass..........	Taylor......	Van Buren.	Pierce.......	Scott	Buchanan..	Fremont....	Fillmore....	Douglas....	Lincoln....
112	73	258	173	565	375	765	699	565	712	8	1008	822	76	1256	1075	1344	1261	22	1446	1590

LIST OF REPRESENTATIVES

To the State Legislature, representing Carroll County since the organization of the county.

1828. Carroll, Montgomery, etc..........Robert Taylor.
1829. " " " ....John Beard.
1830. " " " ....Abel Claypool.
1831. Carroll and Cass......................Walter Wilson.
1832. " " ....Walter Wilson.
1833. " " ....Gillis M'Bean.
1834. " " ....Chauncey Carter.
1835. " " ....Gillis M'Bean.
1836. Carroll....................................Albert G. Hanna.
1837. " ....Samuel Milroy.
1838. " ....Samuel Milroy.
1839. " ....Henry B. Milroy.
1840. " ....James M'Cully.
1841. " ....Andrew L. Robinson.
1842. " ....Andrew L. Robinson.
1843. " ....Andrew L. Robinson.
1844. " ....Andrew L. Robinson.
1845. " ....Henry P. Tedford.
1846. " ....Albert G. Hanna.
1847. " ....Thomas Thompson.
1848. " ....James Odell.
1849. " ....Samuel Weaver.
1850. " ....Thomas Thompson.
1851. " ....Albert G. Hanna.
1852. " ....John B. Milroy.
1854. " ....John T. Gwinn.

1856. Carroll.................................Bernard F. Schermerhorn.
1858. " ....Nathaniel Black.
1860. " ....Thomas Thompson.

LIST OF SENATORS

Representing Carroll County in the Senate from the year 1828.

1829. Putnam, Montgomery, etc.........Joseph Orr.
1830. " " " ....Joseph Orr.
1831. Tippecanoe, Carroll, etc............Othniel L. Clark.
1834. " " " .... Othniel L. Clark.
1836. Carroll and Clinton..................Samuel Milroy.
1837. " " ....Aaron Finch.
1840. " " ....Horatio J. Harris.
1843. " " ....Andrew Major.
1846. " " ....Philip Waters.
1849. " " ....Thomas Kennard.
1854. " " ....James F. Suit.
1858. " " ....James Odell.

LIST OF COUNTY OFFICERS.

JUSTICES OF THE PEACE.

Names.	Date of Commission.	Length of Service.
Henry Robinson	July 14, 1828	Five years.
Isam Adkinson	July 14, 1828	Five years.
William Scott	July 14, 1828	Five years.
William George	August 13, 1829	Five years.
George Julian	October 30, 1830	Five years.
Thomas Gillam	April 19, 1831	Five years.

Names.	Date of Commission.
Joshua Lindsay	Aug. 13, 1831.
Royal Hazleton	Aug. 13, 1831.
Jacob Humerickhouse	Aug. 13, 1831.
John R. Merritt	Jan. 2, 1832.
James H. Stewart	April 17, 1832.
John Law	April 17, 1832.
Samuel Moore	June 15, 1832.
Mahlon Shinn	June 18, 1832.
Moses Alldridge	Feb. 25, 1833.
James B. Larimer	Aug. 17, 1833.
Sam'l I. Moore	Aug. 17, 1833.
William Dawson	Aug. 17, 1833.
Elisha Warden	Aug. 17, 1833.
Solomon M'Cully	Aug. 17, 1833.
Malachi Gray	Jan. 6, 1834.
John Grantham	Jan. 6, 1834.
James Barnes	March 24, 1834.
John Trimble	April 25, 1834.
James H. Barnes	Nov. 17, 1834.
John Chambers	Nov. 28, 1834.
Christopher M'Combs	Feb. 18, 1835.
Simeon L. Stewart	April 13, 1835.
Elisha W. Lake	April 13, 1835.
Samuel L. M'Millin	April 27, 1835.
George Fouts	Aug. 17, 1835.
John H. Marshall	Aug. 17, 1835.
John Phelps	April 15, 1836.
Peter Benham	April 15, 1836.
Michael Kite	April 15, 1836.
Joseph Williamson	June 8, 1836.
Adam Clark	June 13, 1836.
John G. Treen	Aug. 9, 1836.
Matthew Bonesteel	Jan. 2, 1837.
John Lenon	Jan. 7, 1837.
Moses Standley	Feb. 17, 1837.
William George	Feb. 16, 1837.
George Kirkpatrick	May 6, 1837.
John Carey	June 8, 1837.
John Sidenbender	June 9, 1837.
John Calvert	July 15, 1837.
Samuel Moore	Aug. 22, 1837.
Alex. M. Townsend	Sept. 4, 1837.
Reuben G. Munday	Sept. 4, 1837.
William M'Clelland	Oct. 25, 1837.
William Alldridge	April 9, 1838.
John W. Coin	June 23, 1838.
Jacob Humerickhouse	Oct. 6, 1838.
William Dawson	Oct. 26, 1838.
Thomas Thompson	Feb. 6, 1839.
Nathan G. Gillam	April 18, 1839.
Lewis Ewing	Dec. 7, 1839.
Mahlon Shinn	Dec. 7, 1839.
William W. Coshow	Dec. 9, 1839.
John Chambers	Jan. 4, 1840.
George M. Maxwell	Feb. 10, 1840.
Milo Dibble	May 13, 1840.

Names.	Date of Commission.
Daniel Beck	June 22, 1840.
John Harrison	June 24, 1840.
John Bross	Dec. 12, 1840.
John Crowel	Feb. 11, 1841.
Theophilus Bryan	May 12, 1841.
Thomas Barns	May 12, 1841.
John Boggs	May 19, 1841.
Michael Kite	May 19, 1841.
John Ashfield	June 7, 1841.
Adam Clark	July 8, 1841.
Ullery Shively	July 8, 1841.
Alexander M. Townsend	Aug. 11, 1841.
Philip Waters	Aug. 11, 1841.
Hugh Compton	Aug. 18, 1841.
John Lane	Sept. 3, 1841.
John P. Hay	Jan. 7, 1842.
Wm. S. Montgomery	Jan. 7, 1842.
Lorenzo D. Hovey	Jan. 7, 1842.
Archibald Bryson	Jan. 7, 1842.
Moses Thompson	Jan. 7, 1842.
John Cohee	Jan. 7, 1842.
James Lamb	Aug. 8, 1842.
John S. Counts	Aug. 14, 1843.
Gideon Doggett	Aug. 14, 1843.
Samuel Moore	Aug. 14, 1843.
Nathan G. Gillam	April 26, 1844.
John W. Coin	April 26, 1844.
William Saunders	May 15, 1844.
Lewis Gearhart	May 15, 1844.
Peter Mentzer	May 20, 1844.
Levi S. Dale	Nov. 13, 1844.
William Runyan	Feb. 20, 1845.
John M. Longstreth	Feb. 20, 1845.
John Guthrie	March 17, 1845.
Samuel Weaver	May 12, 1845.
Isaac Patty	May 12, 1845.
Allen Reed	Jan. 24, 1846.
Henry R. Glazier	Jan. 24, 1846.
Thomas Gillam	Jan. 24, 1846.
Allen Reed	Jan. 24, 1846.
Samuel Moore	Jan. 24, 1846.
Presley Dunlap	Jan. 24, 1846.
Milo Dibble	April 29, 1846.
Sothey K. Timmons	April 29, 1846.
James C. Todd	May 11, 1846.
William Salsbury	May 11, 1846.
Michael Kite	June 4, 1846.
Norman Newton	Aug. 18, 1846.
Lorenzo D. Hovey	Nov. 27, 1846.
John Davidson	Jan. 16, 1847.
Wm. S. Montgomery	April 17, 1847.
Archibald Bryson	April 17, 1847.
James Lamb	Aug. 20, 1847.
Thomas Ireland	Aug. 20, 1847.
Eli Rogers	Aug. 20, 1847.
John Boggs	Oct. 12, 1847.
Alston Wyatt	April 11, 1848.
Simeon Wilson	June 20, 1848.
Thomas A. Robeson	April 17, 1849.
George Sieres	April 17, 1849.
Zophar W. Bryant	April 17, 1849.
John Boylan	Aug. 17, 1849.
Levi S. Dale	Dec. 7, 1849.
Charles W. Wisehart	April 9, 1850.
Henry C. Sandham	April 9, 1850.
Sothey K. Timmons	April 9, 1850.
James Harmon	April 9, 1850.
Abel Slayback	April 9, 1850.

Names.	Date of Commission.
Erastus W. Hubbard	Oct. 1, 1850.
Samuel Moore	March 14, 1851.
John Harner	April 16, 1851.
James Delzell	April 16, 1851.
Mahlon Shinn	April 16, 1851.
Moses Plank	April 16, 1851.
James C. Todd	April 16, 1851.
Pollard Baldwin	April 16, 1851.
Michael Kite	April 16, 1851.
Samuel Weaver	Oct. 23, 1851.
Lorenzo D. Hovey	Jan. 6, 1852.
Wm. S. Montgomery	April 12, 1852.
Levi M. Graham	April 12, 1852.
James Barrett	April 12, 1852.
Abner Robinson	April 12, 1852.
James R. Laird	April 12, 1852.
William Dillon	April 12, 1852.
George Macfarlane	Oct. 25, 1852.
William J. Sayer	Oct. 25, 1852.
James M. Darnell	Jan. 11, 1853.
Thomas H. Meloy	Sept. 8, 1852.
John Smith	April 10, 1853.
Henry T. Shaffer	April 10, 1853.
Thomas Ireland	April 10, 1853.
John G. Kessler	April 10, 1853.
John Guthrie	April 17, 1854.
David Hiestand	April 17, 1854.
George Sieres	April 17, 1854.
Enoch Stansel	April 12, 1855.
John Lenon	April 12, 1855.
Bilton J. Wilson	April 12, 1855.
Myron M. Southworth	April 12, 1855.
James H. Turner	Nov. 1, 1855.
James Delzell	Nov. 1, 1855.
Moses Plank	Nov. 1, 1855.
James M. Bryant	Nov. 1, 1855.
Joseph Long	Nov. 1, 1855.
Charles Gaumer	Nov. 1, 1855.
William Dawson	Nov. 1, 1855.
Sam'l Moore	Dec. 22, 1855.
Francis S. Morrison	Dec. 22, 1855.
Curtis Hatfield	April 14, 1856.
Abner Robinson	April 14, 1856.
George Macfarlane	April 14, 1856.
Nathaniel Leonard	April 14, 1856.
James R. Laird	April 14, 1856.
William S. Montgomery	April 14, 1856.
John S. Pearson	April 29, 1856.
William Winegardner	April 14, 1856.
Thomas H. Meloy	April 14, 1856.
Joseph H. Taylor	April 15, 1857.
Jonathan Gillam	April 13, 1857.
James E. Smith	April 13, 1857.
Henry F. Shaffer	April 13, 1857.
John G. Kessler	April 13, 1857.
William J. Ewing	April 13, 1857.
David Heistand	April 20, 1858.
John C. Brown	April 20, 1858.
George Sieres	April 20, 1858.
Hamilton Robb	April 20, 1859.
William Mote	April 20, 1859.
John G. Kessler	April 20, 1859.
Henry C. Olds	April 20, 1859.
Hugh Shields	April 20, 1859.
Andrew Robinson	April 20, 1859.
Moses Plank	April 20, 1859.
John Featherhoof	April 20, 1859.
James Delzell	April 20, 1859.

Names.	Date of Commission.
John T. Andrew	April 2, 1860.
Moses M. Lamb	April 2, 1860.
W. Y. Winegardner	April 2, 1860.
George B. Royster	April 14, 1860.
William S. Montgomery	April 14, 1860.
Henry Seibert	April 14, 1860.
David Leonard	April 14, 1860.
George Macfarlane	Oct. 27, 1860.
John S. Pearson	Dec. 16, 1860.
Jonathan Gillam	April 27, 1861.
James Lawell	May 31, 1861.

LIST OF COMMISSIONS ISSUED TO CLERKS OF THE CIRCUIT COURT.

Names.	Date of Commission.	Length of Service.
Daniel F. Vandeventer	May 8, 1828	Seven years.
James H. Stewart	May 8, 1835	Seven years.
" "	August 8, 1842	Seven years.
" "	August 17, 1848	Seven years.
" "	November 1, 1855	Four years.
Matthew Simpson	November 1, 1859	Four years.

LIST OF COUNTY TREASURERS.

Names.	Date of Commission.
Daniel Baum	May 12, 1828.
" "	May 21, 1829.
William George	Nov. 10, 1830.
" "	March 28, 1831.
" "	March 5, 1832.
" "	Jan. 7, 1833.
" "	March 3, 1834.
" "	March 2, 1835.
" "	March 7, 1836.
" "	March 6, 1837.
" "	March 6, 1838.
" "	March 5, 1839.
William Simpson	March 2, 1840.
William Simpson	March 3, 1841.
" "	Aug. 12, 1841.
" "	Dec. 8, 1843.
" "	July 12, 1844.
Milo Dibble	Sept. 6, 1847.
" "	Sept. 3, 1850.
Levi S. Dale	Sept. 1, 1851.
C. M. D. Wilson	Nov. 8, 1852.
Matthew Simpson	Nov. 4, 1854.
" "	Nov. 5, 1856.
John S. Case	Oct. 26, 1858.
" "	Nov. 5, 1860.

LIST OF CONSTABLES.

Names.	Date of Commission.
David M'Combs	Nov. 11, 1828.
Jonah T. Hopkinson	Nov. 14, 1829.
Jacob Humerickhouse	Sept. 8, 1830.
William Olinger	Nov. 8, 1830.
Oliver D. Butler	Nov. 9, 1830.
James Alldridge	Feb. 14, 1830.
John Thompson	April 9, 1830.
Jacob Humerickhouse	April 19, 1831.
William Olinger	April 21, 1831.
James B. Larimer	Nov. 7, 1831.
Obadiah Corder	Jan. 12, 1832.
John Thompson	April 6, 1832.
James B. Larimer	April 21, 1832.
John Comer	May 7, 1832.
William Adkinson	May 26, 1832.
Robert Dunlap	May 26, 1832.
John Mills	June 22, 1832.
James Alldridge	Sept. 3, 1832.
George W. Goodlander	Jan. 7, 1833.
Christian Hermon	May 4, 1833.
Simeon L. Stewart	April 5, 1833.
Matthew Bonesteel	May 13, 1833.
Samuel D. Gresham	Nov. 5, 1833.
" "	April 12, 1834.
James Alldridge	April 30, 1834.
Simeon L. Stewart	May 5, 1834.
James Young	June 27, 1834.
Daniel Yount	April 14, 1834.
James Clark	Jan. 4, 1835.
Thomas Pike	April 20, 1835.
James C. Hooper	May 4, 1835.
Isaac Wilson	July 8, 1835.
David Foster	July 21, 1835.
Abner Shanks	Sept. 23, 1835.
George W. Goodlander	Nov. 2, 1835.
James Clark	Nov. 21, 1835.
Thomas Green	Jan. 4, 1836.
James R. Pile	April 7, 1836.
John Burget	April 11, 1836.
David Hamilton	April 15, 1836.
Stephen A. Daniel	April 18, 1836.
William Olinger	April 19, 1836.
Josiah Brown	May 2, 1836.
William Barns	May 27, 1836.
Moses Campbell	May 27, 1836.
A. M. Townsend	July 4, 1836.
Archibald Slane	June 6, 1836.
Jonah T. Hopkinson	June 11, 1836.
John Bross	Jan. 3, 1837.
James M'Niel	April 3, 1837.
William Scott	April 5, 1837.
Curtis Keener	April 5, 1837.
William Burnet	April 5, 1837.
John W. Penn	April 19, 1837.

Names.	Date of Commission.
William Clark	June 5, 1837.
Philip A. Clover	Oct. 2, 1837.
" "	Nov. 6, 1837.
William S. Evans	Nov. 6, 1837.
Curtis Keener	Nov. 6, 1837.
Johnson M'Clelland	Nov. 7, 1837.
George Sherburn	Feb. 1, 1838.
Alfred Ramey	March 6, 1838.
George Sherburn	March 6, 1838.
William W. Scott	April 4, 1838.
Jacob H. Myers	April 4, 1838.
John T. Gee	April 4, 1838.
Philip A. Clover	April 4, 1838.
Curtis Keener	April 4, 1838.
Joseph Buckingham	April 7, 1838.
John Grist	April 23, 1838.
Josiah P. Williams	April 23, 1838.
Robert Bates	April 24, 1838.
Elijah Isaacs	April 28, 1838.
John T. Hoff	May 26, 1838.
James J. M'Bath	July 9, 1838.
Edwin R. Davis	July 23, 1838.
" "	Sept. 3, 1838.
Aquila Jones	Oct. 8, 1838.
Andrew Watts	Nov. 27, 1838.
Aquila Jones	April 9, 1839.
John Bross	April 13, 1839.
William Tedford	June 1, 1840.
John Finley	April 6, 1841.
Elisha Nichols	April 8, 1841.
John Ball	April 9, 1841.
Thomas Cloud	April 12, 1841.
Solomon Morse	April 12, 1841.
John M. Bowman	April 15, 1841.
Henry Devan	April 19, 1841.
Wm. S. Montgomery	April 19, 1841.
Edwin R. Davis	April 15, 1841.
Jacob Whistler	April 24, 1841.
David Weidner	May 3, 1841.
C. P. Freeman	May 19, 1841.
Alexander Aiken	May 22, 1841.
Layton North	June 7, 1841.
John Ball	June 9, 1841.
Lancaster Fenters	June 22, 1841.
Layton North	Sept. 20, 1841.
William W. Scott	Dec. 13, 1841.
Mathias Timmons	April 7, 1842.
John Finley	April 12, 1842.
Jesse Daniel	April 13, 1842.
John M. Bowman	April 13, 1842.
Lewis H. Ross	April 17, 1842.
Silas H. Jack	April 15, 1842.
John T. Penny	May 2, 1842.
Andrew J. Watts	May 2, 1842.
George E. Douglass	May 2, 1842.
Elisha Nichols	May 5, 1842.
Daniel Cline	May 7, 1842.
Thomas Wright	May 14, 1842.
Josiah Yerkes	May 26, 1842.
George W. Williamson	June 5, 1842.
Parker Lucas	June 6, 1842.
John Tilton	June 15, 1842.
Thomas J. Irwin	June 15, 1842.
William Standley	June 20, 1842.
Hugh Snodgrass	April 4, 1843.
Philip A. Clover	April 8, 1843.
Jonathan Barnett	April 12, 1843.
John M'Bride	April 17, 1843.
John Finley	April 21, 1843.
Robert A. Hamell	April 22, 1843.
Josiah Yerkes, Jr	April 27, 1843.
Thomas J. Irwin	May 9, 1843.
Elijah Isaacs	May 27, 1843.
Benjamin Pratt	April 3, 1844.
Walter Billingsby	April 9, 1844.
Jonathan Barnett	April 12, 1844.
Philip A. Clover	April 18, 1844.
John W. Coin	May 3, 1844.
James W. Welch	May 16, 1844.
Jacob Whistler	July 1, 1844.
Benjamin Pratt	April 18, 1845.
John W. Tingley	April 19, 1845.
David A. Thompson	April 22, 1845.
Edwin R. Davis	May 21, 1845.
James Harmon	August 6, 1845.
Edwin R. Davis	April 12, 1846.
Samuel Kepner	April 13, 1846.
Benjamin Steel	April 17, 1846.
Marion Reed	April 17, 1846.
John Burget	April 20, 1846.
Samuel Dawson	April 27, 1846.
James Miller	May 19, 1846.
James M'Neil	June 6, 1846.
Solomon Reigel	June 11, 1846.
John Green	June 21, 1846.
George O. Alsop	June 21, 1846.
Edwin R. Davis	April 9, 1847.
Joseph Hartman	April 15, 1847.
Mathias Timmons	April 16, 1847.
James M'Neil	May 1, 1847.
David Morrison	May 10, 1847.
Stephen Scott	June 7, 1847.
John Green	June 7, 1847.
Oliver H. P. Hanna	June 12, 1847.
Cornelius Berkshire	June 18, 1847.
Benjamin Steel	June 28, 1847.
George O. Alsop	Sept. 6, 1847.
Myron M. Southworth	April 10, 1848.
J. M. Virgin	April 10, 1848.
William R. Chapman	April 11, 1848.
William Campbell	April 29, 1848.
Edwin R. Davis	May 10, 1848.
Samuel White	May 12, 1848.
John Stockton	May 29, 1848.
Ephraim Fry	June 20, 1848.
Allen W. Gillam	June 22, 1848.
Archibald Slane	Sept. 13, 1848.
William R. Chapman	April 5, 1849.
Thomas Crawford	April 10, 1849.
Sylvester M'Farland	April 11, 1849.
Cyrus White	April 11, 1849.
John H. Campbell	April 11, 1849.
Samuel Huff	April 23, 1849.
Benjamin Steel	April 23, 1849.
Jacob Mullendore	June 4, 1849.
Thomas Crawford	April 5, 1850.
William Riley	April 5, 1850.
Samuel M. Shortridge	April 13, 1850.
Abraham Huntsinger	April 15, 1850.
Jesse Osborn	April 22, 1850.
Jacob Mullendore	May 11, 1850.
Cyrus White	May 11, 1850.
John H. Campbell	May 13, 1850.
Philip Shaffer	June 3, 1850.
William Stockton	June 3, 1850.
Benjamin Steel	Sept. 2, 1850.

Names.	Date of Commission.
David Cade	April 10, 1851.
Elias Harner	April 12, 1851.
Nathaniel Sweet	April 14, 1851.
William Riley	April 14, 1851.
William Stockton	April 28, 1851.
John T. Hornback	May 12, 1851.
John Cochran	May 17, 1851.
Nathaniel R. Campbell	May 21, 1851.
Henry T. Sylvester	July 16, 1851.
Joel Garrison	April 10, 1852.
John Cline	April 10, 1852.
William Riley	April 14, 1852.
Lewis J. Royster	April 26, 1852.
James M. Bryant	April 29, 1852.
Philip Shaffer	April 30, 1852.
James W. Stonebraker	August 7, 1852.
John Campbell	Sept. 7, 1852.
Henry M. Graham	Sept. 7, 1852.
James Hinkle	Sept. 14, 1852.
John H. Campbell	Sept. 14, 1852.
Henry M. Graham	April 8, 1853.
James Ryan	April 8, 1853.
Aaron Ford	April 11, 1853.
Philip Shaffer	April 12, 1853.
John N. Miller	April 12, 1853.
Michael Trua	April 16, 1853.
Joseph Norman	April 25, 1853.
Myron M. Southworth	April 26, 1853.
Ludwell G. Huston	April 26, 1853.
Nathaniel M. Ridgway	May 9, 1853.
William Riley	May 27, 1853.
John H. Harman	May 27, 1853.
Joseph D. Hance	April 5, 1854.
William Drepperd	April 6, 1854.
David Paden	April 8, 1854.
Henry M. Graham	April 10, 1854.
James Ryan	April 11, 1854.
William C. Carson	April 12, 1854.
Thomas J. Brown	April 21, 1854.
William R. Timmons	April 29, 1854.
Joseph Norman	April 29, 1854.
Samuel Dawson	June 10, 1854.
Joel Garrison	June 14, 1854.
James C. Stephenson	June 17, 1854.
George W. Friday	July 3, 1854.
George West	April 7, 1855.
Alfred C. Quinn	April 13, 1855.
Aaron Ford	April 13, 1855.
Samuel B. Glover	April 14, 1855.
Henry M. Graham	April 16, 1855.
Ludwell G. Huston	April 18, 1855.
Horace H. Deyo	April 18, 1855.
Elias Brockus	April 18, 1855.
Alexander Lovelace	May 12, 1855.
George W. Horsley	Sept. 6, 1855.
Richard M'Cain	Sept. 12, 1855.
William Riley	April 10, 1856.
Thomas J. Pile	April 11, 1856.
William C. Carson	April 15, 1856.
George W. House	April 26, 1856.
Frankland Barnard	April 26, 1856.
George Miller	May 3, 1856.
David Paden	May 24, 1856.
William W. Ridgell	May 30, 1856.
John Hinkle	May 30, 1856.
James Mathews	June 12, 1856.
Aaron Ford	June 27, 1856.
John B. Caldwell	April 8, 1857.
Nathaniel M. Crawford	April 9, 1857.
Newton H. Gist	April 9, 1857.
Samuel J. Koontz	April 10, 1857.
William Riley	April 10, 1857.
Jacob Burk	April 13, 1857.
Samuel Hildebrand	April 16, 1857.
Joseph Shigley	April 18, 1857.
Benjamin F. Barnard	April 20, 1857.
John Q. Miller	April 27, 1857.
Henry Kendall	April 30, 1857.
William C. Carson	May 2, 1857.
Jonathan Moore	May 12, 1857.
John E. Dunkin	May 12, 1857.
William H. Green	April 6, 1858.
Nathaniel M. Crawford	April 7, 1858.
Daniel Dull	April 10, 1858.
William Riley	April 10, 1858.
Daniel L. Richard	April 12, 1858.
Joseph Shigley	April 13, 1858.
Samuel Hildebrand	April 14, 1858.
Ludwell G. Huston	April 15, 1858.
John B. Hildebrand	April 17, 1858.
John C. Stephenson	April 20, 1858.
William C. Carson	April 21, 1858.
Daniel P. Cline	April 26, 1858.
Samuel Hawley	May 4, 1858.
Jacob Burk	May 5, 1858.
William C. Carson	May 6, 1858.
Michael Shealey	June 11, 1858.
Newton H. Gist	June 12, 1858.
William S. Clark	Sept. 8, 1858.
Myron M. Southworth	April 6, 1859.
Lucas Haines	April 7, 1859.
Thomas M'Dowell	April 8, 1859.
Joseph F. Peck	April 9, 1859.
Michael Trace	April 11, 1859.
Joseph Sampson	April 11, 1859.
Lewellen Shaw	April 13, 1859.
Samuel S. Hawley	April 5, 1859.
Joseph Shigley	April 16, 1859.
James H. Woodward	April 18, 1859.
Wm. P. Montgomery	April 21, 1859.
Samuel Black	April 30, 1859.
William L. Clark	May 12, 1859.
John Curtner	June 4, 1859.
Jehu C. Hannam	Sept. 14, 1859.
Salem P. Eversole	April 2, 1860.
James Hinkle	April 2, 1860.
William D. Schnepp	April 2, 1860.
Benjamin J. M'Afee	April 2, 1860.
James A. Carson	April 2, 1860.
John W. Ireland	April 2, 1860.
Lewellin Shaw	April 2, 1860.
Alexander M'Laughlin	April 2, 1860.
John B. Caldwell	April 2, 1860.
John Scott	April 2, 1860.
Samuel Black	April 2, 1860.
Charles Wright	April 2, 1860.
John Franklin	Dec. 31, 1860.
Moses W. Swain	April 10, 1861.
John W. Ireland	April 15, 1861.
John Frauklin	April 26, 1861.
Joel E. House	May 2, 1861.
Thadeus Guthrie	May 11, 1861.
Ludwell G. Huston	May 9, 1861.
Aaron Ford	May 31, 1861.
Lewis Sutton	June 3, 1861.
Samuel Black	June 13, 1861.

MAYORS OF DELPHI.

Names.	Date of Commission.	Names.	Date of Commission.
Levi S. Dale	March 3, 1847.	William Barnett	Sept. 6, 1851.
Nathan G. Gillam	April 19, 1849.	Ebenezer W. Bolles	Oct. 11, 1853.
Jonathan C. Applegate	Sept. 19, 1849.		

NOTARY PUBLICS.

Names.	Date of Commission.	Names.	Date of Commission.
Lewis B. Sims	March 1, 1848.	Marion A. Parr	March 3, 1855.
Thomas C. Reyburn	Jan. 7, 1850.	B. F. Schermerhorn	May 12, 1855.
John M. Langstreth	Jan. 25, 1850.	Joseph A. Sims	Jan. 14, 1857.
Robert H. Milroy	Jan. 31, 1851.	B. F. Schermerhorn	March 10, 1857.
William J. Sayre	Feb. 7, 1851.	James H. Turner	Aug. 13, 1859.
Jonathan C. Applegate	Sept. 6, 1851.	James H. Stewart	Nov. 25, 1859.
Archibald Bryson	April 27, 1852.	James M. Bryant	Jan. 4, 1860.
James H. Barns	Jan. 9, 1854.	Attalas L. Benham	Feb. 9, 1860.

LIST OF COLLECTORS OF THE REVENUE,

Under a former law of the State.

Names.	Date of Commission	Names.	Date of Commission.
Henry B. Milroy	June 20, 1828.	Samuel D. Gresham	May 4, 1835.
Joseph Dunham	May 13, 1829.	" "	May 3, 1836.
William M'Crery	May 12, 1830.	" "	May 3, 1837.
Nathaniel Wilson	May 16, 1831.	" "	May 8, 1838,
John Carey	May 10, 1832.	" "	May 8, 1839.
James B. Larimer	May 9, 1833.	" "	May 6, 1840.
Levi Cline	June 11, 1834.		

LIST OF CORONERS.

Names.	Date of Commission.	Names.	Date of Commission.
Daniel Baum	Feb. 11, 1828.	Josiah Brown	Aug. 19, 1844.
Benjamin Baxter	Sept. 5, 1828.	" "	Aug. 18, 1846.
John Rohrbaugh	Sept. 8, 1830.	Levi M. Graham	Aug. 17, 1848.
Matthew Bonesteel	Aug. 18, 1832.	Archibald Slane	Aug. 14, 1850.
Henry Orwig	Aug. 22, 1834.	John Finley	Nov. 8, 1852.
Aquila Jones	Aug. 22, 1836.	George Bolles	Nov. 4, 1854.
William H. Buford	Aug. 13, 1838.	John Sidenbender	Nov. 5, 1856.
Thomas C. Hughes	Aug. 12, 1840.	" "	Oct. 26, 1858.
" "	Aug. 8, 1842.	Artemus Merritt	Nov. 1, 1860.

LIST OF COUNTY ASSESSORS,

Under a former law.

Names.	Date of Commission.	Names.	Date of Commission.
Aaron Dewey	May 20, 1828.	Preston Calvert	Jan. 7, 1837.
Robert Cade	Feb. 17, 1829.	John Woodman	Jan. 9, 1837.
William M'Crery	Feb. 22, 1830.	John Grantham	Jan. 14, 1837.
Nathaniel Wilson	Feb. 22, 1831.	Joseph Alldridge	Jan. 19, 1837.
James B. Larimer	Jan. 9, 1832.	John Grist	Jan. 2, 1838.
John M. Ewing	Jan. 11, 1833.	John Grantham	Jan. 6, 1838.
James L. Johnson	March 3, 1834.	Joseph W. Hanna	Jan. 6, 1838.
John Carey	Jan. 5, 1835.	Curtis Keener	Jan. 10, 1838.
James B. Larimer	May 13, 1835.	Joseph Alldridge	Jan 11, 1838.
John Armstrong	May 13, 1835.	Gideon Conklin	Jan. 15, 1839.
James L. Johnson	May 13, 1835.	Samuel Gear	Jan. 10, 1839.
Samuel D. Gresham	May 16, 1835.	Joseph Alldridge	Jan. 13, 1839.
John Lenon	May 16, 1835.	John Calvert	Jan. 16, 1839.
John Armstrong	Jan. 4, 1836.	James M'Bath	Jan. 21, 1839.

Names.	Date of Commission.
John Armstrong	Jan. 16, 1840.
William H. Duffield	Jan. 5, 1840.
John Irwin	Jan. 5, 1841.
John Armstrong	Jan. 5, 1841.
Thomas Cloud	Jan. 16, 1841.
James Alldridge	
James Alldridge	Dec. 2, 1844.
John Armstrong	March 5, 1846.
James Alldridge	Dec. 8, 1846.
James Alldridge	Dec. 4. 1848.
James Alldridge	Dec. 2, 1850.

LIST OF COUNTY AGENTS.

Names.	Date of Commission.
Samuel Milroy	May 8, 1828.
William M'Crery	Aug. 11, 1829.
John M'Curdy	Aug. 11, 1840.
Lewis Johnson	Dec. 8, 1841.
Milo Dibble	June 18, 1842.
William Crooks	Sept. 8, 1847.

LIST OF RECORDERS.

Names.	Date of Commission.
Daniel F. Vandeventer	May 8, 1828.
Chevalier Richardson	Aug. 22, 1844.
James H. Stewart	Aug. 14, 1837.
Nathan G. Gillam	Aug. 19, 1844.
Nathan G. Gillam	Aug. 15, 1851.
Attalas L. Benham	Nov. 1, 1855.
James H. Barns	Nov. 1, 1859.

LIST OF COUNTY AUDITORS.

Names.	Date of Commission.
George W. Pigman	Aug. 25, 1842.
Ebenezer Hedge	Nov. 8, 1852.
Ebenezer Hedge	Nov. 5, 1856.
John B. Milroy	Nov. 24, 1858.
Edwin R. Davis	Nov. 1, 1859.

LIST OF SHERIFFS.

Names.	Date of Commission.
Henry B. Milroy, app'd	Feb. 4, 1828.
" "	Sept. 5, 1828.
James Miller, app'd	Dec. 10, 1829.
John M. Pinkston	Sept. 8, 1830.
Nathaniel Wilson, app'd	Dec. 10, 1831.
Jonah T. Hopkinson	Aug. 18, 1832.
James Odell	Aug. 22, 1834.
Samuel D. Gresham	Aug. 9, 1836.
" "	Aug. 13, 1838.
William H. Buford	Aug. 12, 1840.
William H. Buford	Aug. 8, 1842.
Enoch Rinehart	Aug. 18, 1844.
Enoch Rinehart	Aug. 18, 1846.
John S. Case	Aug. 17, 1848.
Levi M. Graham, app'd	Feb. 20, 1850.
Henry P. Tedford	Aug. 14, 1850.
" "	Nov. 8, 1852.
Jonathan Barnett	Nov. 4, 1854.
Henry M. Wright	Nov. 5, 1856.
Jonathan Barnett	Oct. 26, 1858.
" "	Nov. 5, 1860.

LIST OF SCHOOL COMMISSIONERS.

Names.	Date of Commission.
Enoch Cox	
Nathaniel Wilson	
Henry B. Milroy	Oct. 28, 1834.
William Crooks	Aug. 21, 1839.
Arthur G. Connelly	Sept. 11, 1845.

COUNTY SURVEYORS.

Names.	Date of Commission.
Aaron Dewey	June 26, 1828.
John Armstrong	June 3, 1840.
" "	April 6, 1843.
" "	Aug. 11, 1846.
" "	June 2, 1849.
Thomas B. Helm	Dec. 12, 1851.
James C. Thrawls	Oct. 18, 1852.
James M. Sterritt	Oct. 18, 1854.
" "	Mar. 28, 1857.
William Guthrie	Oct. 3, 1857.
James M. Sterritt	Mar. 27, 1860.
" "	Nov. 15, 1860.

SEMINARY TRUSTEES.

Name.	Date of Commission.	Name.	Date of Commission.
Gavin Black	Dec. 27, 1830.	David Henderson	Mar. 5, 1835.
" "	Jan. 22, 1833.		

SURPLUS REVENUE AGENTS.

Names.	Date of Commission.	Name.	Date of Commission.
Samuel Grimes	Mar. 7, 1837.	James Witherow	Sept. 7, 1842.
William Crooks	Sept. 9, 1840.	" "	Mar. 7, 1843.

Elections.

The list of voters and certificate of the inspector and judges of the election, held at the house of William Wilson, on the 28th day of April, 1828, are given on pages twenty and twenty-one. I proceed now to give the list of voters, etc., at some of the subsequent elections, held in the county.

ELECTION,

At the house of Aaron Merriman, in Rock-creek Township, on the 7th day of June, 1828, for Justice of the Peace.

VOTERS' NAMES.

1 Joseph Patterson,
2 Aaron Hicks,
3 Aaron Merriman,
4 Christopher M'Combs,
5 Isam Adkinson,
6 William Sieres,
7 William Cummins,
8 John Crook,
9 Alexander Sieres,
10 David Lucas,
11 John Searfoss,
12 Moses Scott,
13 David M'Combs,
14 Moses Hicks,
15 Eli Cotner,
16 John Mitchell,
17 Manuel M'Combs,
18 John Mikesel
19 John Kistler.

At the above election, Isam Adkinson received ten votes, and John Bozarth nine votes.

Joseph Patterson, *Inspector.*

C. M'Combs,
Aaron Merriman, } *Judges.*

William Cummins,
Aaron Hicks, } *Clerks.*

ELECTION,

Held at the house of Daniel M'Cain, in Deer-creek Township, on the 7th day of June, 1828, for Justice of the Peace.

VOTERS' NAMES.

1 Joseph M'Cain,	15 Joseph Jackson,
2 John Givins,	16 William M'Cord,
3 Daniel M'Cain,	17 James Odell,
4 Stephen Guyle,	18 George I. Baum,
5 Abner Robinson,	19 David Baum,
6 Coleman Robinson,	20 Moses Alldridge,
7 Jacob Baum,	21 Thomas Stirlin,
8 Samuel Wells,	22 Hugh Manary,
9 Thomas R. M'Cain,	23 Henry Baum,
10 Aaron Dewey,	24 Samuel Milroy,
11 Moses Thompson,	25 John M. Ewing,
12 Henry B. Milroy,	26 John Phillips,
13 Stephen A. Miller,	27 Henry Robinson.
14 Daniel M'Cain,	

Henry Robinson, sixteen; Thomas Stirlin, nine; scattering, two.

WILLIAM M'CORD,
STEPHEN A. MILLER,
DANIEL M'CAIN, } *Judges.*

AARON DEWEY,
MOSES ALLDRIDGE, } *Clerks.*

ELECTION,

Held at the house of Alexander Chamberlain, in Eel Township, Carroll County, on the 7th day of June, 1828, for Justice of the Peace.

VOTERS' NAMES.

1 Cyrus Taber,	11 Reuben Covert,
2 J. B. Duret,	12 Isaac Reubarger,
3 Gillis M'Bean,	13 Henry M. Barbour,
4 H. B. M'Keen,	14 Thomas Hatfield,
5 Daniel Bell,	15 Lemuel Marsh,
6 Robert Hars,	16 Moses Barclay,
7 Jacob Woodcock,	17 Jonathan Craigs,
8 Moses Chilson,	18 Alexander Chamberlain,
9 John Tipton,	19 Peter De Jean,
10 Samuel Edsall,	20 Chauncey Carter.

At the above election, William Scott received *all* the votes (twenty).

DAVID BELL, *Inspector.*

GILLIS M'BEAN,
CYRUS TABER, } *Judges.*

J. B. DURET,
H. B. M'KEEN, } *Clerks.*

AUGUST ELECTION, 1828, IN EEL TOWNSHIP.

VOTERS' NAMES.

1 Laurent Aveline,
2 Lemuel Marsh,
3 A. Q. Jack,
4 William Hughes,
5 Graham Roberts,
6 John Mitchell,
7 John M'Gregor,
8 Willis C. Bunnell,
9 Cyrus Reamy,
10 John Chilson,
11 Samuel M'Clure,
12 Joshua Binney,
13 John Tipton,
14 Peter Johnson,
15 David Lucas,
16 John Smith,
17 James Taster,
18 Joseph Thatcher,
19 Richard Sharp,
20 Isaac Martin,
21 Moses Hicks,
22 Edmond Sapington,
23 John Mikesel,
24 Francis Aveline,
25 Daniel Bell,
26 William Scott,
27 John B. Duret,
28 Moses Chilson,
29 Alexander Chamberlain,
30 Jacob Woodcock,
31 Joel Helvey,
32 Chauncey Carter,
33 F. R. Kintner,
34 Joseph Barren,
35 George Delisle,
36 Gillis M'Bean,
37 James B. Tompkins,
38 William Duffield,
39 Ira Evans,
40 Ephraim Dukes,
41 John Starbuck,
42 John Surface,
43 Francis Lusignaut,
44 Robert Wilson,
45 Thomas Robb,
46 H. B. M'Keen,
47 Moses Barclay,
48 John Lindsey,
49 William Gardner,
50 Jonathan Craigs,
51 Martin Key,
52 John Tuliver,
53 Reuben Covert,
54 Daniel Crumrine,
55 Moses Tullis,
56 John Maxwell,
57 William Thompson,
58 George Cicat,
59 John B. Jontras,
60 Samuel Johnson,
61 James Wymer,
62 Samuel D. Taber,
63 Edward M'Cartney,
64 Cyrus Taber.
65 Charles Smith,
66 Isaac Reubarger,
67 Robert Siddle.

DANIEL BELL, *Inspector*.

CYRUS TABER, WILLIAM SCOTT, } *Judges*.

CHAUNCEY CARTER, J. B. DURET, } *Clerks*.

FOR GOVERNOR.

J. Brown Ray, . . .	4
Harbin H. Moore, . .	10
Israel T. Canby, . . .	52

LIEUTENANT-GOVERNOR.

A. C. Pepper, ...	58
Milton Stapp, ...	7

STATE SENATOR.

Calvin Fletcher, . . .	8
John Beard, ...	5

SHERIFF.

Henry B. Milroy,	56
Stephen A. Miller	7

CONGRESS.		CORONER.	
Jonathan Jennings, . .	60	David Baum, ...	5
Henry S. Handy, . .	—	Robert Cade, ...	5
John H. Thompson, . .	—		

ELECTION,

Held at the house of Daniel M'Cain, in Deer-creek Township, on the 4th day of August, 1828.

VOTERS' NAMES.

1 Moses Thompson,
2 Hugh Manary,
3 John Carey,
4 William Carey,
5 George Baum,
6 Samuel Wells,
7 James Odell,
8 Daniel Baum,
9 Joseph M'Cain,
10 Nathaniel Hamilton,
11 David Hamilton,
12 Daniel M'Cain,
13 Benjamin Baxter,
14 Moses Alldridge,
15 John Phillips,
16 Jacob Baum,
17 Stephen Miller,
18 David Baum,
19 Joseph Jackson,
20 John Adams.
21 John E. Metcalf,
22 Henry B. Milroy,
23 William M'Cord,
24 Peleg Babcock,
25 Thomas Stile,
26 Daniel F. Vandeventer,
27 Thomas Hamilton,
28 James M'Dowell.
29 Aaron Dewey,
30 Thomas R. M'Cain,
31 Andrew M'Coy,
32 Nathan Rose,
33 Henry Robinson,
34 John Givins,
35 John M. Ewing,
36 Thomas Stirlin,
37 Coleman Robinson,
38 John Little,
39 Abner Robinson,
40 William Wilson,
41 Hugh Graham.

FOR GOVERNOR.		CONGRESS.	
Israel T. Canby, . . .	18	Ratliff Boon, ...	17
James B. Ray, . . .	1	Thomas Blake, . . .	22
Harbin H. Moore, . .	22		
LIEUTENANT-GOVERNOR.		**SHERIFF.**	
Abel C. Pepper, . . .	19	Henry B. Milroy, . .	19
Milton Stapp, ...	22	Stephen A. Miller, . .	19

CORONER—Benjamin Baxter, ... 15

ELECTION,

Held at the house of Jacob Sager, in Rock-creek Township, on the 4th day of August, 1828.

VOTERS' NAMES.

1 William Hicks,
2 Joseph Peterson,
3 Christopher M'Combs,
4 William Cummins,
5 Alexander Sieres,
6 Manuel M'Combs,
7 John Kistler,
8 William Price,

VOTERS' NAMES.

9 William Sieres,
10 Moses Scott,
11 David M'Combs,
12 Isam Adkinson,
13 Jacob Sager,
14 Aaron Hicks,
15 Eli Cotner.

FOR GOVERNOR.

Harbin H. Moore, . .	5
James B. Ray, . . .	3
Israel T. Canby, . . .	7

LIEUTENANT-GOVERNOR.

Milton Stapp, ...	6
Abel C. Pepper, . . .	8

SHERIFF.

Henry B. Milroy, . .	14
Stephen A. Miller, . .	1

For Convention, . . .	2
Against Convention, .	13

CONGRESS.

Thomas H. Blake, . .	6
Ratliff Boon, ...	9

ISAM ADKINSON, *Inspector.*

CHRIS. M'COMBS, } *Judges.*
JACOB SAGER, }

J. V. PATTERSON, } *Clerks.*
AARON HICKS, }

ELECTION,

Held at the house of Daniel M'Cain, in Deer-creek Township, on the 3d day of November, 1828, for the election of President and Vice-President of the United States.

VOTERS' NAMES.

1 Graham Roberts,
2 Thomas Strain,
3 Samuel Milroy,
4 Benjamin Baxter,
5 Jacob Baum,
6 Isaac Griffith,
7 Henry B. Milroy,
8 Daniel F. Vandeventer,
9 James Miller
10 Daniel M'Cain,
11 James M'Cain,
12 William Wilson,
13 William M'Cord,
14 John M. Ewing,
15 John Carey,
16 James M'Dowell,
17 Jonah Tullis,
18 William Carey,
19 Jeremiah Ballard,
20 James Odell,
21 John Little,
22 Thomas Stirlin,
23 William George,
24 Hugh Manary,
25 Joseph Beckner,
26 William Hughes,
27 Jacob Harter,
28 Aaron Dewey,
29 Jacob Sager,
30 Joseph Jackson,
31 John Phillips,
32 John Givins,
33 Joseph M'Cain,
34 John Odell,
35 Stephen Guyle,
36 Samuel Wells,
37 Daniel M'Cain,
38 John W. Johnson,
39 James Williams,
40 Thomas M'Cain,
41 James Johnson,
42 Moses Thompson,
43 Thomas Burk,
44 Abner Robinson,
45 James M'Gillard,
46 William Odell,
47 John Adams,
48 William G. Bishop.

At said election, Messrs. Joseph Orr, John Watts, Joseph Bartholomew, Isaac Montgomery, Amaziah Morgan, electors on the *Administration Ticket*, received each twenty-one votes; and Benjamin V. Beckes, Ratliff Boon, Jesse B. Durham, William Low, and Ross Smiley, electors on the *Jacksonian Ticket*, each received twenty-seven votes.

WILLIAM G. BISHOP, *Inspector*.
AARON DEWEY, ROBERT CADE, } *Judges*.
JOHN CAREY, WILLIAM MARTIN, } *Clerks*.

ELECTION,

Held at the house of Nathaniel Hamilton, in Tippecanoe Township, on the 3d day of November, 1828, for the election of President and Vice-President.

VOTERS' NAMES.

1 James S. Riley,
2 Thomas Hamilton,
3 Peleg Babcock,
4 Nathaniel Hamilton,
5 Nathan Rose,
6 David Hamilton,
7 Jesse Fleming,
8 Silas Atchison,
9 William M'Crery,
10 Jacob Zook,
11 James Hamilton,
12 Thomas M'Millin,
13 Hiram Fuloe,
14 Joseph Dunham,
15 George Diffendaffer,
16 John E. Metcalf,
17 Alexander Smith.

The Adams electors received fourteen votes, and the Jackson electors received three votes.

NATHANIEL HAMILTON, *Inspector*.
NATHAN ROSE, DAVID HAMILTON, } *Judges*.
SILAS ATCHISON, PELEG BABCOCK, } *Clerks*.

PRESIDENTIAL ELECTION, 1828,

In Rock-creek Township, at the house of Jacob Sager.

VOTERS' NAMES.

1 William Price,
2 Moses Scott,
3 John Moyer,
4 Henry Bingaman,
5 William Hicks,
6 Moses Hicks,
7 David M'Combs,
8 Lewis Neff,
9 Aaron Hicks,
10 Moses Standley,
11 Isam Adkinson,
12 Manuel M'Combs,

VOTERS' NAMES.

13 Jacob Kuns,	19 David Baum,
14 John Scott,	20 Henry Robinson,
15 Ephraim Denison,	21 Coleman Robinson,
16 John Ballard,	22 Eli Cotner,
17 Alexander Sieres,	23 David Lucas.
18 Joshua Merriman,	

Jackson electors received seventeen; Adams, seven.

ISAM ADKINSON, *Inspector*.

MOSES STANDLEY, MANUEL M'COMBS, } *Judges*.

JOHN CROOK, AARON HICKS, } *Clerks*.

PRESIDENTIAL ELECTION, 1828.

EEL TOWNSHIP.

Jackson electors, . . . 65 | Adams electors, . . . 31

DANIEL BELL, *Inspector*.

SAMUEL M'CLURE, JONATHAN KELLAR, } *Judges*.

JAMES FOSTER, WILLIAM SCOTT, } *Clerks*.

ELECTION,

Held on the 25th day of August, 1828, in Township 45, R. 2 W., to determine whether the School Section 16 should be sold or not.

VOTERS' NAMES.

1 James Odell,	14 William Hughes,
2 John Kistler,	15 Isaac Griffith,
3 Coleman Robinson,	16 Daniel Baum,
4 David Baum,	17 Moses Standley,
5 Henry Baum,	18 David Lucas,
6 Harvey Robinson,	19 Eli Cotner
7 John Givins,	20 Thomas Stirlin,
8 Hugh Manary,	21 William Wilson,
9 Joseph Jackson,	22 Moses Thompson,
10 Samuel Wells,	23 William G. Bishop,
11 Henry B. Milroy,	24 Daniel M'Cain,
12 Thomas Burk,	25 Aaron Dewey,
13 Ira Bacon,	26 William M'Cain,

Sale . . . . 10 | No sale 16

DANIEL M'CAIN, *Inspector*.

WILLIAM WILSON, WILLIAM G. BISHOP, } *Judges*.

AARON DEWEY, THOMAS STIRLIN, } *Clerks*.

LIST OF VOTERS,

At an election held in the Public School-house, in Delphi, Deer-creek Township, on the third day of August, 1830, for the election of State and County Officers.

VOTERS' NAMES.

1 Graham Roberts,
2 James Miller,
3 Wm. Odell,
4 Samuel Wells,
5 Nathan Hewitt,
6 Samuel Williams,
7 Robert Cade,
8 John Cluster,
9 Abner Robinson,
10 Hugh Graham,
11 George I. Baum,
12 Ethan Allen,
13 John Little,
14 Edward Cooley,
15 John M. Ewing,
16 Thomas Hamilton,
17 David Hamilton,
18 James Hamilton,
19 Moses Thompson,
20 Henry Robinson,
21 John Carey,
22 William Carey,
23 William Hance,
24 Daniel M'Cain,
25 Joseph Swalls,
26 Simon Marsh,
27 William Wilson,
28 Hugh Manary,
29 John Swalls,
30 Joseph Jackson,
31 John Odell,
32 David Beard,
33 Ephraim Denison,
34 James Odell,
35 George W. Cannon,
36 William Hughes,
37 Philip Rohrbaugh,
38 Samuel Frasier,
39 James M'Cain,
40 Henry B. Milroy,
41 Jesse Jackson,
42 Thomas Burk,
43 Jacob Baum,
44 Henry Baum,
45 David Lucas,
46 Jacob Mitchell,
47 David Baum,
48 Alexander Sieres,
49 John Ruhl,
50 Jonathan Justice,
51 William George,
52 Jedediah Johnson,
53 Thomas Perry,
54 Peleg Babcock,
55 John Kistler,
56 John Ballard,
57 Samuel E. Carpenter,
58 Thomas Strain,
59 John Givins,
60 Joshua Whitaker,
61 James Crawford,
62 John M. Gillam,
63 James Laughlin,
64 Thomas Gillam,
65 John Briggs,
66 Elias Lowther,
67 John Hays,
68 John M. Pinkston,
69 Richard M'Griff,
70 James M'Dowell,
71 Thomas Stirlin,
72 William Bishop,
73 Albert Heonin,
74 William M'Cord,
75 William M'Crery,
76 John M'Millin,
77 Isaac Griffith,
78 James M'Gilliard,
79 Aaron Dewey,
80 Jeremiah Ballard,
81 Stephen A. Miller,
82 Daniel Baum,
83 John Rohrbaugh,
84 George Diffendaffer,
85 Stephen Guyle,
86 John Adams,

87 Henry Peck,
88 Moses Alldridge,
89 Jacob Harter,
90 Thomas H. Young,
91 Joseph M'Cain,
92 Samuel Wise,
93 Daniel Lenon,
94 Elisha Brown,
95 Solomon Lesley,
96 Samuel Earnest,
97 Daniel M'Cain,
98 John Kerns,
99 Joel B. M'Clellan.

WILLIAM GEORGE, *Inspector.*
HUGH GRAHAM, STEPHEN A. MILLER, } *Judges.*

GRAHAM ROBERTS, JAMES MILLER, } *Clerks.*

At the above election the following is the result:

FOR JUSTICE OF THE PEACE.

William George,	44
Scattering,	2

COMMISSIONER.

Wm. M'Crery,	34
Thomas Stirlin,	64

STATE SENATE.

John B. Chapman,	29
Joseph Orr,	60
—— M'George,	2

PROBATE JUDGE.

Henry Robinson,	34
Aaron Dewey,	13
John Carey,	51

REPRESENTATIVES.

Jesse Osborne,	4
Samuel Milroy,	91
John Beard,	46
—— Clark,	8
Peter B. Patterson,	28
—— Emit,	2

ELECTION,

At the house of Aaron Merriman, in Rock-creek Township, August 3, 1829.

VOTERS' NAMES.

1 Aaron Hicks,
2 Joseph Glasscock,
3 William Hicks,
4 Moses Scott,
5 John Moyer,
6 John Scott,
7 A. Merriman,
8 C. M'Combs,
9 David M'Combs,
10 William Cummins,
11 William Sieres,
12 Isam Adkinson,
13 Coleman Robinson,
14 William Adkinson,
15 Jacob Sager,
16 Jacob Kuns,
17 Daniel Kuns.

SENATOR.

Joseph Orr,	15
J. B. Chapman,	2

PROBATE JUDGE.

Henry Robinson,	12
John Carey,	4
Aaron Dewey,	1

REPRESENTATIVES.		COMMISSIONER.	
Samuel Milroy, . . .	13	Thomas Stirlin, . . .	17
O. L. Clark, ...	5	William M'Crery, . .	0
John Beard, ...	11		
Peter Patterson, . . .	3		

JOHN SCOTT, *Inspector*.

C. M'COMBS, AARON HICKS, } *Clerks*.

ISAM ADKINSON, WILLIAM HICKS, } *Judges*.

SPECIAL ELECTION,

Held at the school-house in Delphi, for Representative to the State Legislature, in place of General Samuel Milroy, resigned.

VOTERS' NAMES.

1 Graham Roberts,
2 James M'Dowell,
3 John Storer,
4 Henry Baum,
5 William Adkinson,
6 Daniel Lesley,
7 James M'Gilliard,
8 James Odrage,
9 James Laughlin,
10 Henry Sidenbender,
11 Isaac Griffith,
12 Daniel Baum,
13 Joseph Dunham,
14 William Hughes,
15 William Craig,
16 Coleman Robinson,
17 Edmund Sappington,
18 John Kistler,
19 Daniel M'Cain,
20 John Knight,
21 Samuel Milroy,
22 William Wilson,
23 James M'Cain,
24 James Miller,
25 William George,
26 William M'Crery,
27 John Carey,
28 Joseph Beckner,
29 Thomas Stirlin,
30 Jacob Stair,
31 Thomas H. Young,
32 J. W. Randall,
33 James Quick,
34 George I. Baum,
35 Albert Hernden,
36 John Hays,
37 George Diffendaffer.

Robert Johnson, . . .	26	Jesse Osborne, ...	9
Scattering, ...	2		

WILLIAM GEORGE, *Inspector*.

JOHN KISTLER, DANIEL M'CAIN, } *Judges*.

SPECIAL ELECTION,

Held at the house of Jacob Sager, in Rock-creek Township, October 31, 1829, *for the purpose of electing one Representative to the State Legislature, in the place of Samuel Milroy, resigned.*

VOTERS' NAMES.

1 John Scott,
2 John Cummins,
3 Lewis Neff,
4 Jacob Sager,
5 C. M'Combs.

JOHN SCOTT, *Inspector*.

C. M'COMBS, JOHN CUMMINS, } *Clerks*.

LEWIS NEFF, JACOB SAGER, } *Judges*.

TALLY—The result not known.

I conclude my account of a few of the first elections held in the county, by giving the result of the first military election, held at the Court-house in Delphi, on the 3d day of May, 1832, for the election of colonel, lieutenant-colonel, and major of the Seventy-seventh Regiment Indiana Militia. It will be seen that Carroll County was "*some military*," even at that early day.

Total number of votes given, one hundred and twenty-five.

FOR COLONEL.		LIEUTENANT-COLONEL.	
Burrell B. Taylor, . .	57	Philip Pollard, ...	70
Albert G. Hanna, . .	68	John Thompson, . . .	50
MAJOR.			
Reuben G. Munday, . .	53	John Dollason, . . .	69

LIST OF MARRIAGE LICENSES

Issued by the Clerk of the Circuit Court from the organization of the county until the 9th day of March, 1831.

June 10, 1828.......John Bozarth, Lathy Mitchell. Married by Judge M'Combs.

July 14, 1828.......John Morrow, Isabella Hamilton. Married by Judge M'Combs.

Sept. 4, 1828.......Jeremiah Ballard, Susanna Baum. Married by Esqr. Adkinson.

Dec. 1. 1828..........John Swalls, Polly Marsh. Married by Esqr. Adkinson.

Dec. 25, 1828.........Charles Polke, Louisa R. Smith. Married by Rev. J. Crawford.

Feb. 4, 1829..........John Wesley Johnson, Ruth Smith. Married by Judge Griffith.

Feb. 2, 1829..........John M. Ewing, Lydia Ann Robinson. Married by Esqr. Robinson.

March 3, 1829.......Moses Scott, Hannah Chambers. Married by Judge M'Combs.

July 28, 1829........David Price, Catherine Moyer. Married by Rev. John Scott.

Sept. 10, 1829.......David Baum, Hannah Green. Married by Rev. James Crawford.

Nov. 8, 1829.........David M'Combs, Sarah Martindale. Married by Esqr. Adkinson.

Nov. 24, 1829.......Thomas M'Millin, Mary Hathaway. Married by Rev. Jas. Crawford.

Dec. 30, 1829........Levi Dix, Sarah Little. Married by Esqr. Robinson.

Dec. 4, 1829.........Abraham Peterson, Esther Lane. Married by Joshua Lindsey, E. C. C.

March 30, 1830.....Adam Porter, Catherine Holeman. Married by Judge Carey.

April 13, 1830......John Adair, Mary Bross. Married by Rev. James Crawford.

May 11, 1830.......John M'Millin, Elizabeth Manary. Married by Rev. James Crawford.

July 15, 1830.......Greenville Parr, Mary Chester. Married by Joshua Lindsey, E. C. C.

July 19, 1830.......John Long, Esther Kuns. Married by Judge M'Combs.

July 22, 1830.......James Brown, Elizabeth Alldridge. Married by Judge Carey.

Aug. 28, 1830......Enoch Mayfield, Sarah Holt. Married by Rev. James Crawford.

Sept. 2, 1830.......Joel Jackson, Rebecca Bozarth. Married by Judge M'Combs.

Oct. 7, 1830........William George, Mary Manary.

Oct. 7, 1830........Moses Alldridge, Magdalina Harter. Married by Rev. Peter Imen.

Nov. 9, 1830.......Thomas H. Young, Polly Adkinson. Married by Judge M'Combs.

Nov. 15, 1830......John E. Metcalf, Mary Ann Cox. Married by Joshua Lindsey, E. C. C.

Nov. 25, 1830.......William Carey, Elizabeth Whitcher. Married by Judge Carey.

Dec. 8, 1830.......John Ballard, Lucinda Robbins. Married by Judge Carey.

Feb. 9, 1831........Christopher Vandeventer, Elizabeth Baum. Married by Joshua Lindsey, E. C. C.

Feb. 22, 1831......Thomas Pike, Martha Patton. Married by Rev. James Crawford.

March 9, 1831....Peleg Babcock, Melinda M'Cart. Married by Rev. John Scott.

CHAPTER XX.

WAR RECORD OF CARROLL COUNTY.

THE author has been at great pains to give the names of all the officers and soldiers of Carroll County, who served in the war of 1846, and also 1861. He is aware that the list is not complete, for the reason that very many of our people volunteered in companies organized in other counties, and are credited to the counties in which they enlisted.

It would have afforded the author great pleasure to have given a history of the various regiments and companies organized in Carroll County; but he has already far exceeded the limits originally designed for his book, and he is compelled reluctantly to forbear.

DYSON BOOTHROYD, a young soldier in the three months' service, a member of Company "A," of the Ninth Regiment, Indiana Volunteers, who was killed in Western Virginia, on the 13th day of July, 1861, is believed to have been the first Union soldier killed after the commencement of the war. He was brought back by his comrades, and buried in the old Delphi grave-yard, with the honors of war. A monument should be erected, by a grateful people, to his memory.

Captain Robert H. Milroy's Company "C,"

OF THE FIRST REGIMENT, INDIANA VOLUNTEERS (MEXICAN WAR).

Names.	Age.	When Enrolled.	Remarks.
Captain.			
Robert H. Milroy	...	June 19, 1846	
First Lieutenant.			
Andrew L. Robinson	...	June 19, 1846	Appointed Aid to Brig. Jo. Lane.
Second Lieutenant.			
William E. Pearsons	...	June 19, 1846	Appointed Adj't of the Regt.
James W. Colvin	...	" " "	Elected additional Second Lieut. from First Serg't.
First Sergeant.			
Henry M. Graham	28	June 19, 1846	Appointed First Serg't from First Corporal.
Sergeants.			
2. James Chittick	29	June 19, 1846	
3. Alonzo Grout	25	" " "	
4. Wm. G. Mullen	25	" " "	Appointed Fourth Serg't from Corporal.
Corporals.			
1. Wm. Barrett	23	June 19, 1846	
2. Wm. Chapman	25	" " "	
3. Barnabas Busby	26	" " "	
4. James Cline	21	" " "	

Names.	Age.	When Enrolled.	Names.	Age.	When Enrolled.
Buglers.			**Privates.**		
1. Samuel L. Milroy	23	June 19, 1846.	Israel, Pleasant R.	19	June 19, 1846.
2. William Moore	28	" " "	Judkins, John	21	" " "
			Jenkins, John	22	" " "
Privates.			Jervis, Isaiah	21	" " "
Armitage, Valerius	18	June 19, 1846.	Kennedy, Thomas	31	" " "
Barngrover, John S.	24	" " "	Mooney, Oabdiah	23	" " "
Baldwin, Thornburg	25	" " "	Mabbitt, Joseph	19	" " "
Caster, Vincent	18	" " "	Maxwell, James W.	22	" " "
Colegrove, Riley	19	" " "	Miller, James	19	" " "
Chittick, Charles	19	" " "	Morgan, John	26	" " "
Chittick, Archibald	33	" " "	Norris, John P.	21	" " "
Dasney, Daniel	18	" " "	Orb, Sebastian	20	" " "
Carr, Peter O.	25	" " "	Patty, Nathan	25	" " "
Carr, Thomas A.	23	" " "	Robinson, B. A.	25	" " "
Erwin Edwin E.	28	" " "	Snyder, Levi	18	" " "
Esders, Joseph B.	25	" " "	Sherman, Mervin	18	" " "
Emley, Anthony	22	" " "	Shultz, Washington A.	25	" " "
Forgy, Andrew J.	22	" " "	Smith, James C.	18	" " "
Gwinn, Norman	27	" " "	Shivar, James R.	22	" " "
Gee, Lewis	18	" " "	Walter, Alpha	22	" " "
Graham, James W.	36	" " "	Weatherholt, Jacob	23	" " "
Guy, Samuel	22	" " "	Yost, Lewis	35	" " "
Hannam, Jehu	21	" " "	Yeager, Samuel	20	" " "
Hoover, Daniel	28	" " "	Hull, John	50	" " "

Names.	Age.	When Enrolled.	Remarks.
Discharged.			
Daniel Davis, Second Lieut.	...	June 21, 1846	Discharged, October 20, 1846; disability.
Armstrong, James H.	22	" 19, "	" " 15, " "
Erwin, George M.	24	" " "	" Sept. 18, " "
Bowen, Hezekiah	28	" " "	" Oct. 15, " "
Chittick, Stephen	21	" " "	" " " " "
Davis, David	18	" " "	" " " " "
Eidson, Barney	25	" " "	" " " " "
Fizer, John W.	20	" " "	" " " " "
Harrison, William C.	19	" " "	" " " " "
House, Lewis	44	" " "	" " " " "
Hance, William C.	20	" " "	" " " " "
Landrum, Isaac	21	" " "	" " " " "
Landrum, Thomas	21	" " "	" " 12 " "
M'Crery, James W.	23	" " "	" " " " "
Manary, Richard	26	" " "	" " " " "
Pulmer, Robert	19	" " "	" " 10 " "
Died.			
Bell, Michael	20	June 19, 1846	Died on the Rio Grande, Oct. 12, 1846.
Craiger, William H.	22	" " "	Died at Matamoras, Mexico, Oct. 26, 1846.
Cox, Alfred W.	23	" " "	" " " " " "
Foster, James W.	26	" " "	" " " " 20 "

Note.—The above is copied from an old muster-roll in the possession of Captain (now General) Milroy, and is believed to be nearly correct. A few more names, perhaps, were contained on the rolls of the company when first mustered into service.

CARROLL COUNTY'S RECORD IN THE WAR OF THE GREAT REBELLION.

COMPANY "A," NINTH REGIMENT, INDIANA VOLUNTEERS.

(THREE MONTHS.)

NAMES AND RANK.	RESIDENCE.	Date of Comm'n.	Date of Muster.	REMARKS.
CAPTAIN.				
Jehu C. Hannam.......	Delphi...........	April 20, 1861	April 25, 1861	Mustered out; term expired; re-entered; served as Captain Second Cavalry.
FIRST LIEUTENANT.				
John H. Gould.........	Delphi...........	April 20, 1861	April 25, 1861	Mustered out; term expired; re-entered; served as Captain in Forty-sixth Reg't.
SECOND LIEUTENANT.				
William A. Pigman...	Delphi...........	April 20, 1861	April 25, 1861	Mustered out; term expired; re-entered; served First Lieutenant in Forty-sixth Reg't.

NON-COMMISSIONED OFFICERS AND PRIVATES.

NAMES AND RANK.	RESIDENCE.	DATE OF MUSTER.	REMARKS.
FIRST SERGEANT.			
Madden, Thomas........................	Carroll County...	April 22, 1861...	Mustered out July 29, 1861; term expired.
SERGEANTS.			
Eversole, Salem P......................	Carroll County...	April 22, 1861...	Mustered out July 29, 1861; term expired.

Jackson Amaziah	Carroll County	April 22, 1861	Mustered out July 29, 1861; term expired.
Cratts, James M	" "	" "	" " " "
CORPORALS.			
Kessler, John G	Carroll County	April 22, 1861	Mustered out July 29, 1861; term expired.
Merritt, Fred. J	" "	" "	" " " "
Pratt, Richard H	" "	" "	" " " "
Cress, Simeon	" "	" "	Died June 23, 1861, at Lockport, Indiana.
MUSICIANS.			
Inglee, William F	Carroll County	April 22, 1861	Mustered out July 29, 1861; term expired.
Beall, Lucius	" "	" "	" " " "
PRIVATES.			
Andrew, William A	Carroll County	April 22, 1861	Mustered out July 29, 1861; term expired.
Arnold, Samuel	" "	" "	" " " "
Austin, Charles M	" "	" "	" " " "
Barnes, Edward M	" "	" "	" " " "
Baum, George W	" "	" "	" " " "
Burdan, John	" "	" "	" " " "
Benson, Andrew W	" "	" "	" " " "
Berger, Frederick E	" "	" "	" " " "
Black, Samuel	" "	" "	" " " "
Black, Thomas	" "	" "	" " " "
Boothroyd, Dyson	" "	" "	Died July 13, 1861; wounded at Laurel Hill.
Brough, James V	" "	" "	Mustered out July 29, 1861; term expired.
Breen, Joseph	" "	" "	" " " "
Buckingham, Anthony W	" "	" "	" " " "
Corbit, Thomas	" "	" "	" " " "
Coller Ebenezer	" "	" "	" " " "

Names and Rank.	Residence.	Date of Muster.	Remarks.
Cupp, John	Carroll County	April 22, 1861	Mustered out July 29, 1861; term expired.
Daily, James	" "	" "	" " " "
Davis, Charles C.	" "	" "	" " " "
Doggett, Leander H.	" "	" "	" " " "
Fost, Philip	" "	" "	" " " "
Generick, Frederick	" "	" "	" " " "
Greenwalt, Levi B.	" "	" "	" " " "
Gros, Lewis	" "	" "	" " " "
Hanna, James M.	" "	" "	" " " "
Haugh, Jerry	" "	" "	" " " "
Hicks, Thomas B.	" "	" "	" " " "
Huffman, Solomon	" "	" "	" " " "
Hughes, Allen	" "	" "	" " " "
Hull, James F.	" "	" "	" " " "
Huntsinger, Rufus	" "	" "	" " " "
Jones, Samuel H.	" "	" "	" " " "
Kessler, Henry	" "	" "	" " " "
Landrey, Joseph L.	" "	" "	" " " "
Landrey, Hugh M.	" "	" "	" " " "
Lapple, Christian	" "	" "	" " " "
Lenon, Edward	" "	" "	Deserted April 23, 1861, at Indianapolis.
Lister, Ezra	" "	" "	Mustered out July 29, 1861; term expired.
Lister, Joshua M.	" "	" "	" " " "
M'Afee, Benjamin F.	" "	" "	" " " "
M'Mininy, Wm.	" "	" "	" " " "
Morton, James D.	" "	" "	" " " "
Mullendore, Jacob	" "	" "	" " " "

Newhouse, James B.	Carroll County	April 22, 1861	Mustered out July 29, 1861; term expired.
Nipper, Isaac	" "	" "	" " " "
Pudgett, Wm. H.	" "	" "	" " " "
Penny, Berl P.	" "	" "	" " " "
Reynolds, Andrew J.	" "	" "	" " " "
Richards, Simon	" "	" "	" " " "
Riesthammon, Val	" "	" "	" " " "
Red, Cornelius	" "	" "	" " " "
Ryan, Pat	" "	" "	" " " "
Savage, John N.	" "	" "	" " " "
Shuvy, Davis	" "	" "	" " " "
Smith, James W.	" "	" "	" " " "
Stokes, Marion	" "	" "	" " " "
Stoner, Jacob	" "	" "	" " " "
Striker, Peter	" "	" "	" " " "
Taffe, Patrick	" "	" "	" " " "
Thayer, John S.	" "	" "	Discharged May 17, 1861; disability.
Thayer, Francis	" "	" "	Mustered out July 29, 1861; term expired.
Tribbet, William	" "	" "	" " " "
Voris, William N.	" "	" "	" " " "
Williams, Henry	" "	" "	" " " "
Wolf, Doniece	" "	" "	" " " "
Young, Isaac	" "	" "	" " " "

Company "A," Ninth Regiment, Indiana Volunteers.

(THREE YEARS.)

Names and Rank.	Residence.	Date of Comm'n.	Date of Muster.	Remarks.
Captains.				
John B. Milroy	Delphi	Aug. 20, 1861	Sept. 5, 1861	Promoted Major.
Thomas Madden	"	Oct. 8, 1861	Oct. 8, 1861	Resigned March 15, 1864.
George K. Marshall	"	March 16, 1864		Resigned as First Lieutenant, Oct. 4, 1864.
Thomas W. Thompson	"	Oct. 5, 1864	Feb. 11, 1865	
First Lieutenants.				
Thomas Madden	Delphi	Aug. 29, 1861	Sept. 5, 1861	Promoted Captain.
Frank P. Gross	Lafayette	Oct. 8, 1861	Oct. 8, 1861	Resigned April 25, 1863.
Samuel Sidenbender	Delphi	April 26, 1863	May 26, 1863	Resigned May 31, 1863; re-enlisted as private 11th Cavalry; promoted Second Lieut.
George K. Marshall	"	June 1, 1863	June 11, 1863	Promoted Captain; Resigned Oct. 4, 1864.
Thomas W. Thompson	"	March 16, 1864		Promoted Captain.
James M. Wharton	"	Jan. 1, 1865	Feb. 11, 1865	
Second Lieutenants.				
Jacob K. Armor	Delphi	Aug. 29, 1861	Sept. 5, 1861	Resigned October 8, 1861.
John A. Savage	"	Oct. 8, 1861	Oct. 8, 1861	Resigned September 28, 1862.
Henry Kessler	"	Dec. 14, 1862	Dec. 14, 1862	Killed at Stone River, December 31, 1862.
Samuel Sidenbender	"	Jan. 1, 1863	April 7, 1863	Promoted First Lieutenant.
George K. Marshall	"	April 26, 1863	May 26, 1863	Promoted First Lieutenant.
Thomas W. Thompson	"	June 1, 1863	June 11, 1863	Promoted First Lieutenant.
Edward L. Ephlin	La Porte	March 16, 1865	March 25, 1865	

NON-COMMISSIONED OFFICERS AND PRIVATES.

Names and Rank.	Residence.	Date of Muster.	Remarks.
First Sergeant.			
Tantlinger, John S.	Carroll County	Sept. 5, 1861	Killed at Shiloh, April 7, 1862.
Sergeants.			
Deils, Gustave	Carroll County	Sept. 5, 1861	Discharged November 25, 1861; disability.
Kessler, Henry	" "	" "	Appointed First Sergeant; promoted Second Lieut.
Berger, Frederick E.	" "	" "	Reduced; transferred Regular Army, Dec. 21, 1862.
Goodwin, Henry	" "	" "	
Corporals.			
Sidenbender, Samuel	Carroll County	Sept. 5, 1861	Appointed First Sergeant; promoted Second Lieut.
Savage, John N.	" "	" "	Promoted Second Lieutenant.
Johnson, Harrison R.	" "	" "	Died September 10, 1862; disease.
Young, William H.	" "	" "	Mustered out as private, September 15, 1864.
Marshall, George K.	" "	" "	Appointed First Sergeant; Promoted Second Lieut.
Smith, Charles L.	" "	" "	Reduced; Promoted Chaplain.
Fox, Henry	" "	" "	Discharged January 30, 1862; wounded.
Franklin, Noah	" "	" "	Discharged June 1, 1862; disability.
Musicians.			
Lamphler, Jared	Carroll County	Sept. 5, 1861	Discharged August 13, 1862; disability.
Armor, George E.	" "	" "	Discharged June 30, 1862; disability.
Wagoner.			
Shroth, George	Carroll County	Sept. 5, 1861	Discharged as private, July 2, 1862; disability.

Names and Rank.	Residence.	Date of Muster.	Remarks.
Privates.			
Baker, George	Carroll County	Sept. 5, 1861	Veteran; mustered out September 28, 1865.
Beaty, Samuel F.	" "	" "	Veteran; appt'd Corp.; mustered out Sept. 28, 1865.
Beckworth, Thomas C.	" "	" "	Deserted at Nashville, July 18, 1862.
Billingsby, George	" "	" "	Veteran; appt'd Corp.; must'd out Sept. 28, 1865.
Black, William	" "	" "	Dicharged March 11, 1863, to enlist in Marine Corps.
Borer, William H.	" "	" "	Deserted in face of enemy, October 3, 1862.
Brugh, George P.	" "	" "	Deserted from Hospital, July, 1862.
Burns, Sinesia J.	" "	" "	Died April 24, 1862; wounded at Shiloh.
Burr, Lafayette	" "	" "	Appointed Q. M. Sergt.; veteran; promoted Adjutant.
Carr, Alexander	" "	" "	Discharged June 1, 1862; disability.
Chandler, James	" "	" "	" " " "
Chapman, Jacob	" "	" "	" " " "
Coats, John	" "	" "	Mustered out September 6, 1864.
Compton, Nestor	" "	" "	Veteran; appt'd Corp. and Sergt.; killed at Kennesaw.
Creekpaum, Eli	" "	" "	Deserted at Nashville, July, 1862.
Crocker, Henry	" "	" "	Deserted October 5, 1862.
Darby, John	" "	" "	Veteran; appointed Corporal; reduced.
Dani, Christopher C.	" "	" "	Veteran; appointed Corporal; transferred V. R. C.
Drepperd, John	" "	" "	Veteran; mustered out September 28, 1865.
Elbutt, Theodore F	" "	" "	Veteran; appointed Corp.; must'd out Sept. 25, 1865.
English, John I.	" "	" "	Died January 2, 1863; wounded at Stone River.
Fox, John, Sr.	" "	" "	Died March 28, 1863; disease.
Fox, John, Jr.	" "	" "	Veteran; appt'd Corp., Sergt.; must'd out Sept. 1865.
Fogle, Samuel B.	" "	" "	Died at La Porte, Indiana, September 20, 1861.
Ferquer, Landon S.	" "	" "	Appt'd Corp., Sergt.; killed at Stone River, Dec. 1862.
Franklin, James S.	" "	" "	Veteran; appt'd Corp.; killed near Atlanta.

Name	Residence	Date	Remarks
Franklin, Artemus P.	Carroll County	Sept. 5, 1861	Veteran; appointed Corp.; deserted June 20, 1865.
Gates, Abraham	" "	" "	Died September 18, 1863; disease.
George, John	" "	" "	Died June 20, 1863; disease.
George, George	" "	" "	Killed at Chickamauga, September 19, 1863.
Greiss, Theodore	" "	" "	Discharged December 25, 1862; disability.
Gruber, Lewis	" "	" "	Discharged July 11, 1862; wounded at Shiloh.
Guthrie, James	" "	" "	Veteran; appt'd Corp., Sergt.; mustered out Sept. 1865.
Haley, Michael C.	" "	" "	Deserted May 9, 1863.
Hamling, Paul	" "	" "	Veteran; appt'd Corp.; mustered out Sept. 28, 1865.
Hilander, John	" "	" "	Died at Delphi, Indiana, Nov. 20, 1862; disease.
Harrington, Benjamin	" "	" "	Deserted October 1, 1862.
Hutchinson, James N.	" "	" "	Died April 20, 1863; disease.
James, George E.	" "	" "	Transferred to Invalid Corps, March 11, 1864.
Keilty, Patrick	" "	" "	Appointed Corp.; discharged Jan. 17, 1863; disability.
Kendall, James M.	" "	" "	Transferred to V. R. C., May 28, 1864.
Kendall, William	" "	" "	Discharged May 11, 1862; disability.
Kessler, Eli	" "	" "	Veteran; appointed First Sergeant.
Kilmer, Jackson	" "	" "	Killed at Buffalo Mountain, December 13, 1861.
Keiste, Adam	" "	" "	Appt'd Corp., Sergt.; captured at Chickamauga; died in prison.
Lane, Archer	" "	" "	Veteran; appt'd Corp.; mustered out Sept. 28, 1865.
Lathrop, Harrison T.	" "	" "	Discharged March 19, 1862; disability.
Lenon, Wm. G.	" "	" "	Appt'd Comp'y Q. M. Sergt.; transferred to Comp'y F.
Lewis, Alfred	" "	" "	Discharged January 21, 1862; disability.
M'Combs, William	" "	" "	Discharged August 10, 1862; disability.
M'Cormick, Asbury S.	" "	" "	Appointed Corp.; captured at Chickamauga; mustered out February, 1865.
M'Nulty, John	" "	" "	Discharged February 21, 1862; minority.
Merica, Henry	" "	" "	Veteran; mustered out September 28, 1865.
Merica, Lewis	" "	" "	Mustered out September 28, 1865.

Names and Rank.	Residence.	Date of Muster.	Remarks.
Privates.			
Micky, James R.	Carroll County	Sept. 5, 1861	Mustered out September 28, 1865.
Nicholas, John L.	" "	" "	Veteran; Discharged March 8, 1865; disability.
Perkins, John.	" "	" "	Deserted October 1, 1862.
Peterson, Class.	" "	" "	Veteran; died June 20, 1864; wounded at Pine Mt.
Potter, Edwin H.	" "	" "	Veteran; appt'd Corp., Sergt.; must'd out Sept. 1865.
Randals, William.	" "	" "	Discharged November 29, 1861; disability.
Reuber, Henry.	" "	" "	Veteran; mustered out September 28, 1865.
Rinier, Peter.	" "	" "	Veteran; appointed Corp.; must'd out Sept. 28, 1865.
Robb, Charles H.	" "	" "	Mustered out September 15, 1864.
Robinson, William.	" "	" "	Veteran; appt'd Corp., Sergt.; must'd out Sept. 28, 1865.
Robinson, John S.	" "	" "	Discharged May 26, 1862; disability.
Rose, William.	" "	" "	Veteran; transferred to First U. S. Engineers.
Roth, Christian.	" "	" "	Deserted at Louisville, April 1, 1863.
Rosengarter, Jacob.	" "	" "	Transferred to Invalid Corps, December 23, 1863.
Shaffer, Josiah.	" "	" "	Discharged April 30, 1862; disability.
Shaffer, William H.	" "	" "	Captured and paroled, Sept. 5, 1862; never returned.
Shaw, Jeremiah.	" "	" "	Deserted in the face of the enemy, Oct. 3, 1863.
Sinks, Isaac.	" "	" "	Killed at Stone River, December 31, 1862.
Smith, Frank.	" "	" "	Mustered out September 15, 1864.
Souder, David S.	" "	" "	Killed at Buffalo Mountain, December 13, 1861.
Sterritt, Thomas B.	" "	" "	Wounded at Shiloh; sent to hospital.
Thompson, Thomas W.	" "	" "	Appt'd Corp., Sergt., First Sergt.; prom'd Second Lieut.
Tilsey, Charles.	" "	" "	Mustered out September 15, 1864.
Watkins, Abner.	" "	" "	Discharged November 24, 1861; disability.
Wharton, James M.	" "	" "	Appt'd Corp., Sergt., First Sergt.; prom'd First Lieut.
Wilkins, Charles A.	" "	" "	Killed at Chickamauga, September 19, 1863.

Worley, Charles	Carroll County	Sept. 5, 1861	Discharged November 24, 1861; disability.
Young, Christopher	" "	" "	Mustered out September 15, 1864.
RECRUITS.			
Booth, Abraham B	Delphi	March 17, 1862.	Discharged August 21, 1862; disability.
Bovier, Lewis H	Carroll County	Jan. 16, 1864	Mustered out September 28, 1865.
Breene, Joseph	" "	March 17, 1862.	Transferred to Regular Army, December 2, 1862.
Drepperd, Ben. F	" "	Jan. 16, 1864	Mustered out September 28, 1865.
Ewing, John M	" "	Dec. 29, 1861	Died at Spring Hill, Tennessee, March 30, 1862.
Gardner, Anthony	" "	Dec. 29, 1861	Deserted at Nashville, July 18, 1862.
Halthous, Joseph	" "	March 8, 1864	Mustered out September 28, 1865.
Horn, George W	" "	Dec. 29, 1863	Mustered out May 24, 1865.
Hummer, Jacob S	" "	Jan. 1, 1864	" " "
Keilty, Thomas	" "	" "	Veteran; discharged March 22, 1865; disability.
Kellogg, Nelson T	" "	March 14, 1862	Transferred to Invalid Corps, March 29, 1864.
M'Donald, Richard W	" "	Jan. 29, 1864	Mustered out September 28, 1865.
Mader, Christian C	" "	Feb. 11, 1864	" " "
Merica, Charles	" "	Jan. 16, 1864	" " "
Morgan, George C	" "	March 14, 1862.	Veteran; died near Atlanta, August 31, 1864.
Morgan, William H	" "	March 26, 1862.	Veteran; appointed principal musician.
Roseberry, Lemuel	" "	Dec. 11, 1863	Killed at Dallas, May 31, 1864.
Southworth, Valerius N	" "	Jan. 24, 1864	Mustered out September 28, 1865.
Stoner, Solomon	" "	March 17, 1862.	Mustered out March 20, 1865.
Wallace, George	" "	March 17, 1862.	Discharged February 11, 1863.
Williamson, James K	" "	Jan. 24, 1864	Died at Nashville, July 29, 1864; sun-stroke.
Wright, Charles	" "	Feb. 11, 1864	Deserted at Nashville, June 17, 1865.

FORTY-SIXTH REGIMENT, INDIANA VOLUNTEERS.

Name and Rank.	Residence.	Date of Commission.	Date of Muster.	Remarks.
Lieutenant-Colonel.				
John H. Gould	Delphi	Aug. 6, 1862	Aug. 6, 1862	Resigned Feb. 9, 1863; re-entered service Lieut.-Col. 135th Reg't.
Majors.				
John H. Gould	Delphi	May 25, 1862	May 25, 1862	Promoted Lieutenant-Colonel.
Bernard F. Schermerhorn	"	Feb. 11, 1863	Aug. 25, 1863	Mustered out December 14, 1864.
Adjutant.				
James M. Watts	Delphi	Oct. 20, 1862	Oct. 20, 1862	Promoted Major 150th Regiment.
Quartermaster.				
Elza J. Downey	Delphi	June 12, 1862	June 12, 1862	Resigned June 15, 1863.
Chaplain.				
Hamilton Robb	Delphi	Dec. 16, 1862	Jan. 10, 1863	Mustered out with Regiment.

COMPANY "A," FORTY-SIXTH REGIMENT, INDIANA VOLUNTEERS.

Name and Rank.	Residence.	Date of Muster.	Remarks.
Captains.			
John H. Gould	Delphi	Nov. 1, 1861	Promoted Major.
William A. Pigman	"	July 1, 1862	Honorably discharged December 18, 1864.
James V. Brough	"	Feb. 15, 1865	Mustered out with regiment.

First Lieutenants.			
William A. Pigman	Delphi	Nov. 1, 1861	Promoted Captain.
James M. Watts	"	July 1, 1862	Promoted Adjutant.
James V. Brough	"	Oct. 20, 1862	Promoted Captain.
Jonathan Moore	Burlington	Feb. 15, 1865	Mustered out with regiment.
Second Lieutenants.			
James M. Watts	Delphi	Nov. 1, 1861	Promoted First Lieutenant.
James V. Brough	"	July 1, 1862	Promoted First Lieutenant.
William Andrews	"	Oct. 20, 1862	Died May 22, 1863, of wounds.
Jonathan Moore	Burlington	May 23, 1863	Promoted First Lieutenant.
Levi C. Le Sourd	Pittsburg	June 1, 1865	Mustered out with regiment.
First Sergeant.			
Brough, James V	Delphi	Nov. 1, 1861	Promoted Second Lieutenant.
Sergeants.			
Andrew, William A	Delphi	Nov. 1, 1861	Promoted Second Lieutenant.
Penny, Berl P	"	" "	Veteran; mustered out July 8, 1865.
Haslitt, James	"	" "	Discharged October 9, 1862; disability.
Downey, Elza	"	" "	Appointed Commissary Sergeant.
Corporals.			
Ballard, Amos M	Delphi	Nov. 1, 1861	Discharged May 30, 1862.
Thayer, Francis	"	" "	Mustered out December 1, 1864.
Padget, William H	"	" "	Died May 3, 1863, wounds received Port Gibson.
Carter, Lewis	Poplar Grove	" "	Veteran; mustered out Sept. 4, 1865, as Sergeant.
Moore, Jonathan	Burlington	" "	Promoted Second Lieutenant.
Baum, Francis H	Delphi	" "	Discharged May 19, 1862; disability.

Name and Rank.	Residence.	Date of Muster.	Remarks.
Duncan, Michael	Delphi	Nov. 1, 1861	Mustered out December 1, 1864.
Franklin, James T	"	" "	Veteran; mustered out Sept. 4, 1865; Serg't Major.
Musicians.			
Barnes, William W	Lockport	Nov. 1, 1861	Mustered out December 1, 1864.
Randolph, Benjamin F	Pittsburg	" "	" " " "
Wagoner.			
Smock, George C	Delphi	Nov. 1, 1861	Discharged May 19, 1862; disability.
Privates.			
Aker, Jacob	Delphi	Nov. 1, 1861	Veteran; mustered out Sept. 4, 1865, as Sergeant.
Anderson, Alfred J	Rockfield	" "	Discharged May 30, 1862; disability.
Anderson, Samuel T	Pittsburg	" "	Wounded at Champion Hills; transferred V. R. C.
Ashba, Andrew	Delphi	" "	Discharged October 16, 1862; disability.
Beaver, John	Pittsburg	" "	Wounded at Port Gibson; killed at Champion Hills.
Billiard, Lewis	Carroll County	" "	Disch'd July 29, 1863, wounds rec'd Champion Hills.
Bowman, Amos	Delphi	" "	Mustered out December 1, 1864.
Brough, George W	Pittsburg	" "	" " " "
Campbell, James D	Featherhoff Mill	" "	Veteran; mustered out Sept. 4, 1865; Sergeant.
Canter, Levi	Poplar Grove	" "	Veteran; mustered out September 4, 1865.
Corns, John	Pittsburg	" "	Discharged February 5, 1863; disability.
Creson, George W	Burlington	" "	Died at Helena, Arkansas, October 4, 1862.
Creson, John W	"	" "	Veteran; mustered out September 4, 1865.
Davidson, William T	Pittsburg	" "	Discharged May 30, 1862; disability.
Davidson, Robert W	"	" "	Died at Pittsburg, Indiana, May 15, 1863.
Davis, Silas	Burlington	" "	Killed at Champion Hills, May 16, 1863.

Deyo, Horace H	Delphi	Nov. 1, 1861	Veteran; mustered out September 4, 1865.
Dunkin, William H	Burlington	" "	Wounded, Champion Hills; must'd out Dec. 1, 1864.
Evans, Robert B	Pittsburg	" "	Died in Carroll County, Indiana, March 18, 1862.
Ewing, Jasper L	Carroll County	" "	Mustered out December 1, 1864.
Faucett, Charles B	" "	" "	" " "
Fisher, John F	Pittsburg	" "	Died at Columbus, Ky., September 20, 1862.
Freed, John	Delphi	" "	Died at Vicksburg, July 4, 1863.
Freed, Richard T	"	" "	Veteran; mustered out September 4, 1865.
Fry, John	Rossville	" "	Discharged May 30, 1862; disability.
Gibson, Thomas S	Pittsburg	" "	Veteran; mustered out Sept. 4, 1865, as Corporal.
Ginn, Francis M	"	" "	Discharged February 3, 1863; disability.
Ginn, Thomas B	Idaville	" "	Mustered out December 1, 1864.
Greider, John M	Pittsburg	" "	Discharged May 30, 1862; disability.
Hardy, Alfred H	Camden	" "	Died July 18, 1863; wound received at Jackson.
Hay, James	Indianapolis	" "	Mustered out December 1, 1864.
Heartzog, William C	Pittsburg	" "	Died July 2, 1863; wounded at Champion Hills.
Hornback, Jeremiah	"	" "	Mustered out December 1, 1864.
Jay, Solomon	Kokomo	" "	" " "
Jay, Enos	Indianapolis	" "	" " "
Johnson, Robert G	Pittsburg	" "	" " "
Johnson, Samuel N	"	" "	" " "
Julien, Albert A	Delphi	" "	Mustered out December 1, 1864, as Sergeant.
Julien, William F	"	" "	Discharged January 20, 1863; disability.
Kinsey, William A	Rockfield	" "	Discharged Oct. 6, 1863; wounded, Champion Hills.
Kirkpatrick, Samuel A	Burlington	" "	Mustered out December 1, 1864.
Le Sourd, Levi C	Pittsburg	" "	Veteran; promoted Second Lieutenant.
Le Sourd, Benjamin	"	" "	Discharged October 4, 1862; disability.
Lister, Elias J	"	" "	Wounded at Champion Hills; mustered out December 1, 1864, as Corporal.
Malcom, William M	"	" "	Died October 8, 1862.

Names and Rank.	Residence.	Date of Muster.	Remarks.
M'Mahon, Ralph	Delphi	Nov. 1, 1861	Veteran; died at Jeffersonville, July 18, 1865.
M'Namar, Jacob V	North Waverly	" "	Veteran; mustered out Sept. 4, 1865, as Corporal.
Melsern, James F	Delphi	" "	Discharged May 30, 1862; disability.
Montgomery, Isaac W	"	" "	Mustered out December 1, 1864.
Murphy, David C	"	" "	Veteran; mustered out Sept. 4, 1865, as Sergeant.
Nelson, Swain H	"	" "	Killed at Champion Hills, May 16, 1863.
Newell, John	Pittsburg	" "	Died June 2, 1863; wounds rec'd at Champion Hills.
O'Farrell, Peter	P. William	" "	Discharged February 11, 1863; disability.
Patterson, Samuel B	Delphi	" "	Mustered out December 1, 1864.
Parker, Charles M	Pittsburg	" "	Discharged July 20, 1863; wounded and arm amputated at Champion Hills.
Pettit, Wilson H	Delphi	" "	Died at St. Louis, January 2, 1863.
Preston, Francis M	Pittsburg	" "	Mustered out December 1, 1864.
Ransom, Hiram V	"	" "	Discharged September 8, 1862; disability.
Reed, Adoniram J	Battle Ground	" "	Discharged July, 1862; disability.
Rees, John T	Pittsburg	" "	Veteran; mustered out September 4, 1865.
Richcreek, Absalom	Delphi	" "	Deserted at Helena, Arkansas, August 2, 1862.
Robison, Hezekiah	Camden	" "	Mustered out December 1, 1864, as Corporal.
Ruter, Martin L	Pittsburg	" "	Killed by Guerrillas, near Helena, October 8, 1862.
Shafer, Noah	Delphi	" "	Died at St. Louis, December 31, 1862.
Shafer, Ephraim F	"	" "	Mustered out December 1, 1864.
Shaffer, John	Burlington	" "	Died at White River, Ark., July 12, 1862, of wounds.
Sheridan, John F	Rossville	" "	Wounded, Champion Hills; must'd out Dec. 1, 1864.
Shirar, Charles	Delphi	" "	Discharged October 14, 1862; disability.
Sleeth, Thomas W	Brookston	" "	Wounded, Champion Hills; must'd out Dec. 1, 1864.
Smith, Zach. T	Delphi	" "	Discharged June 19, 1863; disability.
Smith, Henry L	"	" "	Killed at Champion Hills, May 16, 1863.

Smock, Archibald	Delphi	Nov. 1, 1861	Veteran; killed at Sabine X Roads, April 8, 1864.
Snyder, Daniel P	Pittsburg	" "	Mustered out December 1, 1864.
Strain, Andrew L	Delphi	" "	Discharged February 7, 1863; disability.
Stoops, John N	"	" "	Mustered out December 1, 1864.
Swatts, Andrew J	Pittsburg	" "	Discharged December 20, 1862.
Tea, Theodore	Delphi	" "	Mustered out December 1, 1864.
Viney, John J	Burlington	" "	Wound'd, Carrion-crow Bayou; must'd out Dec. 1, '64.
Whitcher, George A	Delphi	" "	Discharged November 14, 1863; disability.
White, Reuben	"	" "	Mustered out December 1, 1864.
White, Thomas	"	" "	" " "
Wilson, Ports	Brookston	" "	" " "
RECRUITS.			
Arnot, James A	Delphi	Feb. 21, 1865	Mustered out September 4, 1865.
Ball, Harvey J	"	Jan. 20, 1864	" " "
Canter, Henry C	Poplar Grove	March 10, 1862	Discharged July 16, 1863; disability.
Crockett, Hugh T	Frankfort	Oct. 31, 1862	Mustered out May 29, 1865.
Dern, William M	Delphi	July 29, 1864	Mustered out September 4, 1865.
Dern, Isaac N	"	Feb. 21, 1865	" " "
Franklin, William G	"	Jan. 21, 1864	Died at New Orleans October 3, 1864.
Franklin, Carter	"	March 8, 1864	Died at Lexington, Ky., February 28, 1865.
Guseman, George W	"	Feb. 21, 1865	Mustered out September 4, 1865.
Gwinn, Elijah F	Burlington	March 8, 1864	Mustered out June 26, 1865.
Gwinn, William H	"	" " "	Mustered out September 4, 1865.
Gwinn, James M	"	Jan. 25, 1865	" " "
Gibson, Henry	"	Nov. 11, 1864	" " "
Hamill, John A	Pittsburg	Feb. 21, 1865	" " "
Maxwell, Grandison A	Delphi	July 29, 1864	" " "
Montgomery, Thomas K	Brookston	Dec. 23, 1863	" " "
Moore, George A	Burlington	July 29, 1864	Mustered out July 17, 1865.

Names and Rank.	Residence.	Date of Muster.	Remarks.
Patton, Thomas W	Pittsburg	Nov. 12, 1862	Mustered out July 17, 1865.
Ryhn, Jerome C	Delphi	Jan. 29, 1864	Mustered out July 3, 1865.
Shafer, William	"	July 29, 1864	Mustered out July 5, 1865.
Thompson, Horace M	"	July 13, 1864	Mustered out September 4, 1865.
Underhill, William H	"	July 29, 1864	" " "

Company "C," Forty-Sixth Regiment, Indiana Volunteers.

Captains.			
Bernard F. Schermerhorn	Delphi	Nov. 19, 1861	Promoted Major.
Andrew B. Robertson	"	Feb. 11, 1863	Resigned July 28, 1863.
John G. Troxell	Pittsburg	Nov. 12, 1863	Discharged Dec. 28, 1864; term expired.
Joseph Henderson	Idaville	April 14, 1865	Mustered out with Regiment.
First Lieutenants.			
Anthony Garrett	Delphi	Nov. 7, 1861	Resigned April 26, 1862.
Andrew B. Robertson	"	April 30, 1862	Promoted Captain.
John G. Troxell	Pittsburg	Aug. 1, 1863	Promoted Captain.
William Schnepp	Delphi	Nov. 12, 1863	Honorably discharged, September 14, 1864.
Joseph Henderson	Idaville	Dec. 1, 1864	Promoted Captain.
William Bacome	Delphi		Mustered out August 1, 1865, as Sergeant.
Daniel Harner	"		Mustered out as First Sergeant with Regt.
Second Lieutenants.			
Andrew B. Robertson	Delphi	Nov. 19, 1861	Promoted First Lieutenant.

John G. Troxell	Pittsburg	April 30, 1862	Promoted First Lieutenant.
William Schnepp	Delphi	Feb. 11, 1863	" " "
William Bacome	"	June 1, 1865	" " "
Daniel Harner	"	June 2, 1865	" " "
First Sergeant.			
Troxell, John G	Pittsburg	Nov. 7, 1861	Promoted First Lieutenant.
Sergeants.			
Doggett, Leander H	Delphi	Nov. 7, 1861	Mustered out December 1, 1864.
Benson, Andrew W	"	" "	Drowned in Mississippi River, July 20, 1862.
Case, John S., Jr	"	" "	Mustered out December 1, 1864.
Schnepp, Wm. D	"	" "	Promoted First Lieutenant.
Corporals.			
M'Dowell, Resin V	Delphi	Nov. 7, 1861	Died at New Orleans, January 6, 1865.
Morton, James D	"	" "	Discharged May 20, 1862, by order Gen. Halleck.
Shaffer, George W	"	" "	Died at Riddle's Point, Mo., April 9, 1862.
Willis, Benj. L	"	" "	Mustered out December 1, 1864.
Evans, Thomas S	Pittsburg	" "	Vet.; died in prison at Tyler, Texas, Sept. 1, 1864.
Gibson, Robert	Burnettville	" "	Discharged Dec. 24, 1863; disability.
Vianco, Michael	Delphi	" "	Mustered out December 1, 1864.
Ankrum, John A	"	" "	" " "
Musicians.			
Garrett, Charles	Delphi	Nov. 7, 1861	Discharged March 1, 1862; General Order No. 14.
Pond, George	"	" "	Veteran; mustered out September 4, 1865.

Names and Rank.	Residence.	Date of Muster.	Remarks.
Wagoner.			
Snethen, John	Delphi	Nov. 7, 1861	Died at Helena, Arkansas, February 16, 1863.
Privates.			
Addis, Benjamin	Delphi	Nov. 7, 1861	Transferred to Invalid Corps, Jan. 25, 1864.
Andrews, John T.	Pittsburg	" "	Died on steamer, July 24, 1862.
Babanoe, Anthony	Delphi	" "	Veteran; mustered out September 4, 1865.
Bacome, William	"	" "	Veteran; mustered out August 1, 1865, as Sergt.
Burley, Thornton A	Logansport	" "	Mustered out December 1, 1864.
Burns, John B.	Delphi	" "	Discharged October 10, 1862; disability.
Burns, Benjamin	"	" "	Veteran; mustered out September 4, 1865.
Casad, David S.	Pittsburg	" "	Died at St. Louis, Mo., December 25, 1862.
Chilcot, Benj. B.	Logansport	" "	Veteran; mustered out September 4, 1865,
Clark, Samuel	Delphi	" "	Died on U. S. Hospital Boat, Oct. 2, 1862.
Clark, George W.	"	" "	Died at Helena, Arkansas, Nov. 12, 1862.
Collins, George	"	" "	Died at Helena, Arkansas, Dec. 1, 1862.
Crane, Abel	"	" "	Veteran; mustered out Sept. 4, 1865.
Cripe, David	"	" "	Killed at Magnolia Church.
Davidson, Joseph N	Pittsburg	" "	Veteran; must'd out Sept. 4, 1865, as Sergt.
Davidson, Wm	"	" "	Died at Vicksburg, June 27, 1863.
Dickson, Roswell	"	" "	Mustered out December 1, 1864.
Dougherton, Milton	"	" "	Veteran; mustered out September 4, 1865.
Duke, Alexander H.	Kokomo	" "	Mustered out December 1, 1864.
Egan, John	Delphi	" "	Discharged October 2, 1862; disability.
Galloway, Jonathan N.	Idaville	" "	Veteran; mustered out September 4, 1865.
Gerard, Edward M.	Delphi	" "	Discharged December 25, 1862; disability.
Gibson, Joshua	Burnettville	" "	Discharged April 25, 1862; disability.

Gilligan, John	Delphi	Nov. 7, 1861	Mustered out December 1, 1864.
Goslee, William	Pittsburg	" "	Supposed to have been discharged, Dec. 17, 1861.
Graham, Henry C.	Delphi	" "	
Grandstaff, John D.	Lockport	" "	Discharged August 1, 1862; disability.
Hamilton, George W.	Burlington	" "	Discharged July 12, 1863; disability.
Hamer, Daniel	Delphi	" "	Veteran, mustered out Sept. 4, 1865; First Sergt.
Harrison, James D.	"	" "	Discharged July 8, 1862; disability.
Hazlegrove, James M.	Pittsburg	" "	Veteran; mustered out September 4, 1865.
Henderson, Joseph	Idaville	" "	Promoted First Lieutenant.
Huntley, Whitely	Delphi	" "	Died at Helena, Arkansas, October 28, 1862.
Huntsinger, George	Pittsburg	" "	Veteran; killed at Sabine Cross-roads, April 8, 1864.
Johnson, William	"	" "	Died at Memphis, July 11, 1863.
Kashner, Jacob	Delphi	" "	Veteran; mustered out Sept. 4, 1865, as Sergeant.
Kite, Philip	"	" "	Mustered out December 1, 1864.
Lane, Alexander	"	" "	Died May 1, 1863; wounds rec'd at Magnolia Church.
Lane, George	"	" "	Veteran; died in prison, at Camp Ford, Texas.
Lane, Henry S.	"	" "	Veteran; mustered out Sept. 4, 1865, as Sergeant.
Lewis, Robert	Pittsburg	" "	Veteran; died in prison, at Camp Ford, Texas.
Love, John	Lockport	" "	Died in U. S. Hospital Boat, October 12, 1862.
Lovejoy, Edward	Pittsburg	" "	Discharged Nov. 11, 1862; disability.
Maden, John	Delphi	" "	Mustered out December 1, 1864.
Maxwell, John	"	" "	" " "
Mikesel, David	"	" "	Died at Riddle's Point, Mo., April 19, 1862.
Mitchell, John E.	"	" "	Mustered out December 1, 1864.
Moore, Eli C.	"	" "	Died at Natchez, Miss., August 12, 1863.
M'Glennin, William	"	" "	Killed at Algiers, La., May 26, 1864.
M'Dowell, Parker	"	" "	Died at Terre Haute, Ind., May 14, 1862.
M'Mahon, William	"	" "	Tranferred to Invalid Corps, January 15, 1864.
Neal, John G.	"	" "	Drowned in Mississippi River, July 25, 1862.
Neville, James	"	" "	Discharged June 17, 1862, by order.

Names and Rank.	Residence.	Date of Muster.	Remarks.
Newhouse, John N	Delphi	Nov. 7, 1861	Killed at Champion Hills, May 16, 1863.
Peterson, John W	"	" "	Veteran; mustered out Sept. 4, 1865, as Corporal.
Pickard, Benjamin S	"	" "	Discharged; disability.
Pippinger, Simon P	"	" "	Discharged June 29, 1863; disability.
Pring, Jesse S	Pittsburg	" "	Died May 20, 1862, on way home.
Reaf, Benedict	Delphi	" "	Mustered out December 1, 1864.
Rapse, Josiah	"	" "	" " "
Robinson, Wilson H	"	" "	Discharged November 15, 1862; disability.
Rutter, Jacob	Pittsburg	" "	Veteran; transferred to Tentth Ohio Battery, December, 1863.
Ryan, Edward	Delphi	" "	Mustered out December 1, 1864.
Shepherd, John	Pittsburg	" "	Veteran; mustered out Sept. 4, 1865, as Corporal.
Schriner, George	Burnettville	" "	Discharged; disability.
Shaeffer, John R	Delphi	" "	Died of wounds rec'd at Magnolia Hills, May 17, 1863.
Sharp, John P	"	" "	Mustered out December 1, 1864.
Smock, Isaac E	"	" "	Died May 17, 1863: wounds rec'd at Magnolia Church.
Smith, Harvey	Pittsburg	" "	Discharged June 12, 1862, by order.
Smith, John W	"	" "	Discharged March 4, 1862, by order.
Snethen, John A	"	" "	Discharged March 13, 1863; disability.
Speece, Francis M	"	" "	Veteran; mustered out Sept. 4, 1865, as Corporal.
Stinebaugh, Daniel	Delphi	" "	Mustered out December 1, 1864.
Ten, Joseph E	Pittsburg	" "	" " "
Thayer, Ferdinand A	"	" "	Discharged; disability.
Thomas, John R	Delphi	" "	Died at Nashville, May 17, 1863.
Thompson, James N	"	" "	Died May 16, 1863; wounds rec'd at Champion Hills.
Vianco, Edward	"	" "	Mustered out December 1, 1864.
Waymire, Austin	"	" "	Died May 17, 1863; wounds rec'd at Magnolia Church.

Waymire, Edward	Delphi	Nov. 7, 1861	Discharged March 8, 1864; disability.
Williams, Waldo W	"	" "	Transferred to Veteran Reserve Corps.
Wilson, Amos W	Logansport	" "	Veteran; mustered out Sept. 4, 1865.
RECRUITS.			
Ashba, Andrew	Delphi	Feb. 13, 1865	Mustered out Sept. 4, 1865.
Ashba, John W	"	" "	" " "
Arthur, Alfred	"	Oct. 31, 1862	Discharged January 14, 1864; disability.
Ashba, James M	"	Feb. 24, 1865	Died at Lexington, Ky., April 18, 1865.
Bush, Daniel M	"	March 15, 1864	
Doggett, Silas B	"	Jan. 1, 1864	
Dow, Peter	"	Jan. 28, 1864	
Foster, John M	"	Nov. 16, 1864	
Hughes, Allen	"	Dec. 24, 1861	Mustered out December 1, 1864.
Hardesty, John	"	Nov. 16, 1864	Mustered out May 11, 1865.
Jackman, Henry W	"	Oct. 28, 1862	Deserted April 13, 1665.
Kilgore, Joseph	"	Jan. 12, 1864	
Kaufman, Charles M	"	May 29, 1864	Died at Lexington, Ky., January, 1865.
Lynch, John	"	Jan. 16, 1864	
Lynch, David	"	Feb. 24, 1864	Mustered out June 7, 1865.
Lepper, Edward	"	Aug. 12, 1864	Mustered out.
Lane, Richard	"	Feb. 13, 1865	Mustered out June 7, 1865.
Ruhl, Martin	"	Jan. 12, 1864	Mustered out May 16, 1865.
Shaeffer, Alonzo	"	Dec. 16, 1863	Died at home, May 27, 1864.
Shepherd, Ithia	"	March 26, 1864	Mustered out May 15, 1865.
Todd, George M	"	Aug. 15, 1862	Died on Hospital Steamer, September 29, 1862.
Tomoson, Jasper	"	Sept. 13, 1862	Discharged July 22, 1865; disability.

Company "F," Forty-Sixth Regiment, Indiana Volunteers.

Names and Rank.	Residence.	Date of Muster.	Remarks.
Captains.			
David Howell	Delphi	Nov. 19, 1861	Resigned Feb. 5, 1862; re-entered as Capt. 74th Reg't.
Samuel Osbourne	Indianapolis	Feb. 15, 1862	Resigned May 26, 1862.
Bernard B. Dailey	Delphi	May 30, 1862	Resigned July 26, 1863.
Joseph C. Plumb	Indianapolis	Nov. 12, 1863	Resigned March 2, 1864.
John Shaffer	Delphi		Discharged July 19, 1865, as Sergeant.
Michael Rader	"	Aug. 18, 1865	Mustered out with Regiment.
First Lieutenants.			
Bernard B. Dailey	Delphi	Nov. 14, 1861	Promoted Captain.
Joel Ferris	Burnettville	May 30, 1862	Killed at Champion Hills, May 16, 1863.
Joseph C. Plumb	Indianapolis	Aug. 26, 1863	Promoted Captain.
George W. Stone	Dayton, O.	Nov. 13, 1863	Dismissed August 10, 1864.
Michael Rader	Delphi	Jan. 2, 1865	Promoted Captain.
George W. Yates	Logansport		Mustered out as Sergeant with Regiment.
Second Lieutenants.			
Attalas L. Benham	Delphi	Nov. 19, 1861	Died April 4, 1862, near Point Pleasant, Mo.
Joel Ferris	Burnettville	April 7, 1862	Promoted First Lieutenant.
James Perkins	Monticello	May 30, 1862	Resigned February 14, 1863.
Joseph C. Plumb	Indianapolis	March 1, 1863	Promoted First Lieutenant.
George W. Stone	Dayton, O.		" " "
George W. Yates	Logansport		" " "
First Sergeant.			
Joel Ferris	Burnettville	Nov. 14, 1861	Promoted Second Lieutenant.

Name	Residence	Date of muster	Remarks
SERGEANTS.			
Yates, George W	Logansport	Nov. 14, 1861	Veteran; mustered out Sept. 4, 1865, as Sergeant.
Shaffer, John	Delphi	" "	Mustered out July 11, 1865.
M'Cormick, George	Camden	" "	Mustered out December 1, 1864.
Tilton, Anthony J	Monticello	" "	Deserted August 8, 1862.
CORPORALS.			
Perkins, James M	Monticello	Nov. 14, 1861	Promoted Second Lieutenant.
Snoeberger, David	Camden	" "	Discharged December 18, 1862.
Sutton, Lewis	Idaville	" "	Discharged April 8, 1862.
Herman, Joseph	Burnettville	" "	Discharged February 2, 1863.
Rader, Michael	Delphi	" "	Promoted First Lieutenant.
Porter, George W	Camden	" "	Died at home, November 24, 1862.
Fry, Daniel	Idaville	" "	Veteran; mustered out September 4, 1865.
Quinn, Jacob	Camden	" "	Died at Milliken's Bend, April 15, 1863.
MUSICIANS.			
Paden, William	Camden	Nov. 14, 1861	Discharged February 1, 1863.
Blue, Michael	"	" "	Died at Helena.
WAGONER.			
Eastwood, Matthias	Logansport	Nov. 14, 1861	Died May 14, 1862.
PRIVATES.			
Atchison, Silas		Nov. 14, 1861	Discharged August 25, 1862.
Barr, William	Logansport	" "	Died at New Madrid, April, 1862.
Berry, Henry E	Delphi	" "	Veteran; mustered out Sept. 4, 1865.
Blanger, Daniel L	Huntington	" "	Mustered out December 1, 1864, as absent, sick.
Black, Ferdinand		" "	Discharged December 15, 1861.
Butler, William	Camden	" "	Killed at Champion Hills, May 16, 1863.

Names and Rank.	Residence.	Date of Muster.	Remarks.
Campbell, James	Camden	Nov. 14, 1861	Mustered out December 1, 1864.
Camden, Tilman A	"	" "	Veteran; mustered out Sept. 4, 1865.
Cately, William	"	" "	Transferred to Veteran Reserve Corps, Dec. 8, 1862.
Coleman, James S	Delphi	" "	Veteran; mustered out September 4, 1865.
Collins, Joseph S	"	" "	Discharged September 3, 1862; disability.
Compton, John	"	" "	Died at Bardstown, Ky., January 28, 1862.
Connell, David	"	" "	Died at Milliken's Bend, June 12, 1864.
Cook, Riley		" "	Discharged, 1862.
Cook, John		" "	Discharged April 12, 1862.
Corrigan, Lawrence	Logansport	" "	Mustered out December 1, 1864.
Culham, Patrick	Detroit	" "	" " "
Cox, Abraham	Delphi	" "	Died at Helena, Ark., October 24, 1862.
Crippen, James	Walton	" "	Mustered out December 1, 1864.
Dickey, Nath	"	" "	Veteran; mustered out September 4, 1865.
Dix Ephraim	Camden	" "	Transferred to Veteran Reserve Corps, January, 1864.
Douglass, William	Kokomo	" "	Veteran; mustered out Sept. 4, 1865, as Corporal.
Eastwood, James H	Logansport	" "	Died at Memphis, June 20, 1862.
Foust, Samuel D	Delphi	" "	Veteran; mustered out September 4, 1865.
Franklin, Matthias S	"	" "	Died at home, June 24, 1862.
Gable, Samuel	Warsaw	" "	Veteran; mustered out September 4, 1865.
Gillam, Albert J	Delphi	" "	Discharged February 6, 1863; disability.
Gates, Jacob	Idaville	" "	Veteran; mustered out Sept. 4, 1865, as Corporal.
Hastings, James	"	" "	Veteran; died while a prisoner.
Hastings, Benjamin	"	" "	Veteran; mustered out Sept. 4, 1865, as Corporal.
Hastings, Peter	"	" "	Transferred to Marine Corps, January, 1865.
Heiny, Jacob	"	" "	Veteran; mustered out Sept. 4, 1865, as Sergeant.
Heiny, Jonathan	"	" "	" " " " "

Hogelan, Alexander	Camden	Nov. 14, 1861	Transferred to V. R. C., 1863.
Hoover, Levi	"	" "	Died in Hospital April 2, 1862.
Huffman, George	Monticello	" "	Mustered out September 4, 1865, as Sergeant.
Hurley, Silas	Marion	" "	Died at Helena, Arkansas, Aug. 20, 1862.
Howell, John W	Dayton, Ohio	" "	Mustered out December 1, 1864.
Ireland, Seth	Burnettville	" "	Discharged March 14, 1863; disability.
Jerome, Samuel	Logansport	" "	Dropped from rolls; absence from Regt.
Kellar, Samuel	Delphi	" "	Discharged Nov. 13, 1862; disability.
Knettle, William H	"	" "	Veteran; mustered out Sept. 4, 1865.
Kuhn, Thomas J	Camden	" "	Discharged Sept. 14, 1862; disability.
Leslie, Daniel	Idaville	" "	Veteran; discharged July 12, 1865; wounded.
Mathers, Wm	Camden	" "	Veteran; mustered out Sept. 4, 1865.
M'Cray, Samuel W	Lockport	" "	Discharged May 19, 1862; disability.
Meredith, John	Burnettville	" "	Veteran; died while prisoner, July 16, 1864.
Millard, Henry	Camden	" "	Died at Helena, Arkansas, Dec. 1, 1862.
Moran, James	Delphi	" "	Died at Indianapolis, June 14, 1863.
Nace, Thomas	"	" "	Killed at Champion Hills, May 16, 1863.
Nace, William F	"	" "	Mustered out Dec. 1, 1864.
Nearhoff, Joseph	Monticello	" "	Mustered out Dec. 12, 1864.
Noble, William	Camden	" "	Died at Helena, Arkansas, 1862.
Osbourne, Theoph	Warsaw	" "	Veteran; mustered out Sept. 4, 1865.
Pletcher, David	Delphi	" "	Veteran; mustered out Sept. 4, 1865, as Corp.
Pruett, Henry C	"	" "	Discharged Sept. 11, 1862; disability.
Ridinger, Wm. J	Camden	" "	Died at Memphis, Aug. 11, 1862.
Robinson, John	Idaville	" "	Mustered out Dec. 1, 1864.
Rinier, Isaac	"	" "	Died of wounds rec'd at Vicksburg, June 15, 1863.
Sell, Jacob	Winnemac	" "	Veteran; mustered out Sept. 4, 1865.
Scott, Joseph	Warsaw	" "	" " " "
Shaffer, Francis M	Delphi	" "	Veteran; mustered out Sept. 4, 1865, as Corp.
Stone, George W	"	" "	Promoted First Lieutenant.

Names and Rank.	Residence.	Date of Muster.	Remarks.
Swanger, Wm. F	Warsaw	Nov. 14, 1861	Veteran; mustered out Sept. 4, 1865.
Sharpe, Beecher	Lafayette	" "	Mustered out Dec. 1, 1864.
Shuey Sampson	Idaville	" "	Veteran; mustered out Sept. 4, 1865.
Spence, John	Lockport	" "	Dropped from rolls by order.
Spence, Andrew	"	" "	Veteran; mustered out Sept. 4, 1865.
Sloniker, Jonas	Warsaw	" "	" " " "
Taffe, Michael	Logansport	" "	Killed at Champion Hills, May 16, 1863.
Thompson, Samuel	Camden	" "	Died at Madison Indiana, July 15, 1863.
Tripp, James S	Logansport	" "	Died at Memphis, 1862.
Tripp, Albert W	"	" "	" " "
Wickham, George	Delphi	" "	Discharged April 10, 1863; disability.
Willis, Joseph	Logansport	" "	Discharged Dec. 16, 1862; disability.
Young, Hezekiah E	"	" "	Died December 2, 1861.
Zerns, Joseph	Dayton, Ohio	" "	Mustered out Dec. 1, 1864.
Unassigned Recruits.			
Anderson, John		Sept. 19, 1864.	
Bragg, Melis W		Aug. 5, 1864.	
Castle, John T		Sept. 17, 1862.	
Castle, Thomas W. M		" "	
Crofoot, Orson A		Oct. 23, 1862.	
Elkins, John		Feb. 1, 1865.	
Layton, Joseph		Oct. 29, 1862.	
M'Beth, William		Nov. 4, 1864.	
Plumb, Joseph C		Feb. 2, 1862	Promoted Second Lieutenant.
Plant, Julius		Jan. 4, 1864.	
Rex, Maxwell		Feb. 26, 1862.	

Ryan, John		Nov. 15, 1864.	
Shepherd, Ithia		March 31, 1864.	

COMPANY "D," TWELFTH REGIMENT, INDIANA VOLUNTEERS.

CAPTAIN.			
George Bowman	Delphi	Aug. 12, 1862.	
CORPORAL.			
Sandifer, Ben. F.			
PRIVATES.			
Dern, Silas	Delphi	Aug. 10, 1862	Died at Grand Junction, Feb. 17, 1863.
Elliott, Geo. W	"	" "	Mustered out June 8, 1865.
Glasscock, John W	"	" "	Discharged April 20, 1863; wounded.
Gillam, Allen W	"	July 26, 1862	Died at Indianapolis, Nov. 3, 1862.
Herron, Cornelius	"	Aug. 10, 1862	Deserted at Indianapolis, Nov. 22, 1862.
Irelan, Thomas W	Idaville	Aug. 9, 1862	Mustered out June 8, 1865.
Lunbeck, Isaac J. K	Delphi	Aug. 11, 1862	Discharged Feb. 19, 1863; wounded.
M'Farland, Larry D	"	Aug. 1, 1862	Appointed Sergeant-Major; died.
M'Mahon, Robert	"	July 9, 1862	Transferred to V. R. C.; must'd out June 17, 1865.
Sines, James W	"	July 26, 1862	Mustered out June 8, 1865.
Shoemaker, Wm. H	"	Aug. 10, 1862	" " "
Todd, Harvey R	"	Aug. 9, 1862	" " "
Le Sourd, David G	Pittsburg	Aug. 8, 1862	" " "

COMPANY "K," FIFTEENTH REGIMENT, INDIANA VOLUNTEERS.

Jones, John M	Delphi	June 14, 1861	Promoted Second Lieutenant.

COMPANY "A," FORTY-FIRST REGIMENT, INDIANA VOLUNTEERS (SECOND CAVALRY).

NAMES AND RANK.	Residence.	Date of Muster.	REMARKS.
CAPTAINS.			
Jehu C. Hannam	Delphi	Sept. 18, 1861	Promoted Major.
John G. Kessler	"	May 25, 1862	Honorably discharged, Dec. 19, 1864; wounded; paroled a prisoner.
RESIDUARY BAT.—CO. "A."			
CAPTAIN.			
Samuel T. Ferrier	Delphi	Nov. 1, 1864	Mustered out with Battalion.
FIRST LIEUTENANTS.			
Hiram Sampson	Delphi	Sept. 18, 1861	Resigned March 4, 1862.
Edward M. Barnes	"	May 25, 1862	Mustered out Oct. 4, 1864.
RESIDUARY BAT.—CO. "A."			
FIRST LIEUTENANT.			
John Lathrop	Delphi	June 1, 1865	Mustered out as Second Lieutenant with Battalion.
SECOND LIEUTENANTS.			
John G. Kessler	Delphi	Sept. 18, 1861	Promoted Captain.
Samuel T. Ferrier	"	June 25, 1862	Mustered out Oct. 4, 1864, and promoted Captain.
RESIDUARY BAT.—CO. "A."			
SECOND LIEUTENANT.			
John Lathrop	Delphi	Nov. 18, 1864	Promoted First Lieutenant.

FIRST SERGEANT.			
Barnes, Edward M.	Delphi	Sept. 18, 1861	Promoted First Lieut.; mustered out Oct. 4, 1864.
QUARTERMASTER SERGEANT.			
Martin, Robert K.	Delphi	Sept. 18, 1861	Promoted Adjutant Eleventh Cavalry.
SERGEANTS.			
Ferrier, Samuel T.	Delphi	Sept. 18, 1861	Promoted Second Lieutenant.
Davis, Charles C.	"	" "	Mustered out Oct. 4, 1864, as private.
Pratt, Richard H.	"	" "	Promoted First Lieutent of Eleventh Cavalry.
Gurick, Frederick	"	" "	Transferred to Second Cavalry, reorganized.
CORPORALS.			
Stoner, Jacob A.	Delphi	Sept. 18, 1861	Mustered out Oct. 4, 1864, as Sergt.
Graham, Samuel M.	"	" "	" " " "
Williams, Henry C.	"	" "	Mustered out Oct. 4, 1864, as Sergt.
Baum, George W.	"	" "	Promoted Commissary Sergeant.
Martin William B.	"	" "	Mustered out Oct. 4, 1864.
Peck, John C.	"	" "	Promoted Quartermaster
Elliott, William S.	"	" "	Promoted Quartermaster Eleventh Cavalry.
Barr, Irwin	"	" "	Mustered out Oct. 4, 1864.
BUGLERS.			
Lockwood, Nathan S.	Delphi,	Sept. 18, 1861	Mustered out Oct. 4, 1864.
Wescott, Burgan P.	"	" "	Discharged Oct. 3, 1862.
FARRIER AND BLACKSMITHS.			
Peck, George W.	Delphi	Sept. 18, 1861	Discharged July 19, 1862.
Sische, Reuben	"	" "	Discharged Aug. 31, 1862.

NAMES AND RANK.	Residence.	Date of Muster.	REMARKS.
SADDLER.			
Huston, Ludwell G	Camden	Sept. 18, 1861	Mustered out Oct. 4, 1864.
WAGONER.			
Stoner, David A	Delphi	Sept. 18, 1861	Discharged June 2, 1862.
PRIVATES.			
Abel, John	Carroll County	Sept. 18, 1861	Mustered out Oct. 4, 1864.
Barnes, James	" "	" "	Died at Madison, Indiana, March 6, 1864.
Black, Thomas M	" "	" "	Mustered out Oct. 4, 1864.
Robs, Calvin	" "	" "	" " "
Bragunier, John	" "	" "	Discharged Feb. 5, 1863; wounded.
Bean, Patrick	" "	" "	Discharged September 15, 1862.
Brough, Benj. F	" "	" "	Mustered out Oct. 4, 1864.
Bush, John	" "	" "	Died at Vinegar Hills, Ky., Sept. 28, 1864.
Buckley, William	" "	" "	Discharged Aug. 18, 1862.
Buckley, John M	" "	" "	Mustered out Oct. 4, 1864, as Corporal.
Byers, George W	" "	" "	Mustered out Oct. 4, 1864.
Byers, Ephraim L	" "	" "	" " "
Byram, Augustus F	" "	" "	
Chaney, Albert H	" "	" "	Promoted Lieut. Twelfth Tenn. Cav., Oct. 29, 1863.
Crooks, Charles M	" "	" "	Discharged Nov. 15, 1863; disability; Com. Sergt.
Davis, Owen C	" "	" "	Mustered out Oct. 4, 1864.
Dick, John	" "	" "	" " "
Duker, Henry	" "	" "	Discharged Jan. 7, 1863.
Durfield, Frederick	" "	" "	Mustered out Oct. 4, 1864.
Earhart, Lewis	" "	" "	" " "

Elsroth, Aaron	Carroll County	Sept. 18, 1861	Mustered out Oct. 4, 1864.
Etter, Franklin G	" "	" "	" " "
Fost, Philip	" "	" "	Died at Knoxville, March 12, 1864; wounded.
Foughty, Samuel	" "	" "	Discharged June 21, 1862.
Goodwin, William	" "	" "	Tranferred Second Cavalry, reorganized.
Gross, Morris	" "	" "	Mustered out Oct. 4, 1864.
Gross, Martin	" "	" "	" " "
Heskin, Mervin S	" "	" "	" " "
Hought, Benj. K	" "	" "	Discharged July, 1862.
Hoover, Jacob C	" "	" "	Mustered out Oct. 4, 1864, as Corporal.
Hornaday, Aaron	" "	" "	Discharged November 14, 1862.
Horn, John	" "	" "	Discharged July 15, 1862.
Huffman, Solomon	" "	" "	Discharged June 6, 1862.
Inglee, Wm. F	" "	" "	Wounded; mustered out Oct. 4, 1864, as Sergt.
Judd, George	" "	" "	Died June 21, 1864.
Judd, William	" "	" "	Transferred Second Cavalry, reorganized.
Kendall, Thomas J	" "	" "	Mustered out Oct. 4, 1864, as Corporal.
Lafferty, William	" "	" "	Discharged February 19, 1864.
Lampy, Francis	" "	" "	Missing in action at Motley's Ford, March 13, 1864.
Lasselle, Christian	" "	" "	Discharged March 14, 1864; disability.
Loveland, Linus	" "	" "	Mustered out October 4, 1864, as Corporal.
Martin, Hugh	" "	" "	Mustered out October 4, 1864.
M'Dowell, Robertson	" "	" "	Transferred to Second Cavalry, reorganized.
M'Mininy, William	" "	" "	Died at Nashville, Tennessee, November, 4, 1863.
Mitchell, George W	" "	" "	Died at Bardstown, Kentucky, February 3, 1862.
Montgomery, James	" "	" "	Mustered out October 4, 1864, as Sergeant.
Morrow, Elihu Y	" "	" "	Mustered out October 4, 1864.
Mohr, Henry	" "	" "	Capt. Newman, Ga., July 30, '64; must. out May 24, '65.
Mullendore, William	" "	" "	Mustered out October 4, 1864.
Plant, Peter	" "	" "	" " " "

Names and Rank.	Residence.	Date of Muster.	Remarks.
Point, John	Carroll County	Sept. 18, 1861	Died at Louisville, Kentucky, April 15, 1862.
Redding, Allen	" "	" "	Discharged October 30, 1862.
Sanderson, James I.	" "	" "	" " "
Schoonover, Alfred	" "	" "	Discharged August 31, 1863.
Shaw, Llewellen	" "	" "	Mustered out October 4, 1864.
Shaffer, David	" "	" "	" " " "
Sidenbender, Henry	" "	" "	Discharged January 7, 1863.
Smith, Newton	" "	" "	Discharged October 16, 1862.
Smith, William	" "	" "	Transferred to Second Cavalry, reorganized.
Smith, Alexander	" "	" "	Mustered out October 4, 1864, as Blacksmith.
Skifey, William L.	" "	" "	Deserted January 15, 1863.
Stephens, Henry	" "	" "	Capt'd at Newman, Ga.; must'd out May 24, 1865.
Sterling, Matthew	" "	" "	Mustered out October 4, 1864, as Sergeant.
Straight, William	" "	" "	Discharged October 30, 1862.
Trobaugh, William W.	" "	" "	
Veron, Francis	" "	" "	Died March 13, 1864; wounds.
Wellman, Ferdinand	" "	" "	Mustered out October 4, 1864, as Farrier.
Webb, Francis	" "	" "	Mustered out October 4, 1864.
Wilson, Perry	" "	" "	Transferred to Second Cavalry, reorganized.
Woods, Albert L.	" "	" "	Mustered out October 4, 1864.
Young, Isam A.	" "	" "	Capt'd at Newman, Ga.; must'd out April 4, 1865.
Zaring, Jacob	" "	" "	Transferred to Second Cavalry, reorganized.
Recruits.			
Allen, Hiram W.	Carroll County	March 2, 1864	Transferred to Second Cavalry, reorganized.
Altrip, Hugh L.	" "	Jan. 18, 1864	" " " "
Bowen, Francis M.	" "	March 2, 1864	" " " "

Name	Residence	Date of muster	Remarks
Beaver, Samuel	Carroll County	Dec. 23, 1863	Transferred to Second Cavalry, reorganized.
Booth, Charles	" "	Jan. 13, 1864	" " " "
Booth, Abram	" "	" "	" " " "
Buckingham, James	" "	Jan. 18, 1864	" " " "
Caldwell, James	" "	Jan. 8, 1864	" " " "
Carr, Robert	" "	March 2, 1864	" " " "
Clifford, William	" "	Dec. 26, 1863	" " " "
Cox, Henry	" "	Jan. 2, 1864	" " " "
Day, Joseph	" "	Sept. 18, 1864	" " " "
Davis, Francis M	" "	Sept. 1, 1863	" " " "
Diles, Augustus	" "	Aug. 1, 1862	Discharged February 9, 1863.
Etler, Franklin	" "	April 16, 1864	Transferred to Second Cavalry, reorganized.
Eucking, John B	" "	Jan. 1, 1862	" " " "
Fleetwood, George I	" "	Dec. 1, 1863	Died at Madisonville, Tennessee.
Gardner, Stephen C	" "	Oct. 15, 1862	Transferred to Second Cavalry, reorganized.
Gee, Solomon	" "	Jan. 27, 1864	" " " "
Gross, Othias	" "	Jan. 2, 1864	" " " "
Hattery, Abraham	" "	Dec. 26, 1863	" " " "
Henley, Andrew	" "	Oct. 16, 1862	" " " "
Johnson, James	" "	Jan. 2, 1864	Captured Newman, Georgia, July 30, 1864.
Koontz, Samuel	" "	Dec. 26, 1863	Transferred to Second Cavalry, reorganized.
Lathrop, John	" "	Nov. 7, 1863	" " " "
Large, Harvey	" "	Jan. 2, 1864	" " " "
Loomer, George	" "	March 2, 1864	" " " "
Mayhood, John	" "	Dec. 26, 1863	" " " "
M'Lane, James	" "	Jan. 20, 1864	Died at Madisonville, Tennessee.
Metzker, Enoch	" "	Feb. 23, 1864	Transferred to Second Cavalry, reorganized.
Mongaver, Matthew	" "	Nov. 23, 1863	Captured Newman, Georgia, July 30, 1864.
M'Coshon, James	" "	Nov. 28, 1863	Transferred to Second Cavalry, reorganized.
Mitchell, Daniel	" "	Oct. 15, 1862	" " " "

Names and Rank.	Residence.	Date of Muster.	Remarks.
Miller, John	Carroll County	Jan. 28, 1864	Transferred to Second Cavalry, reorganized.
Moore, John	" "	Nov. 24, 1863	" " " "
Moore, David F	" "	March 2, 1864	" " " "
Mosier, Jacob	" "	Oct. 15, 1862	" " " "
Murphy, Patrick	" "	" "	" " " "
Patterson, James I	" "	March 2, 1864	" " " "
Pratt, Jeremiah	" "	Dec. 26, 1863	" " " "
Schwartz, Jacob M	" "	Oct. 15, 1862	" " " "
Short, Silas	" "	" "	" " " "
Stiles, Isaac	" "	Jan. 2, 1864	" " " "
Smalley, Daniel	" "	Oct. 15, 1862	" " " "
Smith, Jack	" "	" "	Deserted May 9, 1864.
Stoner, Philip	" "	Jan. 2, 1864	Captured Newman, Georgia.
Stoner, George	" "	" "	" " "
Thompson, George R	" "	Nov. 26, 1863	Transferred to Second Cavalry, reorganized.
Tomlin, Isam	" "	Jan. 18, 1864	Captured Centerville, Georgia, September, 1864.
Trumel, Jonathan H	" "	Jan. 2, 1864	Captured Newman, Ga.; must'd out July 31, 1865.
Ingraham, Orrion	" "	Dec. 20, 1863	Deserted September 5, 1864.
Wassaman, Dietrich	" "	Jan. 25, 1864	Transferred to Second Cavalry, reorganized.

Company "K," Forty-first Regiment, Second Cavalry, Indiana Volunteers.

Second Lieutenants.			
Andrew H. Evans	Delphi	Jan. 27, 1862	Resigned June 18, 1862.
Samuel Montgomery	"	April 27, 1863	Mustered out with Regiment.

PRIVATES.			
Buckingham, John	Delphi	Dec. 24, 1861	Mustered out October 4, 1864.
Cupp, John	"	" "	Mustered out October 4, 1864, as Sergeant.
Caldwell, William G	"	" "	Discharged February 7, 1863.
Crawford, Lemuel	"	" "	Died at Nashville, April 5, 1862.
Clawson, Vine	"	" "	Died at Nashville, May 16, 1862.
Davis, William E	"	" "	Died at Camp Wickliffe, Ky., May 5, 1862.
Edson, Ansel M	"	" "	Mustered out October 4, 1864.
Ferrier, Daniel T	"	" "	Captured at Varnell's Station, Ga., May 9, 1864.
Grandstaff, Jos	"	" "	Died at Munfordville, Ky., April 17, 1862.
Gruber, Henry S	"	" "	Veteran, transferred to Second Cavalry, reorganized.
Hall, Tobias	"	" "	Mustered out Oct. 4, 1864, as Corporal; absent, sick.
Hall, George	"	" "	Mustered out October 4, 1864, as Corporal.
Hoff, Eli	"	" "	
Moore, Jacob	"	" "	Mustered out October 4, 1864.
Mullendore, Jacob	"	" "	Discharged February 7, 1863; disability.
Monroe, William H	"	" "	Discharged September 10, 1862; disability.
Merriman, Jasper	"	" "	Died at Louisville, Ky., December 13, 1862.
Plant Lemuel B	"	" "	Discharged December 22, 1862; disability.
Swalls, Daniel G	"	" "	Mustered out October 4, 1864.
Smith, Joseph M	"	" "	" " "
Shoup, Benjamin	"	" "	Discharged November 12, 1863; disability.
Saulsbury, Matthew	"	" "	Discharged August 5, 1862; disability.
Thrasher, Greenbury	"	" "	Discharged January 6, 1864; disability.
Whetstone, John	"	" "	Died at Camp Wickliffe, Ky., February 26, 1862.

Company "K," Sixtieth Regiment, Indiana Volunteers.

Names and Rank.	Residence.	Date of Muster.	Remarks.
Captain.			
William B. Givens	Delphi	April 17, 1862	Resigned April 2, 1863; re-enter as Capt. 11th Cav.

As the residence of the Privates mustered into this Company is not given in the Adjutant-General's Report, I am unable to give the names of the Carroll County soldiers belonging to this Company.

SEVENTY-SECOND REGIMENT, INDIANA VOLUNTEERS.

Names and Rank.	Residence.	Date of Muster.	Remarks.
Lieutenant-Colonel.			
John B. Milroy	Delphi	Aug. 14, 1862	Declined.
Quartermaster.			
Henry S. Dewey	Delphi	July 22, 1862	Mustered out with Regiment.
Surgeon.			
James L. Morrow	Pittsburg	Aug. 15, 1862	Resigned December 17, 1863.
Assistant Surgeon.			
James L. Morrow	Pittsburg	Aug. 4, 1862	Promoted Surgeon.

Company "A," Seventy-second Regiment, Indiana Volunteers.

Names and Rank.	Residence.	Date of Muster.	Remarks.
Captain.			
Nathaniel Herron	Camden	Aug. 16, 1862	Resigned December 17, 1862.

Name	Residence	Date	Remarks
Milton W. Newton	Delphi	Dec. 23, 1862	Resigned February 1, 1863.
Andrew J. Klepser	"	Feb. 24, 1863	Discharged October 6, 1864.
Lewis Gros	"	Dec. 4, 1864	Mustered out with Regiment.
FIRST LIEUTENANT.			
Milton W. Newton	Delphi	Aug. 16, 1862	Promoted Captain.
Andrew J. Klepser	"	Dec. 23, 1862	" "
Lewis Gros	"	April 13, 1863	" "
Mark Aschaffenburg	Lafayette	Dec. 23, 1864	Resigned Second Lieutenant to avoid dismissal.
James H. Barnes	Delphi	Dec. 27, 1864	Mustered out with Regiment.
SECOND LIEUTENANT.			
Andrew J. Klepser	Delphi	Aug. 16, 1862	Promoted to First Lieutenant.
Mark Aschaffenburg	Lafayette	Dec. 29, 1862	" " "
James H. Barnes	Delphi	Dec. 11, 1864	" " "
Richard W. Pilling	Camden	Dec. 27, 1864	Mustered out with Regiment.
FIRST SERGEANT.			
Aschaffenburg, Mark	Lafayette	July 23, 1862	Promoted to Second Lieutenant.
SERGEANTS.			
Pilling, Richard W	Camden	July 12, 1862	Promoted Second Lieutenant.
Gros, Lewis	Delphi	July 16, 1862	Promoted First Lieutenant.
Knight, Jonathan L	"	July 20, 1862	Discharged December 27, 1862.
Stewart, Samuel	Camden	July 15, 1862	Mustered out July 24, 1865.
CORPORALS.			
Barnes, James H	Delphi	July 15, 1862	Promoted to Second Lieutenant.
Stewart, William R	Camden	" "	Mustered out July 24, 1865, as First Sergeant.
Robinson, James T	Delphi	July 18, 1862	Died at Chattanooga, Sept. 16, 1863, of wounds.

Names and Rank.	Residence.	Date of Muster.	Remarks.
Higgenbotham, Joseph R	Delphi	July 16, 1862	Died at Corinth, Miss., January 14, 1864.
Pilling, Samuel G	Camden	July 22, 1862	Mustered out July 24, 1865, as Hospital Steward.
Stokes, Marion F	Danville	July 17, 1862	Mustered out July 24, 1865, as Sergeant.
Faughty, Samuel	Delphi	July 14, 1862	Mustered out July 24, 1865, as private.
Huntsinger, Rufus	Rockfield	" "	Mustered out July 24, 1865, as Sergeant.
Musicians.			
Smith, Arthur A	Delphi	July 16, 1862	Discharged October 28, 1862.
Stoner, George	"	" "	Discharged May 28, 1863.
Wagoner.			
Wellack, Benjamin	Delphi	July 16, 1862	Mustered out July 24, 1865.
Privates.			
Allen, George W	Delphi	July 13, 1862	Mustered out July 24, 1865, as Corporal.
Bailey, George	Idaville	July 18, 1862	Died in Andersonville Prison, August 8, 1864.
Barnard, John M	Camden	July 20, 1862	Mustered out July 24, 1865, as Sergeant.
Bowers, Daniel	Carroll	" "	Mustered out July 24, 1865.
Boyd, John	Delphi	July 16, 1862	Killed at Pilot Shoals, Ga., July 28, 1864.
Brown, Harvey A	Montez	July 21, 1862	Transferred to Veteran Reserve Corps, Sept. 16, 1863.
Burton, Jeremiah	Lockport	" "	Mustered out July 24, 1865.
Cantner, George W	Poplar Grove	July 19, 1862	Discharged January 31, 1863.
Cline, Daniel H	Camden	July 17, 1862	Mustered out July 24, 1865.
Cline, Daniel	"	" "	" " "
Cline, Thomas	"	" "	Transferred to Veteran Reserve Corps, July 1, 1863.
Comer Thomas,	Delphi	" "	Discharged October 11, 1862.
Culler, Jacob	"	July 14, 1862	Transferred to Veteran Reserve Corps, July 1, 1863.

Culler, George	Delphi	July 14, 1862	Transferred to Veteran Reserve Corps, Aug. 1, 1864.
Dimmitt, Benoni	"	July 18, 1862	Mustered out July 24, 1865.
Dimmitt, John	"	July 19, 1862	" " "
Dimmitt, William H	"	July 18, 1862	Mustered out July 24, 1865, as Corporal.
Etskin, Joseph	"	July 16, 1862	Killed at M'Elmore's Cave, Ga., Sept. 12, 1863.
Felix, Leonard G	Feath's Mill	July 23, 1862	Discharged May 7, 1864.
Franklin, Nelson	Delphi	July 22, 1862	Discharged June 2, 1865, as Sergeant.
Frederick, John	Feath's Mill	" "	Transferred to Veteran Reserve Corps, Jan. 15, 1864.
Gard, Stephen J	Lafayette	July 19, 1862	Mustered out July 24, 1865, as Corporal.
Ghear, Elijah	Feath's Mill	July 12, 1862	Discharged May 19, 1863.
Gee, Jeremiah	Delphi	July 13, 1862	Mustered out July 24, 1865.
Gaumer, Harrison	Camden	July 17, 1862	" " "
Gaumer, William	"	July 19, 1862	Died at Nashville, August 13, 1863
Grantham, William H	"	July 17, 1862	Discharged October 26, 1862.
Hare, Joseph L	Cicero	" "	Mustered out July 24, 1865.
Heiney, Henry	Idaville	July 20, 1862	Mustered out July 24, 1865, as Corporal.
Huntsinger, Isaac	Rockfield	July 16, 1862	Mustered out July 24, 1865.
Huntsinger, Samuel K	"	" "	" " "
Jones, Daniel H	Burlington	" "	" " "
Kahl, Ezra	Shelby	July 17, 1862	" " "
King, William J	Delphi	July 20, 1862	Mustered out July 24, 1865, as Commissary Sergeant.
Landes, John R	Carroll	July 21, 1862	Mustered out July 24, 1865.
Landes, Frederick	"	" "	Mustered out July 24, 1865, as Corporal.
Lane, Eli	Delphi	" "	Deserted January 10, 1864.
Lathrop, Harrison T	Christiansburg	July 19, 1862	Mustered out July 24, 1865.
Lesler, William	Feath's Mill	July 12, 1862	Discharged March 28, 1863.
Lewis, Wilson	Lockport	July 13, 1862	" " "
Martin, Thomas	Delphi	July 12, 1862	" " "
Melson, James F	Anderson	July 12, 1862	" " "
Mills, Thomas	Camden	July 11, 1862	" " "

Names and Rank.	Residence.	Date of Muster.	Remarks.
Mills, Daniel	Camden	July 11, 1862	Mustered out July 24, 1865, as Sergeant.
Moore, Peter J	Delphi	July 12, 1862	Discharged December 15, 1863.
Murphy, Francis	Feath's Mill	July 13, 1862	Mustered out July 24, 1865, as Corporal.
M'Ardle, Philip	Delphi	" "	Tranferred to Veteran Reserve Corps, Jan. 15, 1864.
M'Clurg, Cyrus	"	July 16, 1862	Died at Louisville, Ky., September 20, 1862.
Neff, James A	"	July 21, 1862	Discharged February 17, 1863.
Neville, James	Pittsburg	" "	Discharged February 9, 1863.
Nipper, Isaac	Delphi	July 13, 1862	Mustered out July 24, 1865.
Nokes, William	Camden	" "	Died at Murfreesboro, Tenn., March 29, 1863.
Nye, John P	Delphi	July 21, 1862	Discharged March 1, 1863.
Oliver, James K	Pittsburg	July 23, 1862	Mustered out July 24, 1865.
Paxon, John	"	" "	Deserted September 26, 1862.
Pilling, Robert W	Camden	July 11, 1862	Mustered out July 24, 1865.
Pruitt, James H	Delphi	July 15, 1862	Transferred to Veteran Reserve Corps, July 1, 1863.
Riley, Dennis	Feath's Mill	July 25, 1862	Mustered out July 24, 1865.
Riley, Daniel	" "	" "	" " "
Reigel, Simon	Lockport	" "	" " "
Scott, William W	Delphi	July 26, 1862	Discharged February 8, 1863.
Seagraves, William E	Camden	" "	Died while prisoner at Andersonville.
Sance, Isaac	Poplar Grove	July 19, 1862	Mustered out July 24, 1865.
Shirar, Peter	Camden	July 17, 1862	Transferred to Veteran Reserve Corps, July 1, 1863.
Shaw, Henry C	Delphi	July 15, 1862	Mustered out July 24, 1865.
Sigars, Albert	"	July 13, 1862	Killed at Mooresville, Ala., Nov. 21, 1863.
Spitler, Benjamin	Burlington	July 24, 1862	Mustered out July 24, 1865, as Corporal.
Smith, Samuel H	Feath's Mill	" "	" " " "
Salsberry, John A	Camden	July 19, 1862	Mustered out July 24, 1865.
Stoner, Philip	Delphi	July 12, 1862	Discharged March 26, 1863.

Stoley, George	Delphi	July 24, 1862	Mustered out July 24, 1865.
Tolbey, Berry	"	July 18, 1862	Died at Bowling Green, Ky., Nov. 8, 1862.
Vich, Lucian A	Lafayette	July 19, 1862	Mustered out July 24, 1865.
Wayts, Isaac	Delphi	July 20, 1862	" " "
Wilkinson, Isaac	Montez	July 17, 1862	Died at Murfreesboro, Tenn., April 7, 1863.
Yonker, Benjamin F	Battle Creek	July 25, 1862	Died March 1, 1863.
Recruits.			
Adams, James R	Lockport	March 22, 1864	Transferred to Veteran Reserve Corps, Dec. 28, 1864.
Brice, Asbury	"	March 3, 1864	Transferred to Forty-fourth Regiment.
Chapman, Wyman	Delphi	Dec. 26, 1863	" " "
Crousehorn, Elias	"	Jan. 10, 1864	" " "
Foust, George	Lockport	Dec. 26, 1863	" " "
Grandstaff, James	"	Dec. 29, 1863	Discharged January 5, 1865.
Herron, Henry H	Camden	Dec. 20, 1863	Transferred tc Forty-fourth Regiment.
Henderson, Andrew	Delphi	March 11, 1864	" " "
Irwin, Henry	Rock Creek	Dec. 11. 1863	Died at Jeffersonville, Ind., May 22, 1865.
Malatt, Jacob	Lockport	Dec. 26, 1863	Transferred to Forty-fourth Regiment.
M'Farland, David	Monticello	Dec. 24, 1863	Died at Marietta, Ga., August 9, 1864.
Noyce, John F	Pittsburg	" "	Transferred to Forty-fourth Regiment.
Newman, Mark A	Lockport	" "	" " "
Sinks, David	"	Feb. 20, 1865	" " "
Thompson, Robert H	Pittsburg	" "	" " "
Thomas, John D	Lockport	" "	" " "
Timmons, James W	"		

Company "B," Eighty-Sixth Regiment, Indiana Volunteers.

Names and Rank.	Residence.	Date of Muster.	Remarks.
Captains.			
Francis J. Mattler	Delphi	Sept. 4, 1862	Dismissed November 6, 1863; reinstated January 6, 1864; discharged January 3, 1865.
Jeremiah Hough	"	Jan. 31, 1865	Mustered out with regiment.
First Lieutenants.			
John S. Armitage	Delphi	Sept. 4, 1862	
Jeremiah Hough	"	April 3, 1863	Promoted Captain.
Matthew M'Inerny	"	Nov. 7, 1863	Promoted Captain of Company H.
John L. Bullock	"	March 28, 1865	Mustered out with regiment.
Second Lieutenant.			
Jeremiah Hough	Delphi	Sept. 4, 1862	Promoted First Lieutenant.
Matthew M'Inerny	"	April 3, 1863	" " "
John T. Whitcher	Pittsburg	June 1, 1865	Mustered out as First Sergeant with regiment.
First Sergeant.			
M'Inerny, Matthew	Delphi	July 15, 1862	Promoted Second Lieutenant.
Sergeants.			
Gist, Newton H	Delphi	July 15, 1862	Mustered out June 6, 1865, as private.
Reed, James	"	" "	Discharged February 14, 1863.
Heintz, Lewis	"	" "	Killed at Stone River, December 31, 1862.
Smiley, William L	Pittsburg	" "	Deserted; mustered out May 14, 1865.

CORPORALS.			
Crowell, James M	Lockport	July 15, 1862	Died at Nashville, Tennessee, December 22, 1862.
Penny, Henry W	Pittsburg	" "	Mustered out June 6, 1865, as private.
Spitznagh, Frank H	Delphi	" "	Mustered out May 10, 1865.
Chandler, Robert	Lockport	" "	Mustered out May 6, 1865.
Watters, Charles	Buck Creek	" "	Died December 1, 1863; wounds.
Bullock, John L	Delphi	" "	Promoted First Lieutenant.
Houk, David	Lockport	" "	Deserted March 1, 1863.
York, Samuel	Prince William	" "	Transferred Veteran Reserve Corps, July 29, 1864.
MUSICIANS.			
Edgerly, James H	Pittsburg	July 20, 1862	Discharged March 25, 1863.
Beaver, Henry	Monticello	" "	Mustered out June 6, 1865.
WAGONER.			
Stevenson, James C	Prince William	July 20, 1862	Deserted October 18, 1862.
PRIVATES.			
Armor, George E	Delphi	July 20, 1862	Killed at Stone River, December 31, 1862.
Armstrong, James F	Prince William	" "	Mustered out June 6, 1865, as Corporal.
Ashba, Benjamin A	" "	" "	Died at Nashville, Tennessee, October 1, 1863.
Ashba, Jonathan	" "	" "	Transferred to V. R. C.; must'd out June 29, 1865.
Baker, John	Delphi	" "	Mustered out June 6, 1865, as absent, sick.
Bealer, Christian	"	" "	Deserted April 15, 1863.
Bierman, Christian	"	" "	Died at Richmond, Virginia, December 6, 1863.
Blue, John	"	" "	Mustered out June 6, 1865.
Bowen, George W	"	" "	Discharged March 13, 1863.
Bundy, Benjamin	"	" "	Mustered out June 6, 1865.
Casad, John A	Pittsburg	" "	Died at Nashville, Tenn., Jan. 31, 1863; wounds.

Names and Rank.	Residence.	Date of Muster.	Remarks.
Chittick, Jasper	Prince William	July 20, 1862	Mustered out June 6, 1865.
Chittick, Andrew J	" "	" "	" " " "
Clark, Hiram	Delphi	" "	Died at Murfreesboro, Tenn., February 11, 1863.
Clifford, Con	"	" "	Mustered out June 6, 1865, as Corporal.
Condon, Garrett	"	" "	Mustered out June 6, 1865.
Copstick, John M	Prince William	" "	" " " "
Crow, Thomas	Delphi	July 25, 1862	Died at Chattanooga, October 28, 1863.
Crowell, Richard C	Lockport	" "	Killed at Stone River, December 31, 1862.
Davis, Albert	Delphi	" "	Died at Murfreesboro, February 6, 1863.
Denman, Joseph	"	" "	Deserted April 15, 1863.
Dittmer, Frederick	"	" "	Mustered out June 6, 1865, as Sergeant.
Donahoe, John	"	" "	Discharged March 17, 1863.
Eisley, Barney	"	" "	Mustered out June 6, 1865.
Farrier, Robert	Camden	" "	Discharged May 6, 1863.
Felthoof, Henry	Prince William	" "	Transferred to Veteran Reserve Corps, Jan. 4, 1865.
German, John S	Lockport	" "	Discharged April 1, 1863.
German, Southey K	"	" "	Died at Chattanooga, November 4, 1863.
Green, John	Delphi	" "	Deserted December 31, 1863.
Grider, John M	Pittsburg	" "	Deserted October 6, 1862.
Haiffe, Joseph	Delphi	" "	Died at Murfreesboro, February 9, 1863.
Hart James J	"	" "	Mustered out June 6, 1865.
Harshman, Henry	Lafayette	" "	Mustered out June 12, 1865.
Hauk, Jacob	Cleveland, O.	" "	Mustered out June 6, 1865.
Hauk, George H	Lockport	" "	" " " "
Hoover, Joseph	Colfax	" "	" " " "
Huntley, James H	Prince William	" "	Supposed to be dead.
Kekkefoet, Albert	Delphi	" "	Mustered out June 6, 1865.

Kough, Richard	Lafayette	July 25, 1862	Transferred to Vet. Reserve Corps, March 17, 1864.
Lunenburg, Frederick	Delphi	" "	Died at Chattanooga, November 26, 1863.
Magee, John	New York City	" "	Discharged May 15, 1865.
Marshall, Humphrey	Rockfield	" "	Mustered out June 6, 1865.
Miller, Frederick	Delphi	July 26, 1862	Discharged March 12, 1863.
Misner, Usual	Prince William	" "	Died at Louisville, Kentucky, December 29, 1862.
Morton, Harrison P.	Delphi	" "	Mustered out June 6, 1865.
M'Mahon, Patrick	"	" "	Transferred to Veteran Reserve Corps, Jan. 27, 1865.
M'Quillen, William	Rockfield	" "	Mustered out May 17, 1865.
Ohime, John	Lafayette	" "	Discharged October 15, 1862.
Oliver, Lemuel W	Pittsburg	July 27, 1862	Died at Danville Prison, Va., December 6, 1863.
Ratliff, Salathiel	Prince William	" "	Mustered out June 7, 1865.
Ratliff, John	" "	" "	Mustered out June 6, 1865.
Ratliff, Lewis C.	" "	" "	" " " "
Rogers, George	Idaville	" "	" " " "
Rose, William	Lafayette	" "	Died at Silver Springs, Tenn., Nov. 11, 1862.
Rose, Benjamin F.	Transitville	" "	Killed at Kennesaw Mountain, June 28, 1864.
Saxon, Anthony M.	Rockfield	" "	Killed at Stone River, December 31, 1862.
Saylor, Wilson	P. William	" "	Died at Stone River, Nov. 20, 1863.
Scott, Elias	" "	" "	Died at Bowling Green, Ky., Nov. 8, 1862.
Sharp, James W. P.	Lafayette	" "	Mustered out June 17, 1865.
Shay, Thomas	Crawfordsville	Aug. 2, 1862	Mustered out June 6, 1865.
Spies, Matthias	P. William	" "	" " "
Starne, Levi M.	" "	" "	Discharged February 19, 1863.
Stoner, Abraham	Delphi	" "	Transf'd to Vet. Res. Corps; must'd out June 29, 1865.
Stoner, Cyrus	Rockfield	" "	Discharged March 12, 1863.
Swarts, Samuel	P. William	" "	Transferred to Veteran Reserve Corps, Aug. 1, 1863.
Thirtyacre, John	Delphi	" "	Discharged November 4, 1862.
Tucker, Abraham	Rockfield	" "	Transf'd to Vet. Res, Corps; must'd out June 29, 1865.
Tubberty, Thomas	Lafayette	" "	Mustered out June 6, 1865, as Sergeant.

Names and Rank.	Residence.	Date of Muster.	Remarks.
Turner, John W.	Pittsburg	Aug. 2, 1862	Missing at Franklin, Tenn., Nov. 24, 1864.
Welch, John	Delphi	" "	Discharged March 17, 1863.
Whitcher, John T.	Pittsburg	" "	Mustered out June 6, 1865, as First Sergeant.
White, John	Delphi	" "	Mustered out June 6, 1865.
Wolford, Henry	Francisville	" "	" " "
Woster, John	Rockfield	" "	" " "
York, Andrew J.	Prince William	" "	Mustered out June 6, 1865, as Corporal.

Twenty-Fourth Battery, Indiana Volunteers.

Captains.			
Joseph A. Sims	Delphi	Oct. 27, 1862	Resigned December 7, 1863.
Alexander Hardy	"	April 25, 1864	Mustered out with Battery.
First Lieutenants.			
Alexander Hardy	Delphi	July 1, 1863	Promoted Captain.
Hiram Allen	"	May 1, 1864	Mustered out as Second Lieutenant with Battery.
Second Lieutenants.			
Alexander Hardy	Delphi	Nov. 29, 1862	Promoted First Lieutenant.
Hiram Allen	"	July 1, 1863	" " "
James C. Smith	"	May 2, 1863	Mustered out as First Sergeant with Battery.
William S. Ramey	"	March 1, 1864	Mustered out as Sergeant with Battery.
First Sergeant.			
James C. Smith	Delphi	Nov. 20, 1862	Mustered out August 3, 1865.

Quartermaster Sergeant.			
M'Laughlin, Alexander	Delphi	Nov. 29, 1862	Mustered out August 3, 1865.
Sergeants.			
Ramey, William S	Delphi	Nov. 29, 1862	Mustered out August 3, 1865.
Kirkpatrick, Robert	"	" "	" " "
Willard, Frank L	"	" "	" " "
Wallace, George W	"	" "	" " "
Hughes, William H	"	" "	Mustered out June 21, 1865.
Shigley, Jacob	Carroll County	" "	Died at home, November 4, 1864.
Smith, John W	Pittsburg	" "	Mustered out August 3, 1865.
Bugler.			
Jackson, William L	Delphi	Nov. 29, 1862	Mustered out August 3, 1865.
Privates.			
Boles, William T	Burlington	Nov. 29, 1862	Mustered out August 3, 1865.
Bowdell, Jesse W	"	" "	Deserted February 12, 1863.
Ballard, Amos	Carroll County	" "	
Chase, Abel S	" "	" "	Transferred to Veteran Reserve Corps.
Clark, John	" "	" "	Mustered out August 3, 1865.
Callam, Thomas	" "	" "	" " "
Campbell Robert	" "	" "	Deserted January 15, 1863.
Chatten, William F	Burlington	" "	Mustered out August 3, 1865.
Collins, William H	Delphi	" "	" " "
Dick, Levi	Pittsburg	" "	" "
Deford, Elias	Delphi	" "	" "
Dewey, George B	"	" "	" " "
Frevert, Frederick	Burlington	" "	" " "
Farran, Abraham	Carroll County	" "	Died at Knoxville, Tenn., February 15, 1864.

Names and Rank.	Residence.	Date of Muster.	Remarks.
Gates, Jacob R.	Carroll County	Nov. 29, 1862	Died at home, April 8, 1864.
Gwinn, Joseph L.	Burlington	" "	Mustered out August 3, 1865.
Hibbeson, George M.	Camden	" "	Mustered out May 22, 1865.
Holden, Samuel	"	" "	Deserted December 5, 1862.
Hendricks, Samuel	Rossville	" "	Mustered out May 24, 1865.
Jabe, Justice	Carroll County	" "	Mustered out August 3, 1865.
Julien, Madison	Pittsburg	" "	Mustered out August 3, 1865, as Corporal.
Kennell, George	Carroll County	" "	Deserted March 15, 1863.
Koonsman, John M.	Delphi	" "	Discharged July 11, 1865.
Lawson, Curtis	"	" "	Mustered out August 3, 1865.
Long, Enos	"	" "	" " "
Lane, Allen	"	" "	Died at Indianapolis, March 19, 1863.
Lane, William G.	"	" "	Mustered out August 3, 1865.
Myers, John F.	"	" "	Discharged, 1862.
Moore, Augustus	"	" "	Transferred to Veteran Reserve Corps.
Mickley, Uriah A.	"	" "	Mustered out August 3, 1865.
Myers, John F.	"	" "	" " "
Pire, Allen F.	"	" "	Deserted December 10, 1863.
Pratt, George	"	" "	Transferred to V. R. C., Dec. 28, 1864.
Standley, Charles M.	"	" "	Died at Lebanon, Kentucky.
Standley, Moses M.	"	" "	Mustered out August 3, 1865.
Shigley, Robert	"	" "	" " "
Stonebrook, Joseph	"	" "	Died on steamer, April 6 1865.
Tribbett, George	"	....	Never mustered.
Thayer, John S.	"	Nov. 29, 1862	
Wilson, Harrison	"	" "	Mustered out August 3, 1865.
Woodward, John	"	....	Never mustered.

Wickel, Philip	Carroll County	Nov. 29, 1862	Mustered out August 3, 1865.
Walton, Samuel L.	" "	" "	" " "
Wade, David	" "	" "	" " "
Williams, James	" "	" "	" " "
Recruits.			
Appenzeller, John S.	Carroll County	March 9, 1864	Lost on steamer *Sultana*, April 27, 1865.
Alldridge, Marion	" "	Nov. 29, 1862	Mustered out July 24, 1865.
Archer, William J.	" "	Dec. 21, 1863	Mustered out August 3, 1865.
Bryant, James	" "	" "	" " "
Bright, Isaac	" "	March 11, 1863	" " "
Bright, Peacha	" "	Nov. 29, 1862	" " "
Busling, George	" "	March 19, 1863	" " "
Bennett, George	" "	Nov. 20, 1862	" " "
Branch, Barney	" "	Jan. 9, 1864	Died at Kingston, Ga., Sept. 1864.
Cantner, George	" "	Feb. 9, 1863	Mustered out August 3, 1865.
Culler, John T.	" "	Jan. 1, 1864	" " "
Collar, Washington	" "	Jan. 9, 1864	" " "
Cosand, Cornelius	" "	" "	" " "
Cox, Aaron	" "	March 20, 1863	Deserted June 14, 1865.
Deford, Edward	" "	Feb. 8, 1864.	
Denny, William	" "	March 11, 1863	Discharged July 15, 1865.
Eikenberry, Peter	" "	March 9, 1864	Mustered out July 13, 1865.
Ewing, Henry	" "	" "	Mustered out August 3, 1865.
Fife, Kilas	" "	March 25, 1864	" " "
Flora, Jonas	" "	Feb. 11, 1863	Died at Knoxville, Tenn., Feb. 1864.
Gergeous, Conrad	" "	March 11, 1863	Mustered out August 11, 1865.
Guthrie, Joseph	" "	Dec. 27, 1862	Mustered out August 3, 1865.
Hubbell, Albert	" "	March 11, 1863	" " "
Hull, James F.	" "	Jan. 26, 1864	" " "

Names and Rank.	Residence.	Date of Muster.	Remarks.
Hartzog, Samuel	Carroll County	Nov. 16, 1864	Mustered out August 3, 1865.
Hornaday, Francis M	" "	Feb. 11, 1863	Died at Munfordville, Ky.
Linton, George A	" "	Feb. 13, 1863	Mustered out August 3, 1865.
Maxwell, Alonzo	" "	Dec. 6, 1862	" " "
M'Kinny, Elijah	" "	Dec. 21, 1863	" " "
Miller, Joseph	" "	" "	" " "
Matthews, Paul P	" "	Nov. 11, 1864	" " "
Matthews, Clark	" "	Nov. 20, 1864	Died at Louisville, Ky., July 21, 1865.
Matthews, Thomas	" "	Nov. 29, 1864	Died at Chattanooga, Tenn., March 14, 1865.
Miller, George	" "	Jan. 13, 1862	Deserted August 1, 1863.
Newer, Benj. A	" "	Dec. 23, 1862	Died in rebel prison.
Prewitt, William A	" "	March 9, 1864	Mustered out August 3, 1865.
Rhodes, James H	" "	Jan. 9, 1864	" " "
Roach, William H	" "	April 13, 1864	Never reported to Battery.
Ramsay, Joseph	" "	" "	" " "
Shields, James	" "	Feb. 13, 1863	Mustered out August 3, 1865.
Salisbury, Martin M	" "	" "	" " "
Shelley, Phineas	" "	Dec. 6, 1862	Died at Kingston, Ga., July 10, 1864.
Wall, Andrew	" "	Jan. 26, 1864	Mustered out August 3, 1865.

ONE HUNDRED AND THIRTY-FIFTH REGIMENT, INDIANA VOLUNTEERS.

(ONE HUNDRED DAYS.)

Lieutenant Colonel.			
John H. Gould	Delphi	May 25, 1864	Mustered out with Regiment.

COMPANY "C," ONE HUNDRED THIRTY-FIFTH REGIMENT, INDIANA VOLUNTEERS.

CAPTAIN.			
James S. Case	Delphi	May 23, 1864	Mustered out with Regiment.
FIRST LIEUTENANT.			
John C. Colton	Delphi	May 23, 1864	Mustered out with Regiment.
SECOND LIEUTENANT.			
James W. Griffith	Delphi	May 23, 1864	Mustered out with Regiment.
PRIVATES.			
Akins, John C.	Carroll County	May 23, 1864	Mustered out September 29, 1864.
Anderson, John J.	" "	" "	" " "
Anderson, James T.	" "	" "	" " "
Anderson, David J.	" "		Never mustered.
Barnett, Samuel W.	" "	May 23, 1864	Mustered out September 29, 1864.
Baum, Zachary T.	" "	" "	" " "
Blanchard, William L.	" "	" "	" " "
Bowen, Frank M.	" "	" "	Mustered out September 29, 1864, as Sergt.
Brewster, John S.	" "	" "	Mustered out September 29, 1864.
Brought, Alvan M.	" "	" "	" " "
Brown, Isaac W.	" "	" "	" " "
Burr, John H.	" "	" "	Mustered out Sept. 29, 1864, as First Sergt.
Burntrager, Aaron	" "	" "	Mustered out September 29, 1864, as Sergt.
Campbell, Henry E.	" "	" "	Mustered out September 29, 1864.
Case, Reed	" "	" "	Mustered out September 29, 1864, as Corp.
Couch, William	" "	" "	Mustered out September 29, 1864.
Casad, Peter A.	" "	" "	" " "

Names and Rank.	Residence.	Date of Muster.	Remarks.
Clifford, Michael	Carroll County	May 23, 1864	Mustered out September 29, 1864.
Cline, John	" "	" "	" " "
Corey, Aaron P	" "	" "	" " "
Cobb, Richard	" "	" "	" " "
Cress, Ira	" "	" "	" " "
Cook, Jasper J	" "	" "	Mustered out September 29, 1864, as Corporal.
Curson Elijah	" "	" "	Mustered out September 29, 1864.
Cooper, James	" "	" "	" " "
Davidson, William L	" "	" "	Mustered out September 29, 1864, as Corporal.
Durling, William	" "	" "	Died at Bridgeport, Ala., July 25, 1864.
Dunkle, Theodore F	" "	" "	Mustered out September 29, 1864.
Dunkle, William F	" "	" "	" " "
Elston, Jonas	" "	" "	" " "
Evans, John H	" "	" "	" " "
Farthing, Wm. H	" "	" "	" " "
Foley, Theodore	" "	" "	" " "
Fisher, Jacob B	" "	" "	" " "
Flory, Henry	" "	" "	" " "
Griffith, James W	" "	" "	" " "
Gresham, Edward H	" "	" "	Mustered out September 29, 1864, as Corp.
Graham, John	" "	" "	Mustered out September 29, 1864.
Groninger, Joseph R	" "	" "	" " "
Gibson, Henry	" "	" "	Mustered out September 29, 1864, as Sergt.
Gwinn, Thomas J	" "	" "	Mustered out September 29, 1864.
Harley, Charles	" "	" "	" " "
Hamillin, William	" "	" "	" " "
Hartzog, Jacob	" "	" "	" " "

Hammill, John A.	Carroll County	May 23, 1864	Mustered out September 29, 1864.
Harner, Thomas L.	" "	" "	Died at Stephenson, Ala., August 29, 1864.
Hill, George	" "	" "	Died at Nashville, Tenn., August 18, 1864.
Hoan, Calvin	" "	" "	Mustered out September 29, 1864.
Holmes, Charles J	" "	" "	Mustered out September 29, 1864, as Corporal.
Hubbard, Henry	" "	" "	Mustered out September 29, 1864.
Hanna, Joseph W	" "	" "	" " "
Ireland, James	" "	" "	" " "
Julien, Stephen	" "	" "	" " "
Leonard, James H.	" "	" "	" " "
Lyon, Charles	" "	" "	" " "
Merritt, Henry L.	" "	" "	" " "
Messner, Charles B.	" "	" "	" " "
M'Beth, Robert R	" "	" "	" " "
M'Farland, John	" "	" "	" " "
Morgan, William	" "	" "	" " "
Moore, Cyrus W.	" "	" "	" " "
Mount, Charles	" "	" "	" " "
M'Cord, William	" "	" "	" " "
Newman, Jacob	" "	" "	" " "
Nigh, David C.	" "	" "	" " "
Nipper, Robert	" "	" "	" " "
Potter, Frank	" "	" "	Mustered out September 29, 1864, as Musician.
Patterson, Robert	" "	" "	Mustered out September 29, 1864, as Corporal.
Ransom, Hiram V.	" "	" "	Mustered out September 29, 1864.
Robertson, Charles B.	" "	" "	Mustered out September 29, 1864, as Sergeant.
Roblyer, William H.	" "	" "	Mustered out September 29, 1864.
Rickard, William H.	" "	" "	Died at Bridgeport, Ala., July 3, 1864.
Ruffing, Louis	" "	" "	Mustered out September 29, 1864.
Seabring, William	" "	" "	" " "

Names and Rank.	Residence.	Date of Muster.	Remarks.
Sheets, George F.	Carroll County	May 23, 1864	Mustered out September 29, 1864.
Shelton, Howard	" "	" "	" " "
Smith, Lucius J.	" "	" "	Mustered out September 29, 1864, as Musician.
Swalin, John I.	" "	" "	Mustered out September 29, 1864.
Scott, Francis M.	" "	" "	" " "
Templeton, William E.	" "	" "	Mustered out September 29, 1864, as Corporal.
Todd, Jasper M.	" "	" "	Mustered out September 29, 1864.
Thayer, Charles	" "	" "	" " "
Tucker, James B.	" "	" "	" " "
Thayer, Ferdinand A.	" "	" "	" " "
Varnes, Harrison R.	" "	" "	" " "
Wagoner, Isaiah J	" "	" "	" " "
York, James M.	" "	" "	" " "
Recruit.			
Homer Joshua		June 3, 1864	

Company "F," Ninety-Ninth Regiment, Indiana Volunteers.

Names and Rank.	Residence.	Date of Muster.	Remarks.
Downs, William G.	Pittsburg	Aug. 22, 1862	Discharged January 28, 1863.
Downs, Jacob H.	"	Aug. 19, 1862	" " "
Davenport, Clark S.	"	" "	Mustered out June 5, 1865.
Striker, Richard	"	Aug. 22, 1862	" " "

Company "H," One Hundred and Fiftieth Regiment, Indiana Volunteers.

(ONE YEAR.)

Names and Rank.	Residence.	Date of Muster.	Remarks.
Captain.			
Henry E. W. Campbell	Delphi	March 6, 1865	Mustered out with Regiment.
First Lieutenant.			
Edward H. Gresham	Delphi	March 6, 1865	Mustered out with Regiment.
Second Lieutenant.			
Thomas J. Voliva	Attica	March 7, 1865	Mustered out with Regiment.
Privates.			
Angell, Fountain H	Carroll County	Feb. 16, 1865	Mustered out August 5, 1865, as Corporal.
Beebles, Jacob S	" "	Feb. 8, 1865	Mustered out August 5, 1865.
Baum, Jasper N	" "	Feb. 28, 1865	" " " "
Barkhurst, G. L	" "	Feb. 15, 1865	" " " "
Bunker, Samuel	" "	Feb. 28, 1865	" " " "
Close, Harrison	" "	Feb. 6, 1865	Mustered out August 5, 1865, as Corporal.
Camp, William	" "	Feb. 15, 1865	Mustered out August 5, 1865.
Cline, John	" "	Feb. 3, 1865	" " " "
Denton, Benjamin N	" "	Feb. 13, 1865	Mustered out August 5, 1865, as Corporal.
Draper, Jeremiah	" "	Feb. 3, 1865	Mustered out August 6, 1865.
Ferris, William	" "	Feb. 6, 1865	Died at Wheeling, Virginia, March 29, 1865.
Gustin, George M	" "	Feb. 15, 1865	Mustered out August 5, 1865.
Ginden, Joseph	" "	Feb. 17, 1865	" " " "
Groninger, Austin	" "	Feb. 27, 1865	" " " "
Groninger, Stewart S	" "	Feb. 28, 1865	" " " "

Names and Rank.	Residence.	Date of Muster.	Remarks.
Howell, Samuel	Carroll County	Feb. 8, 1865	Mustered out August 5, 1865, as Corporal.
Huston, Jeremiah	" "	Feb. 15, 1865	Died at Stephenson, Virginia, May 22, 1865.
Henemetler, Jacob	" "	Feb. 21, 1865	Mustered out August 5, 1865, as Corporal.
Hines, John N	" "	Feb. 3, 1865	Mustered out August 5, 1865.
Hoan, Calvin	" "	" "	" " " "
Herron, Nathaniel	" "	Feb. 28, 1865	Mustered out August 5, 1865, as Commiss'y Serg't.
Koontze, James H	" "	" "	Mustered out August 5, 1865.
M'Ahvon, Jacob L	" "	Feb. 8, 1865	Mustered out August 5, 1865, as Corporal.
Moore, George W	" "	Feb. 17, 1865	Mustered out August 1, 1865, as Sergeant.
Newman, Charles H	" "	Feb. 13, 1865	Mustered out August 5, 1865.
Nichols, Jacob L	" "	Feb. 15, 1865	" " " "
Olinger, John	" "	Feb. 6, 1865	" " " "
Sweetzer, Daniel W	" "	Feb. 8, 1865	Died at Wheeling, Virginia, April 24, 1865.
Stout, Lloyd	" "	" "	Died at Indianapolis, Indiana, March 15, 1865.
Storms, Owen	" "	Feb. 28, 1865	Mustered out August 5, 1865.
Shroyer, Hiram W	" "	" "	" " " "
Tribbett, George W	" "	Feb. 10, 1865	" " " "
Thompson, William J	" "	Jan. 25, 1865	" " " "
Tucker, John I	" "	Feb. 15, 1865	" " " "
Thomas, John M	" "	" "	" " " "
Wilson, Elza R	" "	Feb. 3, 1865	" " " "
Walker, Samuel C	" "	" "	" " " "
Wilson, Joseph	" "	" "	" " " "
Wilson, Smith	" "	Feb. 11, 1865	" " " "
Recruits.			
Allison, Hiram	Carroll County	March 4, 1865	Mustered out June 10, 1865.

Gorner, Peter	Carroll County	March 9, 1865	Mustered out August 5, 1865.
Hadley, Charles	" "	March 10, 1865	" " " "
Holts, Marion	" "	March 8, 1865	" " " "
Moore, John G	" "	March 9, 1865	" " " "
Potter, Frank A	" "	March 10, 1865	" " " "
Simpson, Charles B	" "	March 11, 1865	" " " "

Company "D," One Hundred and Fifty-Fourth Regiment, Indiana Volunteers.

(ONE YEAR.)

Captain.			
Sylvester Berry	Delphi	April 21, 1865	Mustered out with Regiment.
First Lieutenant.			
Joseph Sampson	Pittsburg	April 18, 1865	Mustered out with Regiment.
Second Lieutenant.			
Benjamin F. Brough	Delphi	April 18, 1865	Mustered out with Regiment.
Privates.			
Allen, James M	Carroll County	March 31, 1865	Mustered out August 4, 1865, as Corporal.
Appenzeller, George M	" "	" "	Mustered out August 4, 1865.
Anderson, John J	" "	March 23, 1865	" " "
Anderson, William R	" "	" "	" "
Bales, Robert J	" "	March 21, 1865	" " "
Bauley, Archibald	" "	" "	" " "
Breyer, Isaiah	" "	" "	Mustered out May 31, 1865.
Buck, Charles	" "	" "	Mustered out August 4, 1865.
Brockhouse, William	" "	" "	" " "

Names and Rank.	Residence.	Date of Muster.	Remarks.
Bugher, Daniel P	Carroll County	March 28, 1865	Mustered out August 4, 1865.
Blue, Isaiah C	" "	March 29, 1865	" " "
Barns, Albert H	" "	April 7, 1865	" " "
Brough, Theodore	" "	April 10, 1865	" " "
Boles, John A. J	" "	May 29, 1865	Mustered out August 4, 1865, as Corporal.
Brown, George W	" "	May 21, 1865	Mustered out August 4, 1865.
Brough, Benjamin F	" "	April 11, 1865	Promoted Second Lieutenant.
Clark, Joseph B	" "	March 28, 1865	Mustered out August 4, 1865, as Sergeant.
Cook, James J	" "	April 1, 1865	" " " "
Cochan, Charles W	" "	March 27, 1865	Mustered out August 4, 1865.
Colwell, John S	" "	April 1, 1865	" " "
Duncan, William	" "	March 15, 1865	" "
Downes, John C	Fountain Co	" "	" "
Depugh, Garrett, A	Carroll County	" "	" " "
Everman, Andrew	" "	March 21, 1865	Mustered out August 4, 1865, as Sergeant.
Elston, Jonas	" "	March 23, 1865	Mustered out August 4, 1865, as Corporal.
Fellows, John M	" "	March 28, 1865	Mustered out August 4, 1865.
Flattery, William S	" "	March 15, 1865	" " "
Fichthorn, Daniel	" "	April 11, 1865	Mustered out August 4, 1865, as First Sergeant.
Griss, Theodore	" "	March 20, 1865	Mustered out August 4, 1865.
Gasaway, James M	" "	April 16, 1865	" " "
Garrison, John K	" "	April 11, 1865	" " "
Graham, John W	" "	" "	" " "
Gwinn, Thomas J	Fountain Co	March 14, 1865	" " "
Grant, Amandus M	Carroll County	March 28, 1865	" " "
Heatley, William E	" "	March 21, 1865	" " "
Harvey, William S	" "	March 23, 1865	" " "

Hamilton, William	Carroll County	March 23, 1865	Mustered out August 4, 1865.
Hartzog, Jacob C	" "	" "	" " "
Hoshow, Henry	" "	March 31, 1865	" " "
Hoshow, George	" "	" "	" " "
Harrell, Alexander	" "	March 22, 1865	" " "
Harter, Moses	" "	April 11, 1865	Mustered out August 8, 1865.
James, William F	Fountain Co	March 27, 1865	Deserted April 13, 1865.
Kinsley, Samuel H	Clinton County	April 10, 1865	Mustered out August 4, 1865, as Corporal.
Lesly, Eli	Tippecanoe Co	March 21, 1865	Mustered out August 4, 1865.
Lesly, Samuel	" "	" "	" " "
Lucas, Alfred	Carroll County	March 31, 1865	" " "
Landry, John R	" "	March 17, 1865	" " "
Millholland, John	" "	March 20, 1865	Deserted April 29, 1865.
Miller, George F	" "	March 23, 1865	Mustered out May 23, 1865.
Morgan, William	" "	" "	Mustered out August 4, 1865.
Moore, Stephen W	" "	" "	Mustered out May 18, 1865.
M'Feters, William	Montgomery Co.	March 31, 1865	Mustered out August 4, 1865.
Myer, Lewis S	Carroll County	March 28, 1865	" " "
Morrow, Elihu S	" "	March 22, 1865	Mustered out June 6, 1865.
M'Cormick, Asbury S	" "	April 11, 1865	Promoted Adjutant.
Moyer, Franklin	" "	" "	Mustered out August 4, 1865.
Mills, Isaac W	" "	" "	Mustered out August 4, 1865, as Sergeant.
Nipper, John	" "	March 23, 1865	Mustered out June 7, 1865.
Nearhoff, Henry	" "	April 3, 1865	Mustered out August 4, 1865, as Corporal.
Northcut, Joseph	" "	March 22, 1865	Mustered out August 4, 1865.
Prutis, Charles S	" "	March 23, 1865	Mustered out August 4, 1865, as Corporal.
Panton, Ira	" "	March 29, 1865	Mustered out August 4, 1865.
Phillips, Isaac	Tippecanoe Co	March 17, 1865	" " "
Riley, John	Fountain Co	March 31, 1865	" " "
Rush, Harvey	Montgomery Co.	March 30, 1865	" " "

Names and Rank.	Residence.	Date of Muster.	Remarks.
Ray, Leander	Tippecanoe Co	March 22, 1865	Deserted April 13, 1865.
Robinson, Mahlon	Carroll County	" "	Mustered out August 4, 1865, as Corporal.
Rohrbaugh, John B	" "	April 12, 1865	Mustered out August 4, 1865.
Schnepp, Andrew	" "	March 21, 1865	" " "
Shinn, Isaac R	" "	" "	" " "
Stocdon, James	" "	" "	" " "
Schofield, William	" "	March 23, 1865	" " "
Schopp, Abraham	" "	" "	" " "
Schopp, Elias	" "	April 3, 1865	" " "
Say, Henry L	Warren County	March 29, 1865	Deserted April 13, 1865.
Shafer, Eaton	Carroll County	April 11, 1865	Mustered out August 4, 1865.
Swain, William	" "	April 27, 1865	" " "
Sherfey, Henry B	" "	" "	" " "
Smith, John B	" "	" "	" " "
Swain, Isaiah	" "	March 15, 1865	" " "
Shaw, James	" "	" "	" "
Schnepp, Isaac	" "	March 21, 1865	" " "
Thorn, John W	....	....	Deserted April 13, 1865.
Troxell, John M	Carroll County	April 11, 1865	Mustered out August 4, 1865.
Thayer, Ferdinand A	Fountain Co	March 14, 1865	" " "
Thomas, John W. F	Carroll County	April 11, 1865	Mustered out August 4, 1865, as Corporal.
Wallace, George	" "	March 23, 1865	Mustered out August 4, 1865.
Wallsmith, Marion	" "	March 27, 1865	Mustered out June 28, 1865.
Witham, Wilson	" "	March 15, 1865	Mustered out August 4, 1865.
Young, Christopher	Tippecanoe Co	March 17, 1865	" " "

COMPANY "M," ONE HUNDRED AND TWENTY-SIXTH REGIMENT, INDIANA VOLUNTEERS (ELEVENTH CAVALRY).

(THREE YEARS.)

CAPTAINS.			
William B. Givins	Delphi	Jan. 25, 1864	Resigned May 31, 1865.
John Larabee	Cincinnati	June 24, 1865	Mustered out with Regiment.
FIRST LIEUTENANTS.			
Henry E. Olds	Delphi	Jan. 30, 1864	Resigned April 7, 1865.
John Larabee	Cincinnati	May 19, 1865	Promoted Captain.
Samuel Sidenbender	Paris, Ill	June 26, 1865	Mustered out with Regiment.
SECOND LIEUTENANTS.			
John Larabee	Cincinnati	Feb. 17, 1864	Promoted First Lieutenant.
Samuel Sidenbender	Paris, Ill	May 26, 1865	" "
Joseph A. Hamilton	Indianapolis	June 16, 1865	Mustered out with Regiment.
PRIVATES.			
Adkinson, Thomas J	Delphi	Jan. 30, 1864	Mustered out September 19, 1865.
Allen, William	Darlington	" "	" " "
Beckner, George W	Delphi	" "	" " "
Barr, Ivan	"	Jan. 14, 1864	" " "
Cave, James E	Clarks H	Jan. 30, 1864	Mustered out Sept. 19, 1865, as Q. M. Sergt.
Corns, Joseph	Delphi	" "	Mustered out Sept. 19, 1865, as Corporal.
Cooper, George A	Darlington	" "	Mustered out September 19, 1865.
Chandler, James E	Delphi	Feb. 17, 1864	Mustered out September 19, 1865, as Sergt.
Deardorf, John	"	Jan. 30, 1864	Died at Larkinsville, Ala., Jan. 2, 1865.

Names and Rank.	Residence.	Date of Muster.	Remarks.
Dick, Levi	Delphi	Jan. 30, 1864	Mustered out September 19, 1865.
Drollinger, Albert G	Darlington	" "	" " "
Doster, Alfred F	Colfax	Feb. 17, 1864	Mustered out September 19, 1865, as Corp.
Evans, David W	Crawfordsville	Jan. 30, 1864	Mustered out Sept. 19, 1865, as Bugler.
Ellis, Thomas	Colfax	April 20, 1864	Deserted June 16, 1865.
Forney, James A	Delphi	Jan. 30, 1864	Mustered out September 19, 1865.
Frazee, Samuel	Colfax	" "	Mustered out Sept. 19, 1865, as Corp.
Foster, Martin	Rockfield	" "	Mustered out September 19, 1865.
Friedley, James C	Rossville	Feb. 17, 1864	Discharged June 2, 1865.
Ferrier, John	Wild-cat	" "	Mustered out September 19, 1865.
Fair, David	Lockport	March 14, 1864	Died at Indianapolis, Ind., April 15, 1864.
Givins, James F	Delphi	Feb. 17, 1864	Discharged June 6, 1865, as Sergt.
Gardner, Joshua J	"	" "	Discharged March 18, 1865.
Gant, John E	Clark's Hill	" "	Deserted June 16, 1865.
Hannam, Jehu C	Delphi	Jan. 30, 1864	Promoted Major.
Harlan, Aaron	Colfax	" "	Mustered out September 19, 1865.
Hamilton Joseph A	"	" "	Promoted Second Lieutenant.
Hopkins, Thomas F	Delphi	" "	Mustered out Sept. 16, 1865, as First Sergt.
Harrison, Eli S	"	" "	Mustered out September 19, 1865.
Hamilton, John W	Colfax	" "	" " "
Harris, John H	Harrisonburg	Feb. 17, 1864	" " "
Haslet, James	Delphi	" "	Discharged June 16, 1865, as Sergt.
Hutcheson, Samuel W	"	March 14, 1864	Mustered out September 19, 1865.
Heil, Noah D	"	April 20, 1864	" " "
Jackson, Elcanah	Darling	Jan. 30, 1864	" " "
Johnson, George W			
Joyce, Marcellus E	St. Louis, Mo	March 14, 1864	Discharged May 29, 1865.

Kerlin, Isaac	Delphi	Jan. 30, 1864	Mustered out September 19, 1865.
Kious, James	Colfax	" "	" " "
Koontz, John H.	Delphi	" "	Mustered out Sept. 19, 1865, as Corp.
Kidd, George W	"	" "	Deserted September 26, 1865.
Leach, John M.	Kokomo	April 7, 1864	Mustered out Sept. 19, 1865, as Vet. Surg.
Loughten, Charles	Lafayette	Jan. 30, 1864	Mustered out September 19, 1865.
Ledman, Alvinus M	Delphi	March 14, 1864	Mustered out Sept. 19, 1865, as Sergt.
Lister, Joshua M.	Rockfield	Feb. 17, 1864	Discharged June 6, 1865.
Loveless, James N.	Colfax	" "	Mustered out Sept. 19, 1865, as Corp.
Miller, A. E.	Rockfield	Jan. 30, 1864	Mustered out September 19, 1865.
Mullendore, John	"	" "	Discharged June 6, 1865.
Martin, John C.	Delphi	" "	Mustered out September 19, 1865.
Myers, Robert	Rockfield	" "	Discharged June 6, 1865.
Martin, Samuel S.	Bellefontaine	" "	Promoted Regimental Commissary.
M'Dowell, Marion C.	Colfax	" "	Discharged June 6, 1865.
Moore, Aaron R.	"	" "	Mustered out Sept. 19, 1865, as Com. Sergt.
M'Dowell, Samuel O.	"	" "	Discharged May 9, 1865.
M'Farland, Alfred	"	" "	Deserted June 4, 1865.
M'Farland, Ezekiel W.	"	" "	Deserted June 16, 1865.
Moore, Joseph	Delphi	" "	Deserted March 26, 1864.
M'Gregor, Rover	"	Feb. 17, 1864	Deserted March 26, 1864.
Minor, Marcus	"	" "	Deserted June 16, 1865.
Nicewonder, Joseph C.	Clark's Hill	Jan. 30, 1864	Discharged March 12, 1865.
Prichard Hugh	Delphi	" "	Mustered out May 27, 1865.
Pickard, Benjamin S.	"	" "	Mustered out September 19, 1865.
Perry, George	Rossville	Feb. 17, 1864	Discharged June 6, 1865.
Quick, John D.	Lebanon	Jan. 30, 1864	Mustered out Sept. 19, 1865, as Sergt.
Quick, William S.	Colfax	Feb. 17, 1864	Mustered out Sept. 19, 1865, Bugler.
Rinehart, William R.	Delphi	" "	" " "
Rightlinger, George W.	"	Jan. 30, 1864	" " "

Names and Rank.	Residence.	Date of Muster.	Remarks.
Ray, Smith	Delphi	Jan. 30, 1864	Mustered out September 19, 1865.
Ray, William D	Rockfield	" "	Mustered out September 19, 1865.
Rine, William D		" "	Died at Fort Leavenworth, Kan., Aug 14, 1865.
Ruggs, John G	Ladoga	" "	Mustered out September 19, 1865.
Rees, David B	Delphi	" "	Promoted First Lieutenant Co. " D."
Roberts, Morris D	"	" "	Discharged Aug. 24, 1865, as Sergt.-Major.
Sidenbender, Henry	"	" "	Mustered out Sept. 19, 1865, as Sergt.
Sampson, George	"	" "	Discharged June 6, 1865, as Sergt.
Shuey, David	"	" "	Discharged June 6, 1865.
Shuey, Daniel	Wabash	" "	Mustered out July 19, 1865.
Scott, James R	Colfax	" "	Mustered out May 30, 1865.
Scott, Jesse	Warsaw	" "	Deserted June 16, 1865.
Stewart, Joseph	Crawfordsville	" "	Mustered out September 19, 1865.
Shepperd, William C		" "	Died at New Albany, Ind., Feb. 28, 1865.
Scott, Cornelius	Rossville	" "	Deserted June 1, 1865.
Shelley, George W. A	Athea	Feb. 17, 1864	Deserted March 26, 1864.
Shelley, James S	Newtown	" "	Mustered out September 19, 1865.
Sidenbender, Samuel	Delphi	" "	Promoted Second Lieutenant.
Sands, Edward	Colfax	" "	Mustered out September 19, 1865.
Sucksdorf, Frederick K	Delphi	" "	Mustered out September 19, 1865, as Corp.
Thomas, Lewis	"	" "	Mustered out September 19, 1865.
Thomas, Charles L	Battle Ground	April 20, 1864	Mustered out June 6, 1865.
Tool, Nelson B	Ladoga	Jan. 30, 1864	Mustered out September 19, 1865.
Tull, James	Delphi	" "	" " "
Tribbitt, William	"	" "	Discharged June 6, 1865.
Tribbitt, Robert K	Rockfield	March 14, 1864	Mustered out Sept. 19, 1865, as Corp.
Woodward, C. P	Delphi	Jan. 30, 1864	Mustered out June 2, 1865.

Wecht, Jacob	Rockfield	Jan. 30, 1864	Mustered out Sept. 19, 1865.
Wells, Benoni	Colfax	" "	Mustered out May 8, 1865.
Wright, Joseph M	Thorntown	" "	Mustered out Sept. 19, 1865.
Winkler, Christ	Ladoga	" "	Mustered out June 16, 1865.
Wilson, John W	Crawfordsville	" "	Promoted to First Lieutenant.
Westcott, Bergan B	Delphi	" "	Dicharged May 8, 1865, as Chief Bugler.
Wolp, Samuel	"	April 20, 1864	Mustered out Sept. 19, 1865, as Corp.
Young, Leonard	Rockfield	Feb. 17, 1864	Mustered out September 19, 1865.
Moore, Cyrus W	Carroll County	Nov. 11, 1864	Died at Jeffersonville, Ind., April 9, 1865.
Wells, John	" "	" "	Mustered out September 19, 1865.

Company "K," One Hundred and Forty-Seventh Regiment, Indiana Volunteers.

Privates.			
Cline, Solomon	Camden	March 8, 1865	Died at Cumberland, Md., April 10, 1865.
Maxwell, Henry J	"	" "	Mustered out August 8, 1865.
Maxwell, Henry	"	" "	Died at Summit Point, Va., July 8, 1865.
Miller, Samuel	"	" "	Mustered out August 4, 1865.

Company "H," Forty-Fifth Regiment, Indiana Volunteers (Third Cavalry).

First Sergeant.			
Shanklin, Robert P	Carroll County	Sept. 12, 1861	Promoted Second Lieutenant.
Corporal.			
Shanklin, George W	Carroll County	Sept. 12, 1861	

Names and Rank.	Residence.	Date of Muster.	Remarks.
Privates.			
Collane, Richard	Carroll County	Sept. 12, 1861.	
Cook, James	" "	" "	Mustered out 1864.
Ford, Absalom	" "	" "	Transferred to Eighth Cavalry.
Ford, Benjamin	" "	" "	Captured at Calhoun, Ga., trans. to Eighth Cav.
Glasscock, Harvey	" "	" "	
Jordon, William	" "	" "	
Jordon, Willis	" "	" "	
Johnston, Jeremiah	" "	" "	
Landes, John A	" "	" "	
Ledman, Alva B	" "	" "	
Overbalser, John	" "	" "	
Ross, Samuel P. W	" "	" "	
Spitler, Jonathan	" "	" "	Transferred to Eighth Cavalry.
Sheets, Salathiel	" "	" "	
Recruits.			
Barnard, Leroy	Carroll County	Aug. 26, 1862	Transferred to Eighth Cavalry.
Brown, Jacob H	" "	" "	" " "
Cook, William	" "	" "	" " "
Copstick, James H	" "	" "	" " "
Jordon, William	" "	Aug. 27, 1862	Captured June 10, 1864; must'd out June 19, 1865.
Marsh, Alexander W	" "	Sept. 9, 1862	Transferred to Eighth Cav.; must'd out June 9, 1865.
Miller, John S	" "	Aug. 28, 1862	Captured August 3, 1864; Transferred Eighth Cav.
Quinn, William H	" "	Aug. 26, 1862	Transferred to Eighth Cavalry.
Young, Martin V	" "	Aug. 29, 1862	" " "
Young, Robert	" "	Aug. 20, 1862	" " "

COMPANY "G," ONE HUNDRED AND FIFTY-FOURTH REGIMENT, INDIANA VOLUNTEERS.

Evans, John F.	Carroll County	April 3, 1865	Mustered out August 4, 1865.
Green, Leroy W.	" "	April 16, 1865	Promoted Captain.
Munn, Jesse.	" "	April 11, 1865	Mustered out August 4, 1865.
Penrod, William.	" "	March 14, 1865	Died at Indianapolis, May 8, 1865.
Smith, Michael.	" "	March 28, 1865	Mustered out May 16, 1865.

COMPANY "I," FIFTY-FIRST REGIMENT, INDIANA VOLUNTEERS.

PRIVATES—RECRUITS.			
Fellers, George.	Burlington	Oct. 19, 1864	Mustered out December 13, 1865; drafted.
Foutz, John W.	Carroll County	" "	Mustered out August 26, 1865; drafted.
Quinn, John.	" "	" "	Mustered out October 19, 1865; drafted.
Rotraff, Emanuel H.	" "	" "	Died at Jeffersonville, January 1, 1865; drafted.
Snell, Joseph N.	" "	" "	Mustered out November 14, 1865; drafted.
Welty, David.	" "	" "	Died December 28, 1864; wounds; drafted.

COMPANY "E," ONE HUNDRED AND FIFTIETH REGIMENT, INDIANA VOLUNTEERS. OO

Barr, William H.	Carroll County	Feb. 8, 1865	Mustered out August 5, 1865, as Corporal.
Brannon, John.	" "	" "	" " " "
Bell, John W.	" "	Feb. 6, 1865	" " " "
Buntin, William R.	" "	Feb. 13, 1865	" " " "
Currans, Dennis.	" "	Feb. 15, 1865	" " " "
Collar, Oscar B.	" "	Feb. 6, 1865	Died at home, March 8, 1865.

Names and Rank.	Residence.	Date of Muster.	Remarks.
Cleary, John	Carroll County	Feb. 6, 1865	Mustered out August 5, 1865.
Dailey, James	" "	Feb. 8, 1865	" " " "
Farthing, Thomas	" "	Feb. 6, 1865	" " " "
Fury, John	" "	" "	" " " "
Galbreth, Milton	" "	" "	Promoted Second Lieutenant.
Hannaman, John	" "	" "	Mustered out August 5, 1865.
Hudson, Levi	" "	" "	Mustered out August 5, 1865, as Corporal.
Jackson, James	" "	" "	Mustered out June 28, 1865.
Lewis, Oliver	" "	" "	Deserted July 3, 1865.
Lockwood, Fred K.	" "	Feb. 15, 1865	Mustered out August 5, 1865.
M'Carty, Patrick	" "	" "	" " " "
Miller, David	" "	Feb. 8, 1865	" " " "
M'Donald, Andrew	" "	Feb. 6, 1865	" " " "
M'Clernand, Frank	" "	Feb. 8, 1865	" " " "
M'Nerney, Hugh	" "	Feb. 6, 1865	" " " "
Marley, Joseph	" "	" "	" " " "
Nicholson, Elihu	" "	Feb. 17, 1865	Mustered out August 5, 1865, as Sergeant.
Nunely, John R.	" "	Feb. 6, 1865	Mustered out August 5, 1865.
Neff, John S.	" "	" "	" " " "
Rush, John	" "	Feb. 13, 1865	" " " "
Swanton, William	" "	Feb. 6, 1865	Mustered out August 5, 1865, as Corporal.
Sowers, John T.	" "	" "	Mustered out August 5, 1865.
Tucker, Issachar B.	" "	Feb. 8, 1865	Mustered out August 5, 1865, as Sergeant.
Terry, David	" "	Feb. 6, 1865	Mustered out August 5, 1865.
Wallace, Patrick	" "	" "	" " " "

COMPANY "K," ONE HUNDRED AND TWENTY-EIGHTH REGIMENT, INDIANA VOLUNTEERS.

Richards, John	Camden	March 7, 1864	Died at Nashville, Tennessee, October 8, 1864.
Shuman, Jacob	Burlington	" "	Mustered out January 4, 1866.
Woodward, John	Montezuma	" "	Mustered out April 10, 1866.

COMPANY "E," NINETY-NINTH REGIMENT, INDIANA VOLUNTEERS.

Brown, Albert G	Carroll		Never mustered.
Cripe, Joseph	Burlington	Aug. 15, 1862	Mustered out June 5, 1865.
Dillman, Jonathan	"	" "	" " "
Dillman, Jacob	"	" "	" " "
Ewing, George W	"	" "	Mustered out May 31, 1865.
Note, Elijah	"	" "	Died at Lagrange, Tenn., February 28, 1863.
Parker, Joseph	"	" "	Killed August 25, 1864.
Robertson, George W	"	" "	Mustered out June 5, 1865.
Shelton, Howard	"	" "	Discharged March 21, 1863.
Shelton, John	"	" "	Discharged September 6th, 1863.
RECRUITS.			
Jones, George	Delphi		Deserted March 7, 1864.
Young, Ephraim	"	Sept. 27, 1862	Died at Lagrange, Tenn., June 14, 1863.

COMPANY "H," THIRTY-FOURTH REGIMENT, INDIANA VOLUNTEERS.

Creson, Leander	Burlington	Oct. 7, 1861	Veteran; mustered out February 3, 1866.
Ramey, Samuel M	Galveston	" "	Died June 23, 1863, of wounds rec'd Champion Hills.

Company "E," Forty-Sixth Regiment, Indiana Volunteers.

Names and Rank.	Residence.	Date of Muster.	Remarks.
Corporal.			
Armstrong, Clinton J.	Delphi	Nov. 5, 1861	Died at Burnettville, July 25, 1862.
Privates.			
Armstrong, Elza E	Delphi	Nov. 5, 1861	Discharged June 14, 1863; disability.
Baum, Charles	"	" "	Mustered out December 1, 1864.
Gosley, Milton M.	Monticello	" "	Veteran; mustered out September 4, 1865.
Itskin, Henry	Delphi	" "	" " " "
Nicholas, Nathaniel	Burnettville	" "	Mustered out December 1, 1864.
Nicholas, William	Monticello	" "	Discharged March 10, 1863; disability.
Stogdell, Robert	"	" "	Discharged Oct. 10, 1863, of wounds, at Ft. Gibson.

Company "K," Seventy-Second Regiment, Indiana Volunteers.

Names and Rank.	Residence.	Date of Muster.	Remarks.
Privates.			
Hoff, Eli	Carroll County	Aug. 7, 1862	Died at Louisville, August 7, 1862.
Waldron, Joseph D.	Delphi	Aug. 15, 1862	Mustered out July 24, 1865.

CARROLL COUNTY COMPANIES—INDIANA LEGION.

ROUGH AND READY GUARDS.

Names.	Rank.	Residence.	Date of Com'n.
John A. Barnes	Captain	Pittsburg	July 25, 1861.
John G. Troxell	First Lieut	"	" "
Wm. Dillinger	Second Lieut	"	" "

TIPPECANOE UNION RIFLES.

Names.	Rank.	Residence.	Date of Com'n.
J. H. M'Connell	Captain	Pittsburg	July 25, 1861.
W. W. Penny	First Lieut	"	" "
W. S. Stewart	Second Lieut	"	" "

JACKSON HOME GUARDS.

Names.	Rank.	Residence.	Date of Com'n.
Peter M. Marks	Captain	Camden	July 25, 1861.
David Paden	First Lieut	"	" "
George Kuns	Second Lieut	"	" "

WILD-CAT RANGERS.

Names.	Rank.	Residence.	Date of Com'n.
Joseph Shigley	Captain		July 26, 1861.
Philip Hemming	First Lieut		" "
James Robinson	Second Lieut		" "

ROCKFIELD STATE GUARDS.

Names.	Rank.	Residence.	Date of Com'n.
J. T. Landry	Captain	Rockfield	Sept. 26, 1861.
J. M. Lister	First Lieut	"	" "
Thomas M'Dowell	Second Lieut	"	" "

BURLINGTON HOME GUARDS.

Names.	Rank.	Residence.	Date of Com'n.
J. M. Darnall	Captain	Burlington	Sept. 28, 1861.
Andrew Bowman	First Lieut	"	" "
J. M. Grant	Second Lieut	"	" "

TIPPECANOE RANGERS.

Names.	Rank.	Residence.	Date of Com'n.
Henry C. Williams	Captain	Pittsburg	Oct. 6, 1862.
Walker M'Beth	First Lieut	"	" "
John M'Connell	Second Lieut	"	" "

REED CASE RIFLES.

Names.	Rank.	Residence.	Date of Com'n.
Jehu C. Hannam	Captain	Delphi	July 25, 1863.
Fred. J. Merritt	First Lieut	"	" "
Milton W. Newton	Second Lieut	"	" "

ELLSWORTH GUARDS.

Names.	Rank.	Residence.	Date of Com'n.
John H. M'Connell	Captain	Pittsburg	Aug. 22, 1863.
Charles Parker	First Lieut	"	" "
John C. Colton	Second Lieut	"	" "

DR. E. W. H. BECK.

This gentleman was appointed Assistant Surgeon of the First Regiment, Indiana Volunteers, in the Mexican War, and transferred to the General Hospital at Matamoras.

In the War of 1861, he was commissioned Surgeon of the Third Cavalry, and served as Brigade and Division Surgeon in the Army of the Potomac.

R-104—Have data on following people of Carroll County in 1891, biographies and some photos: Dr. Charles ANGELL; Franklin G. ARMSTRONG; Daniel BAUM Sr.; David BAUM; Abner H. BOWEN; Andrew BURNTRAGER; Preston B. CALVERT; John S. CASE; Reed CASE Sr.; James P. DUGAN; Dr. John M. EWING; Amanda GILLIAM; John Wesley GILLAM; Samuel G. GREENUP; Mrs. Elizabeth GREGG and Christian GROS Sr.

Also David T. HILDEBRAND; (Colonel) Ziba HOLT; Eleanor JACKSON; Isaac JACKSON; Richard MANARY; William McCAIN; Magdalene McCAIN; Gen. Samual MILROY; James ODELL; Adam PORTER; Enoch RINEHART; Abner ROBINSON; Henry ROBINSON; James B. SCOTT; Ezekiel B. SQUIRER; Thomas STERLING; James H. STEWART; Mrs. Mary TURPIE; Samuel WEAVER; A. W. WOLEVER, and names of related people.—Mrs. R. L. Hunter, 404 Eighth Street North, Nampa, Idaho.

CPSIA information can be obtained
at www.ICGtesting.com
Printed in the USA
LVHW031257060423
743358LV00019B/79

9 783382 133559